Maximum Range-Perfect Shot

J.M. Schneider

Hold Fast Publishing, LLC

This book contains scenes of violence, adult language, and scenes of an adult nature. Reader discretion is advised.

Published by Hold Fast Publishing, LLC February 20, 2026

Book Cover by Elizabeth Berry Mackenney

Contents

Copyrights V

Sunday, October 29 1

1. Chapter 1 -- A Moment in History 2
2. Chapter 2 – An Unlikely Scenario 10
3. Chapter 3 – Partners 25
4. Chapter 4 – Making New Friends 36
5. Chapter 5 – Disclosures 41
6. Chapter 6 – First Contact 59
7. Chapter 7 – Working the Crowd 77
8. Chapter 8 – A Daring Plan 89
9. Chapter 9 – Headaches 96
10. Chapter 10 – Flying Blind 108
11. Chapter 11 – Trouble Everywhere 121
12. Chapter 12 – Politics Versus Reality 140
13. Chapter 13 – Tales and Revelations 151
14. Chapter 14 – Blood Evidence 163

Chapter 1 -- A Moment in History

Senator and Democratic presidential nominee Samuel Brandt Armstrong stepped briskly to the podium like a man half his age. Shaking hands with New York City Mayor Scott Geary, he proceeded to the largest tip of the eleven-point star that supported the Statue of Liberty and waved to the crowd with both hands. The deafening roar he received in response was expected. He held the pose for several seconds, showing off his beaming, perfect smile to the throng of supporters and, more importantly, to the cameras transmitting his image across the country.

After a moment, the crowd grew quiet and gave the senator the chance to speak. "Thank you, thank you," Armstrong responded in his powerful, yet humble tone. "I am so delighted to be here today, in the shadow of Lady Liberty, perhaps the greatest symbol of freedom and our country, on this beautiful fall afternoon. She has stood here for over a century, bravely enduring wars, terrible tragedies, hardships—and, somewhat to my amazement, the last four years."

The friendly crowd responded with slightly forced laughter right on cue, which drew the mischievous, subtle grin and cocked eyebrow Armstrong often used to put a fine point on one of his thinly veiled insults. "What better place to speak about the ways we are going to put this country back on the right path to being a global leader!"

The dais was positioned perfectly so every camera would capture the image of the statue rising like a majestic force behind Armstrong. Photographers amassed on the lower platform used wide-angle lenses to catch the entire scene. Armstrong's Chief of Staff, Dr. Voight Stafford, had cajoled, demanded, and negotiated to put his candidate in the right position to give the cameras the perfect angle.

Armstrong had secured the Democratic nomination fairly easily, but now faced an uphill battle to unseat incumbent Roland Sharpe. Stafford knew that, by placing the regal statue directly behind his candidate, anyone watching the speech would make a subconscious connection between the candidate and the inherent nobility of the blue-green statue. It would help his image among swing voters; otherwise known to Stafford and Armstrong as moderates. And polling indicated there were a lot of swing votes to be had.

Armstrong got to the meat of his speech. A skilled orator, he altered the pace and tone of his words to build up to the points he wanted to make. Even his staunchest Republican detractors had to admit he could command a crowd better than an orchestra conductor while expressing salient points with brevity and clarity.

Armstrong liked to show off his vigor, and Stafford couldn't argue with the man's political instincts. He came off as young and powerful in comparison to President Sharpe, whose mostly gray hair and slight paunch suggested advanced age. Striding between the point and both sides of the triangle, timing his steps to reach the critical part of whatever point he was making just as he reached the edge, Armstrong was in his element.

"… and THAT," Armstrong boomed through the wireless microphone on his lapel as he reached the east-facing side, "is exactly why we need someone in the Oval Office who isn't comfortable with the status quo, who looks forward to new opportunities, who understands this country is at its best when every single citizen is empowered and inspired to make their lives, their communities, and their country a BETTER PLACE!"

Of the 2,000 or so witnesses, most would stubbornly stick to the impossible claim that they heard the report of the shot before they saw the right collar of Armstrong's light-gray suit jacket puff out, followed by a misty cloud of dark red spray shooting both from his upper chest and back. Armstrong's body twisted violently to the right and he staggered back two steps before sinking to his right knee, his face contorting with confusion and pain. He put his right hand on the ground and looked like he might try to return to his feet, but his arm folded at the elbow and he collapsed. Things seemed to freeze as every person asked their eyes to confirm what they thought they just witnessed.

And then all hell broke loose.

Cody Jacobs, the Secret Service agent nearest to the candidate and the man most directly responsible for his safety, reacted before the echo of the shot faded, even though he would spend the next weeks and months angry at himself for not moving more quickly. He bolted from his position just out of the view of the news cameras and dove on the prone man, covering Armstrong with his body to selflessly absorb any further shots that might be intended for his principal.

The remaining four agents of the detail, although a tick of the clock slower, moved with the alacrity of a Super Bowl-caliber NFL backfield, forming a defensive square around Armstrong and Jacobs, their FN Five-SeveN pistols pointed outward, safeties off and fingers on triggers. Another detail, tasked with the protection of vice-presidential candidate Zach Holland, pretty much threw him toward the stairs. The mayor and other dignitaries scattered in panic, hands on their heads in an instinctive but misguided attempt to protect themselves.

"Sir! Sir! Are you OK?" Jacobs yelled. Armstrong turned his head toward the noise, but his response was the raspy sound of a man trying to take a breath and failing.

The question was rhetorical; blood was staining the shoulder of his shirt, telling Jacobs everything he needed to know. "Sir, we're gonna get you out of here!" He screamed into the tiny microphone clipped to the cuff of his white shirt. *"Iceberg! Iceberg! Iceberg! Point Guard is hit! Point Guard is hit! Iceberg! I say again, Iceberg!"*

"Get off me!" Armstrong croaked, and Jacobs realized he was lying on a man with a serious shoulder or chest injury. He shifted his weight to provide some relief.

"Sorry, Sir! Don't move! We have help on the way!" As he spoke, two agents pushed him away to roll the injured senator over onto the stretcher they'd just laid next to him. With little regard for his shriek of pain, they lifted the gurney and started running as fast as they could toward the stairs at the other side of the base, where the whine of a turboshaft engine and the *whop* of rotor blades grew louder every second.

***

The huge black dog, teeth bared, crouched before taking one bounding step and leaping to attack. Kane Logan was ready for it, though he knew being ready might not be enough. With all 150 pounds of the Black Labrador/Great Dane mix coming right for him, if he didn't time things just right, he'd probably lose his hand and maybe the entire arm with it. Using skills he'd spent years perfecting, he waited until the hellhound was in full flight before pivoting away. He still felt the hot breath as the beast turned his enormous head and snapped his jaws shut in with the expectation that something would be between them.

The dog stopped the second he hit the ground and turned once more. Kane faced him and was rewarded with the delighted, high-pitched yip only a dog having fun with his owner and friend could emit.

"Good boy, Jay!" Kane tossed the tennis ball to another part of the large yard, and Jay took off after it, his footfalls resounding like those of a Clydesdale as he pounded through the short grass. He chased the ball down and proudly brought it back, dropping it right at Kane's feet and looking up for praise.

"Very good, Jay! C'mon," he said, picking it up and starting back toward his house. "Time to go in." Jay made a half-hearted attempt to steal the ball back, so Kane chucked it in the direction he was walking. He hated leaving Jay for any extended period—he was the source of most of his joy since his divorce over three years ago—but the nondescript cars would be here soon. He was already dressed in the black suit, white shirt, and gray tie ubiquitous to the Secret Service.

He'd been in his home office at his simple ranch house in southern New Jersey, working at his cybersecurity consulting job, when the news flash about Sam Armstrong's shooting came over the radio. He listened for a couple of minutes to get any details he could (knowing that most of them would be wrong) and then went into the living room and turned on CNN to watch the shooting from every imaginable angle. He could see it was a rifle shot and, more importantly, that it came from a direction where there was nothing but water for some distance. That meant they were going to need him.

Right on cue, his cell rang. The display showed a 202 area code, telling him how his next hours—and maybe days—were going to be spent. "Logan."

"Identification?" an emotionless voice requested. Kane gave his agent number, his access code, and his authentication password as per standard procedure. "Thank you. Agent Logan. You are on expedited recall. What is your present location?"

He'd expected them to tell him to get in his truck and haul ass to either New York or D.C., but the expedited recall phrase meant they were sending someone to pick him up. "Home address on file." There was a brief pause on the line.

"Understood. Expect pickup three-zero minutes. Confirm."

"Order confirmed." The line went dead. *Thirty minutes? That's fast.*

He made two calls. The first was to Brittany from Jay's doggy daycare, who agreed to come by and pick him up as soon as she could. The second was to his boss at the cybersecurity firm to tell him he wouldn't be available for a while. His manager took the news in stride; the company was merely a cover for the CIA, and a little cross-agency agreement with the Secret Service had put Kane in the role.

Pulling out his suit, he decided it was pressed enough to be presentable, so he dressed and dropped his go-bag right by the front door. With nothing further to do but wait for the arrival of his ride, he took his best friend out back for some quality time. After about ten minutes of fetch, Jay was panting like a landed bluefish and Kane had a light sheen of sweat on his forehead, so he figured it was time to head in.

He and Jay paused upon hearing the unmistakable sound of a V-H3D Sky King helicopter flying fast and low. *Wow. They're really worked up about this.* By itself, that wasn't surprising; when the Democratic nominee for the highest office in the land got shot, everything moved fast. But Kane wasn't important enough to have such a conveyance—the same type that was designated Marine One when the president was on board—sent out for little ol' him.

In a few seconds, the aircraft with "United States of America" written on the side appeared just above the treetops, flaring to assess the feasibility of landing in his backyard while lowering its landing gear. Jay flipped out, barking at the strange beast that threatened his home territory. The pilot made a rapid but perfect landing about 100 feet away from the house.

The rear door popped open and none other than Brent Douglas, the deputy director of the Secret Service, leaped from the craft so quickly he barely touched the steps, running over to Kane at a near sprint. Kane was surprised but hardly pleased; their relationship had been downright frosty for several years.

Having been here before, Brent offered his hand to Jay, allowing him to sniff. Satisfied Douglas was a friendly, he quieted down.

"Well, this is the first time the 'DD' himself ever came to fetch me," Kane said.

"A lot of confused agents on site. FBI has the lead, of course, and we're supporting. We've got Holland in a safe location and doubled the security detail around him. FBI wants you to be part of the investigation because of your experience with shooting. You still answer to me and Director Schultz." Adrian Schultz was the Secret Service director, but he was a political appointee. "In the end, though, you fall under the authority of the bureau, as they have jurisdiction." Both his tone and clipped speech told Kane everything he needed to know; Brent wasn't thrilled to be here, nor was he pleased to be acting as a gofer, and it didn't take a genius to figure out what office that order *really* came from.

Kane nodded toward Jay. "Let me put him inside and get my bag. Give me a minute."

"Forty-five seconds." There was no hint of a smile on his face, and the pilot was already revving the engine back up to take-off thrust.

After giving Jay a pat on his head and telling him to lie down in his bed, Kane tossed his bag through the aircraft door and took a spot on one of the bench seats. The chopper was airborne and turning north before he could get his four-point harness buckled.

Chapter 2 – An Unlikely Scenario

Liberty Island was a madhouse. From Kane's vantage point a couple hundred feet above in the chopper, which had run flat-out all the way up the New Jersey coast, people scurried about like termites attacking a log. The pilot spiraled down and landed on a patch of grass that had been hastily marked with a ragged white "X," giving little consideration to the comfort or stomachs of anyone onboard.

Both passengers removed their seat belts before the aircraft stopped bouncing on its landing gear and were out the door in a second, where another agent met them. Kane tossed his go-bag to him, wondering if he would ever see it again. At the police line surrounding the steps to the monument, Kane held up the ID the deputy director had given him during the ride.

The people on the stone base of the statue were members of the FBI, the Secret Service, and a few local police. When Kane and Douglas got around to the front, they halted so as not to interfere with the recreation of the shooting. An FBI agent, standing at the exact point of impact and wearing a small sandwich board that identified him from front and back as "Armstrong" was moving his body in tiny increments as directed by two other agents, who were staring intently at a monitor under a sunshade. The general angle suggested the shot came from Governor's Island—maybe.

A second team was working near the southernmost point of the base, so Kane headed over to find them staring at and poking small instruments into a crater in the granite wall. He flashed his badge at the supervisory agent. "Is there anything you can tell me yet?"

"Yes, sir. It looks like we have the projectile embedded in the stone. We got a little lucky. About a foot to the left, and it would have ended up in the harbor."

"What do we know about the round?"

"Nothing confirmed because it's still embedded, but it looks like we have a 6.5 millimeter Creedmoor that hit the granite at a relatively low velocity. It was probably tumbling at impact, which makes sense considering it went through Armstrong."

"Creedmoor?" Kane repeated. "That's a big boy round with a lot of range, and that means a fairly specialized weapon."

"That's very likely."

"Thanks." He returned to the deputy director, who was talking with several agents all at once. The pair stepped a short distance away from them. "First thoughts?"

"The shot wasn't local, and it wasn't some Elmer Fudd," he responded. "This was a well-informed, patient, and motivated shooter who probably had some funding and training. What do we know about bogeys in the area?"

Brent flipped through a clipboard of documents. "Airspace was off-limits for three hours beforehand as per SOP, and that was confirmed by radar, which was a bitch to pull off with three major airports not ten miles away. Boat traffic was not permitted in a zone from the tip of Manhattan to Morris Canal Park in Jersey City and the tip of Governor's Island. And a drone..."

"Right." The kick of even a small-caliber weapon fired from the heaviest and most powerful drone would destroy any kind of aim, sending the bullet who knew where.

"Hey! I think we've got a trajectory!" Kane, Douglas, and a handful of other agents trotted over to the scene where measurements had been taken with hand lasers based on video images. Two tripods were set up in place of the agent impersonating Armstrong, with telescoping antennas and tiny rings at the top, representing the entrance and exit wounds and making it possible to see the path of the bullet.

Kane stood in front of the tripods. They lined up with the impact crater in the granite. That gave them three data points, meaning they could determine the location from which the shot originated with extreme accuracy. An agent was already pounding numbers into his laptop.

"Confirmed," he proclaimed within a few seconds. "Based on the path from those impacts, we have a bearing of 62.87 degrees with an elevation of 7.91 degrees above the horizon. That's to within 93.1% accuracy based on the model data." Staring intently at the numbers on his monitor, the young man failed to notice the uneasy glances the others shared.

Douglas strode purposefully back to the impact crater in the wall, bending so he could put one eye as close as possible to it. After a few seconds of twisting his neck this way and that, he stood up, looking like he was going to blow a gasket. "Agent, what's your name?" he called to the young man who had made the proclamation.

"Lucas Foster, sir."

"Agent Foster, can you join me over here?" Foster stood and, with a quick look around as if sensing the tension of the moment, hesitated. But when the deputy director of the Secret Service "asks" you to join him, you do so, and Foster obeyed with all the enthusiasm of a child on the way to the principal's office.

"Yes, sir?"

"Agent, do me a favor and eyeball the entry and exit wound positions from the vantage point of the impact crater, would you?" Brent's voice was eerily calm, but his entire face and neck were a bright red, and he hadn't had time to get a sunburn today.

Foster bent down warily, probably suspecting this event was going to hurt. It took about one second to see the problem. The path the bullet had to have taken based on the physical observations and the model pointed up into the sky right down the East River between Manhattan and Brooklyn. Foster's model may have been mathematically accurate, but it simply did not reflect reality. "Ah, shit."

"What's that, agent?" Douglas asked.

Foster stood and tried to retain what he could of his dignity. "Sir, I can't explain it. The data is clear, but obviously the shooting position can't be where the model says it is, because there's nowhere to shoot from that matches the trajectory."

"No, no, agent. We just have to look for a suspect who's about 500 feet tall." Foster closed his eyes at the comment. "So why don't you go back to your computer and give me something I can fucking use!" Foster scurried away to obey the command, passing Kane as he made his way over to Douglas.

"Not a great way to manage people, Brent."

"Too damned bad. I need answers, not bullshit. And this makes absolutely no goddamned sense!"

Kane shared his frustration if not his disposition. "I know but, like he said, the information is solid. We're missing something." He raised his head and yelled to the assembled group. "Can I get a spotting scope over here?" Within seconds, a member of the forensics team was setting one up and aligning it with the path of the projectile.

He handed Kane a small remote control. "The bullet path is locked in. You can move the scope along the vertical or horizontal axes using these controls here, or press 'Home' to return to the path. Just don't touch the scope or move the tripod."

"Thanks." Kane looked through the powerful optics. Sure enough, all he saw was bright blue sky. He panned down, wondering if whatever was under the line of fire on the ground would give him some kind of lead, though he doubted it.

The servo motor worked far too slowly for Kane's taste but, sooner than he expected, something swam into view. He stopped the scope and pulled his head away, confirming he was seeing things correctly. He was, and it was a much better lead than he had ever expected from his wild-ass guess.

Douglas saw his actions. "What is it?"

Kane yelled out another question to the amassed group. "Anyone know how far away the Brooklyn Bridge is from here, straight line?"

"About three miles, sir," came the answer. He didn't see who responded, but the thick Queens accent suggested one of NYPD's finest, so for now he would treat the information as fact.

"What was the coverage plan there?"

"We did daily sweeps of the maintenance areas for the last three days," another voice answered.

"Jacobs?" Douglas asked.

"Yes, sir." Cole Jacobs had only just finished being debriefed after diving on top of his principal to protect him and had insisted on returning to the site. His frustration was palpable.

"That's perfectly reasonable, agent. No one is blaming you." Jacobs' expression demonstrated his disagreement.

Douglas turned to Kane. "I'm not sure where you're going with this Brooklyn Bridge thing. Are you trying to say the shot came from there? No way."

Kane hesitated. He had to be nuts to even consider his theory. It was still taking shape as he spoke about it. "I know it's off-the-wall. This is a long shot, pun intended. A *real* long shot."

Douglas continued to frown. "No one could make that shot. You've got a breeze that changes direction, variable humidity, a moving target—shit, if it's three miles from here, that's..." he paused to do the math. "That's like 5,200 yards. Not feet, Kane. *Yards*."

"What other leads we got, Brent?" His trump card was effective; Douglas had absolutely nothing, and Kane knew it. The bridge was a stretch, to be sure, but right now it was the only option they had.

"Dammit," the deputy director finally said. "OK. Get over there, and bring Jacobs and his advance team, but be quick about it. I don't want you fucking around over there, understand? I need to run this one down yesterday."

"I'm on it," Kane responded, heading over to Jacobs to commandeer his team. It struck him as vaguely funny—he'd lived within two hours of the city for a good portion of his thirty-five years and had been to Manhattan at least three dozen times, but he'd never set foot on the iconic bridge. Come to think of it, he'd never been on Liberty Island before today either. "Well," Kane mumbled to himself, "there's a first time for everything."

He had no idea how prescient his statement would prove to be.

***

It may have only been about three miles as the crow flies, but even with the sirens and lights of both NYC patrol cars and the black government SUVs of the convoy, Manhattan was still Manhattan. It would have been faster to helicopter over, but none had been available, so they were forced to use one of the police boats to race over to New Jersey and climb into two black and whites and two Chevy Suburbans. For reasons no sociologist had ever been able to fully explain, New Yorkers are simply unimpressed by most everything, and even the loud parade of official vehicles less than three hours after an attempted assassination was insufficient to get them to scramble out of the way. The trip took almost an hour.

At least the transit time gave him a chance to do some research. The portion of the tower closest to Liberty Island was roughly 4,800 yards from where Armstrong had been standing. That wasn't just far—it was ridiculous. That number alone reinforced Douglas' contention that Kane was jerking off, and he had to admit the deputy director had a case.

In order to gain access to the eastern tower, they had to go over the bridge itself and into Brooklyn. Kane stared out the right side of the vehicle during the ride, looking toward Liberty Island. The statue came into view about a third of the way across the bridge, confirming the east tower was a possible location for the shot. In a fit of impatience, he turned to the driver just as they were nearing it. "Stop next to the tower. I want to look around." The driver spoke into his wrist, and in a minute all four cars jammed on the brakes. Logan jumped out, followed by Jacobs and the other agents in the second SUV.

He walked to the riveted metal edge and looked out at the distant figure, ignoring the loud and earnest suggestions from other drivers that the agents engage in all kinds of creative sexual endeavors with their mothers, sisters, and even a few farm animals for blocking traffic. There was no way anyone could have taken the shot from right here—with no walkway, anyone trying to stand here would have been run down long before they got the chance.

They piled back into their vehicles and proceeded toward the Brooklyn side, and the serenade of horn blasts faded into the background.

They arrived at the east anchor structure of the bridge next to an exit ramp off Old Fulton Street. Several other police cars were already there, and an officer escorted a middle-aged man wearing a yellow hard hat and denim coveralls to them as soon as they stopped. "I'm Terry Wriggins, maintenance supervisor. What do you need?"

"Kane Logan, Secret Service. Thank you for coming out. I need to get to the top of the east tower."

Wriggins nodded. "No problem. Your agents have had access for several days, so they know what to do. We can use the cables to get to the top of the towers, but you better let me escort you. It's dangerous if you aren't experienced."

"That's fine. Let's go." Wriggins nodded and unlocked a set of double doors.

"Is this the only way someone could get access to the service walkway?" Kane asked.

"Well, they could get in from the Manhattan side and walk over. There's a similar access point there. It's just a longer walk. Other than that, they'd have to be one hell of a climber to shimmy up those pipes."

One of the agents on Jacobs' advance team spoke up. "We surveilled that entrance point as well, sir."

Kane looked at the red fire pipes that ran up the stone wall, grabbing one to check it out. It was a little too big around to grip comfortably, even for his larger-than-normal hands, but the cast iron was strong and would carry a lot of weight.

"Understood. Let's get going." Jacobs grabbed the backpack.

"Follow me." Wriggins led Kane and the rest of his team into the dark recesses of the structure and up a metal stairwell. When they reached the walkway, Kane looked down. They were only about fifty feet off the ground—he'd scaled higher walls in the Marines. More importantly, the large blocks of limestone and granite that made up the face of the anchorage would provide good footholds if someone held the pipes as well. An experienced climber could find a way up here without opening the doors at the street level. *Great. More maybes.*

They walked on the metal grates under the roadway for about a quarter mile before climbing a set of stairs that put them right on the edge of the bridge roadway near the massive suspension cables. Everyone except Kane and Jacobs headed further down the passage. Kane wasn't exactly thrilled by the prospect of his upcoming trek. He wasn't overly afraid of heights, but he did have a healthy fear of—as he liked to call it—sudden deceleration poisoning.

Wriggins pulled out two harnesses with cords running from them, each ending in heavy metal clips, and Kane allowed him to secure one of them around his body. He nodded obediently when Wriggins lectured him about having at least one clip secured to a guy wire at all times.

Kane climbed up on the cable right after Wriggins, clipping himself in and wondering why the damn thing was rounded instead of having a flat surface to walk on. With every step, his breathing quickened as the angle steepened until it felt like he was walking up the side of a cliff. The distance between him and Wriggins started widening. He may have been twenty years older than Kane, but apparently that didn't matter.

Finally, they reached the top, and Kane found the energy necessary to get up the short ladder and stand on the level surface far above the roadway. He leaned against the railing to rest and, even though he could feel Wriggins' amused look, took enough time to ensure he could stand without his legs shaking.

Once he felt better, he started scanning the horizon to the south. The statue was clearly visible, and while the higher angle gave him a new perspective, that didn't make it any more likely that the shot was possible.

Grabbing the range finder, he laid down and scooted forward on his stomach until he neared the edge of the platform. Using the scope, he zoomed in on where Armstrong had been standing and pushed the button to see a readout he expected but still didn't like—4,817.4 yards.

He shook his head and crawled back. He pulled out his phone, ran the numbers, and determined the range was 2.737 *miles*. As far as Kane knew, the longest successful shot ever had been about two miles. Distance aside, even through the most powerful scope available, Armstrong would have been a tiny target at that range, probably no more than a centimeter tall. With the variables involved at this distance, being steady enough to hit such a specific point was nearly impossible.

Regardless of those details, the most significant problem was bullet drop. The second a bullet left the barrel, it began to fall at the constant rate dictated by gravity. If a person fired one bullet and dropped a similar bullet from the same height at the same instant, both would hit the ground at the same time. One would just be much farther away. And that alone made this shot damn near impossible.

So what the hell am I doing here? If nothing else, he had to rule it out. An unlikely, nearly amazing shot? Yes. But not yet impossible. *Shit.*

"How high are we above the water?" he asked Wriggins.

"272 feet at mean high tide." Subtracting the height of the star-shaped base upon which Armstrong had stood, any shot from here had a starting elevation of 248 feet, giving the shooter better odds.

There was one more thing he needed to do. He retrieved the dummy rifle from the pack and took a moment to observe his environment, ignoring the numbers. There was only one question—*could I make this shot?* —and his gut feeling one way or the other.

He returned to the edge and went prone once more, extending the bipod legs from the front of the rifle and sighting in on the spot where Armstrong had been. The breeze hit the back of his right ear as it blew steadily. He made the appropriate adjustment to the scope and moved the gun to compensate. Another three clicks to allow for the rotation of the earth as the bullet transited the distance. The waves of the harbor and the East River ran parallel to each other, so the wind was roughly from the same direction.

The muscles in his face went slack as instinct took control. It was much more about feel right now. Subconsciously, he was aware of the technical aspects of the shot, but his body acted without his direction. He barely touched the weapon; just enough to keep it in place. His finger brushed against the trigger with a feathery touch he would use on a lover. *Pull, don't squeeze.* A figure was walking toward the kill zone. Whoever he was, that person would never know his simulated death occurred when the lumbrical muscle in Kane's forearm flexed, making his finger bend around the cool, curved metal. He sensed, more than heard, the *click* of the trigger.

He pulled his head away from the scope and scanned the target area. Nothing had changed, no bullet had flown, but Kane knew he'd simulated a possible kill shot. *Yeah, it's doable.* And if he could do it, someone else could. It was hardly conclusive and nowhere near scientific, but it could not be ignored. "OK," he announced, rising. "Back to the island. We've got some planning to do."

***

The return trip seemed shorter than the one to get there. Perhaps it was because he was about to stand in front of one of the top law enforcement officers in the country and propose they expend time, effort, and money pursuing a theory based on highly implausible mathematical possibilities and his gut instincts.

He was not looking forward to that discussion.

Things had not slowed down much at Liberty Island, but they had changed. Now, with measurements taken and angles understood, the Secret Service was noting exactly where every single person on the stage had been sitting or standing. With no realistic theories yet, such information would be of the utmost value.

Douglas looked even more harried than he had earlier in the day. He spotted Kane and, with a curt nod to the young man briefing him, headed to meet him. He was intercepted by another of the dozens of people racing this way and that, but this one was carrying a dispatch. Douglas snapped it out of his hands.

"Armstrong is out of surgery and is expected to recover," he announced. Regardless of his political leanings, Kane felt relief wash through him; even semi-retired, he never wanted "his" agency to lose a principal. Behind him, Jacobs blew out his breath, likely flush with the same emotion, but on a more personal level.

"It looks like he was incredibly lucky. His shoulder isn't even that bad. The bullet went *between* the subclavian artery and the clavicle but barely damaged either. Primarily, it's a soft tissue injury. He'll have a bad scar and there might be some nerve damage, but nothing more." Douglas returned the sheet of paper to the agent, his eyebrows raised in a "how-bout-that-shit?" expression that Kane shared; from what he'd seen on video, he'd expected that the arm would have to be amputated. "Anyway," he looked directly at Kane. "Are we done over there?"

"Well, no. It's a possibility I can't rule out."

Douglas squeezed the bridge of his nose. "You've got to be shitting me."

"I wish I was, but I'm not. The bullet would be subsonic at impact, but it would still have the needed velocity. The Creedmoor has enough kick, and there are a few guns that would get the job done. With the height of the tower, the bullet drop is acceptable. And," he paused to pull a sheet of scribbled calculations, "the rest of the numbers check out." He offered the piece of paper to his boss, who scanned it.

"Jesus, Kane. Just because the math works out doesn't mean it can be done! And not being able to rule it out does not mean it's realistic! I need hard evidence, not a scientific study from a lab."

"I know, I know. The whole idea is a stretch."

"Then what the fuck are we talking about?!"

Kane let out a breath. "Brent, I simulated the shot myself. I'm not saying it's easy, but I felt I could pull it off."

Douglas stared at Logan, his face devoid of expression. "You want me to call Washington and report that you had some Luke Skywalker kind of 'May the force be with you' moment, so we're going to pursue a scenario that's only slightly more likely than winning the lottery twice in the same week?"

Kane opened his mouth to speak, but the deputy director continued. "I mean, while we're at it, why don't we just ask every random person in Manhattan if they were the shooter?! That's a great fucking plan! Hell, I'm excited to be a part of it! Thanks for choosing me!"

Douglas looked like he wanted to continue but was interrupted by his phone. Without looking away from Kane, he answered the call. Whatever he heard was more than enough to remove the anger from his face and replace it with wide, worried eyes. He paused for a moment, and his next words sounded like those of a schoolboy explaining why he didn't have his homework done.

"Yes, sir. This is Deputy Director Douglas. No, nothing solid yet, sir. We're still investigating." The response was loud enough that Kane could hear, if not the words, the fury from five feet away. "We have a theory, but it's very thin at this time, sir." More yelling. "Yes, sir, he did, but it's barely plausible, and I don't want to spend time or resources chasing down—" By now other agents, unaccustomed to Douglas speaking in such pusillanimous tones, were looking at him, forcing him to turn away to get a tiny bit of privacy.

With both parts of the conversation now muted, Kane was forced to wait until his boss put the phone back in his pocket. "Well, Agent Logan, I don't know what I should thank you for more. While I do enjoy getting reamed out by an angry POTUS, I'm also quite grateful that I've been ordered to the Oval Office to meet with him in person. Better yet, he wants you to join us to discuss your theory, because it's our only active lead. So you and I have to depart for Washington right now."

Kane chose not to voice the single expletive that popped into his brain. If the president was angry enough to pull two agents off a hot investigation for a meeting, no sane person would want to be on the guest list. *Why couldn't I just have resigned and been done with all this?*

Douglas nodded at Kane's reaction. "Yeah. So you better come up with something more than this 'I gotta feeling' bullshit, and you better come up with it fast." The sound of an approaching helicopter filled the air. "That's our ride, and that means we're an hour and a half away from the worst meeting of our lives." He pivoted and stalked off to the landing area.

Probably the first of many, Kane thought as he followed.

Chapter 3 – Partners

Secret Service Agent Lilly Alexander forwarded yet another tidbit of information about the assassination attempt, this time to the Philadelphia field office. She was falling behind; at least a dozen more emails awaited her attention, and they all had to get out lest the trail of the attempted assassin drift away like fog in a gentle breeze.

Lilly had lucked herself right into this unglamorous role. Having successfully closed her second counterfeiting case in seventeen months, she had been rewarded with an amount of paperwork that should have been illegal due to its sheer quantity. While it meant at least a few days not in the field, it got monotonous quickly for the twenty-five-year-old agent accustomed to constant action.

To focus on the forms, she'd put on her headphones to listen to some music. Lilly got so lost in her efforts that the frantic movements of the other agents in the office failed to draw her attention. Only when she felt the breeze of someone racing by her cubicle did she stand and learn about the assassination attempt in New York.

Tim Benton, her Special Agent in Charge, came over. "Lilly, I need you to coordinate comms for the time being while we get our shit together." With a nod, she headed to the communication office and set up shop.

The volume of information coming in was amazing, but Lilly became energized by it. She soon recognized the patterns in the work and found her groove, gaining ground on the backlog. She was down to only eight outstanding messages when her cell phone buzzed. With a silent curse, she answered it. "Agent Alexander."

"Agent, this is Secretary Carlyle." Lilly's eyes bulged; Marion Carlyle was the Secretary of Homeland Security, and that made her the administration official in charge of the Secret Service. An agent at her level getting such a call was like the CEO of Google calling someone in the mail room by name. *Holy shit.*

"Yes, madame secretary?"

"I need you at Democratic National Headquarters ASAP," she stated like a field general ordering a battalion to advance. "Do you know where it is?"

"Yes, ma'am, but my SAC has put me in charge of coordinating comms for the assassination attempt here at Murray Lane. I don't know if anyone else can take over."

"Call your SAC and tell him that he needs to replace you, and then get over here ASAP. Are we clear?"

Benton wouldn't like that, but his objections wouldn't matter in the face of an order from the secretary. "Yes, ma'am. I'll be there as soon as possible."

"Very good." The line went dead. Lilly stared at the device for a second, wondering what fresh hell she was about to step into, before gathering her things and placing a call to Benton. As predicted, he was not pleased.

***

Brent Douglas put his phone away as the helicopter settled on the South Lawn of the White House. He had been working it hard during the ninety-minute flight, nearly pleading with the agents still at the scene for another theory he could present. The way Douglas looked as they landed told Kane everything he needed to know.

He didn't like going into this meeting with only one far-fetched investigative route any more than his boss did, but had nothing more to offer. He kept looking over the scene in his mind's eye but failed to envision another possible scenario.

The agents jumped from the craft the second it touched down and were met by a White House staffer who escorted them along the concrete pathway just north of the putting green that led to the West Colonnade. Outside the door to the secretary's office, both showed identification to an austere Marine officer while two enlisted men stood on either side of the entrance, rifles clenched to their chests. After scrutinizing their Secret Service badges, the major nodded and the Marines moved aside. The secretary waved them right past her desk without the slightest hesitation.

Kane had to quell a burst of nervous nausea as he followed Douglas toward the semi-famous door. Set at a forty-five-degree angle to the passageway to accommodate the eponymous shape of the Oval Office, it swung open as they approached. He had been around long enough to know even high-ranking, fairly regular visitors found the threshold intimidating, and that was if they were delivering *good* news to the president.

President Sharpe was standing to his left, near the Resolute desk, conversing with Secret Service Director Adrian Schultz and FBI Director Patrick MacMurray. It was not surprising to see Schultz or the FBI chief in the room, but it added yet another layer of tension to an atmosphere that practically crackled with frustration and anxiety. Brief handshakes were exchanged, but Kane had never met this president, so introductions were in order.

"Agent Logan, I presume?" President Sharpe said, offering his hand. There was no hint of the politician's "Damn glad to meet ya!" grin on his face. "Thank you for agreeing to be re-activated on such short notice."

"No problem, sir. It's an honor to meet you, although I do wish the circumstances were different."

The president frowned and raised his eyebrows. "Don't we all." He shook his head. "Let's get started." He settled behind his desk while the men sat on the facing couches in the middle of the room; Kane and Douglas on one, MacMurray and Schultz on the other. "Where are we?"

Douglas looked like he wanted to dive out of one of the bulletproof windows behind the president's desk, but opted for a deep breath. "Sir, as I indicated on the phone, we only have one working lead right now. Unfortunately, it's very unlikely, so we are looking for more plausible explanations."

"And you, Agent Logan, are the sponsor of this idea?" Sharpe asked. Kane could swear he saw Douglas' shoulders sag in relief as the spotlight moved to another target.

"Mr. President, I came up with the theory based on the data we had at the scene. I consider it plausible but, as the deputy director said, it stretches the bounds of reality. Still, at this point, it's the only explanation that makes any sense."

"I've heard the basics. Walk me through the reasons why you consider it feasible, and then why you don't."

"Yes, sir. First, we do know the exact direction from which the shot came, and the east tower of the Brooklyn Bridge is the closest thing someone could stand on in that direction. Second, the bullet we recovered can travel the required distance, especially given the height advantage of shooting from the top of the bridge tower.

"But the distance presents other problems. There are many factors that affect the flight of a bullet, and the further the shot, the more pronounced they are. A tiny gust of wind, the temperature of the round itself, the effect of gravity, even the spin of the earth, these must all be accounted for, and a one-millimeter error in aim by the shooter results in yards of difference for a shot this long. To my knowledge, no one has ever successfully hit a target at this range. In fact, the longest successful shot is over 1,000 yards less."

"That's correct," MacMurray said. "At least by anyone in our government or military. It's possible another country or organization could have done so, but unlikely in the extreme." Kane nodded to the director.

The president turned back to Kane. "So your scenario is improbable?"

"Yes, sir. I'd put the odds at one-in-twenty, and that might be optimistic."

The president nodded, paused a second, and then rose. He walked to his desk and picked up two pieces of paper. "This," he said as he raised one document in his right hand, "is yesterday's polling numbers regarding the election. Forty-four percent of registered voters indicated they would vote for me next month, while forty-one percent indicated they would vote for Armstrong. That leaves fifteen percent undecided, which is a pretty big amount so late in the game.

"This," he said, the single word dripping with menace as he held up the other sheet, "was a phone poll executed shortly after Armstrong was wounded, once it was reported he would survive. I got it just before you arrived." He handed the sheet to MacMurray. "Director, please read these results."

It was obvious MacMurray already knew them, but he still looked at the paper as he read. "Today, after hearing of the shooting, forty-two percent remain likely or certain to vote for President Sharpe, while fifty-one percent would vote for Senator Armstrong, with the remainder still undecided."

"Fifty-one percent! From forty-one in only TWO HOURS!" Sharpe's voice boomed off the walls of the office, and Kane was sure the microphones recording the conversation squealed as their circuits were overloaded. "I went from three points up to nine points down in less time than it takes to play a goddamned football game!"

His voice calmed a bit. "Now, I'm not saying it wasn't terrible. It was, and such things should never happen. But the man who was shot is my opponent, and not only are people feeling sorry for him, I am going to look like a horse's ass if we don't find the shooter and put him in jail for life. Armstrong's staff is going to issue a public statement today or tomorrow, saying he is certain I'll put aside any political differences and apply the full weight of the federal government to solve this crime, that he has full confidence in this country's law enforcement, blah blah blah. That means if I don't have someone in custody A-fucking-S-A-P we won't need to hold an election!"

MacMurray, Schultz, and Douglas stared at the Presidential Seal embroidered on the carpet during the executive rant, having already figured that part out for themselves. "I want this thing solved. I want someone in handcuffs by the end of the week." He turned his attention to the FBI director. "Whatever anyone else in the agency is working on, pull them to work on this case. You do whatever you have to do. Pat, do you understand what I'm saying?"

MacMurray nodded. "Yes, sir. Completely." The director had been around the block a few times, and Kane was sure he understood every part of the cryptic order. The president was being intentionally vague while making sure MacMurray knew to break the law if necessary. If an agent violated the rights of a suspect or moved before a warrant was in place or a civilian got hurt, the recording of this conversation would not have Sharpe ordering such illegal action, and he would have the director's head on display in the Rose Garden. He was playing hardball.

Sharpe turned to face Kane. "Agent Logan, I've discussed this with Directors MacMurray and Schultz. The Secret Service doesn't have resources to spare on your unlikely theory, especially this close to the election, but I can't ignore it. Therefore, as of right now, you are working for me with orders to run your idea to earth. If you can discount it with certainty, do so. If possible, find more evidence so we can act on it. The switchboard will have instructions to put your calls through. You'll work under Director MacMurray, but if you run into any problems or obstacles, this office will eliminate them. Are we on the same page?"

"Absolutely, sir." He was on the same page, but the president had just rewritten the book. There was a reason presidents didn't do what Sharpe had just done; it smacked of imperial rule. Even the agents on the presidential protection detail had certain orders the president himself could not countermand, and with good reason, but the terse sentences from Sharpe had just invalidated that long-standing rule. Kane wasn't sure the order was legal, and briefly considered contesting it, but concluded the president had much more to lose than Kane. If it ever got out that Sharpe had hijacked a sworn officer for any reason, the

Democrat-controlled House of Representatives would have Articles of Impeachment drawn up and on the Speaker's desk before the ink dried. He held his tongue.

"Good. You are to report to Secretary Carlyle at Democratic National Committee Headquarters immediately. She will have further instructions for you. So, if you have no questions..."

Only about a thousand. Kane, however, knew better. "None, Mr. President." He took no pleasure from the assignment. If he got lucky and discovered some evidence or actually found the shooter, Sharpe would take all the credit and give Kane a nice little certificate in a plastic frame. If Kane failed miserably, Sharpe would toss him out of the agency on his ear while proudly bragging to the White House Press Corps that he had investigated *every single lead* to bring about justice.

"On your way, then." Kane rose and headed to the door as another agent opened it. He didn't know this man but gave the brief nod one would offer to a colleague as they passed in the hall. He expected and got the same in return, but noticed the message in the other man's eyes as they passed.

Poor bastard.

***

Lilly Alexander zoomed up I-695 in D.C. as fast as she dared given the traffic. It wasn't that she feared being pulled over—she had the red and blue flashers in the car's grill activated—but she could not afford the delay a traffic accident would cause.

Upon trotting into DNC Headquarters, she was escorted immediately to a conference room. In addition to the agents standing against the walls, there were three people present.

Secretary Carlyle nodded in her direction, and Lilly returned the gesture. Although a Republican appointed by President Sharpe, her job was technically apolitical, so it made sense for her to be here.

The secretary was speaking to Vice President Grant Caufield. Even with the extraordinary circumstances of the day, to see the number two Republican in the heart of the other team's headquarters seemed weird—almost sinister.

The man most expected to be there was Voight Stafford, who was on his phone. He looked frazzled, his salt-and-pepper hair unkempt, his collar unbuttoned, his jacket draped over the chair next to him. Alexander couldn't blame him; not only had a bullet passed within a few inches of his chest less than six hours ago, his candidate was lying in the hospital with serious injuries from that same bullet.

Stafford completed his call and put the phone down. After quick introductions and handshakes, everyone sat to attend to business. Vice President Caufield spoke first.

"Agent Alexander, you'll be taking a special assignment with another agent who"—he checked his watch—"should be joining us shortly."

"This is not something we would normally give to a newer agent," Secretary Carlyle interrupted, "but you have demonstrated your ability over the last year and a half." Lilly nodded at the compliment.

For the first time, Stafford spoke up. "Agent Alexander, I cannot stress how important this is to our country, and also to me personally. Senator Armstrong, as you likely know, is a long-time friend of mine." He had a posh, vaguely British-sounding tone that conveyed privilege and money.

The door swung open, admitting a man who, while dressed like any other agent, had the rugged good looks and physique of a leading man. "Agent Logan. Thank you for getting here so quickly," Caufield greeted him. At that moment, Lilly recognized him, but held her tongue. It had no bearing on what was happening.

"Of course, Mr. Vice President," he responded. "But I have to ask why I'm here."

"Considering the unique nature of your assignment, I wanted to introduce you two myself. Agent Kane Logan, this is Agent Lilly Alexander." Logan glanced her way. "She will be working with you on your part of the investigation."

Lilly was about to give him a polite nod and smile but stopped when she saw the irritation all over his face. He turned to the vice president. "Nobody said anything about a partner, especially an inexperienced junior one," he snapped. "I was under the impression I was brought in to work alone."

Lilly blinked with shock at his statement. *Inexperienced? Junior? Fuck you!*

"That is incorrect. Agent Alexander has a great deal of experience," Caufield responded, both his tone and glare icy. "You will work with her, and you will utilize her skill set fully. That's an order. Is there going to be a problem?"

To Lilly, her fellow agent looked like he was being told to take a bite of a turd. "No, sir. No problem."

Lilly managed to keep her face neutral, but her eyes burned. The anger she felt at being demeaned in front of so many high-ranking officials rose inside her like inky black smoke from the hottest fire. She now wanted no part of working with this pompous prick but, as the vice president had just made clear, that was not an option.

Logan looked over at Lilly once again, blinking as he recognized the disdain emanating from her eyes. Maybe he hadn't realized how insulting his words had been, but that was no excuse, Lilly thought.

"Very good," the vice president continued. "You have your orders. Get to it." Both agents nodded and left the meeting room. Lilly walked quickly, determined to make Kane keep up. With his longer legs, he didn't have much of a problem doing so, but she had no doubt he got the message.

When they reached the parking lot, Kane motioned down the road. "My car is right down this way. Let's ride back to HQ together and plan our next steps."

Lilly ignored his suggestion. "What is your fucking problem?"

Kane sighed. "Look. I'm sorry," he stated with all the sincerity of an employee at the DMV. "That had nothing to do with you. It's—" Lilly's quietly furious voice stopped him mid-sentence.

"You're goddamned right it had nothing to do with me! The next time you try and treat me like some rookie fresh out of Glynco," she snapped, referring to the Secret Service training center in Georgia, "I will put my foot right up your ass and break it off. I'm every bit as capable as you, I'm good at what I do, and you will treat me as such—especially in front of the vice president and the secretary of Homeland Security! Am I making myself heard, agent?" She fixed her eyes right on his and dared him to look away.

Kane did not flinch. The way his nostrils flared was a clear indication that he didn't like being called out any more than she did, but he had the mettle to take his medicine. After a few seconds of the standoff, he nodded. "You're right. I was out of line, and the reasons don't matter. It won't happen again."

"Good. But I'll drive myself if you don't mind."

He shrugged. "Fine. See you there in thirty."

She took that cue to turn her back on him and head toward her car. *This is off to a great start.*

Chapter 4 – Making New Friends

Kane arrived at Secret Service headquarters a minute or two before Lilly, due mostly to how angrily he drove. He'd never had such an overwhelming urge to punch anyone right in the face, but he'd also never had another agent speak to him like that. He *had* earned the rebuke, but it didn't matter in the heat of the moment. Rather than take his frustrations out on Alexander when they got back to the office, he abused the accelerator, pushing the speedometer needle into triple digits.

Even after he parked in the underground garage and rode the elevator up into the citadel-like building, he was still fuming. Taking a deep breath, he brutally quashed such violent thoughts as the elevator doors opened. He stopped at reception to ask where he could find his new partner and was directed up one floor to a cubicle at the end of a row, where Agent Alexander was logging onto her laptop.

"Look," he said to her without preamble, "we got off on the wrong foot. Let's start over. We have a job to do, and being angry with each other is going to make things harder. Truce?"

Lilly looked at him with an expression of pure innocence, as if their heated discussion had never happened. "Truce. How about we commandeer a conference room and map out our first steps?"

"Sounds good." It vexed him that, while he'd had to swallow his anger, hers seemed to have evaporated into thin air. She probably appeared so peaceful because she felt she'd won their confrontation.

A few minutes later, they were in a conference room, with Kane describing what he had seen in New York in great detail. They traded ideas, theories, and conjecture, while Kane stood at the whiteboard that covered an entire wall and started an impromptu flowchart of all the factors associated with the crime—both known and unknown. The unknown took up a lot more space.

"And that's the whole of it," Kane concluded.

"One theory that's barely possible," Lilly summarized. "We've got shit."

"That's the consensus today. But it's where we are. What are our next steps?"

"Threat boards?"

"The usual suspects." While there were always countries and groups that wished harm to the United States in some form or another, there was nothing to indicate any of these entities were involved. Of course, that didn't mean they *weren't* involved.

"In that case, I think our first step is to confirm if this shot was even possible," Lilly stated. "What's your confidence level?"

"Maybe five percent."

"Are you qualified to make that assessment?"

"I have experience shooting at long distances, but there are people better than me. And I might..." Kane's voice trailed off as he started scrolling through his phone. "Yup, here he is." He made a call and activated the speaker.

"Hello?"

A grin came over Kane's face at hearing the gruff voice. "Tell me, is this the old jarhead Terry Richards who couldn't hit the broadside of a barn even if Heckler & Koch mounted a pair of bifocals on his rifle?"

"Depends. Who's asking the question?" he responded, amusement creeping through the faux suspicious tone.

"Staff Sergeant Kane Logan, sir."

"Logan!" His voice exploded with pleasure. "How are you? Damn, it's good to hear your voice!"

"I'm doing okay. It's good to talk to you too, Colonel."

"Thanks. But I suspect you didn't call me to chat about old times, especially today. Still working for that 'consulting company?'" Richards had more than enough experience to know exactly who Kane really worked for, and the savvy not to say it out loud.

"Right now I'm TDY, working in D.C. again." Using the term "temporary duty" made it clear he was back with the Secret Service. "My colleague and I, who is on the line, have been tasked with drawing conclusions, or at least ideas, from today's events. I think you might be one of the few people able to help us."

"It really was from that far away?"

"Even further," Kane replied, knowing the retired colonel would catch his meaning. "Are you up for some visitors tomorrow morning?"

"My door is always open for a fellow Marine."

"Thank you, sir. You still up in Morgantown?" Kane asked.

"Yup. Family keeps wanting me to move down to Florida, but I'll shit twice and die before I go down there. Bunch of geriatric pussies wearing cardigans in 100-degree heat, all driving thirty-five in the left lane with their friggin' blinker on."

Kane had to chuckle at that one. "Roger that, colonel. Reveille is gonna be early tomorrow, so we'll be there first thing."

"See you then, Sergeant."

"Who was that?" Lilly asked. She appeared slightly irritated, and Kane realized he was going to have to tell her what he was doing *before* he did it.

"My old sniper instructor from the Marines. He taught me the craft. I was decent at it, but there were a lot of people there who were better than me, and Richards was better than all of them. He's kind of a legend. Some of the shots he's rumored to have pulled off are... well, they're a lot like what we're talking about."

"What are you hoping to learn?"

"Like I said, he's one of the best ever. If there's a way to make this shot more feasible, he'll know it, but he also won't be afraid to call bullshit if it can't be done. I think we either get a lead or report this as a dead end." Despite his desire to make headway on the investigation, it wouldn't trouble him one bit to be off the president's radar.

"Since we have a plan for tomorrow," he continued, "why don't we call it a day? I have a feeling we're going to be busy as shit for quite a while, so let's get all the sleep we can." Kane felt a lot more tired than he should have; stress had a compounding effect on fatigue. This was not a normal assignment, and he wasn't close to being back in the groove.

"Good idea," Lilly agreed.

"What's your address?" Kane punched it into his phone as she relayed it. "I'll pick you up at six at your place. And dress civilian casual. No sense in advertising who we are, even if Richards already knows. He has neighbors."

"OK. See you at six."

Monday, October 30

Eight Days Before the Election

Chapter 5 – Disclosures

Lilly stared straight ahead as if she was daydreaming, but her mind mulled over the case as she and Kane sped northwest toward West Virginia. He wasn't in a talking mood. It would be better for both of them if they established a bit of a rapport, but that wasn't going to happen if silence continued to dominate the inside of the Suburban.

Once they got away from the traffic and the suburban sprawl, Kane became more loquacious. "I read about those counterfeiting cases you were on. Seems like you did some excellent work."

That came out of nowhere. "Thanks, but it wasn't just me. It was a team effort."

"I read the report, and your name popped up again and again. Your SAC made it clear you were the one who saw stuff no one else did. Some of those connections were... I mean, they were pretty much impossible. How the hell did you do it?"

Lilly sighed. "I have an eidetic memory combined with hyperthymesia."

"What's hyperthymesia?"

"Basically, it's eidetic memory but over the long term."

"Really? I thought that was a myth."

"Yes and no. It's real, but it's often misrepresented, and people have a poor understanding of it. Doctors believe I have one of the most acute cases ever recorded."

"How is that different than a photographic memory?"

"To some degree, the terms are related. Everyone has it a little bit, and some more than others. It's just that, while everyone can remember things for a couple of minutes or hours, I can remember every minute and specific detail of every event indefinitely, and I can recognize connections between them."

"Wow. I can see how that would come in handy. But I thought most people with photographic or eidetic or whatever memories had mental and social issues, like the guy who was the inspiration for *Rain Man*. You don't."

And here we go. These conversations always went the same way. "You mean Kim Peek. Yeah, he had some serious social difficulties, but he also had a genetic disorder."

"Right," Kane responded. "So why don't you mumble and rock back and forth and have to watch Judge Wapner at four o'clock?"

"I wasn't always this 'normal'—god, I hate that term. Growing up, I couldn't turn my brain off. I would stay awake for days with every detail of every day running through my mind over and over until I passed out from exhaustion. I couldn't focus on any one thing, because everything that happened or whatever I saw led to more and more details I could never, ever forget.

"I didn't know what to do with myself. My parents took me to shrinks and stuff, and I told them everything I saw or heard—numbers, words, entire articles, images—they all passed by on this movie screen in my head. I'd read or see them, and they'd become permanent memories. But they didn't understand, not really. Most of them diagnosed me with the worst case of Attention Deficit Disorder they'd ever seen and wanted to medicate the shit out of me. My parents resisted at first but, as things got worse and worse, they started talking to me about trying it.

"But one doctor was different. When I told her about the movie screen, she twisted her head kind of funny and asked me to tell her everything I could remember about May 6th, 2008—which was four years prior.'"

"What was special about that day?" Kane asked.

"Nothing. Nothing at all, but my answer lasted *seventy minutes*. It was a normal Tuesday, started out a little overcast but got nicer as the day went on. I told her literally everything from the moment I opened my eyes to the moment I went to bed, what I ate for all three meals, what we learned in school that day, what I wore, what my teacher wore, what every other kid in the class wore, what was in the news. Everything."

"How is that possible?"

"That's the point. I'd done that every single day of my life since I started having conscious memories. I can recite the same level of detail for May 5th or May 7th. If it occupied one of my senses, I remembered it forever. To me, that was perfectly normal. I didn't understand why other people couldn't do it.

"This doctor suggested hypnosis, and after a few sessions everything was different. For the first time in my life, my head was clear. I could remember the entire day but, when it was over, I learned to put everything in a box in my mind and save it for later. I went from a special-ed student failing most of my subjects to correctly answering every single question in advanced classes every single time. The only problem I had was essay questions—I just kept on writing until the bell rang."

"I can see where this is going," Kane said, his eyes wide in shocked admiration. "Having that skill comes in handy when you're tracking counterfeit money."

"Like you don't know. If you show me a stack of fifty bills right now, one at a time, I could recite every serial number and denomination back to you, backward or forward, and I could tell you the number on the forty-third bill you showed me once you were done. More important for counterfeiting, I can see patterns in the numbers if they exist."

"You mean, like sequential numbers?" Kane looked a little confused.

"Well, yeah, but that's easy. I can tell you if a sequence exists if you show them to me out of order. I can tell you if, out of the first ten bills in a bunch, the odd ones are sequentially related to the even ones in the last ten. In the first counterfeiting ring I busted, the guy had about forty different plates with different serial numbers, but he thought he was cute. Every serial number added up to 202 if you grouped the numbers into four two-digit groups."

"Christ, you should be in cryptoanalysis. Those NSA guys would love you."

"I thought about doing that, among other things, but decided this would be the most interesting way to use my gift. Sitting in a room reading ciphers sounds kind of boring, but here I get to match wits with pretty good criminals on the fly, and I get to carry a gun."

Kane chuckled at that one. "Any other superpowers you want to share with me? X-ray vision, invisibility, eye-lasers, anything like that?"

"Geez, don't I bring enough to the table?" She kept her tone playful; if this was what it took to establish a pleasant working relationship with him, she was all in.

"True," Kane replied. "I'm sure it will come in handy sooner or later."

A pause followed, and Lilly jumped in to keep the conversation from lapsing back into silence. "Now that you know my story, what about you? I did a little checking myself. Seems you were hot shit in the agency for a while, but a few years ago you just disappeared. Best I can tell, this is your first fieldwork since then."

Kane nodded for several seconds. "It's all true," he finally said, as if that explained everything.

"Why?"

His response was flat and formal. "Based on certain executive decisions, there was a reallocation of resources and assignments, and my duties were realigned."

"What the hell does that mean?"

"It means I went into semi-retirement, and this is the first time I was recalled from it. That's all."

"But—"

"But nothing. That's how things worked out. The details won't make a bit of difference to this investigation, so there's nothing more to discuss about the topic."

Lilly frowned at him, but he seemed a lot more interested in the road. She gave him a second to reconsider, but for whatever reason, he'd shut and locked that door and thrown the key out the window.

"Thanks for sharing," she said to the side of his head, not attempting to hide the bitterness toward him that had just started to fade.

***

Two silent hours later, they passed over the Monongahela River and navigated to the driveway of a simple but well-kept ranch home surrounded by red maple trees. *Finally.* The tension in the car after their chat had been palpable, bad enough that Kane had to force himself not to apologize for his curt demeanor. He could see why his partner was pissed. Lilly had shared something with him to establish a connection and had gotten jack squat in return.

They hopped out of the car and headed over the uneven walkway to knock on the front door. After a brief wait, Kane heard a series of *clicks* as locks were disengaged. But, when it opened, he got the warmest of greetings.

"Logan! You look like you could go out on patrol right now!" The colonel had a worn face and leaned on a cane but shook Kane's hand with enough force to make the bigger man's shoulder shake. "Get in here! I've got coffee ready for ya!" Kane turned to introduce his partner, but his host pulled him through the door so quickly he didn't have a chance to do so.

Once inside, however, the older gentleman looked at Lilly like he'd committed the most egregious of mistakes. "Pardon me," he said with crestfallen eyes. "I haven't seen Sergeant Logan in about eight years, but that's no reason to be rude to a lady." He came to a semblance of attention. "I'm Lieutenant Colonel Terry Richards, U.S. Marines, Retired, ma'am. I hope you'll forgive my atrocious behavior."

Lilly smiled at him. "That's all right, Colonel. I'm Agent Lilly Alexander, working with Agent Logan on this assignment. It's nice to meet you." They shook hands.

"We'll blame it on Logan. He never understood the part where you're supposed to be polite to a lady." Kane pulled a face at the remark, and Lilly gave him a quick look, letting him know just how much she enjoyed the little jab in his direction.

"Sounds like a good solution to me." They laughed—even Kane, although his was a bit forced. Richards showed them to the couch before ambling into the adjoining kitchen to get the promised coffee, waving off Kane when he offered to help.

"Someone important must have their balls caught in a vice for you guys to shoot out here this early," he called through the open door. Kane cringed, but Lilly smiled. He'd forgotten how Richards could be obliviously rude one second, a gallant gentleman the next, and then transition seamlessly into spewing profanity in the way only a Marine could in front of someone he didn't know.

"Yes, sir," Kane responded. "This comes from up high on the chain."

"How high?"

"Direct from NCA, actually."

Richards was walking out of the kitchen slowly carrying a tray with a carafe, three mugs, and cream and sugar on it when he heard the acronym for National Command Authority—also known as the president. "No shit?"

"No shit and a half, Colonel."

Richards set the tray down. "Guess I better get serious here."

"I certainly am."

Lilly poured the black drink into her mug and raised it for a sip while Kane added a copious amount of cream to his coffee. He snickered when her eyes went wide at the overwhelmingly bitter taste. He leaned over and spoke to her *sotto voce*, "You'll want to use some cream."

"No kidding," she whispered back.

"Anyway," the Marine said, oblivious to Lilly's reaction, "what can I do for you?"

Kane gave Richards a detailed rundown of the situation, some of which was known to the general public, some not. He could see the wheels turning in the older man's head as he presented facts and figures on handwritten sheets.

"How far again?" Richards asked when Kane finished with the deluge of information.

"The tower is 4,817 yards away, with 248 feet of elevation." Richards blew his breath out; he was having as much trouble with this theory as everyone else.

"It was easy to figure out the direction the shot came from, so I looked on the Google Maps and saw the same thing—the bridge was the closest point to shoot from. When you called, I really thought you were going to give me something new so this would be more realistic."

Lilly jumped in. "So you're saying this shot isn't possible?"

Richards turned his attention to her. "No, Agent, I'm saying something much worse. This shot *is* possible."

"How is it possible, and why is that worse?"

"It's a damn hard shot, but it absolutely can be done. I can 100 percent verify that shots at that range have been successful."

She turned to Kane. "But I thought you said last night the longest successful shot on record was like 1,000 yards less than this one."

"Exactly," Kane answered. "*On record*. Why would we advertise to any potential enemies our exact capabilities in this area? That's like developing a secret submarine or jet fighter with amazing capabilities and then putting a commercial about it on during the Super Bowl."

"Okay, point taken."

Kane turned back to his old commanding officer. "I kinda figured you were going to say something along those lines. But I need something more concrete to take back to the boss." He sounded just like Brent Douglas the previous day. *Perspective is a bitch.*

"Your numbers are dead on," he responded, "but I could make them better."

"How?"

"You have a ballistics report for the projectile?"

Kane held up his file folder. "Yeah, in here."

"What does it say about the back of the round and the weight?"

Kane shuffled the pages. "'Posterior end of the projectile shows signs of alteration in a manner consistent with shaving or sanding.' The weight is... 102 grain. I didn't know Creedmoor 6.5's came that low."

"They don't." It took Kane a second to see the light, but when he did he felt his eyes go wide.

"There you go," Richards said, in a tone suggesting the bland terminology explained everything.

"What does that all mean?" Lilly asked.

Richards fielded the question. "You shave down the projectile to save a few grams of weight, fill that new space with a little more powder—you have to be real careful not to overfill—and you'll get higher velocity and better distance. Basic physics. More velocity equals a straighter and longer shot that's less subject to other forces changing the trajectory, especially wind and bullet drop. Now, on the flip side, the lighter weight makes it more vulnerable to those same forces."

Lilly frowned, clearly not recognizing the portent of all this. "If that's true, it's a wash, right?" Kane shook his head.

"No," he responded. "The faster, lighter aspects of the projectile will win out every time."

"Then it's *not* a wash, and this makes the shot more possible, right?" Lilly's frustration was palpable.

"Yes, but that's not the worst of it," Kane said.

"Goddammit!" Lilly said in a huff. "Will one of you guys get me up to speed?!"

"Agent," Richards responded, "the issue is multi-faceted. First, whoever altered the bullet and reloaded the round has an extremely rare combination of knowledge and ability. That person knew *exactly* what he was doing and understood that the advantages of lower weight would supersede the disadvantages, and he altered the bullet for that purpose but did so in a way that didn't affect its ballistics. That's not easy to pull off. And the shot itself requires an epic level of skill. This individual is *highly* educated and well-trained." He looked over at Kane.

The senior agent picked up the narrative. "That means, if all this is accurate, there was no luck involved. It means this guy was a foot off of a perfect shot at an amazing distance, so we've got a motivated, skilled person somewhere out there with the ability to take out pretty much any target from almost *three miles* away. All he needs is elevation to give him a clear line of sight."

Lilly nodded, acknowledging the import of the situation. The Secret Service was the country's premier protection entity, and they would be unable to cover a three-mile bubble around every senior politician in the country at all times; the logistics and manpower requirements alone made that impossible. Anyone else—like a CEO, a celebrity, or even just a regular guy on the street—would have less of a barrier between themselves and such a shot. "Oh, shit."

"Yeah. As bad as this was," Kane said, "it just got a lot worse. We have to call this in. This is a real threat."

"Yeah, but I don't know what we do with this," Lilly pointed out.

Kane said nothing. *Shit. She's right.*

Colonel Richards jumped into the discussion. "I have a suggestion."

"What's that, Colonel?"

"About a year after you were discharged, I had another guy come through sniper school, Ethan Doyle. Just made E-5 when I met him. Cocky son of a bitch, but he could shoot like no one's business. No disrespect intended, but he was *way* better than you, Kane. Almost as good as me. First week in he nailed a 1,500-yard shot three times in a row."

"Should we check him out?" Lilly asked.

"I'm sure you will, but that's not the reason I brought him up. After he rotated out of school, I would get word about what he was up to, and it sounded a little sketchy."

"Sketchy how?" Kane prompted.

"Like he was a little too eager to shoot. More accurately, he was a little too eager to kill."

"Wait," Lilly interjected. "Isn't that what he's supposed to do?"

"Yeah," Richards responded, "but your objective as a sniper is to complete the mission. Of course that means killing your target, but that shouldn't be why you're shooting. It's like he relished the *killing* part rather than the *completing the mission* part. Professional soldiers—stable ones, anyway—don't actually like taking a life. Doyle would start talking about a shot he took, and it would morph from technical details into this gross description of what it looked like through the scope in gory detail. Honestly, I'm amazed he passed his FITREPS saying some of that shit.

"Then, after he rotated out, he started calling me with all kinds of anti-government stuff. I got an awfully strong Timothy McVeigh vibe from him, and thought about cutting him off, but decided against it. You know, keep your friends close and your enemies closer, that sort of thing. I went along with what he said but never really committed myself.

"But the whole reason I brought him up is because he has one of those camps somewhere way up in New Hampshire, kind of like a weekend survival thing. You need a recommendation from someone he trusts to get in, and guess what their specialty is?"

"Sniper shooting," Kane answered.

"You win the prize, sergeant. He takes rich assholes with their new, expensive rifles and teaches them how to hit targets at 1,000-plus yards."

"How do you know about it?" Lilly asked.

"Because he calls me every six months or so like he's keeping in touch, but it's really him just reminding me I'm always welcome as a guest instructor. He's got this fixation on me, but I'm too old for that."

"We don't have any reason to think our shooter is from there or anywhere else specific," Kane objected.

"No, I get it. But these guys often stick together, at least the leaders. It's kind of the self-fulfilling 'you sound like me so we must both be right' deal, and they talk. Just a guess, but if one of them had a shooter good enough to pull this shot off, he'd be bragging to all the other guys in the club."

Kane thought about it. They didn't have much else, and at the very least visiting one of these camps would give them some insight into what they might be dealing with. He looked at Lilly with his eyebrows raised, and she nodded.

"Can you get us in?" Kane asked.

Richards shrugged. "Probably. You sure you wanna do that?"

Lilly seemed surprised. "Why wouldn't we?"

"You might get your ass shot off if he finds out who you work for."

"He won't," Lilly said. "We'll go undercover—husband and wife. We've got a cabin out in Nowhere, USA, and we want to take care of invaders while they're still a mile away."

Richards apparently agreed. "Shit. He'll eat that up. I'll get my phone."

"Slow your roll, Colonel," Kane said. "We need to figure some things out—like who we are, where we're from, create false backgrounds, stuff like that."

An hour later, they looked over the profiles of the fictional characters they had created. "Hi," Kane said in a conversational tone. "I'm Kane Walsh, from Wilmington, Delaware, and this is my wife, Lilly."

"It's really good to meet y'all," Lilly said. Lilith Walsh's profile indicated she was a transplant from Macon, Georgia, and had never been able to rid her speech of the occasional Southern colloquialism.

"I'd buy that," Richards said.

"Great, but we don't have to convince you, Colonel," Lilly responded in her normal voice. "He sounds like the suspicious type."

"We'll rehearse on the way up." He looked over the handwritten form in front of him. "Ready?"

"Go for it," Kane answered.

Richards dialed. "Hey, Sarge. It's Terry Richards here." He smiled and nodded, spending the next few minutes on small talk. This friendly banter part taxed Kane's patience, but it was necessary; if Richards sounded too eager, suspicions might be aroused.

Finally, though, the colonel found his opening. "No, Ethan, I'm just too damned old to be doing that shit anymore, but I do have something for you. I have an acquaintance who is looking to get a little better at his long-distance shooting, especially after what went down in New York yesterday, and if you're not the man to help him with that, I don't know who is."

A barrage of questions followed, but Richards handled it well, giving "honest" answers when their profiles indicated as such, saying he didn't know when necessary. His performance must have been good enough, because after twenty-five minutes of back-and-forth with Doyle that included a couple of "as a favor to me" statements, Richards slapped his leg and offered his thanks.

"I'll let them know. Thanks a million, Ethan. Yup, five thou in cash, not refundable, and they bring their own ammo. I think you guys will hit it off." He stopped to scribble down an address. "I'll pass it on. You want me to have him call you?" A pause. "Okay, no, I get it. Gotta be cautious. Thanks for getting them in at the last minute. I'll tell him right now so he can get ready. Perfect. I really appreciate this." He ended the call.

"OK. Lucky break—they started a class this week, but he'll let you come tomorrow morning. You gotta be there by oh eight hundred." He tore off the sheet and gave it to Lilly. "He said to go to this address and wait until he shows up. And no cell phones, period."

Kane didn't like that, and he could tell Lilly didn't either. They'd be absolutely on their own if anything went sideways. *Well, that's why they pay us the big bucks.*

"Thanks a lot, Colonel. If this helps us, I'll really owe you one."

"Shit, you already owe me one. If this pans out, I'll expect a fine bottle of Scotch every month until I croak!"

Everyone laughed. "You got it, sir." He turned to Lilly. "We better get moving. We've got to get back to requisition and organize a ton of shit. It's going to be a long-ass day."

"Sounds like it," she agreed.

Kane shook his former commander's hand before turning to leave, but Richards wasn't quite done.

"Kane?"

He turned. "Sir?"

The older man hesitated. An uncomfortable look covered his face, but finally some words came out. "Whatever this is, it sounds like trouble to me. Make sure you check six."

"Always do, sir. Always do."

***

Heading back to D.C., Kane and Lilly discussed what they would need for the trip. With a basic outline, they divided their tasks, calling in to request new identities, IDs, false backgrounds, and everything else that could be tracked in today's connected society.

Shortly after they passed back into Maryland, red lights glowed in all three lanes in front of them, forcing Kane to break with enough enthusiasm to throw them into their seat belts. Lilly saw the cars behind them doing the same, but the sounds of metal and glass smashing into one another never materialized despite the screech of rubber on pavement.

Whatever had happened in front of them must not have been too serious; the traffic started moving again in under a minute. It was slow going as the cars resumed their highway spacing, but Lilly caught the drastic motion of what looked like an SUV aggressively changing lanes behind them. Her eyes went out of focus for a second as she searched her mental inventory.

"We're being followed," she said simply.

"What? How do you know?"

"See that light gray Ford Explorer about four cars back in the middle lane? It was behind us this morning for most of the drive out. He got too close because of all the brakes and is trying to back off."

Kane searched his side mirror until he spotted the vehicle. "How can you be sure?"

"New Jersey plates, WVB-183. I saw the same license plate on the same truck behind us on the way to Morgantown."

"You can remember license plates too?" Kane asked, incredulity in his voice. "No way."

Lilly glared at him with a clenched jaw before bowing her head and shielding her eyes from the outside. "Counter-clockwise starting with the car right in front of us:

"Blue Honda Civic, Maryland plates 376-ACH.

"Black BMW 528i, Delaware plates, 746332.

"Next to us, white Buick Encore, DC plates BG-1847 that you can't see now.

"Gold Chevy Colorado pickup, Maryland 'Treasure the Chesapeake' plates TEG-349.

"Gray Ford F-150, Virginia plates, VRJ-3832.

"Beat up multi-color Toyota Celica, Maryland plates SCJ-432.

"Black Oldsmobile, New Jersey 'Shore to Please' custom plates, ACHOME.

"Red Pontiac Fiero, West Virginia 'Wild Wonderful' plates, 8JE-293."

She lifted her head. "We are being followed," she reiterated.

Kane looked like he wanted to challenge her further but held his tongue. "OK, I'll eat crow later. Thoughts?"

"It's not good that someone has eyes on us this early in the investigation. And that begs the question of how they know what we're doing."

"Agreed."

"So," Lilly asked, "do we find out who they are?"

Kane pondered for a minute. "I'm going to say no. Right now our primary advantage is they don't know we know they're watching us. That gives us the upper hand."

"We're just going to let them drive behind us all the way back to Murray Lane?"

"Yup, if they want. When and where they break off could tell us a lot about who they are."

The rest of the ride passed in relative silence, save for the occasional discussion or question about their tail. Unsurprisingly, the Explorer broke off when Kane took the exit that led to their headquarters. That meant they had exceptionally good intel, and that was not good.

Everything they had so far was bad news, unanswered questions, and vague leads offering little or no promise. That had to change.

Tuesday, October 31

Seven Days Before the Election

Chapter 6 – First Contact

Kane and Lilly sailed up Route 95 in Maryland under a black sky and a crescent moon to their left. It wasn't quite midnight, and they'd already been on the road for over an hour, with eight more to go.

The agents were tired. They'd gotten little more than a short nap before their departure. Most of the previous afternoon and evening had been spent frantically procuring everything a well-to-do couple would own. They needed to look as if they thought they could buy whatever they needed, including skill, to survive the invasion of the unwashed masses that seemed to be coming closer every day.

Kane couldn't complain about the ride they'd ended up with—a 2021 Range Rover Westminster—which was about as smooth and comfortable as anything he'd ever driven. When he pushed the pedal down, the engine flung them back in their seats. The only thing he didn't care for was that, instead of the normal lever on the center console for the transmission, there was one of those dials. Oh well—he'd just have to get used to it.

Just before going over the Delaware Memorial Bridge into New Jersey, the highway was better lit, and the increased visibility paid dividends. "We've got a friend," Lilly announced.

"What's up?"

"Same New Jersey plates, but now they're on a light blue Toyota minivan."

Kane nodded, assessing the development. Whoever was following them had access to multiple vehicles but felt it necessary to use the same license plate two days in a row. Was that due to a limited supply of plates? "If it was the same car with different plates, would you pick up on that as easily as the plate numbers?"

"Not as easily, no, unless it had a unique feature, like a dent or a broken taillight. Numbers and words are unique, so they stand out to me, but one red Honda looks like the next red Honda. I can't say I wouldn't figure it out, but you'd have a better chance of throwing one by me with different plates on the same car than the other way around."

"Okay. So whoever is onto us doesn't know anything about your superpower." He flashed a quick smile at Lilly.

"No one does. That's why I don't go around advertising it."

"On top of that, it suggests limited manpower where the same guy took the plates off one car and put them on another. Those might be advantages we can exploit."

"Definitely."

Like the previous day, their tail followed at a smart distance, and Kane made no attempt to shake them, making the ride fairly uneventful. Even though nothing untoward occurred, the fact that they were being followed again bothered him like an annoying mosquito he could not kill.

***

The further north they traveled through the rural areas of the Granite State, the worse the roads got, the fewer structures they encountered, and the bigger the mountains became. Their tail bailed out when they took the turn for State Route 145 near the Canadian border. Lilly, now behind the wheel, discussed that development with Kane; either the Toyota figured it would be too easily spotted after all this time, which was likely, or he'd confirmed their destination and no longer needed to follow, which was unsettling.

When they reached a barely graded stretch of scree and talus, Lilly couldn't help herself. "Ba-da bing-bing, bing-bing, bing-bing," she sang quietly, poorly mimicking the dueling banjos in *Deliverance* and following that up with nervous laughter. Kane nodded in agreement.

Trees closed in on both sides, making a turn-around impossible. "How you feeling?" she asked, just to get Kane's read on the tactical situation.

"Exposed and trapped at the same time." Lilly watched his head swivel and his eyes dart about like a nervous gazelle. "This is the kind of road that you see the victims take in bad slasher movies."

Glorious. "We're about three miles or so from the meeting point."

"Okay. Keep us ready to move when we stop."

"Copy." They continued in silence, bouncing around in their seats as the road took on the characteristics of a proving ground.

After five or six interminable minutes, an increase in daylight ahead suggested the trees might be thinning, and shortly afterward Lilly entered a small circular clearing about fifty yards across. Three other trails radiated in different directions that looked even worse than the one they'd just traveled.

Lilly could see two mountain peaks from the clearing, and if she could see, she could be seen. Circling the perimeter at low speed, she discovered there was no place where the truck wasn't subject to possible observation. "Shit. We're super-exposed and in a perfect position for an easy shot." Moving into the middle of the area so they didn't look like they were trying to hide, she turned the console dial of the transmission to "P" but kept the truck running.

Lilly touched her pistol, knowing how useless it would be against a rifle at long range. Kane noted her action. "It's all good," he said, but to Lilly he sounded like he was trying to reassure both of them. "Just stay in the truck. The glass is our friend, remember?" Lilly nodded. Shooting through windows almost always guaranteed a miss; contact with the glass sent the bullet off on a different course. Now, if these guys used a two-shot method, where one bullet cleared the glass for the second to get to its target, well...

They sat and kept watch for several minutes until Kane spoke up. "Someone's got eyes on us," he said, barely moving his head.

"Where?"

"East peak, near the top. Light off a scope."

"Could be binoculars," Lilly said with a lot of hope but little conviction.

"Could be, but why would it be?"

Lilly didn't answer. Kane was right—a long-range sniper wouldn't bother with binoculars when a high-quality scope mounted on top of his rifle would do the job. She caught motion off to her left and identified at least two vehicles coming toward them. "Here's our welcoming committee."

"Okay. Remember, we have no reason to think they're anything other than friendly patriots. And we are *so* happy to see them." Lilly almost chuckled until she remembered the consequences of failing to sell their personas.

Two pickup trucks with extended cabs and enormous wheels pulled into the clearing, and two men got out of each. They carried Kel-Tec SU16 rifles with shoulder straps long enough to permit them to raise and fire their weapons quickly.

One of them waved and gestured. It appeared friendly enough at first glance, but it wasn't casual. It conveyed that Kane and Lilly should exit their vehicles and approach without hesitation. If the message was unclear, the staggered column formation that the quartet formed—a fairly common military setup that men such as these would likely know—was threatening enough.

Kane smiled and waved back, reaching for his door handle. "One in the woods, two o'clock," he muttered through the grin. Lilly didn't dare look, but Kane had spotted a shooter to his right and slightly ahead, putting them in a potential crossfire.

Kane was either less concerned or a better actor than she was. Once Lilly took his hand, he strode forward, the perfect picture of a self-appointed alpha male entering a situation with every intention of dominating it. "Hi guys! You must be Mr. Doyle's men. I'm glad we found you! We're so far north of nowhere that we thought we might be lost!"

The lead man did not react to Kane's blather. "You're the Walshes?"

"Yes. I'm Kane, and this is my wife, Lilly." He extended his hand in greeting, but it was ignored.

"Are you carrying?" he asked, no mirth in his voice.

"Carrying?" Kane asked, appearing baffled. "Oh, you mean our sidearms! Yeah, we always carry—at least lately. Why?"

"We'll take them for the moment if you don't mind. Safety protocol."

Kane blinked. "Oh, okay, sure." He raised his untucked polo shirt and pulled his handgun from its holster. Lilly did the same. On the drive up, they'd decided that her best play was to appear slightly submissive to her husband, following his lead at all times. That, along with a hint of bubble-headedness, would make her appear less of a threat to these likely misogynistic men, giving her a little leeway and putting them off-balance just enough that they might let something important slip out.

For that reason, Lilly neither ejected the magazine nor racked the action to clear the chamber, instead presenting her weapon like a loaf of bread. All four men tensed slightly; it would be much too easy for Lilly to turn her hand an inch or two and, intentionally or not, discharge a bullet. She saw Kane look over when the men from the camp reacted to her error, and his surprise seemed genuine.

"Lilly, honey, you've got to clear your gun first."

She gave her husband a horrified look. "Oh! Oh, I'm sorry." She turned to the other man. "I'm really sorry. I'm just nervous, that's all, and I didn't want you to think I was messing around with it and being a threat to you." Kane appeared angry at being embarrassed in front of these men.

"I understand, Mrs. Walsh, but we'd prefer that you follow your husband's example if you don't mind. Weapons safety is followed at all times here."

"Right, of course." With a slight hesitation that suggested a less-than-perfect familiarity with firearms, she complied with his directive.

The man collected both guns and magazines, checked them quickly, and placed them in a small pouch at his waist. "Thank you." His comment was accompanied by a slight smile that was aimed mostly at Lilly, who beamed back at him.

"I am *so* sorry about that. Totally my mistake. It won't happen again, Mister... sorry, I didn't get your name."

"You can call me Ike," he said.

Even though she'd not gotten a real name for a background check, her smile did not fade, but it did change to one of puzzlement. "Just Ike? Is that your first or last name?"

"It's my whole name."

Lilly shrugged, more amused than anything. "Okay, then, Ike. Where's Mr. Doyle?"

"Mr. Doyle doesn't attend these meetings. There are too many people from different organizations who don't think we should be doing what we do here. That's why I need ID for both of you."

"Why do you need ID?" Kane asked. "We have cash like you asked."

"It's not about the payment, but we will need that as well once we get to camp," Ike said. "It's about being certain you are who you say you are." Kane reached into his wallet and pulled out his license, while Lilly returned to the car, grabbed her purse, and offered hers.

Ike glanced at them before adding them to the satchel in which he'd placed their guns. "Great. Last thing, and this is standard practice, we don't allow first-time visitors to see the exact location of the camp, so one of us will drive your car and you two'll ride in my pickup wearing hoods."

"You mean, so we won't be able to see?" Lilly asked.

"Exactly."

"But that will ruin my makeup!"

Ike blinked, and the men behind him smiled. "I'm sorry about that, Mrs. Walsh, but our operational safety supersedes your mascara."

"Honey, you're pretty enough that it doesn't matter," Kane told her. "But isn't that a little over-the-top, guys?"

"Not to us. In any case, it's non-negotiable."

Kane frowned, looking at Lilly to see how much convincing she would need. They weren't about to back out at this point, but to appear eager to be defenseless and blind was unrealistic. She shrugged her shoulders in a "whatever you think" response. "Okay."

Five minutes later, they sat in the back seat of one of the pickup trucks, black hoods covering their heads, holding hands like a frightened couple as they left the clearing.

***

"Jesus, this hood is hot as hell," Lilly carped, the words muffled by the hood. "I'm sweating. How much longer?"

"Just a couple minutes more, Mrs. Walsh," Ike answered. His voice had already lost the hard edge it carried when he first spoke to her, reinforcing how well she was charming these guys right out of their socks with her ditzy behavior. Kane's questions garnered nothing more than short, gruff responses.

Kane wasn't thrilled with their situation, but at least the road was smooth. It still undulated, making the truck rise and fall like a ship in a storm, but they no longer slammed into holes that threatened to swallow the vehicle. The entrance that he and Lilly had used on the way in must have been for new clients only. The camp members likely had multiple escape routes just like this one which they could use to get out of town in a hurry.

In about ten minutes, they slowed. Lilly squeezed Kane's hand a couple of times, prompting him. "It's gonna be fine, sweetie." He kept his voice low, trying to make it seem like he was being secretive, but knew they heard him. Just like Lilly's character, he wanted them to think they were smarter than he was.

"I know." Her voice quavered.

The truck came to a halt. "You guys can take your hoods off." Kane saw a scene that looked like any number of lodges or hunting camps he'd seen—twelve small cabins facing each other with a bigger building at the north end. They parked in front of the large cabin.

"Welcome to Camp Liberty, where America thrives," Ike said as he turned around. His demeanor was much more relaxed and friendly now that he was on his home turf. "Everyone's having breakfast, so let's introduce you."

"How many people are here?" Lilly asked.

"We've got eight clients; you guys make ten." They hopped out and headed inside. The second they stepped through the threshold, all conversation ceased and every head turned their way.

One man stood, his hand extended in greeting. "Hi. I'm Ethan Doyle. You must be Kane and Lilly." He was solidly built, with pale skin and a recent crew cut, but what struck Kane was the hyper-intense way he stared at his new clients like he was trying to peer into their souls.

"Yes, hi. Thanks for getting us in on such short notice." He averted his eyes from the challenging gaze.

Doyle's smile intensified at Kane's docility. "Not a problem. Not only is it my honor to do a favor for Colonel Richards, but I'm always happy to meet a couple of patriots interested in defending their family and country." He went around the room, introducing two couples and four unaccompanied men, using first names only. "You'll find that we're quite friendly here and, while we take our shooting seriously, we don't mind having a little fun as well, especially at chow. Everyone has been here before, so we're pretty relaxed around each other. Don't worry—you'll blend right in with us."

"That's what we're hoping for," Kane responded enthusiastically. Lilly nodded.

"The mess table's right over there. Grab what you want and join us."

Between bites of the surprisingly good fare, Kane and Lilly gave an overview of their fake identities. They'd tweaked the profiles they'd created to ensure they would fit in, and first impressions seemed to confirm that.

"OK," Doyle said, clapping his hands. "Enough chit-chat. Let's get the day started. I'll stay here with Lilly and Kane to bring them up to speed, and we'll join you on the range in a little while. Jefferson, Ike, and Reagan, you guys go to the range and supervise until I'm done with our newest patriots."

"You have three other instructors?" Kane asked as everyone filed out. "That seems like a lot for ten people."

"Four," Doyle corrected, "plus two guys for working the targets, and a cook. Adams, our fourth instructor, had guard duty last night, so he's sacked out. We can accommodate up to twenty-four clients if we fill all the cabins. We never do, not yet, but people are paying serious dollars for the highest level of instruction, and I want to give it to them." He walked to a whiteboard on an easel. "But right now, my focus is on finding out what you know, what you don't know, and then getting you shooting better than you ever have."

Kane nodded firmly. "I'm in. Let's go!"

With a nod, Doyle launched into his lesson. Both his demeanor and voice changed from vehement to sober as he started explaining terms and concepts that Kane knew verbatim. He might have been ardently anti-government to the point of seeing spies everywhere, but he certainly knew everything there was to know about long-range shooting. Kane did his best to trip him up without letting on that he knew more than he should, but Doyle rose to the challenge and provided the correct explanation every time. In another scenario, Kane would have wanted to hang out with him just to talk shooting and ballistics.

Soon, however, his clipped, dry delivery gave way to more effusive descriptions, anthropomorphizing the gun, the bullet, and the actual event of the shot. He could see why his old commanding officer had suspicions regarding his sanity. He employed elegant and flowery prose (*the sniper's version of Shakespeare's Sonnets?*) and Kane had to suppress a giggle here and there at some of his turns of phrase. Worse, the rifle fire from the range was audible in the cabin, and every so often Doyle would close his eyes for a second or two and just listen, as if he were sampling the finest wine or hearing a snippet of one of Mozart's symphonies.

The classroom session lasted just over ninety minutes. Toward the end, one of the doors at the back of the cabin opened and Ike stepped into the room. Doyle excused himself and the two held a quick, hushed conversation, which ended with Ike handing his boss a small duffel bag.

As he headed back to the doorway from which he had come, Kane used his peripheral vision to see Ike glance back at the couple. He didn't react, appearing to focus on Doyle as he diagrammed something on the pedestal chalkboard. A tiny smile creased Ike's mouth for a second before he entered a code in the door lock panel and left. Kane noticed how Doyle's assistant positioned his body to ensure he could not see the code Ike entered, marking the room of some importance. He did not appear to worry about blocking Lilly's view.

Doyle finished the point he'd been making before the interruption and then opened the bag. "Not that I expected anything to the contrary, but you guys check out 100 percent. I'm sorry we have to treat everyone like a potential enemy, but one screw-up is one too many. So here," he started placing items on the desk, "are your pistols and magazines, as well as your IDs. When you leave, we'll show you the real entrance—the one that's better hidden—so you don't have to drive through craters to get here."

"Thanks for that!" Lilly gushed as she put her ID away. "I thought I was going to wreck the distention driving in."

Kane shook his head. "You mean the suspension, Lilly."

"Yeah, that's it!" She slapped the magazine into her gun and put it back in her holster. Kane was already loaded up, and after a few closing remarks from their instructor, they were out the door.

"Sorry for the ask," Doyle said with some embarrassment, "but I have to lock the cabin up until dinner. If you guys could turn around while I enter the code, I'd appreciate it."

"Oh yeah, no problem," Kane answered. He faced the other direction, noting that Lilly did so only after taking a quick, but direct, look at the code lock. A sequence of *clicks* sounded, followed by the rattling of a door being tested.

"All set. Security's important, so thanks. Let's go."

The range was just over a gentle hill about 100 yards behind the western row of cabins. It was set in a slight valley, limiting how far the noise could travel outside of the camp while providing a natural backstop for the shots. Targets were set at intervals all the way back to the base of the far hill. With a cinder block wall behind the shooters, the noise of the high-powered rifles was still muted enough for conversation.

"How long is the range?"

"Three thousand yards," Doyle answered with a hint of pride. "I've got targets out there at different intervals. Two stagers can run the whole show."

Kane was sincerely impressed. "Wow. That's a lot of work for two people."

"Automation helps," Doyle admitted, "and we take a lot of breaks for replacing, raising, and lowering targets during the day."

"Yeah, I can imagine it's not easy to change them out quickly that far away."

"No, it's not. But the really far targets don't get hit too much." Doyle smiled deviously, pulling out his phone. "I do offer an incentive for you to make the long shots. There's a prize if you hit the 3,000-yard marker." He showed the screen to his guests. "That's a Pappy Van Winkle bourbon, twenty-three years old. I've only had one person win it."

Kane raised his eyebrows in admiration, but Lilly seemed unimpressed. "Is that good?"

"Good?" Doyle seemed genuinely offended. "Wow. You need help with more than shooting."

Lilly shrugged. "All I care about is how it tastes with Diet Coke." Kane closed his eyes and shook his head.

"Promise me," Doyle said to him, "if you win the bottle, you won't give her any." He was grinning when he said it, but there was a hint of concern behind his words.

"Don't worry. It's the cheap stuff for her."

"Oh, poo on both of you." She wrinkled her nose and stuck out her tongue, looking far more cute than irritated. The men chuckled.

"Let's get to business," Doyle said enthusiastically. "I took the liberty of having your long guns and ammo bags brought over to the range. We'll take the last two spots down here."

Once they were in place, Doyle used a handheld radio to instruct his range people to raise the first two targets at 100 yards. Kane went first while Doyle and Lilly watched. He could have put every shot in the black outline at the center easily enough—the distance barely tested his ability—but did not. Instead, he missed the first few shots high on purpose, like a nervous shooter who didn't want to embarrass himself in front of others, before putting the next few on paper. The last shots were dead center.

Lilly, on the other hand, wasn't as skilled. Whether she was pretending or not, after watching Kane's performance, she took her turn, missing more than she hit, looking up every couple of shots instead of maintaining her position. Doyle handed her another magazine, gave her a few basic pointers, and let her shoot again. She was a little better the second time around, but there were still several shots that sailed to the hill backstopping the valley.

"You've shot a little before, haven't you?" he asked Kane after Lilly finished her second magazine.

"Yeah, I've been hitting the range on the weekends, getting a few tips here and there," Kane responded in a tone suggesting he liked the compliment. "But I haven't shot anything over 100 yards yet."

"That's okay. You have the basics down and it shows, so now I want to see just how good you are. Load up again." Kane obliged as Doyle spoke into his radio, putting the target out to 500 yards. That would be a little harder, but still within his ability.

As Kane shot, Doyle kept checking his progress but gave him only slight tips. He spent far more time helping Lilly, who was not having the best results. Kane doubted his partner was as poor a shot as her performance suggested. More likely her goal was to garner attention, and it appeared to be working. He watched her while he readied his gun, admiring the way she positioned her body, allowing Doyle to lean into her prone form and make more physical contact than necessary.

"All right," Doyle said, his arm resting on the center of her back, his left leg positioned between hers. "Pull your elbow in a little bit—yeah, just like that—and put more weight on it. That gives you the bipod and both elbows down, so you have more points on the ground at all times. That makes for a more stable platform." Lilly kept her right arm out too far to the side, giving her instructor a reason to grasp her bicep and guide it further into her body, which brought his hand into contact with the side of her breast.

"Oh, my bad," Doyle said, pulling back, but not too quickly. Kane recognized it as the standard "sorry, not sorry" response that a lot of men gave women when they copped a feel while making it appear to have been an accident.

To his surprise, a wave of jealousy swept through him. It shouldn't matter; Lilly could handle herself. Still, he was off-put by his possessive reaction.

"No, don't worry," Lilly responded. "It was an accident, and Kane's not the jealous type. Right, honey?"

"Never have been," he said, forcing a relaxed tone and a smile. "She goes home with me every night, so I must be doing something right."

Lilly beamed at Kane while speaking to Doyle. "See? No issues. Now, how do I position my finger on the trigger?"

Doyle turned back to his student, but not before giving Kane a bro grin that was nothing more than thanks for not getting worked up about what they both knew was an intentional act. Kane responded by jutting his chin out just a shade, but when the instructor turned back to Lilly, he could not control the way his jaw clenched and unclenched several times.

As the day wore on, both Lilly and Kane improved significantly, drawing rave reviews from Doyle, though his praise made him sound more like a salesman than a pleased instructor. During frequent breaks, they got to know the others a little more, and Kane could feel himself being appraised.

After dinner, once everyone got cleaned up and rested, was when tongues truly loosened up. Liquor bottles of all sizes and labels appeared on the tables. Doyle, circulating among his guests, seemed more than eager to act as bartender, and he was not stingy with his portions. Kane nursed a bourbon with a lot of water and observed the conversation.

Kane wondered how he might subtly determine who had enough skill to be a potential suspect, but Doyle did his work for him. "I hope it was a good day for everyone. Let's go around the group with your best distance today and if it's a personal best." The responses varied from 600 to 1,200 yards, and most were stated with pride, taking this group out of the running as suspects.

Predictably, the talk turned to politics. It took only a moment to take the temperature of the room, and the mood was not unexpected; heavily conservative, anti-government, slightly racist, and over-the-top patriotic. Kane contributed a few ideas, trying to keep most of them grounded in reality, but he bounced a few conspiracy theories off the wall to see if any might stick. Most of the time, he got nods of agreement, but he picked up on a few suspicious squints, especially from the other two wives.

Lilly didn't offer much except support, nodding aggressively and tossing out safe platitudes that suggested blind agreement with her husband's statements without a complete understanding of the details. She was flexing her elbow with greater frequency than Kane, and he noticed a slight stumble in her words. So far, her instincts had been solid, but was she playing at being inebriated or going too far?

"Honey, you might want to slow it down a notch," he said in his well-practiced patronizing tone. "You won't be able to shoot for shit tomorrow if you're hung over."

He saw her roll her eyes at the others in their little group. "I'm fine, Kane. We're off the clock now. And," she added, locking her gaze on him, "you know that a drink or three gets me in the mood, so you might want to pour me another." She held her glass out to him and rattled the ice in a most obnoxious manner, but Kane caught the way her eyes went from slightly glazed to laser-focused and back in an instant. She knew what she was doing.

Kane did not indulge her request, but Doyle topped her off using one of the less-expensive bottles. "Thank you, sir," Lilly said with a charming smile. "At least someone here knows how to be a gentleman." She added some RC Cola and took another sip.

The group laughed, and Kane took that opportunity to pull a face. "All I'm saying is watch yourself. Mr. Doyle went to a lot of trouble to get us in here, and I don't want you to spend tomorrow in the cabin with a headache."

"*OK, Dad.*" The two other women, Susan and Michelle, gave him quite a glare to go along with Lilly's response, while their husbands rolled their eyes toward him sympathetically. Gender roles, Kane realized, would be the primary factor in determining who they tried to bond with. He shook his head and gave his newly found allies a rueful, knowing grin.

So far, they'd had very little to go on, and time was not on their side. Finally, though, he had an opportunity. It was a start.

***

Doyle watched the interaction between Kane and Lilly with amusement. Lilly's passive-aggressive reaction to her husband and the top-dog way he spoke to her reminded him of his relationship with his ex-wife, except that Kane seemed unable to keep his partner under wraps entirely. Lilly accepted her place in their marriage, but not too far under the surface was a firecracker who rebelled at her submissive role once in a while. He recalled how she'd allowed him to lean against her on the range, and how accommodating she'd been of his "misplaced" hand. Ethan would not pursue any carnal activities—at least not while they were here. He was a patient man.

Kane, though, was his main focus. *He just needs a little guidance, that's all.* He wasn't military and probably wasn't educated in how a little discipline, judiciously applied, could have beneficial results in a relationship.

And damn, could he shoot! Kane wasn't at Doyle's level, but after only having his rifle for a couple of months, he was hitting 500 yard shots consistently.

Yeah, he sounded a little moderate in his political views, but that just made him a product of the mainstream media and dinner parties thrown by rich, elite liberals. Considering his position and his income, Kane would be part of that group almost by default.

The couple presented unique opportunities. Lilly was part of the Kane package, but she wasn't a bad shot, and having a behind-the-scenes assistant who knew the score was valuable in any organization. He'd talk to his instructors about taking extra-special care of their newest guests.

Welcome to the party, Mr. and Mrs. Walsh.

Chapter 7 – Working the Crowd

Lilly was more exhausted than she'd let on. She wasn't drunk, having consumed just enough alcohol to feel slightly buzzed but, unlike Kane, she'd had to pay close attention to Doyle both in the classroom and at the range, which also took energy. The AR-15 kicked hard enough that her shoulder felt like someone had been hitting it with a mallet. It didn't help her ego that, even though he was trying to appear unschooled in long-distance shooting, Kane had done far better than her despite her best efforts.

Still, her day wasn't over. Lilly had taken note of the two wives who seemed less than enthusiastic in supporting their husbands' positions and sympathetic to Lilly's role as a deferential housewife in a male-dominated household. It would be far easier to connect with them than the men. All she had to do was to get one of them alone for a quiet word, where they might be encouraged to speak more freely. It looked as if the only time to make that happen was after dinner.

Kane was getting ready for bed. Taking his shirt off, she could see the way his back muscles rippled with power just beneath his skin. She'd be lying if she claimed that the idea of getting into bed with that body—even platonically—didn't offer a tiny, if unprofessional, thrill. And, since they couldn't be sure that there wasn't a camera or a microphone in the room, that's exactly what they would do to maintain their cover.

The things a girl must endure to keep up appearances.

But that would have to wait. "Honey, I'm going to take a little walk before bed."

"OK. Better bring a sweater if you're going to be gone long." The advice gave her a reason to turn away and rummage through her suitcase just as Kane dropped his pants. Both relieved and disappointed, she grabbed the garment and headed out. "Be back soon."

Seeing that the lights in most of the cabins were off, Lilly slowly meandered down the center of them, hoping to be noticed, but when no doors opened she chose a path between two of the buildings that led in the general direction of the range. She used a small penlight to make her way safely, but also as a beacon; hopefully, one of the other women would see it and step outside to chat.

After walking a few hundred yards, she noticed a tiny dot of orange light ahead of her. At first, she was uncertain what it might be, but by the way it moved and flared more brightly every few seconds, she realized someone was grabbing a smoke before bed. *But who?* She approached as quietly as she could.

Just as she was able to make out the human form against the soft background glow of the lights from the camp, the person whirled. "Who's there?" a female voice whispered loudly.

"It's me, Lilly. Susan?"

Lilly heard an exhale of relief. "You scared the shit out of me!"

"Sorry. I was just taking a little walk before bed. You too, I guess."

"Yeah," she said, taking a drag on her cigarette while holding out the pack. "You want one?"

"Oh, no thanks. I haven't smoked since college," she lied. Lilly had never smoked but felt that confessing to the habit would create a better rapport between them.

"Good for you. I quit about four years ago, but every time we come here my stress level goes up and I have a few. Rudy hates it, so I sneak off to smoke and let the walk back in the night air get rid of the smell."

"What's so stressful about being here?" Lilly asked, injecting confused innocence into her voice. "During the day it's a little loud, but at night it's so quiet and peaceful."

In the dim light, Lilly saw Susan hesitate. "You and Kane seem pretty normal, but you're the exception, not the rule."

"How do you mean?"

"This is our tenth time here, but our fifth time this year. Everyone here is getting angrier and more distrustful of everything, and that includes Rudy. He spends a lot of time in his office at home these days looking at the news and getting more pissed off about the direction of the country. Democrats, liberals, minorities, immigrants, trannies, atheists, China, Congress, the whole lot of them. The upcoming election has him really riled up. He's not here to become a better shooter anymore. Now it seems like most of the reason for coming here is to bitch about everything with people who will agree with him, and the shooting is an excuse. You heard him at dinner."

"Yeah, but that's just talk. Everyone does it—especially these kinds of men. Kane is the same way; it's just that he's not as comfortable in this group yet, that's all."

"Maybe," Susan hedged, "but the way Rudy is trending, I don't know." She hesitated again.

Lilly placed a hand on her shoulder. "Susan, I don't know you so well, but is there something else going on?" Her new acquaintance looked at her, and Lilly felt herself being assessed for trustworthiness. A pang of guilt flashed through her; she wasn't offering comfort for any altruistic reason. "Anything you tell me won't be repeated. I promise."

Susan nodded. "In autumn of last year, we met a man here named David Park. He seemed nice enough. But recently, I guess sometime in the spring, when he got on the range it was like something switched on inside him when he went to shoot. He became fixated, like a machine on autopilot. I swear I could have set off a bomb behind him and he wouldn't have flinched. It was really strange."

"That's not a big deal, is it? I've only been here one day, and Mr. Doyle talked about calm and laser-focus and single-mindedness a dozen times."

"Yeah, but this was different. I couldn't put my finger on it, but it was *creepy*. David had this really weird blank expression when he looked through the scope, and each time he came here and sighted on a target, he got more and more obsessive.

"The thing was, after he started acting that way, he got so good. He was the best shooter that I've ever seen—even better than Doyle. He was hitting shots over a mile consistently. I saw him hit at 2,000 yards eight times out of ten, and Rudy said he's been on target at 2,500 yards more than once. And he had a serious gun—a TrackingPoint .338 rifle that costs upwards of $15,000. I swear Doyle had an erection when he held it. Everyone was super-impressed with him, but he almost seemed confused when he stepped out of the shooting area, like he didn't understand what all the fuss was about, even after he turned the target into a donut almost two miles away. It was amazing and scary at the same time. But Ethan loved it, and so did Rudy."

Excitement surged through Lilly. This information dripped with potential. She had to keep Susan talking. "Wow. Impressive, and a little weird. But why are you using the past tense?"

"Rudy developed one hell of a man crush on him. They talked on the phone a lot this summer, and I know they emailed each other constantly. They started planning more visits here together—that's why we've been coming more frequently. We were supposed to meet up again here this weekend, but David didn't show up with everyone else. There was no call, no email, nothing from him, and he hasn't answered his phone or responded to email. He just vanished. No one here has heard from him for almost a week, and that got Rudy going with all kinds of conspiracy theories: the government kidnapped him to use him for assassinations, or he was a CIA-trained operative and he'd been coming here to keep tabs on us, or that he was a North Korean spy. Crazy shit." She dragged hard on the cigarette.

"So what are you saying? That this Park guy was some sort of brainwashed robot spy? To what end?"

"I have no idea," Susan admitted. "But with what happened Sunday, and with his abilities, I don't think anything is too far-fetched."

"You really think he shot Armstrong? That's nuts." *C'mon. Give me something solid.*

"Is it? Most people have no idea how hard that shot was. Rudy and I—well, mostly Rudy—are in the better half of the shooters here, and I feel really good if I hit at 500 yards, because it happens rarely enough. Rudy is pretty good out to about 1,200 yards. But David put his shots dead center all the time at twice that far. Who knows how good he really is? And then he disappears a few days before an assassination attempt that he had the right skills to attempt, that only a few people anywhere have? That's awfully unlikely to be a coincidence."

"What did Doyle say? Anything?"

Susan shook her head. “He seems as surprised as anyone and says he can’t reach David either. Ethan is pretty good at hiding his feelings when he wants to, but I believe him.”

“Did he have a wife or family or any connections? Can you ask them?”

“He never mentioned anyone, and he never wore a wedding ring,” Susan stated matter-of-factly. “Rudy didn’t know either, and he talked to him way more than I did. It’s like the guy never existed. That scares me.”

“Why? It’s not like you had anything to do with this, even if he did.” *Keep her talking.*

“No, of course not. But if he *was* part of some coordinated conspiracy, or if he was acting on his own, this place and Ethan are going to come up in discussions.”

“I guess that’s possible,” she hedged, “but if you had nothing to do with it, you won’t be in any trouble.”

Susan snorted a bit. “When the government starts poking around, they’ll find something if they want to. And we have money in less-than-appropriate places.”

“Well, I don’t think you have much to worry about,” Lilly said. “It’s not a crime to have cash in a shoebox in your sock drawer. It might be smelly, but it’s not illegal.” Susan chuckled at the joke. After a slightly awkward pause, she smiled at Lilly.

“Thanks for listening. I’ve been stressing about this all day. It feels good to talk with someone besides Rudy about it.” She stubbed her cigarette out against a tree.

“My pleasure. Everyone needs someone to talk to sometimes.”

“Isn’t that the truth? I’m going to head back to my cabin. You coming?”

"No," Lilly answered. "I'm going to stretch my legs a little more first." They parted ways, with Susan heading back toward the cabins and Lilly strolling in the opposite direction past the range. She took a moment to review the conversation, as well as any non-verbal cues that Susan might have provided. Nothing sprung to mind, but she let the facts dance through her head, waiting for them to form a coherent picture of their own accord. If there was any connection at all, she would find it only by letting her unconscious mind do the heavy lifting.

"Hi. Is everything okay?" The voice was friendly, but Lilly nearly jumped out of her skin.

"What the hell!? Who's there!?"

"It's me, Ike. Are you okay?"

"Jesus, Ike! I was until you made me pee my pants!" Of greater concern to her was that she hadn't been making too much noise and still had not noticed his approach. On top of being expert marksmen, these guys were very good at moving quietly, and that was something else to keep in mind.

"I'm sorry. I just didn't want you to wander too far from the camp and get lost. It's easy to get disoriented out here, and I don't want to spend half the night trying to track you down."

"How did you even see me?" Lilly asked in an attempt to understand Ike's capabilities better.

"Well, I didn't at first," Ike admitted. "I heard you. It's no big deal—the breeze is in my favor, and I'm sure you weren't worried about being super-quiet, so when I heard your footsteps, I used these," he held something up, "and I could see you plain as day."

"What are those?"

"Night vision goggles. Want to try them?"

Lilly was experienced with such tools but stayed in character. "Yeah! I've heard about those things!"

He handed them over. "Just hold them up and look through this end here, like regular binoculars."

Lilly raised them and saw the expected green-tinted image that looked like she was standing around at midday wearing weird sunglasses. Details on trees were clear, even at a distance. "Wow! And I see something walking over there!" She pointed dramatically.

Ike took them back. "Looks like a coyote." The distant light from the camp reflected in the round lenses that extended several inches out from his face, making Ike look like some evil cyborg. The color was a unique hue, a sort of grayish green. Interesting, but hardly relevant.

"So why don't you wear them all the time out here? Seems like the thing to do if you're watching for someone in the dark."

Ike switched them off. "Well, they're battery-operated, so I don't want to waste power. But, more importantly, if you wear them too long, they start to screw with your depth perception."

"Oh. That could be trouble."

"That's why I only turn them on for good reasons, like when I see someone walking around. It's too easy to wander right into Quebec." They both laughed.

"Well, then I'm glad you're out here. My French is rusty!" She touched his arm in the quick, subtle manner that one would employ when flirting.

"It's my job, Mrs. Walsh. You might want to head back soon."

"I will," she replied. "I wouldn't want to be the reason for a rescue mission."

"Please enjoy the rest of your walk and have a good night." Ike turned and headed away. Lilly did the same, figuring she'd go only a little further before heading back. Her short jaunt had been quite productive.

***

Kane was drifting in and out of sleep when he heard the lock on the door being worked. He made sure his right hand was clear in case it became necessary to grab his pistol but, even as the door was swinging open, he heard Lilly's whisper. "Hi, honey."

"Hey," he mumbled, relaxing. "How was your walk?"

"Good. I saw Susan, Rudy's wife, and we talked for a few minutes." She offered no details, meaning there was more she wanted to tell him. He heard her pulling off her clothes, and for one quick second wondered if she was going to stay so in character that she would climb into bed naked or topless. Not that this would have been bad, but it would have been nothing more than a tease, one he couldn't act upon. To his immeasurable relief, the soft cotton of a tank top and briefs pressed into him. He could feel her nipples through the material against his bare back. Must have been chillier outside than he realized.

Lilly kissed his cheek before lying on her side behind him, but she also slid her fingers along the top of his upper thigh. The touch was pleasant and casual, but it was not a come-on. It was a signal. *I've got something.* Kane moved his own hand to cover her forearm. *Go ahead.*

Using her index and middle finger, Lilly started tapping against his skin. It was gentle and subtle enough that, had someone been next to the bed looking right at them, that person would not have noticed the movement. The quick *dots* and *dashes* of the Morse code conveyed her pidgin English to him clearly.

Susan knew guy came here—David Park. Super shooter—2,500 yards-plus. Trance when he shoots. Vanished week ago.

Kane paused, digesting the information. This was a good lead, and the part about the trance wrote a footnote in his mind, one that he would revisit at another time. *He involved?*

Unsure but?

Yup. Real name?

IDK. How ask?

Right. More?

Ike stopped me.

Kane's eyes widened. *Problem?*

No. Make sure I not lost. Quiet AF—scared me.

Kane was not shocked. Sniper skills were one thing, but they weren't of much value in safeguarding a small camp in the middle of the night. These guys were also good at stealth and probably hand-to-hand combat. Just another item on the list of shit to worry about. Fortunately, he was exceptionally good at moving quietly in the dark himself. That might become a necessary skill. He got his mind back to the immediate issue.

K. Next step?

Park info prob in office—big cabin. Get it.

Kane had already reached this conclusion, but he didn't like her answer. The door locks were keyless coded deadbolts, and it would be a time-consuming and noisy endeavor to defeat them if they could be defeated at all. Also, there was no guarantee that all the cameras were on the approach to the camp and not inside. Assuming he or Lilly could get in and out without being spotted, if someone saw any surveillance footage of them sneaking around before they left, they would have to change the name of this place from Camp Liberty to the O.K. Corral.

Kane? Her taps brought him back to the conversation.

Sorry. Surveillance, patrols, coded locks. Big problems.

I saw office combo. Not sure about rest.

Kane was impressed that she had observed at least one combination lock. *Good. Helps me do this.*

Lilly's responded quickly, like she had been expecting his statement. *I go.*

Had Kane been certain that this conversation was private, he would have rolled over and stared at her. Instead, he continued to use code. *No. My thing.* With even one sentry walking the camp all night long, it would be far too easy to be spotted. His time as a Marine gave him a fighting chance of avoiding detection.

He heard her huff in irritation. *No phone for pix. I read faster.*

Dammit, she was right. It was so hard to think of existing without a cell phone that he'd just acted as if he had one, but Lilly didn't need it. She'd memorize Park's entire record in the time it would take him to remember an address. Lilly had the advantage while she was inside. But he'd crawled through so many fields and swamps and deserts with oblivious bogeys ten feet away he could do it in his sleep, and nothing in her personnel jacket suggested she had any skills in that realm. *Yes but I Marine. My area.*

He jerked as she banged out an entire sentence on his hip like she was trying to drive her fingernails through his skin. *U think ur that much better than me?*

Kane froze for a second. Yes, he was that much better—at least in this area—and he knew it. He'd done this kind of thing over and over. Lilly had done a completely different kind of work. He had to remind her of that without pissing her off, so he temporized. *Eyeball tomorrow. Maybe another way.*

Kane felt her hand come off his thigh, only to press into his back at the shoulder. It took him a second to realize she was making a balled fist with a finger—the middle one—extended.

So he'd aggravated her anyway. Well, there wasn't much he could do about it right now, even though he didn't like lying in a bed with a woman who was probably thinking about killing him in his sleep. He took some solace in the way Lilly's breasts pressed into his back and hoped that he would be able to talk some sense into her in the morning.

Wednesday, November 1

Six Days Before the Election

Chapter 8 – A Daring Plan

Lilly opened her eyes. Sometime during the night, she and Kane had reversed positions, with him spooning her and his powerful, heavy arm resting over her body. She took a second to enjoy waking in the embrace of a man until she felt his hips against her body, pressing his rock-hard erection into her. Both flattered and a bit disturbed, she sat up in bed, rousing Kane.

"Is it time to get up?"

"It seems you're already up," she told him with a wry smile. Kane's eyes widened when he realized what she meant but said nothing. There was little conversation as they cleaned up and went to breakfast.

She took a moment to review their status as she picked at her food. While pleased that her flirty, bubblehead act was making inroads with Ethan and his cohorts, Lilly focused on more pressing concerns. Kane might still think he was going to be the one getting Park's information, but she was proceeding like it was her operation. If she resolved the obstacles that they faced, he would have to acquiesce. Or at least he should.

Setting her apprehension about the roving sentries aside for the moment, she focused on the same problem as Kane—defeating the outside lock. She'd been lucky to catch Ike entering the code to the interior office door the previous day, and they could not rely on it for further progress.

They could try to find this Park guy in the system when they got back to D.C., but that was an iffy proposition. He might have used an alias. They had no idea what he looked like. He could have faked his ID—just like Kane and Lilly had done. Too many variables.

Lilly twirled her fork in her hand absent-mindedly as she thought. She felt a tiny dig in the metal neck of the utensil as she stabbed a piece of cantaloupe, noting it was the same fork she'd had at dinner last night, but stopped before getting it to her mouth.

That's it.

Yesterday morning, when Doyle locked the cabin door behind him, Lilly got a good look at the code lock before he asked them to turn around and had seen it again walking in for today's breakfast. Watching her mental recording, it was as clear as day that most of the numbers on the keys were bright white against the black buttons, but the "1", the "6", and the "7" were faded and slick with the wear of fingers pressing them over the years. She couldn't know the sequence, but she now knew which digits made it up. That made for... thirty-six possible combinations. Figure three seconds per attempt, she could enter them all in under two minutes. It wasn't ideal, but it was probably a way in.

Still, something about her solution bothered her, something she couldn't put her finger on. And being unable to recall every single detail she needed was like being flayed alive. Lilly took a deep breath to counter her building frustration. When this happened, her only option was to focus on another topic and let the answer present itself. The stakes were far too high for her to be comfortable with such an approach, but she couldn't see any other way.

She looked up at her husband. Kane was glancing her way, having taken notice of her unnatural movements while eating her melon. She smiled and arched her eyebrows, noting how he returned the gesture like he understood whatever hidden message she was giving him. Of course, he couldn't, but he was going to find out soon enough.

***

Kane was shooting on autopilot, nailing distant targets regularly and earning nods and praise from Doyle and the team of instructors as they walked behind the shooting lanes, but he didn't react, instead focusing on gaining access to the cabin office.

Lilly simply lacked the skill to evade an experienced sentry. Kane couldn't jeopardize her or the mission by sending her out like that. Based on what she'd told him the night before, Ike had pretty much been in her back pocket before she knew he was tracking her. She might be confident, but hubris would be her downfall.

The sticking point, as she had noted, was her far-superior ability to gather the information. He couldn't ignore that. He would have to be in the office far too long, while she would be in and out in seconds. *Should we both go?* It made sense; Kane would get her into and out of the office unseen, and she would use her amazing gift to retain and store what they needed to know as fast as a computer. But was she quiet enough? Moving like a shadow was not something people just did—it took a lot of training that he doubted she had.

Dammit. The roving patrol was fucking everything up. If, instead of relying on stealth, he could eliminate the risk of being detected altogether, this would be a lot easier. He had no idea of the path the night guard would take, nor could he ask, so he couldn't plan for a window where no one was watching.

But maybe he could create one.

Last night, just before ten, Ike had gotten up and headed out of the after-dinner conversation, and Kane couldn't remember him having had any alcohol. Was he the patrol, and was ten o'clock the start time? If Lilly could do the job earlier, she would have a fair chance to get in and out by herself before having to worry about blundering into a suspicious sentinel in the dark.

A diversion. I need a diversion that will occupy everyone and let me send her away from the bonfire early enough. Energized by his realization, he spent the next few minutes kicking around ideas until a simple and obvious plan came to mind. The code lock for the outer door still presented a formidable barrier, but at least he'd resolved part of the problem.

***

Lilly was eager to tell (and brag to) Kane about her ingenuity in solving the code lock problem, deciding they could chat while they cleaned up for dinner. He would see things her way. Of course, he started talking with Doyle after everyone left the range, so she stood obediently but impatiently as they discussed some aspect of his shooting. Kane stared at Doyle with an expression of devout admiration.

"Kane, c'mon. I'm all sweaty!" she complained.

Kane looked at her like he'd forgotten she was standing there. "Oh, sorry. Go ahead and clean up, honey. I'll be there in a second."

"Yeah," Doyle chimed in. "I won't keep him long, I promise."

"Thanks guys." She went to the cabin, grabbing a quick shower and choosing clean clothes. She finished dressing just as Kane joined her. He seemed distracted as he went to his suitcase and started digging through it. "Whatcha lookin' for, hon?"

"Aspirin. I'm a little sore from all the shooting. Did you bring any?"

His request was odd, but he wouldn't have made it without a good reason. "Yeah, I have some Advil with me. Hang on." She opened her toiletries bag and handed him a travel-size pill bottle.

Kane fixed her with a direct look as he made a show of putting the bottle in his pocket. "Thanks."

"Sure."

"Oh," he said. "Gotta get something out of the truck. Be right back." Kane left the door open so Lilly could see him take the bottle from his pocket and put it in the vehicle in the center console.

"I'm gonna wash up real quick," he stated when he returned, tossing his shirt on the bed.

"Okay." He left the bathroom door open halfway when he went in. Lilly wanted to ask about his demonstration at the truck, but she had to provide her info first.

She stepped in behind him. "Sorry, I just need..." She reached over his shoulder to grab something in the medicine cabinet, running her other arm over his bare back. Without waiting for his acknowledgment, she tapped out her message.

I got the door locks. "Where's the damn Q-tips?" she asked simultaneously.

G job! "Are you sure you packed them?"

So I go? "They were on your dresser, Kane." Lilly felt a victory coming but, before Kane could respond, a knock sounded at the door, followed by Rudy's voice. "You guys ready?"

Kane and Lilly shared a look long enough for him to give her a tiny, but definitive, nod. There was more to discuss, and hopefully they could communicate during dinner.

***

Kane felt Lilly jump as his hand slid onto her denim-clad thigh while they were waiting for the main course to come out. She recovered and gave him a little smile before responding to his touch. He didn't have a lot of time to transmit his message, so he didn't dawdle.

Before 10 at fire I'll need meds in truck. U get file then.

U sure?

Y. I solved sentry thing.

Good. Meds?

Y. I'll– He pulled his hand away as the cook came over with two plates for them. It would be impossible to communicate with her while they were eating—you couldn't cut a steak with one hand—but he wasn't sure she fully understood what he was going to do. Perhaps he'd have a few seconds to fill her in later.

That option died a quick death when Doyle came over and clapped his hand on Kane's shoulder. "Hey, Kane. Wanna help us start the bonfire?"

Dammit. "Sure. I'm pretty much done." He turned to his wife. "I'll see you at the fire, honey."

"Okay." While her response was casual, he could tell she was as concerned as he was that she knew only part of the plan, and now it looked like he wouldn't get the chance to get her fully up to speed. He grabbed his coat from the rack as they all filed out into the cool dusk.

Chapter 9 – Headaches

Lilly wasn't nearly as accomplished in fieldwork as Kane, and that made her nervous. Her counterfeiting cases required deceit and caution, but tonight she was going to do the hidden, clandestine work that she'd never experienced beyond a controlled training environment, and only a fool would be calm and confident in such a situation. Worse, Kane had some sort of plan, and she knew only part of it. What if she failed to catch on when he kicked it off?

It took all her control to appear calm as she chatted with the others on the way to the campfire—she could fuck things up long before sneaking around in the dark if someone perceived her as out of sorts in any way. So she did her best to act normally.

The conversation followed the same ebb and flow of dinner, making Lilly wonder what these people would do if anyone ever directly challenged their ideas and beliefs. It was like a fundamental religious service, where nothing contrary to the pre-determined ideology was uttered.

She noticed Kane squint and put his finger to the bridge of his nose, but didn't react. It wouldn't be out of the question for him to be having a stress-related headache—not only was being undercover a burden for anyone, but she was about to embark on a risky action, so she waited to see if this was a real malady or the beginning of tonight's scheduled activity.

A minute later, he pitched his head back and breathed deeply, averting his eyes away from the bright campfire. He stopped participating in the conversation, rolling his neck this way and that. His face, which had only minutes ago shown the enjoyment of being accepted by like-minded companions, contorted in pain. If he were really in distress, Lilly was sure he would have reached out in some way rather than compromising his partner. It was time.

"Honey, you okay?" She put her hands on his shoulder and upper back, noting his normal heartbeat and sinus rhythm.

"Yeah, I'm fine," he said, slurring the word "fine" as if he had been out in icy cold weather for a long time and his face was frozen. A couple of the others took note of his speech and actions.

"Maybe we should call it an early night and head back to the cabin," Lilly suggested.

"I said I'm... I'm *toallee...* totally fine, dammit!" His claim seemed empty as he shook his head before doubling over in what looked like agony. "Fuck!"

A migraine. He's getting a migraine. That's the reason for the meds. "Oh, shit."

Doyle came over. "What's the matter with him? He sounds like he's having a goddammed stroke." His concern seemed genuine.

Lilly allowed her neck and forehead to tighten with concern. "He gets migraines—bad ones."

Doyle knelt next to Kane. "Hey, buddy. You okay? You need something?"

Kane wobbled slightly in his chair. "Nuh, nuh. All gud, need a minute to..." What came out of his mouth next wasn't any language Lilly understood.

"What?" Doyle nearly shouted.

"This happens sometimes. He slurs his words and doesn't make sense." She leaned closer to her husband. "Honey, where are your pills?" Kane responded with more gibberish. "Come on, Kane. Help me. Where are your pills?"

Everyone was looking, but at least they had the good sense to keep their distance. "We can go look for them," Rudy offered. Susan nodded in frantic agreement.

"No, I should go. There's only a few places they can be, and I know them," Lilly protested.

Doyle jumped back in. "Maybe you should stay with Kane, Lilly."

She shook her head, hopeful that no one would challenge a wife who was trying to do right by her husband. "No, I'll do it. This has happened before. These attacks are painful, but they aren't really harmful. Let him put his head down and keep things as dark and quiet around him as possible. Don't cover his head and let him indicate what he needs."

"Sure thing."

She leaned into Kane once again. "Honey, hang in there. I'm going to find your pills and I'll be back soon. Just rest, okay?" Kane didn't react, letting her know that she was following the plan he had tried to communicate. It also meant that the clock was ticking—she'd have to get into the main cabin, gain entrance, find David Park's record, pretend to search for the pills, and get back to give him one before suspicions were raised. She stood up and trotted back toward the cabin.

After she cleared the hill, Lilly glanced back surreptitiously to determine if she was being followed. Having been around the fire, her night vision was about zero, but anyone trailing her would have been outlined by the glow, and no one was visible. For the moment, Kane's plan seemed to be working perfectly.

She moved as quietly as she possibly could, cognizant of the previous night's exchange with Ike. If they saw her working the lock or entering the big cabin through their night vision goggles, she would need a really good story.

It seemed like it took forever to get to her cabin. She raced in, turning on the nightstand lamp and flinging open Kane's suitcase. Starting here, knowing the pills were in the truck, would buy her a little time if anyone got curious. She tossed some of his clothes about to make it appear that she had performed a rushed and frantic search.

Peeking back out around the door jam, she looked for any signs of a nosy neighbor. Seeing no one, Lilly sprinted to the door of the big cabin and knelt at the keypad to begin entering codes.

The first few she entered were unsuccessful, which didn't really surprise her, but after she entered the third value a small yellow light appeared. *Frick. An alarm.* This is what had been troubling her—at a certain point, the lock would either stop taking input or, worse, would alert someone to what she was doing. Entering every possible code was not going to work.

Lilly thought about abandoning the plan and returning to the fire, but decided against doing so. Maybe she could come up with something. *Work the problem.* People used numbers they would easily remember, even those cognizant of security concerns like Doyle, so she concentrated on what she knew about her host. Even an educated guess was better than entering codes willy-nilly. She blinked, running the intelligence they had reviewed back at headquarters through her head. Addresses, birthdays, zip codes, unit names from his military days—there was a ton of information, but she saw nothing that gave her a lead.

What else? Who are we dealing with?

The camp is for shooting. Could it be a type of gun? She only knew of a couple of sniper rifle names with four numbers, but none of them had her three required digits in any sequence.

A bullet caliber? There were a few odd sizes with four or even five digits, but the same problem presented itself—they weren't the right numbers. Oh-for-two.

His longest shot? She reorganized the numbers in her head, but Doyle had said that he'd hit the 3,000-yard target, so there was no realistic combination possible. Every option was either far too short or too long.

The clock in her head started flashing alarms. Any minute, one of Doyle's men would come by to check on her, and she couldn't get caught like this. Lilly took a breath to calm herself, letting her unique skills take over the process. Her vision blurred and everything jumped about as her eyes darted this way and that in their sockets, as they did when she "looked" at each detail floating past her. She started seeing date after date, and that's when it hit her.

It's a year.

Doyle saw himself as an American patriot and a defender of freedom. He ran Camp *Liberty*. And there was one year in the country's history that represented the ideal of patriotic nationalism that he so embraced. Most importantly, it had the right digits.

One. Seven. Seven. Six.

Lilly could not suppress a grin of pride when her mental gymnastics were rewarded with a tiny green light and a soft *click*, immediately after which the door popped open.

***

Doyle listened to Kane's labored breathing as he sat, head down, across from him. His other clients and instructors were at the other tables, talking in hushed tones and glancing over at the problem.

He wished Lilly would hurry up. Doyle didn't enjoy seeing his new pal suffering. Beyond that, there was the question of how this affliction might affect Kane's reliability if things ever devolved to the point that his shooting skill became necessary. He might have to reconsider just how useful Kane could be to him. It was unfortunate, but Doyle knew that such a weakness could get people killed.

Still no Lilly. *This is taking too long.* Their cabin wasn't that far; he could have gotten there, found the medicine, and returned four times by now. Lilly must have gotten disoriented in the dark with worry and was stumbling about just outside the camp. Either that, or... Doyle considered it unlikely that he was being played, but the cost of being wrong was far too high to ignore.

He looked over until he caught Ike's attention and snapped his head up in the direction of the camp. Ike nodded and disengaged from the others quietly and quickly, heading up the trail Lilly had taken a few minutes ago. Doyle hoped there wasn't a problem, that he was being unnecessarily suspicious. His instincts told him he could trust Kane and Lilly, but he'd hate to have to deal with them harshly for betraying that trust.

***

As expected, the dining area was empty. Taking one final look behind her, Lilly bolted to the office door on the far left. This door lock, with only five buttons, was simpler, and she'd had an unobstructed view of Ike's hand as he'd opened it, so it took no time to pass through this barrier.

The room was pitch-black and without windows, so Lilly pulled out her tiny key ring light. As she suspected, there was no computer (computers could be hacked), just a simple desk and a large upright cabinet, which did not have a lock. *Perfect.*

She opened the cabinet, finding the expected box of files on one shelf, but something else caught her attention. It wasn't the collection of rifles, the night vision goggles that she'd seen Ike using yesterday, or the two-way radios, but the collection of M67 hand grenades neatly lined up like eggs in their carton. There had to be a couple hundred sitting there, and the site made her mouth go dry. There was something inherently terrifying about poking around a cabinet containing her body weight in explosives.

Forcing herself to ignore that issue, she pulled the box to the floor and went to the P section. There were three files there, but David Park's was several times thicker than the others. It probably contained a treasure trove of valuable information, but there wasn't time to read it over, and stealing it was far too risky.

Lilly opened the folder. On the inside, taped to the manila material, was a basic bio sheet for Park. Committing the information to memory, she repeated the process with the next few pages, assuming the most pertinent information would be at the front of the file.

Time to go. She went to close the door before looking once more at the little green explosive balls with the lug and safety clip at the top.

Despite her misgivings, such a device might come in handy, so she grabbed two from the back, where they were less likely to be noticed as missing, and put them as gently as possible in the inside pockets of her coat.

Lilly winced when the metal door *clanged* as she closed it a little too quickly, sounding like a brass cymbal in the tiny room. She ignored the noise and scanned the area once she reached the porch. The beam of a flashlight was wobbling its way up from the fire toward the cabins.

Dammit. With a silent curse, she crouched and yanked the heavy door, stopping just before it touched the frame. More gently, she pulled it closed, engaging the door lock. The sound seemed worse than the file cabinet, but she hoped that, if the approaching interloper heard it, he would ascribe it to something else.

Turning to get back to her cabin, Lilly saw that the light had almost reached her. She wasn't going to make it. Thinking quickly and grateful that she'd had the forethought to turn on the cabin light and scatter a few things from Kane's suitcase about, she changed course and pulled the car keys from her pocket, fumbling with them as she got to the door of the Range Rover just as a voice addressed her.

"Lilly? How're you doing?" Susan asked.

"I couldn't find his damned pills in his suitcase," she said without breaking stride, "so I hope they're in the truck."

Susan changed direction toward the SUV. "I'll help you look. But, also, Kane seems a little agitated. He's making hand motions like he wants something, but he's not saying anything, so we don't understand."

"It hurts too much to talk. His pills help him pretty quickly. That's why I've got to find them." She climbed into the driver's seat while Susan pulled open the other door. Both women started digging around the interior.

Lilly located the Advil bottle in the center console compartment. "Here they are!" She held them up.

"Advil?" Susan asked, confused.

"No. He just keeps his pills in an Advil bottle because he thinks prescription drugs are a sign of weakness."

"Weird."

"Well," Lilly responded as she backed out of the truck, "he's a man. There's no understanding them." Susan chuckled in agreement. "Let's get down there." They trotted back toward the fire, but not before Lilly took one more furtive glance around the darkened woods to ensure no one else had followed.

***

Ike watched Lilly's eyes sweep over where he was standing, but he wasn't moving and was therefore invisible to her. Upon arriving from the fire, the light in her cabin drew his attention, but after a minute he realized nothing was moving. He was about to enter the cabin area when the beam of a flashlight bounced up the hill.

He heard Susan call out, but Lilly's answer came from an angle he'd not expected. Perhaps she *had* gotten a little disoriented. He watched from a distance as they climbed through the SUV until they raced back down to the fire.

Ike decided to check the area to make sure nothing was amiss. It was overkill, he knew—Lilly was far too wide-eyed and innocent to do anything devious—but Ethan might have questions. He stuck his head in Kane and Lilly's cabin, seeing clothes strewn about, and then went to look at the truck, training his small light on the ground.

Just off the porch, he paused. Lilly's footprints did not proceed to the Range Rover but turned left toward the next personal cabin, which didn't have a tenant right now. He followed them, and when they didn't turn to that dwelling, he realized they could only have gone one place—right to the main cabin.

***

Lilly raced down the path using Susan's light as a guide but still nearly killed herself about a dozen times by stumbling over pits and roots on the path. She made enough of a racket that everyone was looking in her direction when she entered the circle of the light from the fire. "Got them!"

She put her hand on Kane's shoulder. "Kane, honey? I'm here. I've got your pills. Do you understand?" His body moved slightly and, with what appeared to be great effort, nodded without raising his head.

Lilly shot a look at Doyle. "Water!" she hissed. He scrambled to comply while Lilly shook out two tablets. Lilly convinced her husband to open his mouth just enough for her to place the pills on his tongue and pour a little water between his lips. Some dribbled out, but she saw his throat work as he swallowed.

Like spectators at a golf match waiting for a critical putt, everyone gathered around, keen to see the outcome. The tension was palpable, and for a minute or two no one made a sound, as if doing so would lessen the effectiveness of the medicine Lilly had just administered.

Finally, Kane took a deep breath and raised his head. He appeared exhausted, but his eyes were clear and focused. He looked first at his wife and then back at the anxious faces surrounding him, offering a self-conscious grin. "Hey, everyone."

Faces relaxed in relief. "How you feeling, man?" Doyle asked.

"Better. Not great, but better." He pulled the rest of his body upright, wincing as he did so. "At least I can talk and think now."

"Can you walk, honey?" Lilly asked. "I think you should go lay down." Kane looked like he might protest, but Doyle exerted a little authority.

"Dude, listen to your wife. Rest up. If you rest, maybe you can shoot tomorrow."

Lilly winked at Doyle in thanks for his support. "He's right. If you want to do anything at all tomorrow, you need a lot of sleep."

Kane nodded. "Okay. Guess I've babbled on long enough tonight. Let's head back."

"You need help with him, Lilly?"

"Nah," she said casually, relieved that her husband was feeling better. "He's not as heavy as he looks. I've got this." The pair ambled up the gentle slope toward their cabin with the best wishes of everyone following them into the night.

***

The rest of the group milled about after Kane and Lilly left, unsure of what to do. The jovial atmosphere had faded, and no one was sure if they should go back to their cabins or stay at the fire. Doyle saw it. While he understood their discomfort, he didn't want such a negative pall hanging over the night. "C'mon guys," he urged. "You heard Lilly. Kane's going to be fine with some rest. There's no reason to worry. Relax and have another drink."

Reluctantly, everyone complied—hesitantly, but at least they were sitting back down, and eventually a few gentle smiles appeared. He allowed others to carry the discussion, pleased he didn't have to force it.

Ike stepped silently into camp. Ethan was about to smile and wave him off when he noticed the look on his lieutenant's face. He disengaged from the fire and joined him. "What's up?"

Ike recounted the path of the footprints, but Doyle wasn't ready to draw a conclusion so quickly. "So? Maybe you saw them wrong. She could have gotten disoriented and gone to the big cabin first before going to hers."

"Maybe, but there's something else. I checked the door lock logs. Someone opened the outer lock at 9:36, and the office one a minute later."

"Shit." Doyle looked at his watch. "Seven minutes ago." Ike was looking at him, patiently waiting for his boss to put the pieces together. "Could it be anything else?"

"Can't see what. It was either her or Susan, and I watched Susan come up the path with her flashlight. I didn't see Lilly until she answered Susan, and she was almost at her truck by then. There's no other explanation."

Doyle could see Ike was right. "Fine. Let's go pay them a visit." They turned to head up the hill, stopping when an automobile engine came to life.

Chapter 10 – Flying Blind

Kane looked like he was being supported by Lilly, but he was trying to speed her up. He needed to know what she had accomplished and, more importantly, if she had picked up on her second visitor during her mission. Unknown to Doyle or anyone else, he'd kept his eye on the group and had seen Ike leave.

She had barely shut the door behind her when he started tapping her upper arm. *Ike see you?*

She looked at him, eyes wide. *What?*

Kane pursed his lips and raised his eyebrows. *Doyle sent him. Bet he saw.*

Shit.

Yup.

What do?

U get info?

Yes.

OK. We go now.

Now?

If Ike had seen Lilly anywhere near the main cabin, which was likely, they could expect a visit from their hosts any minute. There was no time to lose. "Yes, right now," he whispered. "Leave the suitcases. Get the guns and get in the truck. Give me the keys."

Lilly blinked at the sound of his voice, as if speaking was *verboten*, but she did not argue and handed over the keys. She grabbed both guns and followed Kane out to their vehicle.

Kane opened his door as quietly as he could and got in, flipping off the overhead cabin light to stay hidden for another moment. When they did start driving and making noise, everything would have to happen with lightning quickness and, since Doyle certainly knew the escape route much better than he did, that meant getting a big head start. They'd haul ass and hope that they didn't get lost or crash on the darkened dirt roads. They closed their doors at the same time. "Ready?" Kane asked.

"Ready as I'll ever be."

"OK... now!" Kane turned the key and, as quiet as the engine was, it sounded to him like a diesel with no muffler in need of an overhaul. Now that they'd made noise, speed took precedence over stealth. He backed out, cutting the wheel as he did so.

The truck rocked on the uneven dirt, and the transmission dial, which had mildly aggravated him during the drive up, now caused more of an inconvenience. The rough surface caused him to lose his grip, forcing him to press the brake and show his brake lights. Cursing, he found the control, selected the "D" setting, and pushed the pedal to the floor. All four wheels spun under the powerful acceleration before they jumped forward. He did not turn on his headlights.

"Know where you're going?" Lilly asked.

"Kind of. After the clearing, I think we drove east before we made a right and got to the camp on this road. So we follow it back until we hit that turn and take a right again."

Lilly took a second to follow Kane's description. "But that's not the way we came in!"

"No, it's not. You want to risk using that potholed mess at ten miles an hour? It'll take forever. Doyle has a much smoother escape route, count on it. When we find it, we'll hit a paved road sooner or later." He jammed on the brake and spun the wheel to follow the sharp bend in the road, nearly hitting the trees.

"And if we take a wrong turn or crash?" Lilly asked.

Kane pushed the accelerator down a little more. "We're fucked."

***

Doyle climbed into his pickup truck and waited impatiently while Ike grabbed his night vision goggles. He saw a flash of red that had to be brake lights in the direction of their primary exit route.

Ike jumped in and Doyle took off. Kane and Lilly already had a sizcable lead, but he was confident he could overtake them in short order. Ike had remarked just how powerful the Range Rover was, and they'd never match its speed once they got to paved, smooth roads. But driving a pickup with bigger tires and beefed-up suspension, combined with their knowledge of the unlit dirt and gravel road to and from camp, they'd catch up quickly.

When they did, Ethan hoped his clients had a reasonable explanation for their actions in the last fifteen minutes.

***

"Headlights," Lilly said as she caught the beam of light in the passenger-side mirror. The twists and turns in the road were becoming less severe, allowing them to see their pursuers. Unfortunately, that made the reverse true as well, even though they were running blacked out.

"Got 'em," Kane answered. "I'm surprised it took this long."

"This isn't the escape route I envisioned," she said. The road, while not riddled with craters, had gradual rises and troughs, and Lilly felt the truck bouncing over every hillock like it was going to take flight. They weren't even doing forty, but her stomach was letting her know it didn't appreciate all the acrobatics. "They're gaining. Can't you go any faster?"

"Those pickup trucks can handle this shit better than us. If we go much faster, sooner or later we're gonna catch air and fly off into the woods the next time we turn. Maybe I can do a little better as my night vision improves, but not much."

"Great." Lilly twisted in her seat to see behind them. Although it was tough to gauge distance at night, the bouncing headlights were getting bigger. She figured they had about two, maybe three minutes before their pursuers were in shooting range. If they didn't get to a real road by then, they might never see one.

Ow! A particularly high crest in the road threw her up and down onto the seat, and she landed on something hard under her left hip. Confused, she reached into her pocket and felt one of the rounded explosives she had taken from the cabinet in the Camp Liberty office. A plan popped into her head. "We're not going to win this race, are we?" she asked Kane.

He was laser-focused on the dark road, so he didn't answer for a second. When he did, his voice was devoid of confidence. "No. But I'm not ready to give up yet."

"Maybe we don't have to outrun them. I've got an idea."

"What?"

She held up one of the hand grenades. "This."

Kane glanced over at Lilly quickly and did a double take. "Is that what I think it is? Where the hell did you find a grenade? Is it live?"

"In the office cabinet. They had hundreds, so I borrowed a couple. And I doubt they're using these things as paperweights."

"That was pretty ballsy," he commented, "but I don't know what you expect to do with it. You think we're going to gain an advantage in a firefight with a grenade?" he asked her.

"No, but it can help us fool them. Next big turn you come to, slow way down. How long does it take for a grenade to go off once you pull the pin?"

"It's not the pin, it's when you release the lever. The standard setting is about four or five seconds."

"Once I throw it, that's how long you have to get out of Dodge. Got it?" Even in the dim light and looking at him in profile, she could see the concern etched into his forehead.

"You better have one hell of an arm, Lilly."

I know. It wasn't exactly easy to throw from a sitting position; the grenade was far heavier than a baseball, and she wouldn't get a second chance. She rolled down the window, ignoring the brisk air as she contemplated how to perform her task without killing them both. She took off her seatbelt and repositioned her body. "Make sure you don't really crash."

Kane remained silent, which didn't fill Lilly with confidence. She wiped her hand on her pants—her palm had grown dangerously sweaty, and she was sure that the M67 user manual had a warning about not dropping it. Once she had a death grip on the annoyingly smooth device (*why the HELL was it smooth?*) and her finger on the lever, she tugged at the pin, delicately at first, but with more and more force until it came free. Lilly felt stupid for deliberately commanding herself to drop the pin in her left hand rather than the grenade in her right hand, but with the consequences of being wrong so severe, she did it anyway. Her fingers started to ache with the pressure, but she wasn't about to try and change her hold.

"Here comes a big turn." She heard the engine RPMs max out as Kane shifted to a low gear, and only when their speed dropped significantly did he get on the brake and turn the wheel. The truck slid sideways toward trees for a second before the wheels bit and re-established traction. Lilly leaned out the window and, with every ounce of strength she possessed, used a backhanded motion to toss the grenade up and out as far as possible. She heard the crack of sticks breaking as the explosive sailed through them.

"*GO! GO! GO!*"

***

"I've got them," Ike said after he flipped on the night vision goggles. "About half a mile. They're bouncing up and down like a pogo stick."

"Yeah, that thing may be a sweet ride, but it's way too fancy for out here," Doyle commented. "Who do you think they are?"

"Don't know. I thought Lilly was a typical dipshit housewife. I coulda smacked her ass before she knew I was there last night, but now she's defeating high-end door locks? That's a well-rehearsed cover."

"Yup, and that pisses me off. I might have to have a little chat with Colonel Richards too. I thought he was on our side, but with him sending them our way, now I'm not so sure."

"Don't jump to conclusions, Ethan. They might have threatened or fooled him. Remember who we're dealing with here. No morals in the fucking government—whoa! I think they saw us. They just stomped on the gas." A second later the truck disappeared over a rise. "Lost 'em. You better get there. We're almost to the road."

A brief, but intense flash of white light pierced the darkness. It lasted only a fraction of a second, ruining Doyle's night vision, but drawing an agonized yell from Ike. Even with filters designed to minimize the effect of such a sudden change, the amplified burst of light overloaded the sensors, making it appear to Ike that he was staring directly at a dozen suns. He ripped the goggles off his head and bent forward.

Doyle blinked away the floating phantom images as he came upon the site of the crash. Several small fires had erupted, but it was hard to see much more. Something about the scene bothered him; not only had they not been going fast enough for the crash to have caused the blast, fuel-fed explosions burned with red and yellow flame for a while, and that wasn't what he'd seen.

He skidded to a stop and jumped out, pulling his sidearm. Ike, still bent forward in pain, didn't follow. Doyle would check on him shortly, but right now the best way to help him was to eliminate whatever threat Kane and Lilly might still present. He took a couple of steps toward the small fires, using the headlights for visibility, but paused as he scanned the area.

There was no truck. There wasn't even a hole in the trees where a truck might have crashed into them and then driven away. His headlights revealed only a few tiny fires burning here and there. He grabbed a branch and studied it, seeing how it had been cut clear through like a well-honed knife had hacked it off in one strike. Ike wobbled over to him, still rubbing his eyes and shaking his head. "I can't see the truck," he stated in a tone suggesting his eyes still weren't right.

"That's because it's not here," Doyle answered, holstering his weapon and dropping the branch to walk back to the dirt road.

"Huh? Where is it?"

"Probably hauling ass down Route 3."

"What the hell are you talking about?"

"This wasn't a crash," he said, staring at the ground. "They threw some kind of explosive into the woods. The branches were cut by shrapnel. Wanna bet there's a grenade missing from the locker in the office?" He stopped and squatted down. "And here's their tire tracks. They skidded, chucked the grenade in the woods, and took off."

"Motherfuckers," Ike said. "Should we go after them?"

"No. We'll never catch them in that truck now, not on the main road. Even if we did, we can't have a damned firefight out in the open."

"So, what now?" Ike demanded.

Doyle didn't like stating the obvious, but he'd started considering it the second he saw there was no crashed vehicle. "We're bugging out."

"What? Are you nuts? Why?"

Doyle looked at his lieutenant askance. He was a good man and could be depended on in any kind of action, but sometimes he couldn't think more than two steps ahead. "Whoever they were, they were trained and motivated, so I'm thinking FBI. With what happened in New York, I'm a little surprised we weren't invaded and arrested already."

"But we didn't have anything to do with that!" Ike protested.

"You sure? Remember that weird call I got, and that big wad of cash we got from Park in April? And now he's up and vanished. I doubt that's a coincidence—that's why I was hoping to see him this weekend. I wanted to get a feel for what he thought about the shoot."

"Just because he's a good shot doesn't make us criminals!"

"Do you think the Feds will care? They'll invade in the morning like fucking Waco, overwhelm us, parade us in front of cameras, call us gun nuts, domestic terrorists, and paramilitaries so every dickhead dumbocrat in the country will be calling for our heads. After we spend a few years in jail on bullshit weapons charges, everything we've created will be gone. You want that?"

Ike pursed his lips, looking as if he wanted to challenge his boss, but gave up after a couple of seconds. "Goddammit. This sucks."

Doyle put his arm around Ike's shoulders. "Yeah, it does. But this is just a setback. Sun Tzu said, 'He will win who knows when to fight and when not to fight.' This is a time not to fight. This is the time to prepare for the coming fight."

"OK, I'm with you. But what about Kane and Lilly? We just let them go?"

"For now, yeah." Now that his plans were cemented in his head, he could afford to indulge his darker side—the one that would not be made a fool of. "We'll find the Walshes, and when we do, I'm gonna have their heads on fucking pikes in front of Camp Liberty II."

***

They emerged from the dirt road and onto asphalt so suddenly that Kane nearly drove off the far side as he struggled to make the turn. The truck fishtailed hard but, back in its paved element, it used the traction control and a slew of other computer-controlled features to return to the path intended by the driver, and they settled between the solid line on the right and the dashed line on the left.

Kane dropped the hammer and the Range Rover rocketed forward into the dark void. His gut tightened up as the speed increased.

Crashing into trees at forty miles an hour was one thing, but necessity dictated speeds of 100 or faster, and he still had the handicap of near blindness. He longed to illuminate the road in front of them, but he didn't see so much as a streetlight anywhere. Turning on his headlights now would just advertise his location, so he plunged through the darkness.

"Anything?" he asked Lilly as she stared out the back.

"No, no one. Nothing." She turned forward in her seat. "But they might be blacked out too."

"I know. We need to put some distance between us." They continued in silence, both of them staring into the void hoping to see as far forward as possible. Kane dared not look away—even blinking seemed a luxury in which he couldn't afford to indulge.

After about ten nerve-wracking miles, however, Kane reasoned he'd created enough separation. The pickup either wasn't following them or couldn't keep up. He snapped on the headlights and brought the speed down. He looked over at Lilly. "Wow."

His partner nodded. "Yeah. You ever get into anything that hairy?"

"No, but I never tried a plan that aggressive while undercover either. Lotta firsts. You?"

"Not even close. I thought we were going to have to ditch the truck and run through the woods, and that's not exactly a strength of mine."

"Well, that may be true, but you nailed it tonight—actually, the whole weekend. You read those guys perfectly, and you were exactly who they wanted you to be. Ike and Doyle looked like they were going to have a fight over you at recess."

"Yeah, I knew I was in his head with that little tit-grab on the range." Lilly was grinning; what would have been incredibly offensive in any normal interaction didn't seem to bother her.

"I wanted to slug him. Did you see how he looked at me afterward?"

"No, but I didn't have to. Why do you think I gave him the opportunity? When a guy like that thinks a girl will let him cop a feel and that her husband won't see it or better yet, is too intimidated to say anything, he's a lot more likely to ignore warning signs about what is going on."

"And you offered it up knowing he'd go for it?" Kane was impressed, but also slightly taken aback at the way she casually used her sexuality to ingratiate herself with their subject.

Lilly's amused look turned skeptical. "C'mon Kane. First, don't try to tell me that you've never flashed those big green eyes and flexed those muscles to get a woman to help you out in some way. Yes, it reeks of reverse sexism, but if letting some Neanderthal barely get to second base helps me solve a case, especially one like this, I'll go topless all day long. And no, I don't feel violated or objectified by those men. I'm using them, even if they don't know it, so if anyone is objectified, it's the man who's thinking with his dick."

Kane considered her words. She spoke with the attitude and authority of a crusty twenty-year agent, not a newbie with a couple of successes under her belt. He realized her exceptional memory was only one of her special abilities; another was the uncanny way she read others. Being young and pretty just made it that much easier to underestimate her. And her willingness to take a hit to get information made her very dangerous. He didn't know whether to be impressed or frightened. *Maybe both?*

He nodded before focusing on more immediate matters. "How about you get some sleep for a while," he advised. "We're going to need to switch off driving, and we'd better watch ourselves all the way home. There's no way to know who they might call to cut us off, or if we'll pick up another tail."

Lilly nodded. “Definitely, but I’m far too amped up to sleep right now.

“Yeah, I feel you. Maybe just close your eyes for a while.”

“OK, but let me know if you start to fade. It would suck to have pulled off such an awesome escape only to have you drive off the road.”

Kane nodded. “Count on it.”

Lilly placed the rifles on the floor in a safe direction and took a deep, cleansing breath.

Ten minutes later, Kane looked over. Lilly’s head lolled back against the headrest, her mouth hanging open slightly, her breathing slow and regular. Even in the dim glow of the dashboard, she looked angelic and innocent, but now that he more fully understood what lay beneath that deceiving exterior, she appeared more attractive to him than ever. No wonder Doyle and Ike developed a crush on her. He didn’t want to look away, but he did have to drive, so he settled for watching the moon as it began to rise over the top of some mountain ahead of them.

Thursday, November 2

Five Days Before the Election

Chapter 11 – Trouble Everywhere

Lilly adjusted the visor to minimize the glare from the sun. The slight jog in Route 495 as it turned to the east pointed the nose of the SUV right at the glaring ball of light, annoying her. At least it kept her awake.

As they neared Murray Lane, Lilly reached over and shook Kane's arm gently. His eyes snapped open and he glanced around, looking as unrefreshed as she felt. "We're almost there."

"Cool." He drew a breath and let it out slowly as he rolled his neck back and forth. "Goddamn, I'm stiff. Anyone catch our tail on the drive home?" he queried.

"No, no one that I saw. Just like you, I was really moving on the way home. I barely dropped below ninety, and no one was keeping up with us."

Kane may have been fatigued, but that didn't prevent his brain from coming up to full working speed almost instantly. "Interesting. They were willing and able to tail us most of the way up there, but either unwilling or unable to pick us up coming back south. Why do you think that is?"

"Last night wasn't exactly a planned departure. Maybe they were expecting us to head out with everyone else on schedule."

"I agree. But we also left D.C. in the middle of the night without much lead time, and they picked us up on the highway almost 100 miles out of town. How did they know that we'd go into Jersey instead of into Philly, or stop in Baltimore?" Lilly remained silent. Kane's question just begat more questions, ones she couldn't answer.

"And," he continued, "what are the odds that they broke off thirty miles from the camp but still knew where we were going, even though Doyle goes out of his way to use word-of-mouth only?"

"You think they knew where we were going and how long we were supposed to be there?"

"Yup."

"That means they have someone inside the agency or another connected branch of the government." Lilly's voice inflection demonstrated her doubt.

Kane wasn't buying into her skepticism. "That's exactly what it means."

"What you're saying," Lilly responded slowly, connecting his dots, "is that you think that someone *inside the United States government*—someone with Republican sympathies, obviously —attempted and almost got away with eliminating a sitting U.S. senator and possibly the next president? And is now actively working to ensure that they aren't caught?"

"Yes, but that's not all. It doesn't have to be Republican versus Democrat. If you expand the idea to consider foreign influence through coercion or blackmail, it goes from a partisan issue to a national security issue. For all we know, some tin pot dictator was afraid that Armstrong would win the election and cut off aid to his country or some shit, figured that killing him was his best plan, and set it up. Maybe he has intel about Senator X or Secretary Y doing something illegal or kinky and not with his or her spouse, and that's the blackmail angle. We'd be foolish to ignore the possibility that this was not domestic in origin, despite no flags saying otherwise."

"Those are just theories, not facts," she protested.

"Agreed. But there's nothing to counter those theories either."

Lilly conceded the point. "If that's true, this is bigger than just the two of us."

"It sure is. I want to get some info on our Mr. Park and then I'm going to call it into NCA. I think there's enough here to warrant some additional assets."

She nodded at his prudent next steps. "Makes sense."

"And, after that, I want to set up a plan to ensure our safety."

Lilly stopped at the red light at the top of the exit ramp before eyeing her partner. "You think they'd come after us?" The onslaught of fear and worry such a thought generated surprised her; she had dealt with some pretty ruthless and dangerous characters in her time at the agency, but to her knowledge they'd never considered her a target. Her mouth went dry and there seemed to be a shortage of oxygen in the now-claustrophobic truck.

"If we get too close, I surely do. This is an all-or-nothing operation. Do you think they'd worry about doing away with two lowly agents?"

That was a lot to digest. She was able to keep herself from scanning the area theatrically for threats, but not by much. Kane's cool and collected assessment of the situation forced her to consider a ruthless plan at the highest levels that they might not see coming. Lilly chose to ignore the still-red traffic signal, leaving behind a din of horns from the drivers who had to stand on their brakes as she sped to Murray Lane and the relative safety of the agency.

***

Once they parked and got upstairs, they headed toward the Computer Information Center, where the hardcore hackers lived and accessed computer records from around the world at lightning speed. Their path took them through the supervisory agent offices, drawing the attention of Lilly's SAC, Tim Benton, who saw them through the window in his door. He nearly knocked his chair over getting to the hall to block their path.

"Jesus," Benton remarked with disdain after giving them a once-over. "Where was your undercover gig—a Brooks Brothers outlet?"

"Tim, not now," Lilly shot back. "We're exhausted, we had a really bad night, and we need to do some work in CIC before anything else."

Benton pulled a face at her words. "Fine. But I want your report before you leave. Three actually—I never saw one for Monday or Tuesday."

Lilly paused. Gently telling her SAC to back off a little wasn't a big deal, but disobeying a direct order from her immediate superior was another matter. She tried to craft a diplomatic response when Kane jumped in. "Your agent is following orders that originated much higher up on the food chain than either of us. She'll get you the reports when she can. Now, move out of the way."

"Not until she gives me what I asked for."

"That's not going to happen right now. Move."

Benton remained fairly calm, but his nose flared at Kane's last sentence. "Look, Logan, I don't take orders from some part-time half-agent who screwed the pooch. I'll get a briefing from Agent Alexander right now or I'll have you removed from the building."

Kane's exhaustion vanished and he straightened his back, using his 6'3" frame to his advantage. "If you think you're going to intimidate me, you are about to find out just how wrong you are." He fixed Benton in his gaze.

Benton didn't take Kane's threat lying down. "No one is going to walk in here and dictate how I run my agents, Logan. I don't give a shit who you work for. Stand down."

A few people walking nearby slowed, taking notice of the raised voices and aggressive postures of both men. Kane ignored them. "Last chance. Move or be moved."

Benton didn't back down, but a tiny flash of doubt passed over his expression, like he knew Kane was ready and willing to escalate the encounter and he wasn't. Without breaking eye contact, he turned his head slightly to address one of the men standing three feet away. "Agent Parker, have Agent Logan escorted from the building right now."

Kane glanced over at Parker. The tall, trim young man seemed frozen in place, with a worried expression. He turned back to Benton and smirked with the knowledge that the SAC had just issued an empty threat.

"Agents!" Kane heard from his left. It took a second for him to realize that it was Lilly using a voice that barely seemed like hers. Authority and power flowed from it, causing both men to look her way. "Kane, you're over there, right now!" She pointed, glaring at him with furious eyes that Kane swore were fire-red. He took two steps back in the direction Lilly indicated as she turned to her SAC. "Tim, do not block the hallway. Agent Logan is right. I will brief you, but not right now, and if you need confirmation of that fact, contact Secretary Carlyle." Benton looked at her, his eyes even angrier at having his subordinate correct him so directly. "Now, sir!" With a shake of his head, he moved to the side. Lilly grabbed Kane's arm and nearly threw the much larger man past Benton and down the hallway.

Once they had turned the corner, she glowered at him as they marched in quick step. "Seriously? What was that about?" She was quiet, but there was no missing the anger and disbelief in her voice.

Kane felt his anger being replaced with embarrassment at his unprofessional words and actions. "He was out of line."

"Yes, he was. But you didn't do anything to diffuse the situation. In fact, you pretty much dared him to punch you! Think that was a good idea?"

Kane stopped and turned to face Lilly directly. "Has he ever been such a pain in the ass about getting a briefing?"

"No, but this is a weird situation. Everyone is stressed to the breaking point."

"Yeah, but he damn well knew who you report to now, and he still tried to force you to debrief him!" Kane lowered his voice even further. "Did it occur to you that *he* might be the inside source?"

Lilly shook her head. "Tim? No way. Not possible."

Kane waited and, when Lilly said nothing further, proceeded. "I'm waiting for your evidence-based justification of that statement." Lilly appeared frustrated trying to come up with a valid response.

"This is a new game," Kane continued. "Everyone is a potential enemy. *Everyone.* You have to get clear on that, and fast. Tell me we're on the same page."

"All right, dammit. I get it."

"Good. I can't do this without you." He saw the hint of a grin. "Yeah, yeah. You know what I mean."

***

The CIC was freezing. The powerful servers and mainframes that performed petaflops of calculations every second generated a massive amount of heat that had to be dispersed constantly, so the room was kept at a frosty fifty-eight degrees. Lilly pulled her Merino wool sweater around her.

They stopped at the front desk and Kane addressed the young man sitting there. "Hello, I'm Agent Kane Logan. I have a Priority One-Alpha clearance, and I need computer time and an operator ASAP please." His voice was polite and reasonable, but the tone and cadence made it clear that challenging him was unwise.

"Certainly, Agent Logan. Let me confirm your status... got it. You should know, however, that we have at least eight such requests pending with the assassination attempt, so it will be a while." He kept his gaze fixed squarely on his monitor, probably expecting the riot act that Kane appeared ready to read him.

Before any such explosion could take place, Lilly took a closer look at the desk supervisor. "Martin?" His head popped up.

"Agent Alexander!" Martin gushed, his eyes lighting up in delight. "Are you with Agent Logan?"

Lilly nudged Kane out of the way and turned her coquettish smile all the way up. "I told you to call me Lilly," she admonished him. "Yes, we're on assignment together. How have you been? And how's your father? He was in rehab from that car accident, right?"

Martin's smile intensified. No straight man could resist the allure of a beautiful woman asking about—and remembering—the details of his life. "Yes! Dad is much better. He's finished therapy and getting around really well."

"That's great. I knew everything would work out." She lowered her voice just a bit. "You know I'm not trying to curry favor with you; you'd see right through that. But we could use a little help getting on a system. This is hot—really hot. You know I wouldn't ask if I didn't need to."

Martin hesitated, but only for a second. "OK, but if anyone ahead of you calls me out, I'm siccing them on you."

She put on her bedroom eyes and tilted her head slightly. Men found it irresistible, and it was a tool she used to close deals like the one she'd just made. "I understand. I would too."

Kane watched the young man look at her wistfully. Lilly was out of his league, but her charm suggested he wasn't that far out. After a second, he snapped out of the spell and returned to business. "Can you tell me the general nature of your inquiry so I can get you the right operator?"

Kane responded. "Citizen identification. Include a connection to shooting and guns, paramilitary groups, or anti-government organizations."

"That's about half the people on our watch lists," he mumbled, checking his display. "You can see Arif Kumar, cubicle 7F. He specializes in that area. I just IMed him."

"Thanks, Martin. Really. Talk to you soon." She winked at her admirer and turned in that direction, leaving a surprised Kane to scurry after her.

"Who the hell are you?" he asked as he caught up to her. "I think you've got multiple personalities. Flirty Lilly to get what she wants,

Bad-Ass Lilly to take charge of fighting agents, and Brainy Lilly who remembers everything. Will I ever get to meet the real Lilly?"

Lilly said nothing until they reached their destination. "Who says I'm not all of them? And a couple more?" Without giving him an opportunity to respond, she knocked on the metal edge of the cubicle.

A young man with a dark complexion, wavy hair, and glasses turned to them. "Agents Alexander and Logan? Hi, I'm Special Analyst Arif Kumar." Quick handshakes were exchanged. "What can I help you with?"

"We need a full profile for a man named David J. Park," Lilly told him. "That may be an alias."

Arif started typing. "Sure, but I'll need more than that. What else can you give me? Birthday? Associations? Locale?"

Kane chuckled. "Careful what you ask for..." Arif looked puzzled until Lilly started rattling off details from the pages she had memorized. He dutifully entered each piece of data as she spoke, but after a minute he turned to her.

"Are you making this up?" he asked, incredulous.

Lilly managed to not sigh in exasperation. "Of course not."

"But you aren't referencing a document or your phone or anything!" Arif protested.

"I have a good memory."

"I'll say. What else?"

Lilly resumed the deluge of data.

"Here we go. David Jackson Park, age forty-four, 68 Winding Creek Drive, Douglasville, Pennsylvania. Owns a fairly large landscaping and snowplowing business in the area. Married in 2018. No kids. Republican, donates a fair amount to local candidates, especially those with hardcore right-wing views. Member of the NRA, National Association for Gun Rights, Gun Owners of America, association to the

Proud Boys and the Oath Keepers, and connections to other extremist groups on watch lists."

"Cool," Kane said to Lilly. "Let's see about getting up there to talk to him."

"Good luck," Arif scoffed as he read further. "He's dead."

"What? When?"

"Friday."

"You mean, like six days ago Friday?" Lilly asked.

"That's what I mean," Arif responded.

Lilly looked at Kane. "Two days before the attempt. No way that's a coincidence."

"Not likely. Do you have anything on cause of death?" he asked Arif.

"Yeah," the technician responded after a few more keystrokes. "Homicide. Shot in his driveway near dawn. I can send you the details."

"Please," Lilly responded, giving Arif her email address. "Send me anything and everything you have."

"Of course. I'm running the search right now." He glanced at the display. "And there's a lot. The system will auto-drop the files to your inbox when it's finished."

"Thanks." The agents headed back up to Lilly's floor to await the promised information, making a detour so that Kane could get an agency laptop to use. Arif's brief explanation indicated it would be a big job; when an analyst said there was a lot of information, that usually meant they were about to be buried in an avalanche of virtual paper.

They grabbed a small conference room. "What's the point of killing Park before the shooting?" Kane asked while awaiting the information from Kumar. "And if he wasn't the shooter, how was he involved?"

Lilly shook her head at the obvious problem. "It makes sense to kill him after he does the job, but before? I don't get it."

Kane squinted as a new thought started to form. "Do you plan for important events, Lilly?"

"Usually, yeah."

"What happens if your original plan doesn't work out?"

"Well, if I'm smart, I have a backup plan, so I go to that if I can." She paused. "So Park was the backup?"

Kane nodded. "If I'm going to take the time and the resources to set up such an elaborate plan like this, I'm damn well going to have a Plan B. My primary shooter might chicken out, get in a car accident, or be abducted by aliens—then where the hell am I? But, once I'm sure I'm ready to go with my Plan A, Plan B becomes a liability, so I eliminate it."

"But the 'kill the killer' plan doesn't really make sense." Lilly objected. "You get rid of the shooter, you've got to kill the guy that killed the shooter, and then you have to kill that guy, and so on. It's a never-ending cycle."

"True, but it does slow up anyone trying to get back to the source, giving someone more time to escape or for the trail to go cold. In something like this, that might be the smart play."

Lilly paused as she mulled over Kane's idea. "Assuming you're correct, what do you think we should be looking for?"

"More leads," Kane responded, sounding none too pleased at losing their primary suspect. "I doubt there will be anything in his info that will directly implicate someone else, so we need a total background check."

"That's going to be a shitload of work."

"Oh yeah," Kane agreed. "I hope you don't like sleep."

A chime from the computer indicated that information was pouring into Lilly's inbox. It took about three minutes for it all to load. There were 165 files. *Sweet Jesus. We'll need a year to go through this mess.*

Kane scanned the list of files, trying to determine what they contained by the name. He saw one that piqued his interest. "How much forensic scene investigation experience do you have?"

"None beyond the classes at Rowley," Lilly responded, referencing the James J. Rowley secondary academy where agency recruits focused on specialized procedures.

"I figured. I've done the work before, so I'll review the details of the shooting scene. You start reviewing and collating all the other stuff, and once I'm done with my part, I'll join you."

"Sounds good." Lilly took up a position at the whiteboard and started making columns: People, Locations, Organizations, Events, Times. There would be many more, but she had to start somewhere. With a sigh, she double-clicked the first file in the endless list.

***

Kane was glad he hadn't grabbed breakfast before he started his task. The horrendous crime scene photos on his computer screen were enough to make the most grizzled investigator queasy.

He'd expected the carnage. The police report indicated that the projectile extracted from the body had been a .223. Such bullets were fast and did an unholy amount of damage, and the pictures he now viewed supported that contention.

The top half of David Park's head was gone, spread about his driveway as a mass of partially congealed blood and shredded tissue.

Kane did not enjoy looking at it but did so to ascertain where the shot came from. The entry wound had been obliterated by the damage, but the pattern of spray and spatter on the concrete indicated that the shooter had been north and slightly east of the victim.

He went back to the police report. Fifteen calls had come into 911 reporting a single shot between 6:56 and 7:02 AM, but later interviews with the callers revealed that no one saw anything else of note, such as a car leaving the area of Park's home.

Opening a browser, he brought up Google Maps and used a ruler to create a line in the direction of the shot. On the north side of Route 562 there was a set of hills, a couple of ponds, and a county park that was sparsely populated, all about 800 to 2,000 yards from the kill spot. Most importantly, such hills would give any shooter the elevation for a clear line of sight into the valley below, and that would likely include 68 Winding Creek Drive.

A long-range rifle shot, timed so there was enough light but not much activity about, and no witnesses. That sounded like a planned operation, and that fit the profile. Park might not be the shooter, but he was sure as shit involved.

He grabbed the autopsy report. It seemed a waste of time—a monkey could figure out the cause of death—but a good investigator checked every lead. He glanced through the basics, like Park's height and weight and what he'd been wearing, as well as the dry medical terminology that described his injury.

The description of Park's body, at least below the neck, was unremarkable as well. Everything about the heart, lungs, stomach, intestines, bones was perfectly normal, but the blood toxicology section had a few interesting details. A few chemicals, such as aripiprazole, a couple of benzodiazepines, and lithium suggested some significant anxiety issues. The presence of ethanol (*drunk at 7 a.m.?*) was something to note but had no bearing on his investigation.

There were several trace elements listed at the bottom that were most decidedly not normal but were familiar to him. Kane, too tired to remember exactly where he'd come across those drugs, circled them on the sheet with a notation to investigate them further.

Lilly was going back and forth from her computer to the whiteboard, adding information every couple of seconds and drawing lines between bits of information that might be connected. Drawing a square to claim an as-of-yet untouched portion of the board, Kane started writing down what he knew. Compared to what she had already noted, his data set looked pathetic. However, it had confirmed Park's involvement in their case, so it was worth doing.

He went to his computer and brought up one of the many files that Lilly had shared with him. It was a list of Park's American Express transactions for the previous year, and it was quite long. Hoping that he'd have half the success rate with this stuff as he had with the crime scene report, he started running his finger through entries that consisted mostly of ammunition purchases, subscriptions to militant websites, and fast food.

***

Four hours and forty minutes later, they finished going through the files that Arif had sent them. Lilly looked at the board as a whole for the first time. It was covered with abbreviations, circled terms connected by solid and dashed lines that jumped over each other, grouped items, arrows pointing in every direction, nearly illegible notations, and hub-and-spoke patterns.

Kane gave his assessment of their creation. "What a mess. It looks like a conspiracy theorist and a flowchart designer had an insane kid, and this was his homework." He pulled the plastic off a generic cafeteria sandwich and bit into it without enthusiasm.

Lilly barely had the energy to poke her fork around her mostly iceberg lettuce salad. "A lot of things repeat over and over again. They fit the profile but don't give us any good leads. He bought tons of ammo, but there's no record of him buying any guns. He visited sketchy websites —mostly political-fringe groups with a smattering of porn—late at night. He had a lot of shitty junk food delivered to his house, and he pretty much put the kids of the local liquor store owner through college. Classic loner, angry at everyone. About the only thing we can use is the organizations he belonged to, and all that gets us is a lot of interviews with guys who are going to be super suspicious of us."

"But the crime scene report fits the situation. It wasn't like he was the victim of a random attack. He was a player in some way, definitely."

Lilly nodded as she looked over at the separate section that Kane had created. "That's your little walled-off section on the right, the crime scene info?"

"Yup, with forensics."

Lilly focused on Kane's work, and some of the words stood out to her. She wasn't sure what was there, but knew to let this process play out, and soon it started paying dividends. Oddly enough, the results weren't visual, but auditory. Like a stereo heard through a wall in the next apartment, sounds started replaying themselves in her head. At first, she couldn't quite make them out, but as things got louder she started hearing the words. It was still partially gibberish, but certain terms and phrases became clear: "Frederick," "in the head," "no witnesses," and "no known motives." Giving her another clue, the voice saying those things was measured, patterned, polished, and rhythmic, like a professional orator.

Or a newscaster.

By now, Kane recognized the look. "What is it?" he asked.

"A .223 round, head shot, before seven a.m., lots of people heard the shot but no witnesses." She was mostly talking to herself rather than Kane, but he answered anyway.

"Yeah."

"Who does the morning rush news on 103.5?" WTOP was one of the more popular news radio stations, and Lilly often listened to it on the way to work. It gave a few minutes of regional and local news every half-hour instead of pure politics.

"Dunno. I don't live around here anymore."

Lilly shrugged and opened the door, sticking her head out and yelling her question to the cubicle-filled room.

"Rick Yanone, six a.m. to ten a.m." came the response. The instant she heard the name, she knew that was the voice.

"What does that have to do with anything?" Kane asked.

Lilly ignored him, activating the speakerphone on the table. "Agent Alexander for Arif Kumar, please."

Only a few seconds passed. "This is Arif Kumar."

"Hi, Arif. It's Agent Alexander again. Can you check one more thing for us?"

"Sure."

"Shootings in the US, say October 12th through the 22nd, with a high-powered rifle shot to the head, during morning or evening rush hour. Witnesses heard the shot but no visual on the shooter or a get-away vehicle. One of them may have happened in Frederick, Maryland or Fredericksburg, Virginia."

"No visual, no vehicle," he mumbled over the sound of his fingers tapping up a storm. "OK, I've got—wow, six hits in that timeframe. And one of them is in Fredericksburg, Virginia."

Kane's mouth fell open.

"Great. Send them over, please."

"You got it." The line went dead.

"How the hell did you come up with that?" Kane asked, sounding both impressed and annoyed.

She smiled with the tiniest hint of satisfaction. "A little luck. Coming into work early last week, I heard a news report about a shooting in Fredericksburg about a guy who was shot in his driveway just as he got home from work. Right in the head—a couple of neighbors saw the guy drop where he stood. No report of a car leaving the scene. It sounded just like what you wrote down, so I figured it was worth the question."

"Well, damn. So, how do we use this?"

She looked at her screen to see Arif's newest delivery. "Here we go. I need a map of the country." Kane left the room, returning shortly with a large, laminated United States map. He taped it up on the wall, and Lilly handed him a fine-point Sharpie. "Mark these down when I call them out."

"October 16th, 6:50 a.m., Texarkana, Texas." It took Kane a moment to find it, but when he did, he put a bold "X" on the map and wrote the date and time below it, followed by "#1".

"October 16th, 5:48 p.m., Jefferson City, Missouri.

"October 17th, 6:03 a.m., Knoxville, Tennessee.

"October 17th, 4:48 p.m., Findlay, Ohio.

"October 18th, 7:00 a.m., Douglasville, Pennsylvania.

"October 18th, 5:14 p.m., Fredericksburg, Virginia."

Kane sat back down and, along with his partner, stared at the map with the six X-marks. "What are you making of this?" he asked.

The pattern started to take shape. "How far of a drive do you think it is between those locations, going in the order I just gave you?"

Kane considered the distances involved. "It's a real loose estimate, but six to eight hours for each. Except the last one; that's more like four hours from southeastern Pennsylvania to northern Virginia." It took him a few more seconds, but then the lightbulb clicked on. "Oh."

Lilly nodded. "I can't think of a better way to make sure your primary shooter is up to the task *and* eliminate your backup shooters than sending your assassin out to kill your Plan Bs. If he fucks up or backs out at any point, you've still got at least one shooter left. If he nails all six and it's efficient and sexy, you know you've got the right guy for the job."

"It fits. It fits down to the last detail," Kane commented, turning her way after a moment of studying the map. "That's nice work, Lilly."

"Well, thanks, but you know what this means, right?"

Kane blew out a breath. "Yeah, a lot of road trips and flights. You want to go to Pennsylvania or Virginia tomorrow?"

"Virginia, I guess. Shorter drive, and there's still lots of pretty foliage to look at," she said, trying to find the bright side of things. "And now we've got five more stiffs that were somehow involved, so we have five more mountains of files to go through. Geez, I don't know when we're going to get to that."

"We can't, not fast enough to suit the situation. But maybe we don't have to. Do you think we have enough evidence to expand this investigation?"

"Absolutely," Lilly said. "At this point, we wouldn't be doing our job if we didn't get more people to run these leads down."

"I agree." He clapped his hands together. "Let's make ourselves presentable. I'm going to make a call, and I suspect we're going to have an appointment at 1600 Pennsylvania Avenue sometime this afternoon."

Low-grade panic flooded through Lilly. "Wait. We're going to go see the president?"

"Well, yeah. We report directly to him now."

Oh boy. "Fine. I'll meet you back here in thirty minutes."

Chapter 12 – Politics Versus Reality

The security checks at the West Wing portico entrance were still tight; not quite as bad as during Kane's last visit, but everything was still being double- and triple-checked. With Lilly having never been to the White House, she was subject to greater scrutiny than he was, but the agents were cleared and on their way to the Oval Office with a few minutes to spare.

Kane was not surprised to see Brent Douglas and FBI Director MacMurray waiting in the secretary's office, but the presence of Voight Stafford was a shock. Keeping Senator Armstrong's chief of staff informed was one thing, but he was unlikely to have any significant security clearance, making Kane unsure of what he could say in front of the man. He longed for a minute alone with either of the other agents, but the three men merely nodded at them before resuming their hushed *kaffeeklatsch*. Neither Kane nor Lilly was invited to participate.

Not thirty seconds later, the secretary's desk phone rang, and she snapped it up with the reflexes of a mongoose. "You can all go in," she said, and an agent opened the door.

The office was empty, which wasn't uncommon. Visitors were often admitted a minute or two before the president got back from wherever he might be to speed things along. Better to waste the time of a governor, congressman, or the head of the Midwest Dairy Council, Kane reasoned, than that of the most powerful man in the world.

Douglas excused himself from the group and came over. "This better be good," he said in a partially-hopeful, partially-aggrieved tone.

"It is. It's worth this meeting," Kane reassured him. "But I have to ask about—"

Conversation ceased as the president entered from his private office. Dressed in a tuxedo minus the jacket and bow tie, he sat behind the Resolute desk while looking squarely at Kane. "Let's keep this short."

"Yes, Mr. President," Kane answered, gesturing toward Lilly. "This is Agent Lilly Alexander. We've developed some leads that, while not definitive proof, do lend credence to the Brooklyn Bridge shooter theory." He hesitated, glancing at Voight Stafford. He was about to reveal information about a criminal investigation to a private citizen who was on the edge of being materially involved in the case.

I've got two sworn senior law officers and the leader of the Executive Branch here. They had to know we'd discuss sensitive information. If they don't stop me, it's their asses. "I want to state, for the record, some of the topics I'm about to bring up might be security sensitive." He couldn't have given them a clearer signal, but no one reacted, so he continued, giving a quick but thorough disclosure of all he and Lilly had learned and pieced together through this morning, *except* for their suspicion of an informant somewhere in the government.

The president listened intently. "Sum it up for me, agent. What do you want?"

"Sir, we're requesting dedicated resources to process all the evidence we've discovered. We simply can't do that and physically chase down our leads in a timely fashion. We're also requesting four agents—one to go to each of the other crime scenes. Agent Alexander and I will go to the other two."

President Sharpe narrowed his eyes. *He's probably calculating any political spin.* He looked at the FBI Director. "Mac? Can you spare that based on Agent Logan's conjecture?"

What the fuck? This isn't conjecture—it's solid evidence. He held his tongue but wondered why the president used that term.

"Going through the paperwork, sure. We've got a bunch of first-year agents who can handle that. I can assign one of the more reliable ones to go over it."

"If I may interject?" Stafford said in a manner that indicated he knew he would be permitted to do so. "One of my graduate students—" he never passed up an opportunity to remind everyone he was the chair of the Political Economics department at Georgetown and held a doctorate in the discipline—"is doing her internship at the FBI. She has a clearance and can offer an unbiased eye with which to review the information that these two have collected—with Director MacMurray's approval, of course."

The president nodded in preliminary approval of the move, but all four of the agents took on concerned expressions. "Uh, that might create a problem, sir," Kane said.

Both the president and Stafford looked right at him, dismissing any chance that Kane could hand the discussion off to one of his bosses. "What sort of problem, Agent Logan?" Sharpe asked.

"My apologies, sir, but not only would such a person lack the experience to properly vet such evidence, but appointing her to such a role is a conflict of interest. Doctor Stafford is closely tied to the victim of this investigation, so he should be excluded from selecting participants."

"Agent," Stafford asked in the tone of someone not accustomed to being questioned by a low-level drone like Kane, "do you, for one second, believe that I don't wish to find the person who nearly killed my candidate and friend?"

"No, sir. I'm suggesting that this student might feel pressure to 'find' connections in the data that aren't there in the assumption that something must be found, or that doing so might curry favor with you—however incorrect that assumption might be."

"In that event," Sharpe said, "I am confident that you will be able to identify such invalid connections and dismiss them in short order." He turned to the director. "Mac, make sure Dr. Stafford's person gets what she needs."

"Yes, sir."

"Now," the president continued, "what about the site investigations?"

"That's tougher," the director responded. "We're already stretched to the max, and that's with Secret Service help. If we reassign agents, those protection details will be compromised, and we cannot risk that. Most other agencies are in the same boat."

"I have to agree with the director," Stafford said. "There is little here to justify much more than a cursory review of the background information currently available."

The president nodded. "Sorry," Sharpe told Kane. "Admin help, but no field help at this time. Just do your best with what you have."

Kane managed to keep his expression neutral despite his growing frustration. "Yes, sir."

"When can you guys be at the first two sites?"

"Sir, by the time we get there, it will be almost dark. I'd request time tonight to go through more of the files and set up an action plan for Dr. Stafford's student. We will visit those sites tomorrow morning."

"OK. We can't just run you 'til you drop. Get some rest, but I want you guys back in action at first light."

"Thank you, sir. We'll be moving before dawn."

"Good." Sharpe pushed himself up from the ancient desk. "If you will excuse me, I've got dinner with King Gustaf of Sweden. Agent Douglas, would you stay behind a minute?"

Kane, Lilly, and MacMurray exited the White House and headed to their cars on West Executive Drive. It wasn't lost on Kane that Voight Stafford had stayed behind as well.

MacMurray caught up with Kane and Lilly. "You almost got your head ripped off in there, Logan. Cue on me next time."

Kane agreed but felt the need to defend himself. "Director, my objection was valid and you know it."

"Not the point." MacMurray shook his head. "Sharpe doesn't like being challenged—not by someone at your level, and definitely not in front of others. It would have been better if you'd let me hang back to convince him, privately, to change his mind. Now he'll stick with his decision no matter what because you backed him into a corner."

I fucking hate politics! "I didn't think of it that way."

"It's all right. You're not paid to worry about that kind of stuff. This student will likely still be objective, and we'll find a rookie agent to vet what she comes up with before we pass it on to you."

"Thank you, sir." He figured that was the end of it, but Lilly spoke up.

"Sir, why is the president listening to Armstrong's chief of staff?"

"Guys, I know you are focused on solving this, but you aren't seeing the bigger picture. The investigation itself is what matters, not the results."

"Come again?" Lilly asked.

"If you find the shooter, great, but right now perception is reality. No one would blame Stafford if he went scorched earth and flayed Sharpe alive in the press for failing to find the attacker, even this early, and the president knows it. That petrifies him politically, so he's doing everything he can to be accommodating. By letting Stafford see that you guys answer directly to him, allowing him to interject little stuff like this kid from Georgetown, and sit in on meetings, Sharpe is begging him for time."

"What you're saying," Lilly responded after taking a second to parse the director's speech, "is that it's better for the president to *look like* he's doing the right thing rather than actually doing the right thing, like give us the resources we need?"

"Now you're catching on," MacMurray said in the tone of a patient teacher. "And, if it's better for the president, it's better for me, better for Douglas, and it's better for you. Keep that in mind."

"I don't have the stomach for this political bullshit. It leaves a bad taste in my mouth," she concluded.

"Believe it or not, me too," MacMurray said. "But keep going. You're doing good work. At least you got your admin support." He hopped into his waiting SUV, which sped away.

Kane watched the vehicle depart. "Mac may be right, but still, that was a weird meeting."

"Yeah, real weird. But at least we're off until tomorrow. I'm kinda shot and could use a night in my own bed."

"Well, prepare to be disappointed. You aren't going home tonight." Kane smiled as Lilly rolled her eyes in exasperation, knowing she thought he was going to suggest they keep working.

"Come on, Kane. I know getting chased by armed paramilitaries is just another weekend for you, but we mortals feel stress when we face death."

"Yeah, I guess you're right. How about you stay with me at the Marriott tonight?"

"With you?" Her eyes displayed suspicion almost immediately. "Why?"

"It's more secure than any house, and we can cover each other more easily in a hotel room. Plus, it's closer."

Apparently, that was enough to convince Lilly. "Yeah, that sounds good. I'd love a little room service."

"Where's your go-bag?"

"In my personal car at HQ."

"Cool," Kane answered. "Let's do this. I need the sleep too."

***

Lilly dragged her tired ass into the decently appointed room. She wanted to pass out, but her body demanded nourishment first.

Kane looked just as worn. He needed a shave;. well, he probably thought he did. Lilly was a sucker for the five o'clock shadow look, and right now stubble decorated his jaw in a way that made him look dangerous and sophisticated at the same time. Reluctantly, she tore her eyes away from him.

"Only one bed, Kane?"

"Yeah, but I don't see a problem; it's not like we haven't slept together." Lilly shot him a look as he continued with a sly smile. "Of course I'll use the sofa. If you wanna shower first, I'll call for dinner. The menu is on the end table. Let me know what you want."

Lilly was quick to decide on a cheeseburger with a side of fries before checking her watch. "I wouldn't mind a little sip of something to chill out before bed. The timing is tight, but I think we've earned it." Agents were not allowed to consume alcohol within ten hours of reporting for duty.

"I've got it. This place knows how to take care of agents without a fuss. Don't worry."

"Thanks, Kane." She tossed her suit jacket on the desk chair and padded her way to the bathroom, hoping the warm shower would help the knots in her shoulders and the concerns floating through her mind.

***

Twenty minutes later, Lilly exited the bathroom in a T-shirt and sweatpants, with her still-damp hair pulled back in a ponytail. Not exactly her best look, but it wasn't like she had to impress anyone with her appearance right now.

Kane was clicking through the channels on the TV when she exited, but tossed the remote on the bed as soon as she appeared. "Food should be here in about fifteen." They brushed by each other, and before he entered the bathroom, he turned back to her. "You smell nice."

Caught off-guard, Lilly didn't respond for a second, and Kane winced. "Sorry, sorry. That wasn't cool. It's just that I'm not used to sharing a room, that's all."

Lilly shook her head. "Forget about it. You're fine." Kane disappeared through the doorway, and she sat at the edge of the bed, wondering what had possessed him to make such a comment. She realized the fatigue was likely hitting him hard too.

Or maybe I just smell nice and he noticed.

She shrugged off both the comment and her reaction when the "Breaking News" logo appeared on the screen. *Please don't let it be another shooting.*

Fortunately, that was not the case, but the news was still of interest to her, and she suspected Kane would feel the same way. "Armstrong's going to make a statement from the hospital in a minute," she said when she heard him exit the bathroom.

"Oh, I'd like to see that." He moved to sit, but a rap on the door indicated their food had arrived. They wolfed down their meals so quickly that they were picking at the remnants when Senator Armstrong came on.

He looked good. A little tired and pale but, considering the trauma he'd undergone, that was understandable. He smiled that million-dollar smile, took the softball questions that the assembled press corps lobbed at him, and provided measured, positive answers devoid of any rancor, interspersed with some low-key humor. His words of thanks to those who had helped him and confidence in President Sharpe sounded sincere.

Lilly and Kane soon lost interest. The speech was nothing more than an opportunity for Armstrong to display how strong he still was and that, yes, he was still very much ready to continue his quest for the presidency.

It was then that Lilly noticed something missing from her evening meal. "I thought you were getting a little something for us to drink," she protested.

Kane grinned at her. "I was wondering when you'd bring that up." Reaching under the tablecloth of the room service cart, he extracted a chrome platter on which a bottle of Johnny Walker Green and a bucket of ice rested. "I guess your superpower took the evening off," he teased.

"That's not how it works and you know it," she pointed out in feigned irritation. "And I was thinking wine, not straight Scotch."

Kane dumped ice into two rock glasses and poured a generous amount of the amber liquor into each. "Like you said, we've earned it. And, considering the way you were drinking at the campfire the other night, don't try to tell me you can't handle it."

Partially in response to his statement, Lilly drained about half of his glass in a single pull. "Most of that was me trying to encourage my 'suitors' to make a pass at the drunk girl, but yeah, I can handle my booze pretty well."

"Good thing. I might have gotten jealous if you jumped in the sack with one of them. Or both." He tossed his drink back with studied indifference.

"Geez, Kane! You've got some imagination!" She refilled her glass and offered the bottle to him. "I know I said I wasn't above using my looks to my advantage, but what kind of slut do you take me for? In any event, I think three-ways are a violation of agency procedure."

"I'll have to take your word for that. I've never had such an opportunity." His smile, now that it appeared without reservation, was extremely becoming, and Lilly found herself unwilling to look away. "In any case, cheers... partner," Kane said. They tapped glasses and took another healthy pull on their drinks.

"Thanks for that," Lilly told him after a pregnant pause.

"For what?"

"For thinking of me as your partner and treating me like an equal."

Kane frowned. "You sure as shit shouldn't thank me for doing what I should have done from the start."

"You're right, of course," Lilly told him. "Knowing how you really feel, why did you flip out when you found out we would be working together? After getting past the whole douchebag phase, you've shown yourself to be a good guy."

Kane paused, leaning over to refill his glass while refreshing Lilly's as well. He wouldn't meet her eyes, but she could see the wrinkles in his skin just above his nose that spoke of...anger? Regret? For the first time since they'd met, this aggressive, powerful agent seemed barely able to contain his emotions. "You can talk to me, Kane. If you want."

For a minute, she thought he was going to walk away from her, even though there was nowhere for him to go except the bathroom. But he didn't run. He faced her, his jaw set in a grim line.

"Are you sure you want to hear this? After you do, you can't unhear it."

Chapter 13 – Tales and Revelations

Kane hoped his warning would scare her away, but her expression didn't change. She probably deserved to know, but telling her might be worse than keeping her in the dark. She might not trust him anymore.

Or are you hoping she'll let you off the hook?

He thought he'd been clear about the magnitude of such a confession, but Lilly was not fazed. "You just told me we're partners. Partners shouldn't keep stuff like this from each other."

"OK. You asked for it." He took another sizable sip of liquid courage. "Like you said on the way to West Virginia, about four years ago I was the golden boy in the service—even more than you," he said with a forced grin. "And, also like you, my success earned me my share of admirers and haters.

"I ignored the haters. They couldn't do a thing to stop me, and it was pretty clear I was going to be the next deputy director. After that, maybe the director. And then, well, I would have been in my mid-forties, and I could've written my own ticket.

"Anyway, cut to an event in Denver. The previous president decided to attend a fundraising dinner to help one of the senators who was facing a serious challenge in the upcoming election. It was super last-minute, meaning yours truly got the call to run the advance team *and* onsite perimeter security because the regular presidential advance detail was already committed and I was so fucking good.

"It was a shit show. I didn't have enough time and I didn't have enough agents to do the job properly, but I ignored those little voices in the back of my head. I was Kane Logan. No matter what, I made things work, solved every issue, and corrected every problem. I could handle this."

The bitterness in his voice increased threefold. "I was wrong. I felt like I was on top of everything, but in hindsight I could see I was barely holding the plan together. And then we got a credible threat, but not enough to pin down the unsub. That just upped the pressure."

"I set up a system of roving agents, figuring that using movement would allow me to multiply the security presence. It felt like the right call, but not with the logistics involved. There were too many connections and too much coordination required between agents. I didn't see it."

"That wasn't your fault, Kane," Lilly interrupted. "You worked with what you had."

"Yeah, maybe, but—" He seethed with anger. He hadn't recounted this tale in several years, and it wasn't any easier than the last time he told it. *Why would it be?*

Lilly wouldn't let it go. "But what?"

Fine. She wants to know, she's gonna hear it. "But something went wrong. I must have directed one of them incorrectly. Maybe I gave one of them bad or unclear orders." He saw himself talking to each member of his small team at the same time, trying to keep each of their directives straight in his head, remembering the vague feeling of unease that permeated the moment. "Whatever orders I gave, I don't really remember, but a service door ended up unchecked and unlocked for who knew how long.

"The threat was real. The perp got in through the unlocked door, almost like he knew no one would be there. We picked him up already in the building, and it ended up in a foot chase." He didn't have to tell Lilly that chasing a perp through a building with the president in it was already a failure.

"He... he ran down a dead-end hall and was shooting when two agents rounded the corner. He hit both of them. Patricia Noecky was hit in the abdomen; she's a paraplegic now. And Sean Oldham was hit as well. He eventually recovered, but he had to take early retirement from his injuries."

"You aren't responsible for that, Kane. They were sworn agents and they knew the risks."

Kane gave her an acerbic grimace. "The agency does not agree with you. The investigative board determined that I was at fault."

"Based on what?" she asked.

"Let's see," Kane responded. He knew the summary verbatim. "'Failure to secure a protected scene. Failure to implement an appropriate protection plan. Negligence regarding the safety of agents under my direct command.' Better than that, they determined my actions were directly responsible for the injuries to Patty and Sean."

To Kane's surprise, Lilly just nodded a little. "I know. I know all about it."

"What? How?" Kane felt betrayed, like he'd been set up.

"That incident was national news, if you remember, and I was at the academy when it happened. We all knew it was about someone in the agency, even though no names were mentioned. When we met, it didn't take me long to figure out you were the one involved."

Kane stared in amazement. "Then why did you ask about it? Why did you make me tell you all about my biggest failure in glorious detail?!"

"Because you needed to let it out. It doesn't take a trained shrink to see that you've internalized this whole thing." She offered a kind look to him, one that was so warm and reassuring he almost felt like crying. "Whether you know it or not, it's still eating at you, and sooner or later those memories are going to finish you off."

"Tell that line of shit to their families," he spat. "I fucked up. That's the bottom line, and the careers of two good agents are over, and one can't walk because of my mistake. That's what eats me up."

"They understand. It's you that doesn't understand. You didn't do anything wrong."

"Bullshit!" he exploded. "I was so fucking arrogant I didn't want to admit I might be in over my head, so I sent an agent the wrong way and left a hole big enough to drive a cruise ship through! I'm lucky it wasn't worse! The only reason I wasn't tossed out completely was because I'd done so much good work otherwise, so I was demoted to standby status. That's almost certainly why they brought me back for this case—that, and my shooting skills."

"Kane, you didn't screw up at all."

Kane wasn't interested in false platitudes. "You don't know that!" he nearly screamed at her. "You can't know that!"

"Yes I can," she stated firmly enough to make a crack in the shell that held his self-recriminations in place. "Did you read the whole report?"

"No," he admitted. "Once I heard the verdict and got the directive, I kind of checked out. I just didn't care anymore. Plus, I was told it was sealed, so I had no chance of getting to it."

"Maybe you couldn't get to it, but I could."

"How did you do that?"

Lilly gave him a pitying look at his underestimation of her abilities. "After we got back from West Virginia, in all the chaos of prepping for Doyle's camp, I called in a couple of favors to see what was up. I got the real story."

Stunned didn't begin to describe Kane's reaction. He was almost afraid to ask his next question. "What did you find out?"

"Mainly that a lot of information was not presented during the hearing. The fact that you were undermanned was glossed over."

Kane shook his head. "But, why? What possible reason could there be to suppress information?"

"You just said you'd earned your share of haters in the agency. Think about the congressional inquiries that would have come up if the board decided that the agency had short-changed a presidential protective detail."

Kane nodded. "Yeah, that would've been a nightmare. A lot of high-level people would've gotten their asses handed to them."

"On a silver platter," Lilly agreed. "Do you remember who the lead agent on the investigation was?"

"Brent Douglas."

"And what position does Agent Douglas now hold?"

"You know who he is," Kane responded automatically before understanding the import of her words. "Are you serious?"

Lilly shrugged. "I don't know, but isn't it an amazing coincidence that he ran an investigation that falsely determined you, not the agency, was at fault, saving them a ton of embarrassment, and then six months later was promoted to the number two position in the agency, getting the gold medal for pole vaulting right over you to do it? And that he's a lock to take over when that useless suit Schultz retires—which will probably happen right after the election if Armstrong wins—while you're safely stuck in the back of the bus where you can't make any noise?"

Kane was silent for a minute as he contemplated this theory. "So you think he did all that to set me up? That's a little hard to believe."

"No, I don't think it was a planned setup. It was an opportunity that someone, maybe Douglas, took advantage of. Now, maybe you were right about being full of yourself. Maybe you needed a little reality check to slow your roll because you were getting too big for your britches, but that's a training issue that's easily addressed by your leadership chain. Ignoring or suppressing valid evidence to let you take the fall for something that was a clusterfuck just waiting to happen was not right. This whole thing was FUBAR from the second you got your orders, and you paid for it."

"You realize you committed a felony by reading a sealed file without authorization?"

She smiled languidly. "Yeah, but I thought it through. Who's going to find out? The only people who know that I went there are the security staff, which is fine because we're allowed in the records room, and the records clerk logged that I pulled a file that wasn't sealed because I asked him real nice. It's all proper."

"You did all that for me?" To say he was touched by her actions was an understatement.

"I did it for us, Kane. Even if you were a total dick to me at first, we were partners the second we got introduced at DNC headquarters. And, after working with you for a few days, it's pretty clear you're not an asshole. At least, not every day." To punctuate her point, she placed her hand over his and offered a smile of comfort.

For what seemed like the tenth time, he saw Lilly in yet another light. She wasn't just some pain-in-the-ass rookie cutting her teeth with him. She wasn't the uber-savant who etched every single thing she saw and heard into her incredible mind either. Nor was she merely the frighteningly effective femme fatale who mixed toughness with sultry innocence to achieve her goals. She was all these, but even more. She was his partner, one who had gone out of her way to show him some compassion and do something for him.

He sensed a profound change in their relationship, not just professionally, but personally. He ignored the second part even though Lilly's eyes sent a similar vibe. "I guess I owe you one."

"Damn right you do."

"Well, while you determine what that might be, I'm going to hit the bathroom." With that profound proclamation, he took his leave of the woman he was now proud to refer to as his partner.

***

Lilly was sitting at the small table near the window when Kane came out of the bathroom, looking at the TV with the sound turned down. The gravity of their conversation was not lost on her; they could not explore it further, but it remained nonetheless.

To spare both of them further, agony, Lilly brought the focus back to business. "How do you think this investigation is going to turn out?"

Kane's relief was palpable. "Best guess is that we never find the shooter, because he's somewhere with no extradition earning interest on a numbered account in the Cayman Islands."

"We can find him," Lilly protested. "Guy like that, he's got to have a past somewhere. That's more an FBI Legal Attaché operation, or maybe the CIA."

"Not if he's a sleeper agent."

"I thought those were myths." The idea that someone could recruit a child or teenager, train them for whatever, and then send them off to live a normal life until they were recalled for dangerous duty was too far-fetched for her.

"I know a lot of people at the FBI. About twice a year someone goes to the Hoover Building and reports that they were recruited in fifth grade by the Russians—well, now the Chinese or the North Koreans—but they are renouncing that and declaring their patriotism. Most of them are bonkers, but there have been a few real sleeper agents that actually could verify their story."

Lilly took a sip of Scotch. "I can't imagine someone sitting on their hands for thirty years without saying a word. The stress alone would kill them, or drive them to drink or do drugs."

"Sometimes they don't even know they've been trained until they're activated."

"Activated?"

"Yeah, like with a code phrase or a picture or something. It flips a switch in them and they instantly remember everything they need to remember, but completely forget it the second the trigger expires or they get the cancel trigger. It's a fugue state."

"I don't know how you'd condition someone to react that way."

Kane shrugged. "There's a lot of 'black ops' in our own government doing things that bend or even outright break the law. Drugs, brainwashing, that sort of scary..." *Wait a minute. Drugs and brainwashing.* He stopped his explanation, squinting in concentration. "What were the drugs that I listed on the whiteboard at the office today? The ones that I found in the autopsy report, that I said were odd."

Lilly did her thing, and it took her a few seconds to recall the requested information. "Phenobarbital, Scopolamine, Risperidone, Triazolam, Clonazepam, and Levi... no, Levothyroxicone—I think. Your handwriting sucks."

"Levothyroxine," Kane corrected, nodding. "I can't believe I didn't see it earlier. It's fucking Burundanga!"

Lilly laughed out loud at the fake-sounding word. "It's what? What the hell is bunga-dunga?"

"No, Burundanga," he enunciated. "That's not the scientific name. It's a street name, like 'Molly' or 'Ice.' This shit is like a date rape drug, but not exactly. It's used a lot in South America—it makes people highly susceptible to suggestion, so criminals target wealthy people and feed them this stuff so they'll give access to their life savings. The victims never know until it's far too late."

"That's fascinating, Kane, but what does it have to do with the shooting?"

"There's a few stories about sketchy black operations fucking around with this stuff for purposes of re-programming people, like tailoring the drug so you would retain what you learned but also forget it. The idea was you get a kid who's maybe on the streets or detached from any support system, you treat him nice, give a sense of purpose and support, feed him good meals with tiny bits of the doctored Burundanga mixed in there, and over time you can convince him of almost anything and slowly bury it in his subconscious. So you teach him whatever ideology you want, teach him how to shoot or make a bomb, or anything else, and he has no idea you did it. Then you send him off to college or work and he lives his life—gets married, buys a house, starts a family, and contributes to his 401K.

"But one day someone calls his cell phone and says something like, 'Armand the cheese monger says it's time to buy some grapes.' Makes no sense, but it's his trigger phrase, and now he's the killing machine he was trained to be, and he goes and blows someone up or takes a shot at his target. And he probably won't remember what he did afterward."

"And you believe those stories?"

"They don't start from nowhere, and I trust my sources. I've coordinated with CIA and other agencies, and you see enough to know the capabilities. Plus, didn't you say that Susan from the camp said David Park would go almost into a trance when he shot?"

"Yeah."

"That fits the profile. It makes sense that you could train him to flake out when his eye went to the scope. In fact, that's a huge deal. I don't care who you are—you point a rifle at a presidential candidate, you're going to get buck fever in a big way. And, at that distance, you can't shake even the tiniest bit."

Lilly nodded. She'd experienced that on the range, where a tiny twitch equaled a two-foot miss, and that was at 500 yards. The shot from the bridge was nine times that distance, so even the beating of his heart would be an issue. Remaining calm and smooth would be paramount. "Sure, but isn't it possible that he was taking something that calmed his nerves so that he could be a better shot? I've heard of most of those drugs. Aren't they available in over-the-counter medications?"

"I'm pretty sure they all require a prescription. I mean, yeah, it *could* be a coincidence, but that's yet another convenient happenstance." He sat back and folded his hands behind his head. "I'm willing to bet that the five other victims have all those drugs in their systems, and at levels equivalent to Park. Did we get the tox screen for any of the other victims?"

"I didn't look," Lilly admitted. "Didn't have a chance." She was already pulling open her laptop. Kane followed her lead.

"Knoxville has one," Lilly called out, "but it doesn't list any of our drugs. It does say 'trace elements of additional foreign substances—no bearing on cause of death.'"

"No surprise there," Kane responded. "I mean, if a guy has half of his head all over the driveway and you know he didn't do it to himself, how much are you going to dig into his blood chemistry?"

Lilly grunted in tacit agreement. The reports for Texarkana and Jefferson City did not have a toxicology report, but both Findlay and Fredericksburg noted that such results were pending.

"Change of plans," Kane stated. "You go up to Pennsylvania tomorrow and check things out. I'm going to Fredericksburg to talk with that medical examiner to see if I can get some preliminary info. We don't need to confirm all six. If we get one other victim with the same cocktail in his veins, I'm gonna say that's proof of concept."

"I'll go with that," Lilly responded, "but that just raises another question. How many private citizens have the resources, the time, and the medical knowledge to customize a complex drug interaction and deliver it to six shooters regularly over months or years?" Something else occurred to her. "And Park was in his forties. That's a lot of time to wait for the opportunity to activate him. And that sounds like a government operation."

Kane rubbed his eyes. "What's more, why would anyone set up this intricate, damn near perfect plan decades in advance and waste it shooting at a presidential candidate with no major crisis happening? You'd wait until there was one and then take out the actual sitting president to gain an advantage, not a candidate. I don't know what to make of it."

It seemed to Lilly that every time either one of them opened their mouth, the situation got more complex and dangerous. She was grateful that Kane had suggested sharing the hotel room for mutual protection. But these newly unearthed ideas might expose the plans of a sovereign nation that had attacked the United States.

For all she knew, solving this case (or failing to solve it) could lead to anything from more assassination attempts to World War III.

Friday, November 3

Four Days Before the Election

Chapter 14 – Blood Evidence

Kane was tired. Tired enough that he didn't set the cruise control, fearing he would drift off to sleep while the car dutifully continued at eighty miles an hour right into a ditch. Rest had not come easy the previous night as he mulled over the case. As serious as the assassination attempt itself was, the potential for further carnage made that worry fade into the background.

He first headed to the shooting site on Downman Avenue. The street was lined with upper-class McMansions, with manicured lawns and German luxury cars in the driveways. A black-and-white police unit was parked in front of the home of the recently deceased Walter DeLong, and a uniformed officer stepped out of it as Kane pulled up.

"Can I help you, sir?" the officer inquired.

"Yes, good morning. I'm Secret Service Agent Kane Logan." He extracted his ID.

"Thank you, sir," the officer said after scrutinizing it closely. "I'm Officer Scott Baker. Why is the Secret Service here?"

"We're running down a lead," Kane responded cautiously. "It's probably nothing, but we can't leave anything unresolved. I didn't expect to see a watch here so many days after the event, though."

Baker shrugged. "Look at the houses. Lotta money, lotta influence with local government, so we're making the residents feel better." He made his statement without rancor, but Kane was sure that he, as a newer officer, was drawing the lion's share of babysitting duty.

"Gotcha," he answered. "I'd like to take a look in the house and around the grounds."

"Certainly, sir. Please let me know if you need anything, like if you want to go on other properties. Everyone here is kind of jumpy still, and I'd be happy to escort you rather than have someone point a shotgun at you."

"Noted. Thanks." The officer got back in his car and Kane walked up the driveway. The scene wasn't all that different from what he'd seen in the Douglasville images, with the dark stain on the concrete that hadn't quite faded.

The interior of the well-appointed house offered no clues, so he headed to the basement, and that's when things became a bit more interesting. Mr. DeLong was either an avid hunter or really liked taxidermy. Head- and body-mounts of elk, black and grizzly bears, mule deer, fallow deer, red deer, eastern cougars, an alligator, and a wild boar were only part of the collection that spread across every inch of the basement, which looked like a mountain hunting cabin, complete with a well-stocked bar. The room could be an advertisement for a safari tour guide.

An ammunition-reloading setup completely covered one table. Kane looked into the large containers, seeing casings, both spent and new, in .416 Remington Magnum, .308 Winchester, .375 H&H, and—not surprisingly—6.5 Creedmoor calibers. Next to it was the biggest gun safe he'd ever seen, but it was empty. Kane estimated it could hold at least fifty long guns and maybe a couple dozen handguns. No question, DeLong had been involved in whatever this was turning into.

Armed with this information, he headed upstairs and back out of the house. Glancing in the direction indicated by the pattern of the bloodstain, he noticed an opening in the trees that exposed the top of a hill or ridge to the north, maybe a mile away. He went back over to the police car. "Hey, Baker. What's up that way, near the summit of that hill?"

Baker climbed out of his vehicle and turned in the direction Kane indicated. "I think there's a bunch of apartments and a baseball field. It's off Route 639." He reached for a map in his glove box. "Yeah. Wicklow Road. A bunch of people heard the shot from the apartment complex, but it was tough to localize."

"Great. Thanks." He returned to his truck and, using a combination of his navigation system and dead reckoning, within a couple of minutes he was pulling off Route 639 and onto residential Wicklow Drive. Townhouses and cookie-cutter homes lined the street, getting newer as he proceeded up the gentle incline until there was nothing more than frames and concrete basement shells. Coming around a turn, he came to a baseball field complex, and scanned the area for the highest point. A large storage building fit the bill, so he pulled up next to it. Grabbing his spotting scope, he jumped first on the hood, then the roof of his truck to reach the apex.

Walking the length of the building, it didn't take long to see this wasn't the spot. Smaller hills, houses, and trees obstructed his view. Had it been the dead of winter, the lack of leaves on the branches might have revealed a couple of opportunities, but the kaleidoscope of yellow, red, and orange made a clear shot impossible. Frustrated, he jumped down and looked for another location.

A dugout on the third-base side of one field was promising. The wood construction would provide stability, and the pitch of the roof provided an excellent shooting platform. Once on it and in a prone position, a glance confirmed it was a valid shooting location. Laid out before him was the valley in which most of Fredericksburg existed. Kneeling on one of the rows, he propped his elbows up and aimed the spotting scope in the right direction. Sure enough, just past the expansive cemetery, he could see the driveway of the house in which Walter DeLong had met his violent end.

If Lilly confirms the shot in Pennsylvania, we're really onto something. Kane checked his watch. She was still probably an hour, more like ninety minutes, from her site, so he could accomplish more before touching base with her. Five minutes later he was back on Route 95, heading to Richmond to take a look at DeLong's autopsy report.

His latest discovery had fully alerted his senses, so he set the cruise control. There was no risk of falling asleep now.

***

Douglasville, Pennsylvania was a pleasant town with a small business center at the south end and a sprawl of houses on tree-lined roads further north. Winding Creek Drive was not much different than the rest of the area. Lilly pulled into the Park driveway and got out, her eyes going right to the bloodstain from the photos she'd seen the previous night.

Forcing that image from her head, she walked to the front door and rang the bell. After almost a minute, the door opened a sliver, just enough for Lilly to see half of a woman's face eyeing her suspiciously. "What?" the woman demanded.

"Hello. I'm Agent Lilly Alexander of the United States Secret Service. Are you Mrs. Park?" She showed her identification, hoping that it would engender a friendlier response.

The strategy failed. "That's me. What. Do. You. Want?"

Ohh-kay. "I'm sorry to bring this up, but I'm investigating a lead that may tie in with your husband's death. May I come in and take a quick look around?"

Park didn't look receptive to the idea. "Do you have a warrant?"

"No, I don't."

"Then no you can't. Get the fuck off my porch and the fuck off my property." She pushed the door shut and Lilly could hear her turn the deadbolt. She didn't understand why the woman directed such venom at her but realized she had just been through a traumatic event and likely was not herself. And some people just hated the government. While it would not be hard for her to get a search warrant, it was neither worth her time nor appropriate to torment this recently widowed woman. Plus, going through Park's home wasn't her primary reason for being here.

She went back to her truck, pausing to look to the north. The hills Kane had suggested as the shooter's vantage point were clearly visible. The shot was possible, having both the elevation and the angle needed. She sighed. *All this way to confirm a line of sight.* It seemed like a waste of time, but wasn't. There was no room for assumption based on a two-dimensional map, not now. They needed to be certain.

Just as she backed out of the driveway, her cell rang, with the dashboard display indicating it was Kane. Lilly hoped he'd been more productive in Virginia than she'd been in Pennsylvania. But when she pushed the Answer button, she heard a loud grunt and a high-pitched tinkling, like heavy sleet hitting a metal railing. The noise lasted for maybe a second before the call died.

What the hell?

***

Kane sat in an unoccupied office in the Virginia Department of Health building off of Jackson Street in Richmond, flipping through the pages of Walter DeLong's autopsy report until he found the "Toxicology Screening" section. The list was far longer than he'd expected, but it wasn't hard to find all six drugs listed as present in his system at the time of death, in quantities significant enough to cause overt physiological reactions.

Kane would have been more surprised if the report *hadn't* contained the drugs. Each suspected coincidence had meant a connection, and the pattern was pointing to his once-dubious theory being quite possible. He wasn't ready to use the term "probable"—at least not yet—but he was getting there.

Below that dry list, however, there was a handwritten paragraph, which usually indicated that there was something else going on, something that the dry sections of the autopsy report might not make clear. More importantly, the note started by listing the very drugs he was searching for.

The combination of benzodiazepines and barbiturates suggests the possibility of unique, pronounced, and unpredictable physiological and psychological reactions. There is no medical justification for this combination, yet each drug is present in significant proportions, enough to induce extreme tardive dyskinesia, paranoia, fugue states, violent outbursts, insomnia, and other overt symptoms that may be difficult or impossible to classify.

"Fugue state" stood out to him. But even more, the paragraph suggested that other symptoms might be present and easily noticeable at other times. He'd not considered that, but if true that fact might make identifying the real shooter that much easier—if he was still alive.

Chapter 15 – Escalation

It took Kane only a few minutes to get back on Route 95 toward D.C. The traffic was sparse, allowing him to escape to more rural areas quickly. He figured he had enough information to call Lilly. He needed to share what was bouncing around in his head so she could analyze it and provide the confluence they had to have. She could mull it over during her longer drive back to HQ, and Kane would give odds that she'd have ten different options about how to proceed by the time they reunited at Murray Lane. He placed the call.

The screen read Connected, and he waited to hear his partner's voice, but it never materialized. A massive jolt sent his truck surging forward, followed by an explosive pressure wave that caused his ears to pop. A hammer blow sent waves of pain through his upper thigh barely a second before the screen went black and shatter marks etched across the glass.

One glance in the rearview mirror clarified everything for him. Most of the back window was gone. An SUV that looked like a Dodge

Durango with a crumpled grill was right on his ass, with the driver holding a black object out the window. As Kane watched, several bright flashes emitted from it in quick succession.

GUN! He jammed the accelerator to the floor, regretting yet ignoring the secondary stab of agony in his leg, and twisting the wheel just enough to alter his course without losing control of his SUV as it accelerated. His pursuer fell back rapidly.

It didn't stay there long. With a surprising demonstration of its power, the Dodge jumped back onto his rear bumper, the driver firing his weapon again. Kane jinked the wheel left and right and was rewarded by seeing the weapon wag as the driver tried to stay with him. It was Kane's only defense.

He felt a slight sag to the left, and his speed dropped a shade. *Probably shot a tire.* While the Kevlar-reinforced run-flats would keep him going a while longer, speeds in excess of 120 would shred a damaged one pretty quickly. He glanced down. A black spot was spreading across his gray pant leg fast enough to indicate rapid blood loss.

I've got to end this. Now. Either someone in another car was going to be shot or he was going to lose consciousness and plow into a family sedan at a speed that would be fatal to everyone.

But how? The Dodge was keeping pace with him, and believing he could shoot his FN backward accurately was a delusional fantasy. He had to get this guy off his tail, and he lacked the power to do so in a straight race.

He looked down, confirming what he already knew; the truck had no manual emergency brake, forcing him to consider an alternative. It was an incredibly risky move he'd never tried, but now was not a time for such irrelevancies.

When a small gap in the traffic presented itself, Kane pulled the wheel hard left while keeping his foot firmly on the accelerator. As he felt the two left wheels getting very light on their springs, he stood on the brake and reversed his steering. The tires that, only a second before, were begging to lift off the roadway, now crashed back to asphalt and squealed under the monumental forces stripping the rubber from them. More importantly, the nose of the massive SUV started coming right.

As soon as the turn started, he got back on the gas pedal and steered into the skid, amazed he had gotten this far. He guided the truck through an arcing turn that took every inch of all three lanes and the right shoulder to complete until he was facing the drivers he had just passed. He checked his mirror.

His pursuer may have had a good command of his vehicle, but he was either untrained or caught by surprise by Kane's maneuver, because the gray Durango was rolling down the highway like a Matchbox car that had fallen out of the pocket of some irresponsible child. It went for over 200 yards, finally coming to rest on the driver's side. Kane slammed his tortured vehicle into reverse and left clouds of rubber smoke hanging in the air as he backed toward the wreck. The wheels and numerous parts of the Dodge were spread across the road, forcing Kane to slalom around them.

Screeching to a halt, he jumped out—and nearly fell flat on his face as his injured leg refused to support his weight. He grabbed the door and held on for dear life until he could stabilize himself and then limped to the Dodge as he pulled his weapon. He could hear the wail of sirens getting closer.

"Get out of the car!" Kane bellowed but heard nothing in response. Walking around to the shattered windshield, he could see the lone occupant, a man hanging from his seat belt. His face was bloody and his arm appeared badly broken near the wrist, but Kane was unsure if he was alive or dead. Something peculiar caught his eye; instead of a normal seat belt, the driver was wearing a four-point harness, like fighter pilots and race car drivers.

The sirens got louder. Knowing police would not react kindly to a man they did not know pointing a gun at the victim of a serious traffic accident, he backed away but did not take his eyes off the driver. Kane fished his agency ID out of his suit jacket and, with both hands raised, awaited the chance to identify himself.

Things went about as expected. When the first Virginia State Trooper vehicle screeched to a stop, the doors popped open. Hats and the tops of two heads appeared above the windows, while guns were pointed right at him. "Drop the gun! *Now!*"

"Dropping it!" Kane yelled back. He put the weapon on the ground and took a step away from it, "I'm United States Secret Service! This is my ID!" He tossed it toward the police and interlaced his hands behind his head, hoping they weren't going to put him on the ground, as his leg was absolutely killing him. "Injured male in the gray truck! He's a suspect of mine, and he needs medical!"

His claim and instant compliance drew the desired response. The troopers stood and, with their weapons still pointed right at him, advanced cautiously, separated from each other by several yards. Other cruisers were racing up to the scene, making Kane feel a little better. Police with backup would feel less threatened and, while there were about to be more guns pointed at him, their numeric advantage would put them more at ease.

One officer picked up his ID. Looking it over quickly, he nodded to his partner and they resumed their advance, picking up his gun on the way.

"I'm going to pat you down!" someone behind him yelled. "Do not move!"

"Not moving!" Kane responded. He heard footsteps, and a second later got a thorough feeling-up.

"He's clear," the man shouted. "You can put your hands down, sir."

"Thank you." Kane turned. "My suspect might be badly injured. He needs an ambulance right now."

"On the way, sir. ETA about one minute." Kane nodded. "I'm Trooper Gary Woodard. What the hell is going on here?" Kane gave him a quick run-through of the events of the last few minutes, stressing that there was a loaded weapon somewhere in the vicinity. During his tale, another trooper had offered him a rag which he pressed against his leg injury to staunch the bleeding. By then, EMTs had ripped the shattered glass of the windshield away and were tending to the suspect.

"Is he alive?" Kane asked.

"Yes!" the emergency responder answered. "He has injuries to the extremities, but he has good respiration and pulse."

Kane nodded. He didn't wish to slow them one bit, but he needed information right away. "Get me his wallet!"

"Not now!" the EMT yelled, irritation in his voice. "First we treat him!"

I don't have time for this. Objectively, the EMT was doing the right thing by putting the life of the man first, but he had to think of the bigger picture, and a delay in identification could cost more lives. He limped over to the officer that had retrieved his ID and gun and held his hand out. "Let me have them." His tone was that of a five-star general giving an order to a buck private. Now that he had established who he was, his words carried the authority to make the trooper comply without question.

Kane holstered his weapon but, keeping his ID out, made his way to the EMT. "I understand your priorities," he stated in a low, vaguely threatening tone as he displayed his badge, "but this is a federal crime scene under my jurisdiction, and I'm giving you a direct order. Note and log it, but either you get me that wallet or I will get it myself."

The EMT, seeing the flushed, angry face of the injured man and realizing that not one of the troopers in the area seemed inclined to stop him, took the path of least resistance. "As soon as I can get to it, you've got it," he said.

"Thank you." He needed to interview this guy as soon as he could, but he had to be alive for that, so he got out of the way and let the EMTs do their job.

"Got the gun!" someone yelled. Kane wobbled over to the grassy median, staring at a handgun with a ridiculously long magazine, at least seven inches long, sticking out of the grip.

"Fuck me," Kane breathed. This was not good. "Any of you know what type of gun this is?"

The trooper standing immediately to his right spoke first. "It looks like a Glock 19, but I've never seen a mag like that."

"Close. That's a Glock 18c, and the reason you've never seen such a mag is because this little switch here," he pointed to a tabbed circle at the back of the slide, "makes it full-auto by design. This is a military gun, and a rare one at that."

He turned back to the assembled officers. "Here's what I need. Contact the Richmond Secret Service field office and get them here. This scene is under the jurisdiction of the United States Secret Service. No traffic moves along this road in either direction until it's cleared by the SAC. Tag and bag that gun, and I want you," he pointed to the man who had almost identified it properly and read his badge, "Trooper Cross, to personally take possession of this weapon until a Secret Service agent *who identifies himself to you and confirms his identity* relieves you of that duty. If you don't know, you keep the gun. Is that clear?"

"Yes, sir," the trooper answered.

"Thanks. I know I'm being a bit of a dick, but I cannot stress how hot this is."

The EMT trotted over, handing him a faded brown wallet. "Here you are."

Kane opened it. Seeing a driver's license, he put it in his pocket. "Thanks for this."

The EMT looked down at the stained-red rag he held to his thigh before turning his head to follow the trail of bloody footprints that Kane had not known he was leaving in his wake. "Sir, you're bleeding pretty bad. I think we should take a look at that leg."

"Yeah, but in a minute. How's he doing?" Kane nodded toward his suspect.

"Stable. Ready for transport. The roll cage and the four-point harness did their jobs."

"There's a roll cage in that car?"

"Yeah," the EMT confirmed. "Pretty substantial one too. Wasn't even slightly bent and that thing looks like it rolled a bunch of times."

"Good to know," Kane answered. His breathing was becoming labored as the pain increased. "Where's he going?"

"Spotsylvania Hospital."

He turned to Trooper Woodard. "You got a team to go with him?"

Woodard looked insulted and sounded just as exasperated. "Yes, Agent. This is not my first day."

"I didn't mean it like that. Please convey the message to your team that this is an incredibly high-value target. I want one of your men in the same room as my suspect at all times until the Secret Service arrives. No one—and I mean *no one at all* except appropriate medical personnel—is allowed in to see him. It is not only possible, but likely, that an attempt will be made on his life. In fact, I'd appreciate it if you'd double your security team until the Secret Service can relieve you."

"Yeah?" His unspoken question was more elaborate. *Are you serious or just batshit crazy?*

"Yes, and the same rule goes for them as for Trooper Cross with that gun. They are not relieved until they confirm and double-check the identity of their relief. If in doubt, their orders remain in effect as per my authority. I don't care how long it takes." Woodard raised his eyebrows and headed away to direct his people. Kane realized he was being over the top, but it would be far too easy for anyone to monitor phone and radio traffic and to insert men or women who could impersonate an agent. Hell, he was pretty sure that Lilly had heard at least the beginning of the attack on him, and she'd probably already pushed the alarm button back at Murray Lane. It wouldn't be hard to impersonate one.

Lilly! If they had gone after him, they could be plotting to take her out too. Without another word to the men gathered around him, he whipped out his phone and made a call.

***

Lilly was going out of her mind with indecision. Something had gone wrong, that much was clear, but should she call back? Would the noise of his phone ringing somehow alert an adversary or give away his position? Or was he too hurt to dial a call, but might be able to answer and tell her where he was so she could send medical attention? The wrong guess could kill or save Kane—or it might not matter one bit. *Dammit!*

There was one thing she could do. She tapped on the screen as fast as she could, glaring at it until the call was picked up. "United States Secret Service, Richmond Office."

"This is Agent Lilly Alexander, access code 28663. I need an immediate track and trace on an agent's cell phone!" She identified Kane and his general location.

The answer came quickly. "His phone is on Route 95 North in Golansville, Virginia."

"Is it moving?"

"Yes, but not at traffic speed." Just then, the display indicated a call coming from Kane's phone.

"Got it. Please dispatch a team to that location for a possible agent down." Without waiting for confirmation, she terminated the call. "Kane?! What the hell is going on?!"

Kane's voice was strained. "Lilly, check your six right now for threats!" She heard other agitated voices in the background and wished to know more, but had the presence of mind to clear her immediate area.

"I'm good! I'm driving. No one around me. Are you okay?"

"I'm okay. I just took heavy gunfire on 95 from an SUV that was chasing me, but we have the driver in custody. Keep your head on a swivel." The rural two-lane road on which she drove was devoid of traffic at the moment, but it was also a great place for someone to cut her off or try a potshot as she went by, so Lilly flipped on her emergency lights and pushed the gas pedal down. Speed was her friend right now.

"What do you need from me?" she asked, but instead of an answer from Kane, she heard a different voice in the background. "Sir, you've been shot!"

What!? "You were shot?" she nearly screamed. The tiny bits of dissonant information randomly trickling in were driving her nuts.

"I know!" Kane's voice lowered in volume as he answered the man, sounding like he'd already had this conversation, before coming back to Lilly. "A shot deflected into my upper thigh. It's pretty shallow. No big deal."

"Let us treat you!" the other voice urged. He sounded much more concerned than Kane, making Lilly wonder if her partner was playing up the bravado for any of the stupid-ass reasons that men did such things.

"Wait a fucking minute!" he snarled to the mystery man. "I've got an address in Bristow, VA. I'll text it to you. Alert the local cops and tear that house apart."

"What am I looking for?"

"Hell if I know. I'm hoping you'll tell me."

Lilly rolled her eyes but understood why Kane was unable to be more specific. "Copy that. I'm still like three hours out, though."

"Understood. I'm taking this asshole back to Murray Lane after he gets fixed up at the hospital, and we're going to have a chat. I'm hoping you'll find something that'll give me the leverage I need."

"I'm on it. Get that leg fixed, Kane," she urged.

His amused snicker was laced with pain, making her want to strangle him. "I will, Mom," he responded sarcastically. "I think this EMT is about to crawl down my pants. We might be engaged soon."

"Well, don't do anything I wouldn't do," Lilly told him. His dark humor was becoming contagious.

"That doesn't rule much out," he shot back. She killed the connection and started perusing her nav system for a highway where she could more safely exceed the posted speed limit.

***

Pear Tree Court in Bristow, VA was a small cul-de-sac with nine houses packed closely together on small lots. Two uniformed officers standing on the porch of one of those houses were speaking with a woman as she screamed and gesticulated wildly, alternating between complaints about her rights being violated and questions about her husband's location. Several neighborhood residents were standing in front of their own homes, watching the show.

Lilly pulled into the driveway behind a gray Buick and approached the porch.

"Who the fuck are you?!" the woman demanded. She gave Lilly no chance to answer, instead leaping to her own conclusion. "FBI? Oh, this is great!" She turned back to the cops. "Now you've got the FBI here because you can't deal with me yourselves!" The officers looked relieved at her arrival, making Lilly wonder how long this little scene had been going on.

Boy, homeowners just love me today. "Hello. I'm Agent Lilly Alexander with the United States Secret Service, not the FBI. Are you Danielle Barnett, wife of Scott Barnett?"

"Yes, I've already told these ignorant assholes that! I want to know what the hell is going on here and where my goddamned husband is!"

"Certainly. Your husband is in custody and is suspected of assaulting a federal officer with a deadly weapon."

"What?! Scott would *never* do anything like that! Where is he?!"

"He is currently at Spotsylvania Hospital getting treatment for injuries sustained during his arrest."

"Injuries? What did you fucking Nazis do to him?!"

"Ma'am, he was injured in a one-car automobile accident while chasing and firing a gun at a federal agent."

"That's crazy! You're crazy!"

"Be that as it may," she said in sedate, measured tones, "that is the situation at this time." It was a little-known guilty pleasure of many law-enforcement personnel to maintain their composure while explaining things and watching a civilian lose his or her shit because of it. Lilly looked at the officers, one of whom held up folded papers and nodded.

"Now, if I'm not mistaken," Lilly continued, "this officer is holding a valid search warrant signed by a judge, giving us the right to search your premises. You will therefore remove any pets or people from the home and step aside so we may conduct our legal search. If you fail to do so, you will be arrested for obstructing a federal officer. Make your decision right now." Her bitchy-sweet smile made it clear that she would enjoy ordering these officers to cuff her and throw her in the back of one of their patrol cars if she persisted, and that she wouldn't worry too much about keeping the house neat while performing her search.

Mrs. Barnett took two symbolic steps away from the threshold of the walkway. "My son is at school, and the only animal in the house is his pet hamster," she said sullenly.

"I appreciate your cooperation," Lilly said with over-the-top gratitude. She headed into the home, followed by the two officers.

"There better not be one thing out of place when you're done, or I'm suing the government!"

Lilly ignored the idle threat. She would, of course, make every effort to keep things in place, as this was someone's home, but she would also do what she had to do to uncover evidence. After all, one of the owners of this house had taken shots at her partner, and his wife might be an accomplice.

The house was, not surprisingly, very normal—neat, but not too neat. A pullover sweatshirt rested on the back of one chair, and a few toys were on the floor of the living room.

"What do you need from us?" one of the officers asked.

"For right now," Lilly answered, "just stick with me. If you see something odd, call it out. It would be helpful if you catalog anything we confiscate."

"Fine. But what are we looking for?"

"I wish I could tell you. We suspect this is part of a coordinated effort, so anything that suggests communication from someone to Mr. Barnett would be like gold to me. I know that's kind of vague. Just follow your instincts," she recommended.

The officers nodded, and all three started opening the drawers, cabinets, and closets. Twenty minutes later, they had nothing of value, so the trio headed upstairs.

The first stop was the master bedroom. If his wife was complicit in the crime her husband committed, this location could be a treasure trove of information, as bedrooms were more private and therefore better hiding spaces.

If this couple was working together, however, they didn't store anything about it here. In fact, with the exception of a drawer full of some fairly elaborate marital aids and sex toys, there was nothing that evoked any reaction at all.

They stuck their heads into two more rooms. One was the kid's bedroom, and the other was a guest bedroom/storage room. They checked both thoroughly but came up empty. Arriving at the last door, Lilly turned the knob to enter, but the door was locked.

The officers called downstairs. Mrs. Barnett claimed she did not have the key, as that room was her husband's office and he didn't like anyone going in it. Lilly could hear the officer explaining that, if she was trying to hinder the progress of the investigation, she would fail, with the only result being a broken door. Either Mrs. Barnett was telling the truth or decided that damage to her house was worth being problematic, because he radioed back to break it down.

Taking a second to size up the situation, Lilly found a good aiming point and delivered a powerful strike just below the knob with the ball of her foot. The door cracked around the knob and plate, swinging open with enough force to bang against the wall. Lilly stepped in and halted as she took in the surroundings. "Oh, sweet hell."

If a room could be said to have a creepy vibe, this one did. A laptop sat in the middle of a desk surrounded by three monitors, each with screen savers running through images of Senator Armstrong in various unflattering poses and expressions. A huge map of the country covered one wall, covered by the tried-and-true method of using twine and thumbtacks to connect topics and locations that may or may not have been related. It looked like a spider had gone berserk. Two enormous trash bins were filled with tiny bits of shredded lined paper.

A simple press-board cabinet, like one you could buy at Wal-Mart, was on the opposite wall, and Lilly made her way over to it. It was not locked, so she pulled it open to reveal an arsenal that looked like it had been plucked directly from a Call Of Duty video game. She'd only heard of some of these weapons, which few private citizens could legally own.

Even with all that firepower, what struck Lilly was the abundance of notepads that were stacked as many as thirty high on every flat surface of the room, including the floor, with only a narrow walking path winding through them. She grabbed the pad on the desk nearest to the computer, the only one that was not part of a pile. Figuring it would be one of the more recently used ones, she flipped through the pages. They contained random doodles and phrases that meant nothing to her (she would still have them analyzed by a behavioral assessment team), but she was fascinated by the diverse and seemingly arbitrary terms and phrases that covered every page.

Kane's theories from the previous evening about brainwashing and triggering phrases rushed back to her. There had to be a million such potential codes scattered about the room on these pages. Even with her gift of recollection, she would be overwhelmed by the sheer quantity of data. This situation called for computer analysis.

"OK," she said to the officers, "I need pretty much everything in this room. Of course, all the guns. I doubt anyone here has a Federal Firearms License. The computer, any thumb drives, pictures of that mess," she said, gesturing to the twine wall, "the contents of the recycling bins, and—sorry to say it guys—every single notepad in here." She saw their eyes widen in despair. "I need them all in the back of my SUV before I head back to my headquarters, and I want to be moving by—" she checked her watch—"1400 hours. Call in anyone you need to help. If you get any resistance, put them through to me." She paused, knowing that enthusiastic help was much more productive than conscripted help. "I know, guys. I do. But this is absolutely critical."

Like Kane, her instincts were good; knowing smiles replaced disgusted expressions. "Yes, ma'am. We understand. Give us a couple of minutes to get things rolling, and we'll have you on your way ASAP."

"I appreciate it. Oh, and this notepad," she said, holding up the one she had just picked up, "is Catalog Item Number One. Mark it as such because I'm going to put it in my truck before I come back to help load all this stuff." She headed downstairs to the landing, where Mrs. Barnett went apoplectic upon seeing Lilly leave her home with something she hadn't had when she entered. "Give me that! You can't take that!"

"Actually, I can," she responded. "And, unless you can provide your FFL documentation, you are under arrest for the possession of illegal firearms."

"WHAT?!"

Stunned, she didn't resist as her hands were cuffed behind her. Lilly sent a quick text to Kane describing her findings before getting to work.

Chapter 16 – Q & A

Kane limped out of the elevator at Murray Lane. It had taken far too long, in his opinion, for the doctor to remove the bullet; he had important work to do. Once they were done, he nearly ran from the hospital, happy that the local anesthetic he'd insisted upon seemed to do its job. In retrospect, however, he wished he'd made the quick stop in the hospital pharmacy to get the pain pills he'd been prescribed.

When he got out of his truck at headquarters, bolts of agony shot from his heel to his ribs, worse than anything he'd ever dealt with in the past. Walking was tough.

He pulled out his phone. *Where r u?* he texted Lilly.

Conf Room 305 unloading evidence.

On my way. He hobbled to the elevator, and only when the doors closed did he grimace in pain and lift his right leg off the ground for a moment of partial relief. He wished the ride was longer.

Two agents, their arms full of notebooks, were entering the conference room, making him hopeful they could develop more leads. His excitement, however, did not prepare him for what he saw when he entered.

The conference table had been pushed into the corner. The notepads covered about sixty square feet of the room to a depth of three feet. Lilly was making notations on each one, checking them off on a clipboard, and moving them from one pile to another.

The pain in his leg was replaced by astonishment. "Holy shit. Is this where I come to buy a term paper?"

Lilly looked up. "Right? Welcome to hell."

"I know you said you had something, but this is everything and my brother's kitchen sink."

"This," she said as she stood and stretched her back, "is what Mr. Scott Barnett does in his downtime." She tossed him the notebook she'd grabbed at the house while explaining what else had been discovered in the home office, especially the repository of illegal guns.

Kane listened as he flipped through a few pages. "That fits. He used a full-auto Glock 18C on me."

Lilly gaped. "And you only got shot once?"

"I know. I should play the lottery tonight. Why did you separate this one?" he asked.

"A hunch. It was closest to his computer, not in a pile, and the last twenty pages or so are blank. I figured it might be the most recently used one. We need something to work with ASAP, and that's our best chance. Where is your suspect?"

"On the way to BridgePoint Hospital. He had to have surgery for a broken arm, so he got a later start than I did. He should be there about 1700."

"Cool. How are you feeling?" She gestured to his leg and his torn suit pants.

"A little sore, but otherwise I'm good."

"Yeah, you look just ducky. You made it sound like a scratch over the phone."

Kane displayed a sardonic frown. "Well, it didn't seem too bad at the time, and the adrenaline was pumping. Plus, as you might have noticed, I don't always let my weaknesses show."

Lilly's eyes went wide and her jaw fell open like a cartoon character. "No! I am shocked! Say it isn't so, Kane!"

He looked down to the side, shaking his head to demonstrate his aggravation, but he had to exert more control to not smile than to stand without cringing in pain. Lilly knew how to break through his personal defenses in a way that made him want to laugh out loud. "Why are you calling me out like that?" he finally asked in a pitiful attempt to save face.

"C'mon. If I had half the injury you're sporting, you and I both know damn well you'd be pushing me in a wheelchair whether I wanted it or not."

"Yeah, you're probably right, although I take issue with the 'whether you wanted it or not' part. You don't have a problem advocating for yourself."

It was Lilly's turn to appear amused. "No, I do not. And, on that topic, I need your help to organize all this before we have to go to the hospital, and there's more coming up. We've got to get it over to Stafford's grad student."

"She's going to crap her pants when she sees how big this job just got," Kane commented, none-too displeased at the development.

"One can hope. Maybe we'll get some real agents on this after all. So pick a pile and a clipboard, Kane, and dig in. You're not about to let me have all the fun, are you?"

Kane scanned the room. "You know, I got shot today, and I'm still sure I've had more fun than you." With that, he pulled up a chair and got to work.

***

BridgePoint Hospital is a small collection of unimpressive, interconnected, light-brown brick buildings. As hospitals in major cities went, it was on the smaller side and for that reason it rarely received any kind of attention or notoriety.

Such conditions also made it a prime location for the Secret Service to hold and treat suspects without fanfare or publicity. Only certain non-medical personnel, and even fewer doctors, nurses, and technicians, were able to pass by the desk in the back corner of the basement and get to the single elevator that did not go up from here.

Arriving shortly after receiving a call that Scott Barnett had been admitted, Kane and Lilly entered through the emergency room, the most direct route to the restricted area. Lilly expected no issues gaining access to the suspect, but both she and her partner took a step back when one of the staff, upon seeing Kane enter with his limp and his discolored, torn slacks, grabbed a wheelchair and ran right toward him. After a quick explanation of Kane's appearance, the overzealous but well-meaning orderly smiled and retreated, allowing them to continue on their way.

"Do I look that bad?" he asked, descending the stairs at a snail's pace.

"Kane, you look like you got mauled by two wombats and a pissed-off gorilla." She wasn't even sure what a wombat was, but the name sounded vicious. "You should be in this hospital as a patient, not to interview a suspect. Are you sure you're up for this? I don't mean it as an insult, but you're hurting and you might not be at your absolute peak right now."

He shot her a look. "Either he's our shooter or he's another link in the chain, and we need to know. Now. Time is not our friend. You remember what's at stake?" He looked determined to the point of anger. "I'll get it done."

They reached the security desk and presented their badges. After a quick radio call, they were admitted with a single instruction. "Room 3."

Despite the pressing nature of the situation, Lilly felt a tiny and very unprofessional thrill at being admitted to a highly secret and secure area that only a few agents would ever see. They proceeded to the appropriate door and pressed the button.

An agent opened the door, with another staring directly through the big window into a small, separate room where Scott Barnett lay on a bed. His eyes were blackened, his face was scraped and scarred, his head was bandaged, and he had a cast on his right arm up to the elbow. His uninjured arm was handcuffed to the railing, an IV line in that forearm.

Perfunctory introductions were exchanged, but before anything else could be said, a dismal wail came over the loudspeaker. "You can't keep me here! I didn't do anything! Who the hell are you people?"

Barnett's tone wasn't defiant. It was scared and confused. Lilly looked at Kane, seeing the same question on his face. *Had they miscalculated?*

"That's about what we've gotten from him since we got here," one of them reported. "We didn't interview him, but he keeps yelling that this is a huge mistake, asking how he got hurt, what is going on, he didn't do anything, that kind of shit."

"Yeah, I have to disagree," Kane answered grimly before spotting a thick manila folder on the small table. "Is this his medical rundown?"

"Yes. We figured you would want to see it, so we brought it up from the hospital."

"Perfect. Thanks." Kane started flipping through it.

"Has he been Mirandized?" Lilly asked.

"He has. It took forever to get him to shut up long enough to hear us and understand, but it's on tape."

"That's great, guys. You can consider yourself relieved. Thanks."

"Sure thing. Just use that phone to call the desk upstairs if you need anything."

Lilly walked over to the one-way mirror. Barnett's expression matched the tone she heard through the speaker. Either he was an Oscar-worthy actor or he didn't know what the hell was going on. "Was he dosed with your cocktail?" she asked Kane the second the door clicked shut.

"And how. These numbers are like five times what we found in Park and DeLong. And, by the levels, I'd say it was recent."

"He was freshly dosed?" Lilly asked. "I thought this was something that was administered over time."

"That's the only way I've ever heard of it being done. Maybe this works differently than I thought. I don't know. We need to get a proper lab analysis." Kane looked as baffled as Lilly felt.

"This doesn't make any sense."

Her partner scowled. "Well, let's go make it make some sense. You ready?" He pointed toward the door.

"Yup." Kane stepped in, Lilly right behind. She did her best to look compassionate; Kane's glare could melt steel and, as overused of a concept as it was, good cop/bad cop could be effective, especially when the good cop had soft eyes and a comforting smile that might coax information out of someone.

They had barely cleared the door jamb when the injured man pounced. "Who are you? Where am I? What is going on?!"

Kane and Lilly stood right next to the bed—intentionally—so they would tower over Barnett. "I'm Agent Kane Logan, and this is my partner, Agent Lilly Alexander. We are with the United States Secret Service. You're at BridgePoint Hospital in Washington D.C."

"Why is the Secret Service interested in me? What did I do?"

Kane and Lilly shared a glance. "Well, for starters, you chased me up Route 95 just north of Richmond this morning and shot up me and my truck with a fully automatic pistol."

"I did what?! You've got the wrong guy!"

"No, we don't. I watched as EMTs pulled you from the mess you made of your Durango. I spent almost an hour in surgery," he said, pulling aside the ripped fabric of his pants to show the bandages and bloodstains that he had not yet washed off his thigh, "so a doctor could pull a 9-millimeter round out of my leg. It matched the gun you used."

"What are you saying?" Barnett nearly screamed.

"I don't know how to be more clear," Kane told him.

"Oh, shit. Was anyone hurt?"

Kane rolled his eyes, and Lilly wasn't sure if he was playing his role or was genuinely frustrated. "Except for me having a gaping hole blasted in my thigh, no."

Barnett stared at Logan like he was a raving lunatic, and Lilly took the chance to jump in. "Mr. Barnett, are you claiming that you don't recall doing any of these things?"

"Absolutely! I remember getting up for work and then, well, that's it. The doctor said that's probably from my head injury. I certainly didn't shoot at anyone. Are you saying my car is wrecked?"

"Completely wrecked, Mr. Barnett. It's a total loss."

Barnett closed his eyes and shook his head. "Danni's gonna kill me."

"Your wife has her own set of problems. She was charged with possession of all your illegal firearms."

"WHAT ILLEGAL FIREARMS?!" His concussion was still fresh enough that the outburst made him wince in agony. The handcuffs clinked as he tried, and failed, to cradle his forehead.

"The ones in the pressboard cabinet in your home office."

"That's nuts! I have a Remington hunting rifle, a .22 rifle for varmints and plinking, and a shotgun. That's it. They are *not* illegal in Virginia."

"No," he responded. "They aren't. But the twelve fully automatic military-grade weapons you own are not registered with state police as required by law. And that's a felony."

Barnett took a deep breath. "Look. I can't even begin to understand what kind of government fuck-up is going on here, but you've made a huge mistake. I don't shoot at people, I don't own a dozen full-auto guns, and I have never done anything wrong besides drive forty-seven in a thirty once. So go back to your office and figure out where you screwed up because you got something wrong." He looked away from Kane and Lilly, dismissing them as much as a seriously injured man who was handcuffed to a bed could. His quivering lips, however, told a very different story.

"Mr. Barnett," Kane continued, "your fingerprints were all over every single one of those guns."

"That's not possible!" Barnett was going to deny and dismiss everything they said from now until the end of time. If they were going to get anywhere, they needed a new tactic.

Lilly picked up the transcript of the interviews with Danielle Barnett. She'd become much more forthcoming about her home life and her husband—specifically, the way they had stopped interacting almost completely. Scott would come home from work and, if he ate dinner with them at all, he would be completely non-verbal, to the point that their son was acting out at home and school. As soon as she started clearing the dishes, he would head upstairs, lock himself in that office, and do whatever he did until the middle of the night, even though he never discussed it with her. This had been going on for several months.

Lilly replayed the home search in her mind, blinking when she recalled the bottom drawer of Mrs. Barnett's dresser, the one that held the sex toys. She'd just assumed that they had been for their shared use. A lot of couples had a porn stash or some other kinky toys somewhere for their mutual entertainment.

But the toys she saw were designed to provide female pleasure when no one else was available or willing. And there had been at least eight of them. While she couldn't rule out any specific type of fetish or fantasy that the Barnetts might use them for as a couple, the smart money made them hers only. It gave her an opportunity to ask a seemingly unrelated question that might give them the opening they needed.

She strolled back to the bed and let Kane finish his latest attempt to engage the recalcitrant suspect before jumping in. "Mr. Barnett, are you and your wife having troubles in the bedroom, sexually?"

His head snapped around. "What?! Why the hell is that any of your business?!"

"Well, I found a fairly extensive collection of sex toys in your wife's dresser, ones that are used primarily by women." She freelanced a little. "They appeared to be fairly well-used, and I doubt that is your doing." Kane looked at her like a dog that heard a high-pitched whistle.

"Our sex life is just fine!"

"I see. Can you tell me the last time you had any form of sexual relations with her?"

"I'm not telling you anything about our sex life!"

She put her hands on the bed railing and leaned down, interposing herself between Kane and Barnett. "Because you don't remember the last time you touched her, right? Because it's been weeks, maybe months. While you've been up in that office night after night working on your notebooks and cleaning your arsenal and developing your conspiracy theories, your wife has been sitting downstairs after your son went to bed, waiting for you to scratch her itch, and it hasn't occurred to you to do a thing about it. That's why she uses that vibrator with the attached clit tickler, isn't it? You're lucky she isn't fucking someone else yet."

A flicker of doubt flashed across Barnett's face. She had broken through the false memories, but that didn't last long. "You fucking bitch," he snarled, concern changing to fury. "Who do you think you are? You tell me I'm a felon, that I'm doing all sorts of illegal things, and now you're saying I can't satisfy my wife because she's some kind of sex freak?! Go to hell. I want a lawyer." This time he put his head back on his pillow and stared at the stark ceiling.

The glimpse of reality that Lilly had brought to his attention was a start. She was about to push harder, to open that door wider, but had another thought. Barnett had lawyered up. Lilly quickly considered all of what was going on and reached a decision. She looked at Kane and directed her eyes toward the door. He hesitated, so she repeated the gesture, and finally he acquiesced. They left the room without a word.

That silence ended the second the soundproof door clicked shut. "What the hell?" he asked. "You had a hit. You missed the chance to exploit it."

"First of all, he asked for a lawyer." She was about to continue when Kane nearly exploded.

"Jesus fucking Christ, Lilly! There are ways around that at this level. We might be holding the guy who nearly killed a presidential candidate, right? Not to mention the shooter of a federal agent with a fully automatic weapon!" He looked like he wanted to punch her.

Lilly was unmoved. "I know you're a little pissed off because of your leg and his stonewalling, but maybe you can let me finish before you read me the riot act." Her calm, measured words threw a wet towel over Kane's ire.

"Leaving when he lawyered up gives him the false impression he's got some leverage, which we will take away when we go back in. That will get him off balance. Right now, and more importantly, I poked a tiny hole in whatever's blocking him. So instead of dealing with us, now he's alone and wondering why his loving wife feels the need to keep a slew of dildoes and vibrators stashed in the back of her underwear drawer." She walked back to the window and gestured to Barnett. "Look at his face, Kane. I'll give you five to one that he's less worried about being arrested than he is about having lost weeks and months of his life."

With each point Lilly made, Kane's expression lost a little more aggravation, and by the time she finished he was nodding softly. "Not bad."

Lilly smiled at him. "Not everything calls for a sledgehammer. Sometimes a tack hammer works better."

"Point taken," he responded and shifted gears. "So you don't think he's lying, and he believes what he's saying?"

"Exactly," Lilly said, plopping down on an uncomfortable chair. "But that leads us to some kind of amnesia, and that's too convenient—both retrograde and anterograde amnesia?"

"It's common with head injuries," Kane responded. "Shooting me happened so recently that it's a blank spot. And the last few months are spotty at best, so he defaults to a happier time further back in his life."

"Is there anything we can do to help restore those memories? Like therapy?"

"Not really. There's been extensive work with hypnosis, but it turns out that most of the restored memories are exaggerated or even completely made up."

"Dammit. So either he's the best liar ever, or he really does have amnesia."

Kane was silent for several seconds. "There was a four-point seat belt in the car, and he was buckled in tight. It also had a roll cage. Why would he have those unless he suspected he was going to crash?"

Lilly shrugged. "A high-speed chase is about the most likely place to have an accident. It sounds like a smart move to me."

Kane's eyes narrowed. "But those aren't factory options. Barnett would have needed to have the harness and roll cage installed or have installed them himself. If he really doesn't know what the hell is going on, why did he have them put in? It's his car—he bought it new and it's registered to him." He pulled his phone out and requested a check on Barnett's finances for any such purchase, waiting while they ran his numbers. "Okay, thank you very much. Yes, please send a team over to talk to them, but it's not high priority." He hung up and focused on Lilly. "Barnett put $4,419.18 on his Visa on August 11th at a Dodge dealership in Chantilly, Virginia for exactly those things."

"Great. So what?" Kane had confirmed his idea, but she didn't see what they could learn from it.

"Barnett has our chemical martini in his system, so it follows that he was being run by someone else, right?" Lilly nodded. "Why would you have someone attack a Secret Service agent but take steps to safeguard his survival?"

"Uh, I'm just spitballing here, but maybe because you don't want him to die?"

Kane was not deterred by her sarcastic response. "If he's not going to come after me, he's not any more likely than normal to get in an accident and die, so the supplemental restraint is superfluous. If he comes after me and dies in the accident, whether he gets me or not, he can't offer much information. But, if he does get in an accident while he's attacking me but doesn't die, he becomes a liability when he's arrested."

Lilly saw where he was going—sort of. "Yeah. Ideally, you'd want him to make the kill but either get away or die in the attempt. You can't question a dead guy." Her voice trailed off as the fuzzy connections came into sharper focus.

"So, why have someone try to kill an agent but install safety features to keep him alive so he can be questioned and become a liability?" Kane repeated.

It hit her like a smack across the cheek. "You want him alive so he can feed you bad information." Kane winked at her. "But then why the amnesia crap? That's the stuff of shitty TV shows. How can he feed us bad information if he doesn't know anything?"

"It might make sense if you consider that he was somehow de-triggered."

"By who?"

"The accident itself could have been the de-triggering."

"I don't follow."

Kane exhaled, drawing the action out for several seconds. "I'm on shaky ground here, but stay with me. When the subject is triggered, I assume it's with a code phrase. That's low-risk and can be delivered remotely, like by phone."

"Sure, that fits," Lilly agreed.

"But, if you want your subject to do his job and go back to normal, he has to be brought out of the trance."

"So that's another phone call with the 'stand-down' code."

Kane tapped on the table. "Yeah, yeah—but no. Think that through. If you're making that call to turn him off, you've got to know exactly when to do it. Expand your thinking to other events—the shooting in New York, for example. After your shooter does the deed, you don't want to turn your guy off until he's in a safe house or somewhere that carries no risk. And to know exactly when to do that, you have to monitor him somehow. That means either watching him, which means you're in the vicinity, or using a tracking device, which can be found. Either way, you're opening yourself up to being discovered."

"Okay. Keep going." Lilly watched Kane work the problem, impressed with his process. She remembered everything and could connect seemingly disparate facts in a way that most people couldn't, but Kane took a single fact and used it to figure out an entire plan. Through experience or some innate ability, he was more devious than those he was pursuing, something she had not yet mastered. It was like he was playing chess against himself. In his way, he had a gift at least as powerful as hers. His train of thought took her to stations that weren't on her map. Yet. *We are one hell of a team.*

Either forgetting or ignoring his leg, he stood up and started limping about the space. "So you use an event that is sure to happen as the de-triggering. When Barnett gets in a serious car accident, he returns to Mr. Normal Guy from the suburbs and has no idea what just happened."

"But what if he doesn't crash?" Lilly asked. "Does he stay a zombie forever?"

"Maybe you have several de-triggers. Number one is the accident. If he doesn't get in an accident, number two is him getting to a safe house, or passing a landmark, or whatever. Maybe you call him with a de-triggering phrase as a last resort. The point is you have enough events to turn him off no matter how things go, and he's no longer a liability."

Lilly smacked her hand on the table. "Right! That's what Susan said when I caught her smoking that night at the camp. David Park acted normal until he stepped into the shooting area, and then he was in a trance, and then the second he stepped out, he was back to normal."

"There you have it. The trigger-by-event might work to turn them off and on, meaning these guys can be triggered, de-triggered, and *re*-triggered, and there are multiple ways to do each," Kane concluded. "The $64,000 question is, how do we re-trigger Mr. Barnett?" He plopped back into his chair.

They sat in silence for a few minutes until Lilly thought of something. She grabbed Barnett's notebook. The first page alone had about a dozen different short sentences and phrases on it, all written at random angles and interspersed with crude drawings. She held it up. "It looks like Mr. Barnett was a doodler and tended to write down phrases he either said or heard. If this is his most recent notebook, what do you think the chances are that he wrote the code phrase down out of habit?"

Kane's gaze shifted between Lilly's self-satisfied grin and the notebook several times. "It's gonna take a lot of time to go through it," he cautioned.

"Then I better get started. Can you get me a fresh notebook and some coffee?"

Chapter 17 – Answers Questioned

Kane watched Lilly fly through each page of Scott Barnett's notebook, adding to the list of options. He couldn't begin to fathom how she could keep it all straight, but he didn't doubt her ability.

"All done," Lilly said, yanking him back to the business at hand so abruptly he had no idea what she was talking about for a second.

"Geez, that was quick," he said upon recovering. "What do we have?"

"One hundred and five nonsensical phrases, some of them repeated over thirty times. I've ranked them by frequency. That's a lot of bullshit to somehow include in one discussion."

"Wait. You want me to come up with a way to use the sentence—" he twisted his head to look over Lilly's shoulder—"'Tomorrow's jack of clubs is yesterday's two of diamonds' into a discussion? And do that 104 more times."

"No, of course not. We don't have that kind of time. We read them off to him, one by one, and ask him what each means until one hits."

Kane chuckled. "I know this guy shot me, but I don't want to kill him from boredom." Lilly smiled back at his joke, but he knew her idea was better. "Let's see how far we can get before he clams up."

"He kind of already did that. Do you think you can get him talking again?" Kane gave her a "hold my beer" look.

Lilly handed him her notes, tearing off a few blank pages for her use and collecting Barnett's notebook as well. "Cool. You run the show using my list. I'll follow along with his notes and see if he says anything that might tip me off, so watch me for a cue."

"You got it." They headed back into the prisoner's room.

Barnett had an expectant look on his face, but it faded when he saw only the two agents enter. "Hey, I said I wanted a lawyer. I'm not talking to either of you without one."

"That's fine," Kane responded as he stepped up to the bed. "We can get you your public defender and watch him crash and burn trying to keep you out of jail after about a million people watched you attack a federal agent with a gun. You know where they send people who shoot at agents? Supermax prisons—the ones where you get shivved for talking to the wrong person, and where you better keep your back to the shower wall to avoid... well, you understand.

"However, we have some info that we don't fully understand, and you might be able to help us make some sense of it. If you do, we can maybe take it easy on you... and your wife. It would be good for your son if he doesn't end up in foster care while you two are doing hard time for attempted murder and possession of illegal weapons. Your choice."

"But I told you, I don't know what the hell is going on. I have no idea how I can help you."

"So your answer is 'no'"? Kane shrugged. "That's your call. It's a pretty stupid one if you ask me, but this is a free country and you are not obligated to help us." He turned around and looked at Lilly. "Told ya. That's twenty you owe me. Let's go." He nearly cracked up at seeing the way Lilly pressed her lips together tightly and shook her head at Barnett before they turned toward the door.

"No! Wait!"

The agents stopped, glancing back at the bedridden man with *what now?* expressions on their faces. "Yeah?"

"I'll listen to what you've got, but you've got to promise to help me and my family out even if I don't know anything." It didn't take the skills of a professional poker player to see he knew he was bluffing.

Kane and Lilly shared another look. Like the first, it was merely for show; they had him and they knew it. "I'll tell you what," Kane said. "If I think you're being honest with me, I'll do that." Putting on a face the scariest Marine drill instructor would find impressive, he stepped forward and got as close as he could to Barnett's head without doing an exam of his tonsils. "But," he growled like a pissed-off Rottweiler, "if I think you're fucking with us, I will make it my mission in life to put you and your wife in the worst federal prison I can find for the next fifty years." He backed away and returned to a normal tone. "Do we have a deal?"

Barnett looked like a vengeful demon had driven a spike right through his soul. "Yeah, yeah. Deal. I'll be straight with you, I promise."

"Very good. Now, I'm going to read some short code phrases to you. If you have any sort of information about the phrase, call it out.

Don't give me interpretation or analysis—you either have information or you don't. Got it?"

Barnett appeared to be recovering from the worst of his shock and nodded obediently. "I'll do my best."

"Perfect. The first phrase is, 'Weeping Willows cry the saddest so ngs.'"

Barnett blinked. "That's it? That's the whole phrase?"

"Yes. I told you they were short. Anything?"

Barnett shook his head firmly. "Sorry, no. Nothing."

"That's fine. The next one is..." Kane continued with the absurd one-liners, but each time Barnett shrugged, bewildered. Kane believed him; he'd half-expected his prisoner to wet the hospital bed when he was threatened. He wouldn't dare lie.

But Barnett's honesty was turning Lilly's theory into a dead end. Two-thirds of the way through her list, they still had nothing. He would, of course, go through them all, but he was already considering his next course of action when he felt Lilly tap him on the shoulder.

***

Lilly sat at the small table, listening to Kane try and fail over and over again as she leafed through Barnett's scribblings. Her idea had been a good one, but they either didn't get the right phrase or Barnett hadn't written it down or something.

She'd memorized every page in the notepad, but she continued to search for anything out of sheer stubbornness. It did not shock her when nothing new materialized. As Kane got near the end of her useless list, she realized it was time to start considering a new approach, so she gave up on the pad and pushed it away.

Once more, she waited for ideas to come to her out of the ether, but something was wrong. It took her a second to recognize that, somewhere in her supposedly empty line of sight, she was reading a word, and that word didn't fit into any paradigm she was considering. It irked her, like a bug crawling on her skin, one she had to deal with right now.

The only thing with written words on it was the damned pad, and she'd read every one of them about a thousand times, so it made no sense that there would be anything new. Still, she gave the front page one more cursory glance without moving in any way. To her amazement, she found the word 'jeans' on it—but not in ink. It was *pressed into the page* from someone writing on the piece of paper above it, and the pressure of the pen had etched itself into the pad like a dinosaur footprint pressed into some mud. The foot that made the print, like the pen, was long gone, but the impression of it remained.

It was far too subtle to be noticed by viewing it directly; only when seeing the pad nearly on edge did the tiny valleys of the phantom word reveal themselves. By tracking left and right at the appropriate angles, she was able to discern a whole sentence, and once she wrote it down and read it to herself, she knew she had one more code phrase. *But would it work?*

Only one way to find out. Standing, she tapped Kane on the shoulder.

***

Kane took the sheet of paper from his partner. He was sick and tired of reading the gibberish and was sure Lilly's latest discovery would fail just like the other ninety-six he'd already read. "Okay, Mr. Barnett, only a few more. The next one is, 'Jordache was to jeans as the Three Stooges were to comedies.'"

The effect was instantaneous. Barnett had been sitting in his bed looking slightly confused, but as Kane finished the phrase, his head dropped and his eyes closed like he had narcolepsy. That lasted for only the briefest instant before he sat up in his bed, his body rigid, his back ramrod straight. He stared at nothing as if watching an invisible individual at the foot of his bed, but his eyes were lifeless and apathetic. "Number 47 active and ready."

Kane was afraid to speak or even move, as if Barnett was a baby deer eating from his open palm and would race off at the slightest disturbance. He looked at Lilly, but she was as frozen as he was. They should have had a plan in place to communicate with Barnett if they triggered him, but should've-ism wasn't going to help them right now. *What do I do?* he mouthed at her.

Lilly shrugged, then jutted her chin toward Barnett. Kane had no idea how to proceed, but anything was better than just standing there like a rube gawking at a pretty painting. *Think!* Whoever had triggered him probably had military training or knowledge and would likely fall back on it for communication purposes. That could work.

"Number 47, report status."

Nothing on Barnett moved except for his mouth. "I declare No Joy for Target K. I say again, No Joy Target K."

He failed to kill me. "Number 47, understood. State intentions."

No answer. He clearly had not asked the right question or not asked it in the right way. What else would his handler need to know? "Number 47, provide location."

That worked. "Unknown. Possible capture. Execute Code 999 Omega?"

Lilly didn't react, but Kane felt a cold blast of fear shoot through his heart. It didn't take too much imagination to figure out that, with Omega being the last letter of the Greek alphabet, that the code signified the end of something or someone. "Number 47, negative on Code 999 Omega. I say again, negative on Code 999 Omega. Confirm order."

"Confirmed. Negative on Code 999 Omega."

Phew.

"What is this nonsense?" Lilly whispered.

Kane held up a finger, looking to see if Barnett reacted, but it was as if he'd heard nothing. That made sense: Kane had uttered the triggering phrase, so Barnett was responding to his voice only. He pulled Lilly to the other side of the room. "Not sure. It sounded to me like he was asking to kill someone, or maybe himself."

"Damn. How screwed up is this guy's head?" Lilly asked.

"I don't know. But, more importantly, how do we get something we can use from him?"

Lilly bit her lip. "This guy is a worker bee. We need to know who he thinks he's talking to or what his next steps are. Can you try to order him to perform his next mission, or maybe go somewhere to debrief, something like that?"

Kane nodded. "So we can follow him? That's a good idea." He went back to the bed. "Number 47, can you execute your next mission?"

No response. "Number 47, what is the location of your next mission?" Still nothing.

Dammit. I've got to get a handle on what he responds to. How do you talk to a foot soldier? Kane had been a Marine sergeant. He'd given subordinates thousands of orders, and he'd taken just as many from officers. Sometimes they were simple and easy to obey and sometimes they were difficult and confusing, but—especially to an enlisted man—they were never, ever requests. "Number 47, execute next mission."

"Unable," Barnett responded. "Current location unknown. Injured. Possible capture."

"Number 47, understood. Return to safe location when possible."

"Confirmed."

Kane walked back to Lilly, who was nodding enthusiastically. "Good work!"

He was about to agree, but realized they couldn't high-five each other just yet. He motioned with his head for her to leave the room, and he followed her out. "We still have a problem."

"What's that? He won't be that hard to follow."

"We have to de-trigger him, and right now we have no idea how to do that."

"Sure we do. We have 105 possible ways to de-trigger him."

Kane had already thought of that but hoped that Lilly had a better idea. Clearly, she did not. " You want me to read through the entire list *again*?"

"Yup." Her teasing smile taunted him.

Kane rolled his eyes and snatched the list away from her. "Fine. But we're not going to be caught with our pants down this time." They discussed how they would respond when and if Barnett came out of his trance, which led to several phone calls to get needed assets in place.

Once everything was set up, they went back into the room where Barnett remained in place like an upright corpse. Success came more quickly this time. At the eighth example of the word salad, Barnett's body exited the fugue state by once again appearing to take the world's shortest nap and falling back on the bed. Shaking his head as if emerging from a deep slumber, he looked at Kane and Lilly with blank eyes. "What?"

Kane transitioned to his script seamlessly. "I said we're sorry, Mr. Barnett. There's been a terrible mistake. We've just arrested another man in a similar vehicle, and it seems I didn't see you collide with him. You were just driving along minding your own business. And the guns and other evidence at your house were clearly planted, so those charges have been dropped as well and your wife is being released. Please accept my apologies, along with those of the United States Secret Service." He removed the handcuffs.

Barnett squinted at Kane before responding somewhat unsteadily. "About time you figured that out."

Kane nodded like a child who knew he did wrong. "Yes, sir. We used a false assumption and went from there, and that skewed our entire investigation. The way I spoke to you was inappropriate and a violation of your civil rights. You have my apologies as well as the agency's." He saw irritation and anger replacing the confusion on Barnett's face.

"What's your name?"

"Agent Kane Logan, sir."

"And you?" He looked in Lilly's direction.

"Agent Lilly Alexander."

"You didn't try to stop Agent... uh, your partner from basically threatening me?"

"Kane Logan, sir," Kane reminded him helpfully.

Lilly shook her head. "No, I didn't."

Barnett grinned viciously. "It seems you're just as guilty as your pal," Barnett concluded. "So neither of you get off."

Kane and Lilly looked at each other mournfully but said nothing further. A knock sounded at the door, and Kane admitted an agent. "Mr. Barnett, I have instructions to drive you wherever you want to go as soon as you're ready." He placed a pile of clothes on the bed. "I got these for you."

Barnett nodded. "Fine. You two," he said to Kane and Lilly, "get out. You'll be hearing from my lawyer soon." They exited the room and went back upstairs to the main part of the hospital and out to the car, with Kane laboring even more than on the way down.

They jumped into Lilly's SUV, waiting for the agency vehicle that would deliver Barnett to wherever he wanted to go. They wouldn't follow right behind him; the driver knew to keep the car's GPS on the entire time.

Lilly broke the silence. "What do you think Barnett's mission will be?"

"I don't know," Kane answered, "but that's a more important question than we realized."

"Why?"

"For all we know, his mission is to poison the water supply of a city, or set off a dirty bomb in D.C., or try to kill another political figure. He's gonna be slowed by his injuries, but if we don't know what he's going to do, we have to be prepared to stop him long before he gets a chance to do it. That means we need people for this op."

Lilly frowned. "Yesterday, Mac said he couldn't spare any field resources."

"They have to now. It's too risky to ignore, and it's criminally negligent to try to run this op with just two of us. We need at least three teams, and maybe a chopper for air surveillance. We need to talk to the White House now."

Lilly nodded, put the SUV in gear, and sped out of the garage, turning north for the executive mansion.

Chapter 18 – Skeleton Crew

The traffic was thick but not insane, enabling Lilly to maintain a brisk pace as Kane spoke to the White House.

"I'm sorry, Agent Logan," the executive secretary responded, "but the president is at a speaking engagement in Philadelphia and will not be available for several hours."

Kane blew out his breath. "OK, is Vice-President Caufield in the Castle?"

"No, agent. The vice-president is with the president."

"Thank you." He terminated the call and looked at her. "What now?"

"Schultz? Hell, he's the director."

Kane shook his head. "He won't go against Mac or Sharpe. Waste of time."

"What about Brent Douglas? He's the deputy director and next in our chain of command." She chanced a look in his direction.

He pulled a face at her idea. She couldn't blame him, not after she basically accused Douglas of sabotaging Kane's career, but differences and rivalries had to be put aside in favor of the risk to the common good. He nodded like a man knowing he had to cut off his finger to save the rest of his hand. "Worth a shot. Let's go."

***

Kane limped to the elevator right behind Lilly. She would check on the progress that Stafford's grad student had made with the evidence while Kane tried to wrangle resources from the deputy director.

She looked at Kane when the doors opened on her floor. "I'll be in my cubicle." Kane nodded and left the elevator, but Lilly wasn't finished. "And play nice," she called after him. "We won't get shit for help with this case if you go all alpha male again." Kane wanted to tell her to shut up, but she was right. He nodded and they parted ways.

Exerting more effort than he cared to admit, he hobbled over to Brent Douglas' office, barely acknowledging the receptionist. Brent did a double-take at Kane's still-disheveled appearance. "Jesus, Kane. Couldn't you have taken five minutes to put on a pair of pants without holes?"

"My go-bag is back at the hotel," Kane answered before cutting to the chase. "We need some resources, Brent. We've got something substantive." He ran through the recent developments, including his intended plan. "I need a couple teams."

Douglas was silent for a moment. "You released him? And gave him free taxi service to wherever? What the hell were you thinking? He committed a felony and could be part of an attempted assassination!"

"Brent, he wasn't going to give us shit. Regular Scott Barnett doesn't know anything, and brainwashed Scott Barnett won't talk even if you peel his fingernails off. This was our only play, so I did it, but I need resources to make it work."

"You fucking prima donna," Brent snarled. "You do realize we have specialists, people who can get what we need from the toughest subjects, right? But no. When things get real, you revert right back to form. You should have let the shrinks take a crack at him."

Kane felt his skin getting hot. "And how long would that take? A week? Longer? Meanwhile, the trail goes cold and we've got nothing. I made a judgment call, and every second we continue this pointless conversation is a second wasted. Why are you dicking around here?"

Brent paused, and when he finally spoke his voice was flat and measured. "You might as well know the whole deal. The president thinks you're manufacturing evidence and drawing conclusions to stretch this out as long as possible, and Mac and I agree. They're getting impatient."

"Why the hell would I do that?!"

"All you have is Agent Alexander's analysis driving this whole investigation, and all you've gotten from that is a loose connection to six stiffs. She's carrying you."

"Having Lilly as my partner wasn't my idea, goddammit! And, in case you forgot, I got shot this morning just after researching the autopsy on one of those stiffs! You think I was the victim of a random act of road rage?"

"No, that was a real lead," Brent conceded. "You had a real living suspect in custody—something I could have taken to the Oval Office as solid evidence—but you *fucking released him* to enact some lunatic plan! It might be the kiss of death for you."

"It's a good plan, and I didn't have time to analyze every little angle!"

"That's what phones are for, Kane! You call and get approval before you jump. Did you forget how high-profile this case is?"

"Approval?" Kane snorted. "You would have called Mac, he would have called Sharpe, and we'd have wasted a couple hours debating the wisdom— and the political expediency— of my idea. By then, whoever was running this whole thing would have figured out his resource was compromised, and our opportunity would be gone. Sometimes groupthink can work against you."

"And sometimes going off half-cocked can work against you. He's going to get rid of you."

Kane tried to resist verbalizing what he was thinking, but he was too tired and frustrated to restrain himself. "Like you tried to after Denver?"

"And there it is," Douglas said as if he'd just discovered the Source of Ultimate Truth. "You're still bitter because you screwed up and I had to call you out on it. Revenge is never a good motivator."

"It's not revenge I'm after, but let's not mince words. You and I both know you suppressed evidence, so don't stand there and act like my moral superior, *Deputy Director* Douglas."

"Look," Douglas responded. "I don't know what the hell you're talking about, but it doesn't matter. I'm not putting my stamp of approval, or the agency's, on your idiotic idea by giving you more agents so you can play Captain America. And, if this psycho harms anyone else, I will make sure the only federal job you'll ever get will be as a mailman somewhere above the Arctic Circle."

Kane wondered if his leg would hold up when he punched Douglas right in the nose. "Don't threaten me. You couldn't get rid of me the first time, so don't try again. If you had a set of balls, you'd drop the political bullshit and give me what I need so we could run this down and maybe get the person behind the attempt on Armstrong, which is also called 'doing our jobs.'"

"That 'political bullshit' is the only reason you're here right now instead of writing mostly useless cybersecurity protocols for some CIA front company. When everyone asked me if we should get you to help out with this case, what do you think I said—even though I suspected you'd do something like this?"

"Gee. Thanks for the ringing endorsement. You want me to get down on my knees and suck your dick as thanks?"

Douglas flashed a grin suggesting he knew he held the better hand. "I think we're done here." He went back to his desk and stared at some piece of paper on it as if he was entirely alone, giving Kane no option but to leave.

***

Lilly was searching the boxes of evidence she'd recovered from Barnett's house. A few ideas and hazy patterns had started to emerge to her, but she had barely started considering it all when Kane returned.

"That was quick. How'd it..." The look on Kane's face made it unnecessary to complete the sentence. "That bad?"

"Apparently we are the only two who think we're making progress on this case." He went on to describe his less-than-productive meeting with Brent Douglas.

Lilly listened to him with equanimity while feeling her jaw tighten. "Perhaps," she said when he finished, "I should have more fully clarified the term 'all alpha male' and how *not* to be that way."

"Don't give me that," he snapped back. "A reasonable review of the facts didn't matter. I knew he wasn't happy about bringing me in when that chopper landed on my lawn. You told me why yesterday. Now I'm sure. He's going to use this situation to get rid of me permanently." His anger changed to something more like regret. "I'm sorry, Lilly. You're going to be collateral damage. I wish I could change that, but I can't." Kane shook his head.

"Are we off the case?" she asked.

"He didn't say that. But he has Mac's ear, and Mac has the ear of Secretary Carlyle and the president, so there we are." He spoke like the scenario was a foregone conclusion.

Lilly stood up and grabbed his tie, pulling his face down to within a few inches of hers. "In that case, Agent Logan, how about you postpone our funeral and come up with a way to solve this fucking case." Her snarl was almost palpable.

Kane wrapped his much larger fist over hers and removed her hand from his tie. The effort wasn't violent, but Lilly could feel the overwhelming strength of his grip. "How?" he responded. "One phone call and we're all done."

"Oh, one call?" She extracted her phone from her pocket and turned it off. "What call?"

"That won't matter and you know it."

He's decided this is over. She needed to do something drastic, something that would reboot his brain. Seizing the first idea that occurred to her, she cupped his crotch in her hand.

Kane's eyes widened for a second before he stepped back, nearly falling. The cubicle wall rocked and threatened to collapse under his weight. Fortunately, this area of the floor was deserted. "Christ, Lilly! What the fuck are you doing?!"

"Just seeing if you were still a man," she answered cruelly. "The way you sound right now, I thought your balls might have gone back up inside you like a toddler. But," she made a show of looking down at Kane's package, "since that doesn't appear to be the case, how about you get your head out of your ass? We can be at Barnett's house in under an hour. Do you want to solve this case and rub Douglas' nose in it, or would you rather go home and have an Appletini?"

Her inappropriate actions and words finally had the desired effect. His mien changed to one of aggravation—and purpose. "I know what you're trying to do, Lilly."

"I hope so. It's pretty obvious. Now, are you in, or do I have to violate a few more HR policies?"

"It's not going to be easy to make this work just by ourselves," Kane temporized.

"I know. That's why I need you at the top of your game. If you're firing on all cylinders, we can do this, but if you're going to act like a whipped puppy we might as well go home. So grow up and let's get to work."

Kane's eyes narrowed. Lilly could see something was still holding him back, but any hesitation disappeared quickly. "All right, I'm ready...no guts, no glory, right?"

"That's fucking-A right. Now get some new pants and let's do this." She stared into his eyes, making sure she'd truly gotten him back on track, and was pleased to see he matched her gaze.

Taking a deep breath, Kane turned for the nearest bathroom, but Lilly, with her emotions running as hard and fast as they ever had, couldn't refrain from one last comment. "Oh, and Kane?"

"Yeah?"

"That's one hell of a package you've got there. Once we get fired for real, maybe we can see how well it performs. See you in the truck."

With that said, she brushed by Kane, blatantly ignoring his raised eyebrows and eyes that were as big as frisbees.

***

Director Pat MacMurray was working on the last folder on his desk, trying not to rush but failing. He was looking forward to getting home at a decent hour tonight, maybe having dinner with his wife and watching a little TV before bed.

Then his phone rang.

"Son of a bitch," he muttered, picking it up without checking the caller ID. "MacMurray."

"Hold for the President, please."

Dammit. It wasn't the upcoming conversation that irritated him; Sharpe was fairly concise, especially when calling after hours. But MacMurray feared the call would result in many more hours in the office tonight. *What's one more night?*

"Mac," the president said, "glad I caught you."

"No problem, sir. What can I do for you?"

"I need a minute of your time to discuss Agents Logan and Alexander..."

Saturday, November 4

Three Days Before the Election

Chapter 19 - Lone Wolves

Scott Barnett sat in the living room of his house in Bristow, Virginia, wondering what the hell had happened over the previous twelve hours. His arm, head, and chest throbbed despite the powerful painkillers he'd taken at the hospital. He'd wanted to see his son when he got home, but now he was pleased that his wife had sent Adam to his uncle's house for a sleepover— especially considering the look on her face as she sat across from him.

"I saw all the guns and shit they took out of your office," Danielle stated. "Where did they all come from?"

"I... really don't know," he admitted. "Those agents said everything was planted."

"Come on, Scott! You've been in that fucking office every night for the last six months! That stuff didn't just show up this morning!"

He put his hands to his head, wincing as his fingers moved against his scalp. "I know it doesn't make much sense, but I'm not lying when I say I don't know. I can't remember a thing about that office except where it is."

Danielle stared at him, her face a mix of disgust, disbelief, and resignation. "Who is she?"

"Who is who?"

"Your girlfriend. Or boyfriend. Whoever you've been cheating on me with."

Scott rolled his eyes. "Huge chunks of my life are blanks to me, I got in an accident I can't remember, arrested by the Secret Service for something I didn't do, you got arrested for a bunch of illegal guns and hundreds of notebooks in my office that I didn't put there, and now you're accusing me of fucking another woman? Are you trying to make this worse—if that's even possible?"

"What do you want me to think?" Danielle said. "This whole family is a mess, you haven't touched me in months, and you can't even be bothered to come up with a terrible excuse! Do you just want me to leave? Or do you want to be the one who moves out? What about our son? Have you even given him a thought?"

"Of course I have!" he exploded. "You know how important Adam is to me!"

"He used to be important to you," Danni yelled back, "but I don't think you've said two words to him since the beginning of the summer! You've been a crummy husband and a crummy father for a long time, Scott!"

Scott's phone buzzed. Thinking it might be his son, he looked at it but didn't recognize the number, so he ignored the call.

"Maybe you're right," he said, feeling the energy drain from his body at his inability to answer his spouse's simple questions. "Maybe I've got a tumor or something."

"You don't have a fucking tumor," Danielle snapped back. "You're just a lying –" She paused as his phone buzzed once more. "Who the hell is calling you!?"

"I don't know the number." He put the phone to his ear and was about to let go of a little anger by yelling at the caller, but before he could say a word, everything went dark.

***

"Game time," Kane said. Lilly expected that; she heard his cryptic commands and knew Kane was getting the response he wanted. He started the car.

"Okay." They'd parked on the side of Route 619 with a view of both exits, and in under a minute a gray Buick sedan pulled out and turned north. Kane gave him a minute and popped an illegal U-turn to follow. Five minutes later both cars had merged onto Route 66 West, with the government SUV settled in about 100 yards behind Barnett's sedan.

***

He terminated the call without a word and sat back to adjust his wire-rimmed glasses. It was something he did before taking the next step in any plan to ensure it was still the best course of action. People always thought they were so smart, and as a consequence of such hubris they stuck to plans that might have been academic masterpieces that fell apart in the real world. The participants in any plan had the most annoying habit of not doing what was expected of them.

After a few seconds of consideration, he dropped the cheap black Alcatel flip phone in favor of the red one and placed a call. No one responded when the connection was made, but he spoke anyway. "Forty-Seven just called in. The target is following as intended. Are you absolutely clear on what is to be done?"

"100%. We're the best in the business, and we're personally invested."

"You'd better be more than invested."

"We understand the consequences. This will be settled by morning."

"See that it is." He terminated the call, confident that the message had been properly received at the other end.

***

With the beep indicating the call had ended, he stepped into the most expansive room of the building and addressed the four men drinking Cokes and munching snacks around the single table. "Mr. Smith just called. We're a 'go.' Do *not* deviate from the plan. Ninety minutes."

They nodded, but the man delivering the news was not finished. He chambered a round in his Desert Eagle for effect. It was a little over the top, but in the near silence the *clack* resounded with great authority. His friends looked at each other and shared thin smiles that signified anything but joy.

"Remember—no mistakes." Ethan Doyle said with a look that could have stopped a tank. "Not this time."

***

Kane was bored, which was about the worst thing he could be right now. Barnett drove monotonously, not changing his speed and rarely changing lanes. Tailing such a target wouldn't tax a teenager with his learning permit.

He caught Lilly looking his way several times, and Kane could tell she had something to say. "What is it?"

Lilly sucked in a lungful of air. "You've got to get this investigation back on track with the higher-ups, Kane. Doesn't matter if we're pulled from the case or tossed out of the agency. This one is too big."

"You think I don't know that?"

"I'm not sure. You keep opening your mouth before you think," Lilly said. "You aren't stupid, but for some reason you think bullying people to get your way is a good idea. I can't believe you got so respected in the agency by cursing out everyone who disagreed with you. You want to burn all your bridges at the agency, fine, but now is not the time for that. You need to remember who you used to be."

"I might have lost that guy forever," Kane answered honestly.

A bleak silence fell over the interior of the car, lasting for several seconds. "If that's true," Lilly finally stated, "a few hundred million people are about to lose a lot more."

Well, that's a great feeling.

***

Kane and Lilly merged onto Route 81 South, cruising through Virginia east of the Shenandoah Mountains that would have been visible off to their right had it not been dark. A little after midnight, Barnett put his blinker on and the target vehicle took an exit about thirty miles southwest of Roanoke.

Lilly took stock of what she could gather about the area as they moved through the secondary roads, but there wasn't much to learn in the dark. Here and there, a single light marked a barn or a house, suggesting farmland, but the fields did not appear plowed. Perhaps they were pastures for grazing cattle, Lilly reasoned.

When Barnett turned onto a gravel road that appeared to be an entrance to one of these farms, Kane continued straight before turning off his lights and coasting to a stop about a quarter mile down the road. Both the darkness and a slight rise in the terrain hid whatever was at the end of the driveway. Lilly used her phone and pulled up a satellite view of the area.

"It looks like there are three buildings clustered at the end of the road about two and a half miles in. There's only the one road in or out."

Kane studied the map. "Okay. What's this here?"

"Looks like a dirt road. Not sure if we can drive it, though. Why?"

"If it's passable, we can probably use it to get about a mile closer and have the trees as cover."

"Cover for what?" Lilly asked.

"We didn't come here because I like the foothills of western Virginia in autumn. We're going in."

"Going in? Just the two of us? To pursue a man who just shot you with a machine pistol? You have no idea who's waiting for us."

"Hey, back at the office you pretty much emasculated me for suggesting we were screwed without agency help, so here we are. This is what 'on our own' really means—going up against an unknown, probably superior force without the element of surprise. Or did you just think we were going to knock on the front door, flash our badges, and everyone will throw their hands in the air?"

"No, now we do what Douglas said we should have done earlier today. We call this in and observe until the cavalry gets here."

"Did you forget that Douglas made it abundantly clear that we weren't getting any help? And that was before I almost slugged him!"

"But your plan paid off! They *have* to listen to us now! We can commandeer local law enforcement to help contain the site until they get here."

"Based on what, Lilly?" Kane was nearly shouting now. "For all we know, Barnett's Uncle Cletus lives there and he came here to relax after a stressful day, maybe drink some moonshine. We have zero knowledge of any illegal activity over that hill. We barely have enough probable cause to justify the gas we used to get here. The locals will reject our request based on that alone! If we don't get something concrete—here, tonight—and do it by ourselves, we absolutely will be out on our ass, and all your noble intentions of solving this case for the greater good will go right down the shitter." The temperature in the car climbed a few degrees.

"Would you rather get your ass shot off when whoever is in there pulls an MP5 and doesn't miss this time?" Lilly snapped back. "You yourself said this could all be a false flag, but now you don't seem to care about that! This couldn't scream 'trap' any louder."

Kane flashed an ugly smile that, in the dim light, appeared satanic. "Yeah, and you were happy to ignore that fact until right now. It's easy to arrest a few counterfeiters armed with Saturday night specials, but it's something different going after military-type personnel with serious weapons, isn't it? A little scarier now, huh?"

When Lilly didn't answer, he plunged ahead. "Unlike you, I'm not about to grab your crotch and wonder where your balls went, but I don't really need to, do I? It seems you've lost your nerve, and at the worst possible time."

Bastard. "Whatever you say, Kane. But I'm calling this in to Mac before I move a muscle. You want to charge that hill like Roosevelt's Rough Riders, be my guest."

Kane made like he was settling into his seat for a pleasant conversation, folding his arms in a display of permanence. "Oh, hell no. I'm not going anywhere until I hear this one."

Lilly thought about smacking that arrogant grin off his face but settled for placing the call to the director's cell phone. The phone rang several times before a steady, firm voice came over the line. "Director MacMurray."

"Director, this is Agent Lilly Alexander. Agent Logan is with me, and you are on speaker. We followed his shooter this morning to a suspicious site near the North Carolina-Virginia border, and we need your authority to request a team from the Charlotte office as well as commandeer local authorities to safely investigate this location."

A pause and a sigh followed. "Did Agent Logan put you up to this call?"

"No, sir. In fact, Agent Logan was against me calling you at all."

"You should learn to follow his lead in that area."

Lilly looked over at Kane, who gave her a "told you so" look. "Sir, I don't understand that statement. We were given a directive to investigate the assassination attempt, and this is where the evidence has led us."

"It hasn't led you anywhere," Mac responded. "You lucked into one potential lead, and you took that lead and did perhaps the worst possible thing that you could with it."

Well, that statement certainly fits Kane's interaction with Douglas. "That action led us to this new lead, sir. Agent Logan had a hunch, an idea that was time-sensitive, so we acted on it. I supported that decision, and now we have a potential payoff."

"All that means, Agent, is that both you and Agent Logan need a refresher in following the rules."

Lilly squeezed the phone in irritation. Although better than Kane at keeping her temper under wraps, she had her own limits, and Mac's statement made her internal pressure gauge soar into the red. "I'm sorry, Director," she snarled, "but I seem to recall something in my training about how good agents take initiative when necessary." Kane shook his head and pursed his lips in a silent whistle at her audacity.

Mac's voice changed to match Lilly's intensity. "And I seem to remember that I'm in charge of the agency that has the lead on this investigation, and when I tell an agent—even one from another agency—that they are out of line, that's the end of the conversation. There are things going on, things you don't know about, meaning I'm not inclined to have my orders questioned. Agent Logan?"

Kane started at being pulled into the conversation. "Sir?"

"You were a Marine sergeant. What happened when some PFC challenged your orders in front of the squad?"

"Well, sir, after I finished ripping him a new one in front of the other troops as an example, I would PT his ass until he dropped. And I'd probably still put an LOR in his jacket."

"Hear that, Agent Alexander? While I can't put you through extensive physical training, rest assured I can choose the agents that represent this organization and can write a Letter Of Reprimand about one."

Realizing she'd likely already torched her career, Lilly had little fear of asking her next question. "Then why haven't we been pulled from the case and replaced with someone more, shall we say, sycophantic, sir?"

"Do you recall our discussion as we left the White House the other day, Agent?"

"Yes, sir, but I don't see what—"

"Tell me how it might look to Voight Stafford if the president pulled you two off this case. Remember how I told you the president works with perception, not reality? There was a little message in that statement, but apparently neither of you picked up on it.

"Therefore," he continued before she could get a word in edgewise, "do whatever you want, but after the election, I would strongly suggest you look into other opportunities in the private sector." With that, the director terminated the call. Lilly stared at the phone, her anger apparent even in the minimal lighting.

Kane clapped his hands slowly. "Bravo, Agent Alexander. Brah-voh. And thank you."

"Thanks for what?"

Kane's smile appeared sincere. "A few hours ago, I was worried that my fight with Douglas was going to cost you your career. But after lecturing me to keep my cool, you did exactly the opposite. What is it—do as I say, not as I do? Anyway, after that little tantrum, you just dug your own grave, meaning I don't have to feel guilty anymore. So, like I said, thanks."

"You're welcome. Now that you have a clear conscience, maybe we should see what's going on in those buildings."

"Wait. Now you want to go in?"

"No," Lilly responded, pulling her sidearm and making sure everything was in order. "I still think it's a kamikaze mission, but you heard our esteemed leader. We are fucked in every sense of the word. The only way to save our asses is to arrest someone definitively connected to the assassination attempt, and that means we check that place out."

"You're giving me whiplash, Lilly," Kane said, all traces of sarcasm gone from his tone. "First you question my manhood when I try to suggest we exercise caution, then you get here and shit your britches because things look dangerous. Then, after you call out the director of the FBI, you suddenly want to storm the castle. What the hell?"

"I'll be damned if some desk-riding, politically motivated executive is going to tell me that my partner and I don't matter when we've busted our asses and gotten this far. Maybe you don't have anything to prove, but I do. So drive the goddamned car and get us up that dirt road as far as you can."

After a second, Kane put the truck in gear and followed Lilly's orders.

***

Kane maneuvered the SUV through the rough trail at a snail's pace, loathe to use his brake lights and announce his presence to anyone around, making the trek into the woods a sixty-minute ordeal. Once they were as close as they were going to get, they exited the truck and started in the general direction of the buildings, Kane in the lead. Because of the pain in his leg, they moved slowly through the woods. It took them another half-hour until a faint glow appeared over a slight rise, indicating they were at the complex, which consisted of a house, a barn, and a feed silo. Grateful for the break, he leaned against a tree.

Lilly came to him. "This is your area, Kane. What's our plan?"

"Well, I'm better at covert, but you're faster, especially right now. I'll take point and go up to the house to observe and act if prudent. This tree line is about half a mile from the compound. Stay back near it and, if things turn to shit, you bail hard and make tracks to report in."

"And leave you behind? No way!"

Kane expected her objection. "I know—it sounds shitty. And I'm not going to make myself a target. But if we're together and they surprise us, that's worse."

"We don't have a bit of intel on who's in there, Kane, besides Barnett. What are you going to do if ten people rush out?" Lilly asked.

"If it's that many, you aren't going to be much help. If I see a crowd, I'll back off. Most likely I observe, see what I can see, and then meet up with you to discuss."

Lilly sighed. "Okay. Let's go. But you better be careful. You're a dick most of the time, but that doesn't mean I'm interested in replacing you. I've almost got you broken in."

Chapter 20 – All War is Deception

Ethan Doyle was getting restless, even though he knew it was normal when awaiting the enemy. He panned his head left and right slowly across the tree line through his night vision goggles.

Discovering their true identities had been easier than expected. A visit to Colonel Richards and about an hour of asking questions while providing just the right kind of encouragement had finally gotten an honest answer out of him.

After that, a quick call to Mr. Smith, who'd given him the handsome tuition to train David Park, bore fruit. The invitation from his benefactor to settle the score with his former guests was too tempting to pass up. He longed to plunge a knife deep into Kane's chest and then slit Lilly's throat with it while it was still covered in his blood, but this would be just as good.

Contact. Barely visible at the extreme left of his field of view, he saw a figure emerge from the trees and proceed downhill. Kane had not come from the expected direction, which Doyle took as a painless lesson. *He's a piece of shit traitor and a Fed, but he's not an easy kill.*

He raised his handheld radio to his face, encrypted so that only four other radios in the world could receive from it. "Target K visual at the wood line, bearing 250. Hold." He got only a double-click of the transmitter in response. Moving before they had both targets in sight was foolhardy and useless.

***

Lilly crouched behind the crest of the hill as Kane had directed, giving him three minutes to move into position. He became hard as hell to track after he went about fifty yards, his dark gray suit blending into the inky blackness. She opened her eyes wide and kept sweeping them left and right in an attempt to catch his movement, and occasionally it worked. But, more often than not, he was an imaginary specter, and if she couldn't see him, neither could their adversaries.

Time. She rose, moving slowly and steadily down the hill toward the objective in the odd half-crouch, half-trot she'd seen Kane employ. Her thighs protested almost immediately. *How the hell can he do this for half a mile with a gunshot wound to the leg?*

She drifted to the left, the opposite of Kane's path, her eyes on the house, and when the door opened she tossed her body down onto the damp grass. Pulling compact binoculars from their case, Lilly trained them on the building.

Four or five men stepped through the front door. Superior numbers, and they were brandishing rifles. Fortunately, even the gentle noise of the door had carried all the way to her, so Kane had to have been alerted as well. Having watched the way he got into position, she was confident that he would be able to avoid them without being detected.

But something glinted off the face of one of the men as he turned in the dim glow of the single light coming from the barn. Her first thought was that he was wearing sunglasses, but that made no sense. The same reflection occurred on two others, giving off an odd sage color. She'd seen that color recently. But when?

Night vision goggles! Oh shit! Ike had been wearing them at the camp when he'd snuck up on her. They could probably already see her, and Kane might as well be jumping up and down in front of them with sparklers in each hand.

Short of digging a hole, she couldn't make herself any less visible unless she sprinted back to the crest of the hill. At least she had a sizable lead if she needed to bolt. Kane did not, and right now he was unlikely to outrun a glacier.

She shook her head to no one, wondering how she was going to get them out of this mess.

***

Dammit. Kane counted five adversaries outlined against the glow of the house, and it looked like they were wearing night vision goggles, which made all of his expertise at evasion about as useless as a flashlight in broad daylight. They would be able to see him long before he could evade, and that put him on the losing end of this situation.

The group dispersed and Kane lost track of three of them as they stepped off the porch. The other two paused for a moment, their heads turning slowly and methodically before they disappeared as well, and

Kane's last sighting showed them headed directly toward him. He had to move—now.

But where? He no longer knew where they were, but picked his path and moved along it with an urgency borne of his survival instinct.

He went about ten paces before he stopped, his path blocked by a shadowy figure and the circle of a gun barrel, which reflected what light there was. At such close range, he had no chance to pull his weapon so, out of options, he raised his hands and waited for the person that controlled his fate to speak.

The voice he heard did not engender a ton of confidence in his future. "How ya' doing, Mr. Walsh? Or should I say Agent Logan?" Ethan Doyle asked. "In either case, I think we need to clear the air a little."

***

Lilly watched two men shove a third into the house while the others headed up the hill in her general direction. *Time to go.* Summoning her courage, she rose and ran for all she was worth.

Faint voices reached her ears. She had been seen. There was nothing she could do about that except pump her legs harder and hope that her pursuers were tasked with defending their location rather than killing or capturing her at all costs. At night, with a sizable head start, she didn't think they would waste the bullets on her.

That theory went right down the tubes when she heard the *crack* of a bullet being fired and the thick, wet *smack* of lead hitting dirt as the projectile ripped up the sod a few yards to her right.

Shit. This shot hadn't hit her, but it was a frightening development. Lilly found another gear, but the tree line was still very far away. She started changing direction at random.

Another shot, but she didn't hear it hit the ground. Lilly thought about returning fire, but that meant stopping and taking time to aim in the dark, and she had a pistol, not a rifle. *Not worth it. Just keep going.* If she could get into the trees, she'd have a fair chance.

Lilly crested the ridgeline like a hurdler and raced into the foliage. With the ground now sloping down and hiding her from her pursuers for the moment, she turned forty-five degrees to her right to throw them off the trail, even though the underbrush made such a racket that a blind person could track her. About seventy-five yards into the cover, she flattened herself behind a tree, trying to quiet her breathing.

She listened for signs of pursuit, but the woods remained silent. Without the immediate threat of being shot, she focused on thinking her way out of this situation.

Moving forward as slowly as she could until she got back to the ridgeline, Lilly poked her eyes and nose over the edge and raised her binoculars to see what she could see. To her surprise, all five went inside. She would have left one man on watch but didn't complain; their questionable actions gave her more options.

Before she could consider those options, a noise from the barn next to the primary structure interrupted her. Two vehicles exited and drove to the road that she and Kane had been on earlier. The cars disappeared over a rise, but Lilly was able to follow the glow of the headlights and see them head in opposite directions on the paved road. The one that went south disappeared into the trees, but the other stopped after a short distance, and the headlights went out. Those cars would sit in place and just wait until she tried to drive out of the area.

It was a lot easier to watch a big SUV than to chase one woman in a dark forest. She was, in essence, just as much of a hostage as Kane.

Fuck this. I'm calling for reinforcements. She grabbed her phone and was about to dial 911 when she saw the complete lack of a signal, just like before. *Are they using a cell blocker?* Frustrated, Lilly took a deep breath. She'd had a signal at the truck. It would be a long walk and take time she didn't have, but it was her only play. With a furtive look around, she got to her feet and started picking her way back to the truck as quickly as she could.

Hang on, Kane. Just hang on.

***

Director MacMurray sat at his desk in his home office, staring at the green blotter under the glow of the brass lamp. He'd spent two hours in bed tossing and turning since the call from Kane and Lilly. Finally, after accidentally waking his wife for the third time, she'd banished him to his office.

He was the director of the most powerful police agency in the country, but he couldn't shake the feeling that he wasn't running anything at the moment. Needing to get another read on the situation, he placed a call. The first thing he heard was the deep, full breath of someone struggling to come fully awake. "Hullo."

"Brent, it's Pat. Sorry to wake you," MacMurray lied.

"No sweat. What's up?"

"I just got a call from Alexander and Logan." He went on to give a quick recap of the acrimonious exchange.

"He went without backup? I thought he had more sense than that."

"It's not in his nature to ignore a challenge. I think he's got a chip on his shoulder, one that's been growing for a couple of years."

"He's showboating, Pat, staying true to form." He paused, and his voice was guarded as he spoke the next words. "Why are you telling me about this?"

Mac sighed. "I need your real opinion on this—not some politically-motivated spin. Just be a cop. What do you think about Logan's work on this? And, for that matter, Alexander's as well?"

"They've come up with questionable leads at best—more like theories that you can't completely discount. They did develop one real lead, but then he screwed it up. I know you haven't had as much contact with him as I have, but that's been his M.O. for years."

"Yeah, but now they are saying it might have paid off."

"I'll bet." MacMurray could hear the sneer through the phone. "And lemme guess—he asked for some sort of full-out assault on this place. With little to no evidence."

"He asked for additional teams to investigate," the director answered. "And, considering the situation, I'd say that's a reasonable request—but Sharpe gave me orders to deny them support."

"I know," Douglas answered.

"How do you know about Sharpe's order to me?"

"When he kept me behind yesterday, he asked me to keep an eye on those two. After I told him about Kane's stunt this afternoon, he said he would talk to you."

Mac's voice increased a few decibels. "This is an FBI investigation! Why the hell are you getting orders from the president behind my back?!"

"It wasn't behind your back. Sharpe told me you were far too busy to focus on one agent, so he asked me to handle it. It was just too small of a detail for you, so I took it." Douglas' explanation was reasonable, but Mac's anger did not subside.

"You, me, and Sharpe are going to have a meeting when this shit storm is over," he promised, the threat clear. "But, putting that aside, we have a situation. What are we going to do about it?"

"Do?" Douglas sounded shocked. "What can we do? We both got direct orders from Sharpe himself to ignore the two of them. You might be pissed, but do you really want us to disobey orders from POTUS?"

"No," Mac responded. "But I don't think it's a violation of those orders to wonder why the president is, against all reason and logic, burying and discounting the only agents making any sort of progress when he almost always gives us free rein to run any sort of investigation."

Brent didn't respond for several seconds, and when he did speak his voice was hushed. "Are you suggesting POTUS is trying to cover up an attempted assassination? Is that what you're driving at?"

Mac wondered how much of this conversation would be repeated in the Oval Office. He had to watch his step here. "Definitely not. I'm suggesting we start asking questions, nothing more."

"I don't even know where to start with that one. Honestly, I don't even know if I should do a thing about it."

"That's your prerogative, but no one ordered me not to investigate. I'll be in my office at seven to brainstorm, and I would think you'd want to join me."

"If you're right, you think this can wait until morning?"

"No," Mac answered honestly. "But right now we have two agents who might be in deep shit. At the very least, I ordered them to ignore a potential lead in a crucial case, and I may have abandoned them to the detriment of their safety. Either way, I failed them once tonight, but I'll be damned if I'll do it again—and *that* can't wait more than anything else." It felt good to say those critically important words.

"So what are you going to do?" the deputy director asked.

"Nothing until I have a better idea of where they are, and that means I've got things to do." He hung up and dialed Kane's number, only to hear, "*The person you are trying to reach is not accepting calls at this time.*" Strange. He tried Lilly and got the same response.

Frustrated, he placed a call to headquarters to request a phone trace, only to learn that not even his agency, with all its technological prowess, could track a cell phone that was out of service.

They're on their own.

Chapter 21 – Coming to Blows

Lilly resisted the urge to look at her phone for a signal. The light from the screen would serve as a homing beacon, even without night vision goggles.

Lilly had lost her mental compass. She'd been walking for about forty-five minutes without seeing any sign of the truck or the rough trail they used to get up here. Opening her eyes as wide as they would go and sweeping her head left and right, she looked for any clue as to her whereabouts. Something to her right drew her attention, so she focused that way and made out a straight and clean horizontal line in the darkness. Shortly, the line gave up its cover and became the hood of their SUV. It was amazing how easily one could get lost.

Relieved, Lilly leaned on the hood only to see she *still* had no cell service. Was someone following her and blocking her phone? She spun in a quick circle but saw no one. Without communication with the outside world, they were screwed.

Lilly would soon lose the cloak of darkness. Kane was in real trouble—if he was even still alive—and so was she, and all she could do was drive out of here and hope she made it. Not a great plan. Lilly tried to come up with another option, but nothing presented itself.

The noise of dry, fallen leaves being disturbed interrupted Lilly's thoughts. The rustle was far too loud to have come from a squirrel or a chipmunk; it sounded to her like a boulder rolling downhill, making it large enough to be a threat. Stashing her phone, she took a position on the other side of the truck and pulled her FN.

A moment later, she made out the shape of a person coming in her general direction. It appeared to be a man, solidly built, but limping. The movements of the dark figure were not those of a stalking predator. They reminded her more of frightened and frantic prey, just like Kane would be. Like her, the other person seemed unaware of the truck. Leveling her weapon at the figure, she remained hidden. If it wasn't her partner, she had a clear shot and would not hesitate to take it. She mustered all the courage she could. "Kane?"

The dark outline turned in her direction. "Lilly?! Where are you?"

"Over here!" He staggered to her, clearly the worse for wear. "I'm so glad you're okay!" Only then did she notice the dark stains of blood on his face. "You are okay, right?"

"I guess," he answered, wiping them away with his sleeve. "They worked me over pretty hard." He sounded vaguely disconnected, his words disjointed. Lilly thought he might have a concussion, but there wasn't time to check right now.

"How'd you get away?" she asked.

"I know how to get out of zip ties, and they ignored me except when they were using my head as a punching bag. When they went into another room for whatever. I got my hands free and took off."

Lilly nodded, grateful and surprised that his captors had been so cavalier about guarding him. "Who were they?"

"Dunno. I didn't recognize any of them. They kept asking what I was doing here, who I'd come with, that sort of crap."

Lilly wanted to turn her attention to getting clear of the area, but something struck her. "Wait. They didn't know why you were here? If they sent Barnett to shoot at you this morning, they have to know what was going on. Did you see Barnett?"

Kane looked confused for a second. "No, didn't see him either. Maybe they were trying to screw with my head, get other info. I don't know."

He's a little off. Lilly couldn't blame him, but he might not be the most reliable asset at the moment. She'd have to keep that in mind. "We can worry about that later. We just have to get out of here, regroup, and think."

"So make the call. Even the local police can help us now." Kane said.

"I don't have a signal, haven't since we started walking. Try your phone?" she suggested.

"They took it," Kane answered. "But if you don't have a signal this far away, they're probably using a powerful cell jammer, or a lot of little ones, so no phone will work." Now he sounded much more like himself. "But so what? We can just drive the hell out of here."

Lilly shook her head. "Not so fast. They spotted me after they took you in the house, and just before I started heading back, two cars left the compound and stopped somewhere on the main road. I think they're waiting for us. We're trapped."

"Well, if we can't make a call, our only option is to run for it. I'm not about to sit here with my dick in my hand and wait for roosters to start crowing so they can find us again."

Kane was right; doing nothing was only delaying the inevitable. But, beaten and bloody, could she count on him? Maybe not, but she didn't have a better strategy. She nodded in agreement.

They got in the truck, Kane taking the driver's seat without hesitation. Lilly got her gun out as he made a K-turn and headed back the way they'd come in. "What's your plan?" she asked.

"You said there were two cars, and they likely parked on either side of the end of this dirt road, right?"

"That's where they stopped, and I didn't hear or see them move," Lilly answered.

"So we'll run into one or the other no matter which way we turn?"

"Yup. There's the problem. I don't see a way out."

He pushed the pedal down and the truck accelerated, bouncing over the bumpy trail. "We can't turn left. We can't turn right. So, what's the obvious answer?"

Lilly's frustration boiled over. "I don't know! What's the goddamned answer?!"

Kane paused, waiting until the road was only about fifty yards away before flooring the engine. As they shot forward, he finally responded. "We don't turn."

He continued straight across the road, blasting over the asphalt, through a flimsy fence, and rocketing into a wide-open field. Lilly's head pitched forward as they bounced, then smacked back into the headrest as they roared over the grass and mud. The truck fishtailed as the wheels tried to find purchase in the soft dirt and mud, but the four-wheel drive took effect and in a few seconds they were tearing up a slight incline at over seventy. Kane waited until they crested the hill before flipping on his lights.

Feeling a bit like a sock that just came out of the dryer, Lilly shook her head to clear it and turned to check behind them but saw no one in pursuit. Kane angled to the south to intercept a real road. He did not slow down, but at least the ride smoothed out.

"Yeah," Lilly said breathlessly. "I guess that was a pretty obvious answer. Nice thinking, Kane."

"I don't untie the knots. I just cut the rope," he stated.

"Great. Where are we headed now?"

"We should probably put a little distance between us and these guys. But first, I've got a thought." They proceeded a couple of miles until they entered the tiny town of Wytheville. Kane yanked the wheel to turn into a Tractor Supply parking lot, screeching to a halt at the back side of the store.

"How is this putting distance between us and them?" Lilly asked.

"Trust me." Kane grabbed a small flashlight from the center console. "Get out and watch for anyone." Again, he moved before Lilly could respond, like he had a schedule to keep, so she followed his direction, facing outward to keep a lookout.

Despite the good hiding space, Lilly's internal alarms were going off as hard as they ever had. Something was wrong. This was dangerous. She had no idea what led her to such a conclusion, but every time she'd had this kind of instinct, it had come to fruition.

Kane was crawling under the truck, shining the light this way and that. "Bingo." Kane pulled himself back out, training the flashlight on a black device about the size of a greeting card, but thicker. "This is a cell signal interrupter, and even money says they're tracking it."

As he spoke, Kane found and removed the battery. The tiny red light on the blocker died instantly.

Lilly's phone, now free from the electronic shackles, blew up. Most were innocuous e-mails, but four calls and six texts from Director MacMurray stood out. Holstering her weapon, she looked at the texts, but they all said the same thing—call me ASAP. He'd left no messages, so there was no way to know what he wanted, but based on their earlier conversation it wasn't likely to be good news. She told Kane anyway.

"Don't call him," Kane advised. "Chances are he got the go-ahead to shit-can us. If we don't hear the order, we aren't disobeying it." Lilly nodded; Mac was far away and unlikely to offer assistance.

"So who should I call?"

Before Kane could suggest a course of action, a call came in. Looking at the screen, she saw a number she did not recognize. With a slight frown, she answered. "Alexander."

An unrecognized male voice responded. "Is Agent Logan with you?"

What the hell? She gave Kane a look to make sure she had his attention and put the call on speaker. "Who is this?" Kane leaned on the hood across from her to listen. He looked as perplexed as she felt.

"That's not important. But is Kane there?" the caller persisted.

"Why should I tell you? I don't even know who you are. Maybe he's got a laser dot trained on your temple right now."

Laughter sounded through the phone. "Unlikely. He's standing right next to you, wondering who this is just like you are. So, agents, hear this; an American in Scotland is as out of place as a Canadian in Brazil."

Lilly barely had time to grasp that the phrase was complete nonsense before Kane's head slumped to one side and popped back to attention almost immediately. His eyes were as dead and lifeless as a shark's, but he strode purposefully around the hood, coming right for her. He said nothing, but Lilly's instincts told her to defend herself.

She retreated, reaching for her gun, but Kane was too fast. Lilly got the FN free of its holster only to have him strike her wrist with a powerful backhanded blow before she could aim. The gun flew from her hand, over the truck hood, and clattered to the pavement nearby.

"Kane! Stop!" He didn't even pause. Lilly back peddled furiously, fear coursing through her. She tripped, catching herself against the truck before she hit the ground, but the delay allowed Kane to throw a punch.

Lilly deflected the blow, but the force pushed her to the ground. She used her momentum to roll back up, ignoring the ache in her forearm. Kane continued his pursuit, firing fists at her, forcing Lilly to back away and block frantically. She would not survive if he hit her cleanly. She had to change the fight.

But how? Kane's assault was relentless. She thought about running, but she didn't want to turn her back on her large, violent attacker. Her breathing came in ragged pants, but Kane's attacks kept coming. While her strength waned, his seemed limitless. Lilly could not stand against the barrage; she needed to find his weakness—if he had one.

The next time he charged, Lilly stepped left and blocked, using his momentum to send him off to her right. Her move gave her time to put a few yards and a few seconds between them.

"Kane, think about what you're doing! Listen to me! Stop! It's Lilly! Listen to my voice!" No effect. He was a machine, a robot, just like Scott Barnett when he was triggered. And she had no idea how to de-trigger him.

She had to find her gun. Lilly hoped the sight of it would give Kane pause—if it didn't, she might be forced to shoot. The idea of taking Kane's life filled her with dread.

But her weapon was nowhere to be found. Moving backward while scanning the area where she thought her gun could have landed, Lilly lost her bearings. When she backed into the building, with a dumpster right next to her, she knew she was trapped.

Oh no.

Kane used her lack of options to his advantage. Faking with his right, he fired off a roundhouse left. Lilly couldn't adapt fast enough, and his massive fist crashed squarely into her ear and upper cheek.

The horizon tilted wildly. Before Lilly could make sense of what was happening, she was on the ground, a high-pitched buzz filling her head. Her mind screamed at her to *get up!* but her limbs would not respond. She rolled onto her back and tried to rise, but all 225 pounds of Kane Logan sat down right on her chest, driving the breath from her body.

Lilly pounded on his chest and upper arms with everything she could muster but might as well have been striking granite. Swatting her fists aside like annoying mosquitoes, he wrapped both hands around her throat and squeezed.

She grabbed at his wrists, trying to pull them off and away, but his grip was vice-like. Muscles in Lilly's neck shifted, making it impossible to draw a breath. She arched her hips in an attempt to throw him off, but Kane absorbed the move like he was riding a rodeo bull. He rocked forward, applying more pressure. Lilly felt her eyeballs bulge.

Panic ripped through her. Finding strength she didn't know she had, Lilly raised her arms over her head and pounded the insides of his elbows with her fists. Kane's arms folded and his body collapsed down. He could neither maintain his grip on her throat nor hold himself up, falling forward and slightly off to one side, his neck pressing against Lilly's cheek.

Drawing one enormous breath to replenish herself, she captured a hunk of his skin between her teeth and chomped down for all she was worth. Kane roared. She kept her jaws clenched until she tasted blood, opening them only when she felt his weight roll off her body.

Coughing and wheezing, Lilly scrambled to her feet. She was disoriented but stumbled in the direction of her gun. Fortunately, the matte-black shape was now visible on the concrete in the increasing pre-dawn light. She retrieved it and headed back to her partner, who was still writhing on the ground.

"Kane!?" Her voice was raspy and it hurt to speak. She kept her distance, not sure if he was playing possum, her gun pointed squarely at him. His head turned a little as he tracked her voice, but he remained down.

"Answer me, Kane!" Lilly ignored the pain in her throat and used the firmest voice she could muster to make sure he understood that she had the upper hand. Better to deter him from acting than being forced to pull the trigger. She repeated the command twice.

Finally, she heard him utter a muffled gasp, like he was trying to speak but couldn't. *I didn't hurt him that bad, did I?* "Say something to me."

More groans. Lilly wasn't sure what to do, but finally Kane pushed himself up to a sitting position, his left hand pressed against the neck wound. He did not look at her.

"Kane, goddammit. Answer me or you're getting a round in the fucking leg!" She was about to threaten him again but stopped when Kane emitted a sharp cry laden with grief.

Lilly's jaw dropped as the unmistakable sound of sobbing reached her ears. "Oh, god, Lilly. I'm so sorry!"

That was the last thing she expected to hear. Shaking off the shock of the surreal moment, Lilly lowered her gun and took a couple of steps toward him, now more concerned than scared. His words were so raw and plaintive that she felt an almost maternal need to offer help. "Talk to me, Kane. What's going on?"He too

He took a deep, shuddering breath. "I'm sorry... that—it wasn't me. I mean, it was, but... I couldn't stop."

"They dosed you, didn't they?"

"Yeah," Kane responded. He sat up further, bringing his legs and arms tightly against his body, still looking off into the distance. Lilly could see the stain of blood on his shirt collar. To her relief, it wasn't gushing.

"And that phone call was the trigger," she said matter-of-factly. "What were you supposed to do?"

His head dropped so low it almost disappeared below his broad shoulders. "Kill you, then something about a fire. I'm not sure." He wasn't outright crying anymore, but his voice told Lilly everything she needed to know.

"It wasn't your fault, Kane. I know it wasn't really you doing that."

"I know, but... you can't understand how it felt. I saw your face, how horrified you were. I heard you trying to reach out to me. I heard the fear. And...." Kane smacked his fist into his thigh. "And none of it mattered. I didn't care who you were. To me, taking your life was like passing the salt. If you hadn't bit me, I would've done it."

Lilly took the remaining steps to him. She wanted to sit with him, to reassure him that he wasn't responsible, but they were still out in the open with hostiles likely in the area. She settled for placing a consoling hand on his shoulder, but Kane jerked his body away as if her touch was poison.

"What else happened?" she probed gently. "Who was it? I counted five outside the house —were there others inside?"

"I can't remember. It's like I knew what they wanted me to do, but I can't recall any part of anyone telling me anything." His tone reminded Lilly of a suspect who had committed unconscionable violence in a fit of rage and was only now grasping the consequences. "I can't see faces or remember voices. The last thing I remember... it was... it was seeing the men come out of the building and recognizing they had night vision goggles. I knew I had to get out of there fast. And then nothing until I came after you."

After several seconds, he turned to face Lilly. His face was tear-streaked, but he was once again composed, even though he still couldn't meet her eyes. "I don't know what the hell to do now."

Ignoring any potential danger, she knelt and placed her hand on his cheek, applying pressure until their eyes met. "You were just traumatized. I was too. I'm going to have one hell of a black eye, and you need stitches. Right now we need to get somewhere safe. So move your ass, Agent."

After a pause and a heavy sigh, Kane nodded and got unsteadily to his feet. He handed the keys over without being asked and Lilly pulled out from behind the building, intent on finding the highway. Leaving the town behind on the way to the interstate, an orange glow—in the direction of the farm they were just at—drew her attention. "What the hell is that?"

Kane, still pulling himself together, jerked his head up. "Looks like a fire," he remarked. "Check it out?" A moment later, they crested a hill; the blaze was definitely at the farm.

It came together for both of them at the same time. "Something about a fire..." Lilly repeated Kane's earlier words. He was looking at her in alarm.

"You think ..." he asked, trailing off.

"That we were supposed to end up in it? Safe bet." She threw the truck into a savage U-turn and roared back toward the small town as Kane called 911 on Lilly's phone.

Chapter 22 – Shoot to Miss?

Kane pointed at the blue sign with white writing identifying the local Virginia State Police barracks. Without comment, Lilly stood on the brakes and whipped the truck to a crooked parking job near the front door. As they raced into the building, Kane grabbed for his ID, but it wasn't there. A hint of a memory crossed his mind at light speed, of hands going through his pockets and emptying them, but it disappeared before he could begin to understand. He shook his head, confused, but let the thought go in favor of what was currently happening.

Lilly went straight to the desk. "Secret Service. We need someone right now." The young trooper pulling the shitty early-morning desk duty blinked but, after scrutinizing her badge through the window, buzzed them in and escorted them down a hall.

On the way, a sergeant was moving purposefully through the desks when he spotted the trooper and the agents. After quick introductions, he dismissed his trooper. "What the hell happened to you guys?"

"There's a big fire up off Route 610," Lilly said.

"Okay. Call the fire department."

"This happened to us there," Kane explained. "It's an unsecured crime scene. We need your help so firefighters can go there safely. How many men do you have?"

The sergeant grabbed the duty roster at the front desk. "Day shift doesn't start until seven, so right now we've got four available officers. I can't leave the barracks unstaffed."

"Got it. Will you assist us, Sergeant....?"

"Novak. What happened there?"

"Short version—people tried to kill us both."

Novak paused. "No shit?"

"No shit," Kane confirmed.

"Fine," Sergeant Novak agreed. "But one of you is going to have to explain this to my captain."

"You won't have a problem justifying this, I promise."

Lilly broke into the conversation. "Sergeant, can we requisition a sidearm for Agent Logan?" Kane looked at her like she had taken leave of her senses.

"Are you nuts?!" Kane hissed at her. "I don't know if I can trust myself to have a gun!"

"What?!" Novak nearly screamed. "What happened to yours, and why shouldn't you have one?!"

Kane gave the trooper a highly condensed version of the evening's events. "That's why I don't have ID either."

"You can get by without that," Lilly said to him, "but you can't go into a potential crime scene unarmed." She shifted her attention to Novak. "Please give him a service pistol. If anything goes wrong, it's on me."

"Great," Novak responded. "You'll be the one to tell the family that he killed their mother or father."

"It won't come to that. You have my word." Lilly sounded convinced, but Kane failed to share her certainty.

"It better not," Novak snarled. He faced Kane and poked a finger in his chest. "You go off the reservation, I'll drop you myself. You understand?"

Kane gave him a sullen nod. "I'd do the same thing if I were you."

The trooper looked him up and down. "Fine. Wait here." He disappeared down a hallway and, when he returned, he carried a Sig Sauer P320 in a shoulder harness and three full magazines, as well as a clipboard. He made Kane sign the document acknowledging receipt of the weapon before handing it over. Kane put the harness on under his suit jacket, loaded the weapon, and holstered the gun. Both Lilly and Novak saw his hands tremble as he did so.

"Thanks," Kane told him, hanging his head like a dog that got caught going through the trash.

"Sure thing." The trooper relaxed a little. "It sounds like you had a hard time. But you're a pro—you wouldn't be where you are otherwise—and your partner has confidence in you. This'll be fine." Kane just looked at him, unconvinced. "More importantly, that receipt you just signed names me as the person giving you the gun, so if one of us has to shoot you, I'll be doing paperwork until spring. Don't make me do that, okay?"

Kane finally smiled a little. "I can't be that cruel. I'll be fine."

"That's better." The tension between the trio faded, and Lilly smacked him in the arm by way of encouragement. "Hey guys," Novak announced to the other troopers, "saddle up. We got a job."

***

All three buildings were engulfed in flames when Kane and Lilly arrived at the scene with the state troopers. Several fire and EMS vehicles were already there with hoses deployed, trying to get ahead of the blaze.

As they checked out the fire, an EMT came over with a bag and asked Kane if he could treat his neck. Kane nodded and pitched his head to the side. The peroxide stung like hell, but in a couple of minutes gauze was taped to the injury.

Seeing them—or more likely, seeing Trooper Novak—the fire chief came over. "The barn is probably screwed," he said without preamble, "but we might be able to save part of the house and the greenhouse. This fire is exceedingly hot, like an accelerant was used."

"There might be important evidence in the house," Kane said. "It's critical to keep it intact."

"We're going to stop the fire as fast as we can. We can't control what it burns."

Kane recognized the foolishness of his statement. "Understood. When you're done, though, please let us help you search."

"That I can do." Someone on one of the trucks yelled a question, and the firefighter turned back to his primary job.

"Sorry, Agents," Trooper Novak said. "I don't think you're going to find much after they put this one out."

"Yeah, maybe," Kane responded noncommittally. The forensic guys forever amazed him, and he was sure they'd be able to find something in the ashes—if he could get a team to the site.

Lilly tapped his arm and inclined her head in the direction of the ridge and slope that had occupied so much of their time only a few short hours ago. "We're kind of exposed here," she mentioned.

Kane trained a critical eye in that direction. At night, visibility was limited, but the sun made everyone here a potential target. He should have recognized that the second they stepped out of the trucks but still wasn't tracking fully. As he looked, his vision blurred and he found himself standing in a small, dim room with three other men. One of them was Ethan Doyle.

"What the fuck?" he mumbled, shaking off the memory.

Lilly, focused on the ridge, barely heard his invective. "Huh?"

"It's Doyle," he stated.

"Ethan Doyle?! Where?!" Lilly swept her head left and right.

"No, before. It was him and his men in the house. They're the ones that dosed me and told me what to do."

Lilly addressed the most pressing issue first. "Sergeant, can you have someone clear that ridgeline, please? The people we're dealing with could make a shot from there with ease."

Novak frowned. "Look, I don't want any surprises here," he told them, lowering his head so the brim of his Stratton hat barely exposed his eyes. "Tell me right now if we need to pull back. I'm gonna be right pissed if I lose a guy because of any 'need-to-know' bullshit."

"No, sir," Lilly answered. "Agent Logan is piecing this together as it comes to him. You know what we know, and we won't keep you out of this loop. There is too much at stake."

Novak turned to one of his people and gave a few curt commands, causing his subordinate to raise his radio. "Okay. It's being taken care of."

"Thank you." Lilly pulled Kane a few feet away. "What exactly do you remember?"

Kane relayed the entirety of the memory. "It was like a flash of memory, not much, but something. It's there, but it doesn't last long. When you mentioned the ridge, all of the sudden I was staring at Doyle's face."

"Why are you remembering things? Barnett didn't."

"I don't know," Kane admitted. "If I had to guess, I'd say it was the rather forceful method you used to snap me out of it."

"Are they real memories?" Lilly asked.

"They feel like it, but who knows? My head is awfully fucked up."

"I say they're real. We discounted Doyle and his gang as fanatics, but maybe they had more to do with this than we know. Since I doubt they expected us to survive, it's unlikely they made any effort to set up false memories. We're going to trust what you recall."

Kane nodded in agreement. "I'll tell you the second I get another flashback and we'll go from there. Thanks."

"No thanks needed." Kane hoped his look conveyed his appreciation of how delicately she handled him without words.

The fire trucks were finally making progress, but there was significant damage to the house. The barn was nothing more than a giant glowing ember, and the greenhouse wasn't much better off. When a car with "Fire Investigator" on the side pulled up, the driver exited with a duffel bag and headed to speak with Sergeant Novak, but Lilly and Kane intercepted him. She flashed her ID to the middle-aged man, which was enough to stop him in his tracks. "Hi, sir. We have good reason to believe this fire was set intentionally."

The inspector responded with a nod. "That's what the fire chief said when he called me. He also thinks an accelerant was used, and the heat from the fire makes me agree." Without another word, the man walked away, digging through his bag.

***

Lilly watched the firefighters work, and it looked like they were getting the upper hand. *Maybe we will get something.* It seemed the house might survive. At this point, she would take just about anything.

Lilly's phone rang. The number, once again, was one she didn't recognize. It was a 202 area code, which was in D.C., but that didn't mean shit. The earlier had come from an 816 number, which was somewhere in Missouri, so this could be more danger.

"Walk away," she told Kane. "Right now." He did not hesitate, stepping out of earshot. Only then did Lilly take the call. "Alexander."

The voice was familiar. "Agent Alexander! It's good to hear your voice! This is Director MacMurray on an unsecured line. Are you and Agent Logan okay?" To say Lilly was surprised to get the call at all was an understatement.

"Uh, yes, we're fine. We had a tough time of it, but we are both okay and in a safe place, sir. What can I do for you?"

"Can you put Agent Logan on the call as well, please?"

Lilly hesitated. It *sounded* like Mac, but voice impersonation was not unheard of, and if this wasn't Mac and he used another trigger phrase on Kane, every trooper on the site would blow him away. "Sir, for reasons that I can't fully explain right now, I'd prefer not to. It's better if I relay your message to him myself."

"Agent, I know we had words the last time we talked, and I apologize for that, but I need to speak to both of you. Consider it an order."

"I understand, sir, but I am respectfully declining that order. I will explain at another time if you want, but right now I'll either listen to your message myself and relay it to Kane or I will terminate this call." Her statement was met with silence, so she tried a softer tack. "Sir, when I'm able to tell you why I'm doing this, you'll understand." Kane, unable to hear but seeing her expression, looked at her curiously.

"All right, I'll accept that—for now." He cleared his voice. "Number one, I was completely out of line earlier with my statements to you. I'm under some influence from some very senior officials." *The president. What is his problem?* "Officially, the two of you are *persona non grata* regarding this investigation. Officially, no one will provide agency assistance or hear what you have to say." He paused, and Lilly couldn't wait for the other shoe to drop.

The shame in his voice was tangible. "That's why I'm calling from my personal phone," he continued. "I lost focus and allowed two agents to go into harm's way without backup or support. That's not the way I do things, and that's not the way my agency operates. So, *unofficially,* you and Agent Logan are back in business, and I'll get you the resources you need."

If she'd been ill-prepared for his first words, this statement left her dumbfounded. "Wow, sir. I have to admit that's the last thing I expected to hear from you right now. Thank you for saying that."

"No, Agent, it's me who should be thanking you. In fact, I owe you much more of an apology than I can offer right now. Do you have any leads?"

"Several, sir."

"Good. Tell me what you need."

"Yes, sir. For starters, we could use...."

***

Lilly put the phone away, amazed at this turn of events. Ten yards away, Kane was standing in place, hands raised and palms open in a bewildered question. Lilly walked to him. "You are not going to believe who that call was from or what it was about," she told him, trying and failing to keep herself from grinning.

***

Kane picked through the remains of the building in which he'd been held. Unqualified to determine what the tiny bits of char had been, he wasn't sure what he was looking for, but he pressed on.

He was tired and fighting off pain in both his leg and his neck, but took heart in knowing that this site would be properly processed. Lilly's news had been the equivalent of a ninth inning walk-off grand slam. Now they could get help from other agents and focus their energies on the core components of the investigation, whatever they were.

All that aside, he was wracked with guilt about what he'd almost done to Lilly. He did not relish the thought of driving back to D.C. with her. Having a purpose kept the worst of those feelings in the background, but that would change during the long, dull ride.

The sound of a low-flying helicopter split the morning air. Kane watched it fly an elliptical orbit around the area, pleased that Sergeant Novak was taking Lilly's concerns and request seriously. The chopper completed its pass before landing about a 100 yards away. A trooper spoke briefly with the pilot and then ran back to Novak and delivered a message. The sergeant came over to Kane.

"The entire area is clear. No one up there now, but there are some signs of people being there recently."

"That might have been us," Kane conceded. "I appreciate you checking. I don't think we can be too cautious right now. We're still trying to get a handle on what's going on here."

"You probably can't tell me, but this is about the assassination attempt in New York, right?"

Kane grinned to get his message across. "I certainly cannot tell you about that."

"Got it. Thanks." The fire investigator took the place of the trooper.

"I did a quick chemical analysis for accelerants. It's preliminary, but this fire was started using diesel fuel, which burns hotter than either gasoline or kerosene. More importantly, there were shavings of magnesium in the fuel, so that jacked the heat up big time. That's why it burned so fast. They wanted to obliterate the structures and everything inside."

Kane nodded. Doyle couldn't risk leaving behind any evidence, and the hottest fire was the best way to eliminate it quickly and irrevocably.

"Did anything survive?"

"Yeah. We caught a break. A big chunk of the structure collapsed and smothered another area of fire, so some things didn't burn. We have to clear away some debris, so we can't be sure what's under it, if anything." He pointed to two firefighters digging away at a pile of charred wood.

Kane nodded, hoping they might catch a break and find something. "Thank you, Marshal... Cooper," Kane said, reading his badge.

Kane turned back to survey the area, and that's when he noticed the four indentations in the ground that were devoid of grass. With his focus no longer on the building itself, they were easily recognizable as spots where shooters had lain prone for target practice. Kane looked downrange. The only backstop was the hill, which was two, maybe three miles distant, and the other hills formed a box canyon. The floor of the valley sloped down and away from the shooting area, dropping several hundred feet. Even better, there appeared to be a wide access road running along the southern slope, and Kane was willing to bet it ran all the way to where human-shaped targets were probably set up. He'd seen this distance and trajectory before.

He spotted Sergeant Novak and limped over to him. "Is there a surveying company in town?"

"You mean, like land surveyors?"

"Yup."

"Uh, yeah. Trick's Land Surveying."

"Great name," he mumbled. "Can you get them here, please? Whatever they're doing, have them drop it. They can bill their time to the Secret Service."

Sergeant Novak squinted at Kane. "What do you need them for?"

Kane gestured to the large area. "What does this look like to you?"

Novak shrugged. "A shooting range. So?"

"So I think I just found where those people I can't talk about were practicing for what they never did, but I need to be sure. Agent Alexander and I are going to find the target area, and I want the survey team to stand right in one of these depressions and tell me how much that slope drops and how far away the target area is. Let me have your cell number. I'll call you when we're in position." Novak looked down the valley as he read off the digits, this time with a more critical view. "And Sergeant, please make sure they know that they were never here and didn't do any such job."

"You got it." Novak grabbed his radio and walked back to his truck.

"Lilly!" She acknowledged hearing him the third time he bellowed. He pointed to the truck and gestured for her to bring it over. She looked confused, but he knew she would figure things out.

***

Lilly followed the wide dirt road that ran the length of the valley at about twenty-five miles an hour, not bothering Kane as he stared out the open passenger window like a dog enjoying the smells of the drive. He hadn't said much beyond asking her to take this road as far as it would go, so she complied. The purpose of the area had been instantly obvious to her.

The road ended at a small opening about the size of a two-car garage, about thirty feet up a slight incline from the bottom of the valley. Kane exited the vehicle, waving for Lilly to follow him while looking back at where they'd come from. He seemed fixated on his task, so Lilly did not interfere. Instead, she took it upon herself to start checking things out. The first thing she noticed were three wood frames that roughly resembled football goalposts. Two eyehooks were secured into the crossbar, with one more on the top of each vertical beam. It didn't take much imagination to figure out that a target had been suspended between those eye hooks. "You think they practiced here?"

"I sure do."

"But what about Doyle's camp? That range wasn't this long."

"Another backup plan, just like the other shooters."

"These guys thought of everything."

He pulled out his phone and dialed. "Is the survey team in place? Can they see me? Great." He stepped backward until he was between two of the wood frames. "I need distance and drop to exactly where I'm standing, please." He waited a moment.

Kane nodded to no one in particular. "Are they absolutely certain of those numbers? Great. Thanks." He hung up and turned to Lilly, a self-satisfied smirk on his face.

"What was that all about?" she asked.

"I asked Novak to call in a surveying team and have them measure the distance and elevation. Wanna guess those numbers?"

Lilly didn't need her eidetic memory to recall the values. "4,817 yards distance and 248 feet of drop."

"You win the prize. And that means they did a lot of work to get everything ready in such an exact fashion, which takes a lot of time—time I'm not sure they had for an operation this extensive."

"When was Armstrong's speech announced?" Lilly asked.

"I don't know, but we get told before it's generally announced, so we probably had six weeks advance notice. So figure John Q. Public had two, maybe three weeks. The perps probably knew the general distances and heights between the Brooklyn Bridge and the Statue of Liberty ahead of time, but they still had to find a remote location matching those general characteristics. They had to secure the location, probably via a legal purchase so as not to alert anyone. Then they'd needed to scrape out the shooting area, the road, and the target site—not the easiest work in the world, so they would need heavy-duty earth-moving equipment. And all that had to happen *before* they could start practicing, but *after* Armstrong's speech at the Statue of Liberty was announced."

"Sounds like way too much work in way too little time," Lilly said. "And that suggests a really big organization."

Kane turned to the earth behind the target frames, which looked like it had been raked through thoroughly, and peered at it. "I'll bet they didn't get all their projectiles from the backstop. We'll have to ask the team to use a metal detector when they get here."

Lilly agreed and started wandering back toward the truck, noting the multitude of wide tire tracks in the loose dirt of the road. It made sense; the occupants had abandoned ship quickly and probably drove down here more than once to collect things that might implicate them.

When she opened the door, she noticed the back wheel of their SUV resting on a flat, rectangular piece of metal about two feet by eighteen inches—roughly the size of a range target, one that would simulate a person's body and head. *Maybe they dropped it in the rush to leave.* It looked like it had indents in it and, more interestingly, a length of chain extended from one corner. Curious, she inspected closer.

Kane noticed her odd behavior and limped over to find Lilly pulling the truck forward just enough so that Kane could pick the item up. Sure as shit, it was a target.

Kane held it up so Lilly could see the front. There were scores of little craters where the paint had been chipped away and formed tiny concave features from the impact of bullets. And every single mark was in a three-inch grouping.

Lilly whistled. "Are those shots from all the way back at that farm?"

"I didn't see another location closer, and that's what I was looking for when we drove up here, so probably."

"So the shooter is just that good?" Lilly surmised.

"Looks like it," Kane responded, "but that's not the whole of it." He paused. "Let's assume he took all these shots during the same session. Nothing hit the target outside the X-ring, so clearly he doesn't miss. But, when it mattered most, he missed. How?"

"Nerves," Lilly answered with a shrug. "I don't care who you are or how many drugs you're pumped full of, you point a gun at a living human, let alone an important political figure, you're gonna get a little jumpy. And it was not an easy shot. The potential for failure is high."

Kane shook his head. "In most cases, I'd agree. But I'm telling you from experience that this drug mix makes you ignore everything except what you were ordered to do. I was looking you in the eye, I knew exactly who you were, and I didn't give a damn about any of that because it simply didn't matter. Nerves didn't factor in. It's the mission and nothing else."

"Yeah, but both you and Doyle told me that a micro-millimeter twitch of the gun barrel matters a lot by the time the round gets to the target for this kind of shot. One tiny little thing goes wrong, maybe something not under his control, and he hits eight inches to the left."

"And yet he overcame every one of those issues and did not miss once on this target. Either that, or the other shots missed the target entirely, but that seems unlikely considering how many perfect hits we have. It doesn't make sense."

Stalemate. His reasoning was valid. So was hers. "Let's call it a question we have to answer," she conceded. "What's our next step?"

Kane scratched his head. "Well, first the basics. We run down who owned this place, who they got it from, and how. Interview neighbors, or what passes for neighbors out here. They might be miles away. See if any large earth-moving machines were rented locally. You said a full-on forensics team was coming down. Let them do their thing."

"Yeah, I know the drill," Lilly stated impatiently. "But what do *we* do?"

Kane frowned. "I don't love it, but we have to change our role. You and I know more about whatever is going on than anyone. Now that we actually have a semblance of a real team, it's time to step back and manage this thing. We go back to Washington and set up shop where we do exactly that." He smiled. "That kind of gives you the lead here."

Lilly let the surprise register on her face. Kane was a front-line kind of guy, and another agent might not have stepped aside so willingly. "Well," she smiled at him, "at least we won't get punched in the face or bit so much anymore."

Kane closed his eyes for a second, and Lilly silently rebuked herself for being so cavalier about what was obviously still a sore spot for him.

To his credit, he at least tried to make light of it. "I hope so. This is starting to hurt." He rubbed the bandage on his neck. "It's my first hickey. I don't see why anyone likes them."

"There's a lot of different ways to do them. That one, it's more for the S&M crowd."

Kane winced. "I am not even going to ask how or why you know that."

Lilly popped her eyebrows up mischievously. "Good choice."

"Inappropriate statements aside, let's head back and see if anyone's arrived. We can bring them up to speed, but we're going to keep this target and take it back with us."

"Why?"

"If you discount the hole in my leg, this is the first piece of physical evidence we have. Not only am I not risking it disappearing, I'm looking forward to dropping it on someone's desk —not sure whose at the moment—and forcing them to admit we've been right all along."

She stepped up to him. "Kane, we've got an ally, a good one, in Mac. You go in there with an attitude and you're just going to screw up this whole thing worse than before. We've finally got some good cards in our hand. Keep them close to the vest until it's time to go all-in."

"I didn't know you knew how to play poker, Lilly."

She smiled. "Of course you didn't. The best players never let on that we can or how good we are. That's how we win." With a wink, she got back in the truck.

Chapter 23 – A Painful Lesson

Several FBI agents were on the scene when Kane and Lilly returned to the site. The firefighters had finally cleared away the collapsed part of the house and were dragging plastic tubs filled with papers clear of the charred remains. Kane made a beeline for them while Lilly went to introduce herself to the other agents.

The bins were covered in soot and the lids were slightly melted, but Kane managed to pry one open. Grabbing a few of the papers, he found receipts for gun supplies, ammunition, deposit slips, and order forms. *Looks like we caught a break.*

Kane closed up his box and pointed to the others. "These are coming with us," he said to the firefighters and troopers. He loaded them in the back of their SUV, leaving room for any others they might find.

He joined Lilly and the other agents. "Hey guys, I'm glad you're here. I know you'll do a standard sweep, but I need a few extra things." He provided details to the team.

The in-charge agent nodded. "The director already filled us in. You've got nothing to worry about."

Kane nodded at the man. "Thanks." He turned to Lilly. "You all set?"

"Yeah, we're good."

"Great. Let's get going." They climbed in their truck and started down the rough dirt road back toward the highway. Lilly sent a quick text to MacMurray's personal phone outlining what they'd done. Shortly thereafter, they were dealing with the ever-present herd of tractor-trailers navigating Route 81 on their way back to Washington.

***

Ethan Doyle ignored the posted speed limit signs and guided his F-250 west on Route 58. The large cab, though spacious, was still crowded with Doyle and his four lieutenants. Their gear and guns filled the bed of the truck.

He wished he'd been able to watch the life fade from their eyes like so many of the others he'd shot in the past years, but that hadn't been the plan. At least they were dead, and that was good enough for him.

Doyle's phone rang. It was a number he didn't recognize, but that was expected. Communication leading up to the previous night had been clandestine in the extreme. He pushed the OK button on the screen, leaving the speaker on for all to hear. "This is Doyle."

"Mr. Doyle," came the not unexpected and slightly creepy, superior voice. "I trust you are well and heading to Alternate One as dictated."

"Yes, Mr. Smith," he answered. "We're all in good shape and about eight hours from our destination."

"I see. I'm assuming that the plan for targets K and L was completed successfully."

"Yes, sir," Doyle responded. "K was dosed, we confirmed his mental state, and he repeated his orders several times. We saw him get in his truck with L and gave them an out. When we saw their vehicle dart behind a store in town, we set the fire at the camp and got out of the area to avoid being spotted."

"Did you confirm termination of the targets?"

"We tried to, but we spotted fire and police activity headed to the scene. Additionally, the sun was coming up fast. We thought it was more important to remain covert, and K is more than capable of taking care of L, so we chose to evacuate." *Where was this going?*

"I see. I'm curious as to what part of your instructions confused you."

"Confused me?"

"Yes, you must have been confused, as YOUR TARGETS WERE JUST SIGHTED LEAVING PRIMARY ONE AND HEADING NORTH! Worse, part of the structure may have survived!"

Doyle blanched, as did the rest of his team at the outburst. "They're alive? And the building's not wrecked?"

"Either that, or they have two body doubles driving back to D.C. This makes me wonder why you did not follow your specific orders."

This man sounded like a desk jockey who didn't understand how things worked in the field. "Sir, it took far longer than we expected for K to implement his orders. Since we had no way to contact you, and daylight was becoming a problem, we made a decision with the information we had at the time."

"Your orders did not allow for leeway, interpretation, or freelancing. I'm quite sure I was very clear on that point."

"You were, but I don't think you realize how the tactical situation was changing—"

"You assured me you would do what was necessary to eliminate the targets and the evidence, and you did neither."

"I made a call to keep my team safe. If it didn't work out, we will make things right."

"No, Mr. Doyle, that won't be necessary. Your services are no longer needed. We have more trustworthy alternatives. Do not go to Alternate One. You are dismissed. And," he said, his voice becoming even more sinister, "I strongly suggest you forget everything about me, where you've been recently, and our association." The call ended.

Doyle and his men shared stares of disbelief. "Who the fuck does that guy think he is?" Ike asked no one in particular.

"What do we do now?" Adams asked.

Doyle shook his head. He felt stupid to have trusted Smith, but proud of his penchant for creating contingency plans in case things didn't work out. "Reagan, you're sure we're all set with the tracking chip on their truck?"

"Damn straight."

"And they can't turn it off?"

"They can, but that's only if they know it's there. And they'll never know."

"Cool," he announced. "Now we do things our way. The right way. Enough of this pussy-footing around."

He didn't need to see the nods of agreement from his lieutenants as he made a U-turn in the median, putting them on a course for Washington.

***

Kane drove silently, exhausted by the lack of sleep but buoyed by the massive quantities of caffeine he bought at Sheetz while they were getting gas. In addition to two large coffees, he'd also grabbed a two-liter bottle of Mountain Dew. The coffees were empty, and he was more than halfway through the fizzy green potion, and they weren't even to Front Royal yet. His heart felt like a bird fluttering in his chest, and he'd have to stop soon for a bathroom break.

He'd countered Lilly's attempts to discuss recent developments with grunts. He couldn't handle Lilly telling him she didn't blame him for his attack, and that's where any conversation would go. At least he couldn't see the side of her head where he'd punched her and the damage he'd caused, but he *could* see her wince every time she swallowed. That was bad enough.

He caught Lilly giving him sidelong glances as he sucked down the stimulants. Finally, she seemed unable to stand it any longer. "Jesus, Kane," she said after another gulp. "You're either going to have a heart attack or get sepsis when your bladder bursts."

"Maybe both," he responded, taking another long pull on the soda to avoid a more substantive response. The rich, sugary mess was starting to bug his stomach, so much so that he let out a rippling belch that lasted several seconds. "Sorry."

"Or that will happen," she remarked. "At least it came out that end and not the other." When Kane barely reacted to the juvenile joke, Lilly took a breath. "Drinking gallons of terrible soda and black coffee won't make it go away, Kane."

"No, I know," he said. "My friend Jack Daniels is going to help me with that later tonight."

"Great. I'm sure you'll make the critical breakthrough we need while drowning in shitty bourbon."

"We've got a real team on this right now, not just the two of us. You can find someone else to partner up with. I'll do some desk-duty time where I can't hurt anyone while you stay more involved."

"That's idiotic," Lilly spat back. "We're a team, Kane. We work well with each other." She touched his arm, but Kane pulled back as if her finger was a live electrical wire. "Tell me what's really bugging you," she implored.

Kane nearly lost his temper. "What's bugging me is that I attacked a smaller fellow agent and nearly killed her!"

Lilly did not miss a beat. "Let's be honest. You may have attacked me, but I won that fight."

Kane glowered at her. "Excuse me?"

"Excuse me nothing. Last time I checked, when someone comes after me and I put them on the ground writhing in agony, that's an old-fashioned ass-whoopin'."

Kane stared at her. He had no idea what to say, but humiliation started crawling around in his head.

"And you don't like it," she continued with a snarl in her words. "So before you start whining about how big bad Kane beat up the weak little woman, you better remember who ended up on her feet while you cried like a little boy who dropped his ice cream. I won that fight straight up."

"Yeah," he said bitterly. "You look like you won. The whites of your eyes are red because I popped every blood vessel in them, your face is blotchy, I wouldn't bet against you having a fractured larynx, and the side of your head is swollen like a cantaloupe. You got lucky."

"Lucky, my ass. Typical man. You can't possibly handle that I took you down, so you're making excuses and acting guilty."

"Are you saying I don't have anything to feel guilty about?"

"Yes, I am. I'm also tired of you moping around like Santa skipped your house on Christmas Eve." She sounded way more pissed than Kane would have expected. He'd been the asshole here; she was just his unfortunate victim.

"Well, fucking excuse me for having a shred of chivalry."

"It's not you being chivalrous. It's you being a stubborn, arrogant asshole!"

Kane sighed. She just didn't get it. "You think calling me names is going to fix any of this? I'm not eight years old."

"Are you embarrassed that a little girl is pointing out what a misogynist you are?" She sounded like a sister getting tired of her brother's teasing.

Kane was nearing the point where he would explode and worry about the resulting collateral damage after the fact. "Fuck you!"

Lilly leaned in and spoke more softly. "If I was a man, would you feel the same way?"

His pain and remorse faded into the background. "What?"

"This whole shame routine is because you still think of me as a woman first and an equal second. If you had a male partner last night and everything went down the same way, you'd have apologized, shaken his hand, and been done with it. But, with me, your attack was a mortal sin in your eyes, and it's all because I've got tits. Tell me I'm wrong."

Kane couldn't do that. The second she stopped baiting him and spoke about her gender, he recognized a fundamental truth about himself. He had nothing but respect for her intelligence, her instincts, her confidence, and her overall skills as an agent. Minus a little experience, she was absolutely his equal. But she was still a woman, the weaker sex, and men did not attack women. Why? Because they couldn't defend themselves—or so he'd been told since he was a boy.

But this one could and wasn't afraid to do so.

Goddammit. "You're right," he told her. "One hundred percent. I didn't give it a thought, but it's all true. I mean, I shouldn't have attacked you no matter who you are, but that's different. I'm acting like I'm superior just because I'm a man." He made eye contact with her. "No more of that. You have my apologies."

The smile that creased her face, even distorted by the injuries he'd inflicted upon her, was perhaps the most beautiful he'd ever seen. "Thank you. I'm sorry about being so direct, but you had your head so far up your ass you didn't even realize what was going on."

Kane nodded, and another thought occurred to him. "That's twice you've put me back on track, and you aren't shy about doing it. Are you like this with all your partners?"

"Just the stubborn, brooding men who think they know better than me," she told him.

"So, you don't think female agents can't be just as hard to work with?"

"Oh, I'm sure they can. Just as hard, if not worse. But I've only had male partners and supervisors. Of all of them, you were the hardest to pin down, but I've got you figured out now."

"You do? Care to share?"

"I'm not sure you're going to like it," Lilly cautioned.

"I didn't like learning about my underlying male chauvinism, but I survived that. What's one more hit to my ego?"

"Well, to put it simply, you care."

To say Kane was disappointed with her diagnosis was an understatement. "I care? What the hell does that mean?"

"It means that, for some reason, you are intent on showing the world that everything bounces off of you and doesn't impact you one bit. The reality is that you take all the criticism, all the mistakes, all the perceived failures and allow them to affect the person you are and how you execute your duties."

"And that's good or bad?"

"In your case, mostly bad, but there's an upside," Lilly told him. "A good agent uses his emotions but doesn't let them override logic. You keep your emotions wrapped up and buried until something like last night happens, then you go off the deep end. You're human, all claims and evidence to the contrary. If you let your feelings out a little more regularly rather than allowing them to build up, I think you'll find this job a lot easier."

Kane just stared; with a few sentences, she'd led him to an epiphany that he'd sought for years.

Thankfully, Lilly broke in before he could continue that line of thought. "That's enough psychoanalysis for one day. Let's do a bathroom break. I'm sure you'll need one soon."

Chapter 24 – Secret Rendezvous

With his remorse eradicated and hopped up on caffeine, Kane was a different person. Now he wouldn't shut up, or even pause, as he bounced from one theory or idea to another. Lilly would take that over a mute, sulking partner any day.

She tried to keep up with the rampant onslaught of ideas, but more often than not Kane dismissed them before Lilly could process everything he said. A couple of times she almost giggled at his runaway train of thought but let him continue in the hope he would come across something of value.

Kane didn't do that, but his frenetic analysis of the situation ruled out many theories. Finally, after babbling for forty-five minutes, he turned to his partner and smiled sheepishly. "Maybe you've got a couple ideas too."

She shook her head in amusement. "Self-awareness finally raises its ugly head," she joked. "Truth be told, you did cover a lot of options, but we haven't put ourselves in a place where we can start working them. We need a plan."

"Which I'm sure you have."

"Of course I do. Doyle and his men are either part of this operation or a clever decoy, and they aren't unique. There had to be other groups that trained backup shooters too, and those backups all want to be compensated for their efforts because mortgages still have to be paid, and kids still need clothes and food. That site was likely bought legally to ensure that dog didn't bark, and that was a huge piece of land. The guns they used, and all the practice ammo, that stuff wasn't cheap. What do these all have in common?"

"Money."

"Big money," Lilly agreed. "I saw amounts in the thousands when I checked out our dead shooters, but we need to expand our horizons by an order of magnitude."

"How do we do that?"

"Off-shore accounts. Foreign governments. Anyone who can write a check for a couple million without thinking about it and have the resources to spread it from hell to breakfast easily."

"I can't think of anything more fun—for you, I mean. This is what you live for, digging through receipts and checks and bank records. I'm going to be about as useless as a blind monkey."

"Don't worry. You take orders pretty well. I'll train you up in no time."

"Of course you will." The mood in the car was almost jovial; compared to what could have happened the previous night, that was nothing short of amazing.

Lilly's phone rang. She gave Kane a look before checking the screen. "It's Mac on his other phone." That was probably good, but she still kept the phone off speaker just in case. "Agent Alexander."

"Hello, Agent. You know who this is?"

"I do, sir."

"Did the team arrive on site?"

"Yes, sir. They are working the scene from several angles. They should have something this afternoon," she added optimistically.

"What's your current status?"

Lilly checked the mile marker. "About two hours out from Murray Lane, sir."

"Kane is with you, still incommunicado?"

"Correct on both, sir."

"Good. Tell him to proceed to Alternate Seneca. He'll know exactly what that means." Lilly relayed the information to Kane, who nodded.

"Text me at this number when you cross the bridge. And remain extra vigilant while traveling. Your personal threat board is off-the-charts high right now."

Personal threat board? Lilly had no idea what he meant, but she knew how to watch her back and would do so. "I'll do that, sir."

"I'll fill you in when we meet up." He terminated the call, and Lilly filled Kane in on the conversation.

"He said that? 'Off-the-charts high?'"

"Verbatim," Lilly confirmed. "Why?"

"That's an unofficial term used by some teams," Kane said. "It means things are as bad as they can get—pretty much you should be expecting a horde of maniacs to take a shot at your principal the second you enter the venue. If Mac used that terminology, and he is coming out to meet us himself, he's either really worried about something, or..."

"Or what?"

"Or it's a setup."

The disdain in Lilly's voice said it all. "So the director himself is going to take us out?"

"Well, it would be easy. Our guard would be down."

Lilly raised her eyebrows and tilted her head slightly. "Too risky. Why have the director do the dirty work that any number of lower-level peons could handle?"

"It wouldn't have to be the director. Hell, he might not even be there. Mac travels with a bodyguard."

"And of course he would sign right up for the cold-blooded murder of two federal agents."

Kane had to concede the point. "You don't see this meeting as potentially dangerous?"

"I didn't say that. I said having Mac take us out himself is about the worst possible way of doing the job, if that's what this is."

Kane shot her an approving look. "What do you think is going on?"

Lilly bit her lip. "Well, we should at least consider that this may be exactly as advertised —a meet-up to warn us. But we shouldn't bet on that."

"Agreed."

"It would help if I knew what Alternate Seneca is."

"It's a safe house northwest of the city," Kane told her. "Surrounded by forest, well-hidden. I've used it a few times, usually when we needed information in a hurry and couldn't afford to worry about things like due process." He said it matter-of-factly, but Lilly shivered thinking about what might have transpired there.

"Remote?" she asked.

"Big time."

"So there could be shooters in the woods just waiting for us to show up?"

"Sure could be."

"Making it a bad idea to traipse up to the meeting like everything is on the level. That means we need to change things up so radically that they won't expect it. How do we do that?"

They fell silent for a moment. After about a mile, Kane spoke up. "At Doyle's camp, when you were shooting, I know you weren't doing your best on purpose, but what do you feel your max range was?"

Lilly paused. "At three, maybe 400 yards, I felt like I could be on paper with every shot. Five hundred or more, things got iffy."

Kane nodded. "I think that works. Even if you're close enough to hit a car or something like that, it should scare them enough if needed."

"Oh, I'll more than scare them."

"Cool. So I think we play it this way...."

***

Alternate Seneca was further away than D.C., so it took longer to get there. After discussing their plan and the possible outcomes, they became silent once more as tensions increased. Kane focused on his driving, allowing Lilly to watch out for unwelcome tails, but she saw nothing, so he didn't worry about it.

As morning became afternoon, they crossed the American Legion Memorial Bridge passing over the greenish-brown waters of the Potomac River. Lilly did not send a text to Mac or anyone else.

Kane navigated the bucolic roads as houses became nicer and separated by wider strips of sycamore trees. When he started slowing, Lilly gave him a look of confusion until she saw the well-concealed driveway on the right. "Wow," she stated. "I've been by here a dozen times, and I've never noticed that entrance."

"No one does." He changed subjects abruptly. "You ready for this?"

Lilly took a deep breath. "As much as I can be." She picked up the rifle and double-checked that it was ready to fire.

"Okay. Right after this rise, the house'll be about 100 yards away. Mac will be parked next to it. One bodyguard, maybe two."

Lilly cracked the passenger door open. "Here we go." Kane slowed just before the apex of the hill, and when the speed dropped below five miles per hour, she jumped out. Rolling once, she popped to her feet and sprinted behind the truck and into the woods. Kane pulled the door shut and proceeded up the driveway.

The other car was just where he predicted, with Mac and his bodyguard standing next to it. Kane halted about twenty yards from his welcoming committee and got out, his hand near his weapon.

The bodyguard tensed and moved as if to reach under his suit jacket, but Mac raised his hand. "Easy, Ian. Stand down." Ian did as ordered, but Kane could see just how much he didn't like it. He extended his hands away from his body, just as the director did.

"Thank you," Kane said sincerely to Ian. "And thank you for understanding my actions, sir."

Mac smiled. "Please don't make me regret it, Agent."

"No, sir. There's too much at stake."

The director looked around. "Where's Agent Alexander?"

"Covering all contingencies until we've secured the site, sir. Our opponents have proven to be very resourceful in gaining the upper hand. I'm not about to make it easy for them."

"That's a better decision than you realize," he answered, surprising Kane.

***

Lilly watched through the scope as Kane and Mac spoke. She thought she might have to fire when she saw the reaction of Mac's bodyguard, but fortunately for him he stopped in time.

It had only taken her a few seconds to find a safe location from which she could observe and hopefully not shoot. Of course, "safe" was a relative term. For all she knew, these forested acres were crawling with enemies. It was hard not to think of the rifle, the one aimed at her head right this second with a bullet in the chamber, and realize that it would take nothing more than the flexing of a finger to end her. But she had a job to do, so she did it.

She was encouraged by the body language, and more so by the director and his bodyguard placing their guns on the hood of their vehicle. Kane followed the bodyguard into the small safehouse while Lilly kept her sights trained squarely on Mac. If someone else was waiting inside, Kane was unlikely to come back out. Her insurance policy was that Kane had made it clear to the director what would occur if that scenario played out.

She waited for a few interminable moments before the door opened and the broad shoulders of her partner filled the doorway. He faced in her general direction and gave her the all-clear signal. Lilly was glad to see it but couldn't help but feel like her coach was telling her to steal second base. She emerged from her hiding spot and started the trek toward the building.

Kane went back inside with the director, and Lilly joined them in a stark basement room. Kane and the director sat on straight-back chairs at a plain table that, under other circumstances, had probably been used for interrogation rather than a meeting. Quick pleasantries were exchanged, and they got down to business.

Kane started. "Sir, the first thing I've got to ask is why our threat boards are 'off-the-charts high.'"

The director smiled. "I knew that would get your attention. Unfortunately, it's true. As I indicated on the phone the other evening, I'm kind of limited by my higher-ups as to what I can do with this situation." Mac only had two higher-ups, and it was clear which one he meant.

"I've been meaning to ask about that," Lilly interrupted. "According to Kane, last week our instructions—from POTUS himself—were to take any action necessary, just short of declaring war on another nation, to get to the bottom of this. Now it's like we're being put out on the curb with a 'free' sign on our backs. What changed?"

Mac nodded. "That's a simple question and a complicated answer. First of all, investigations are still ongoing and are being readily supported. It's *your* investigation that is being curtailed. Yours only."

"Why?" Kane asked. "Are we that far off the mark?"

"Not to my way of thinking," Mac answered. "In fact, you seem to be developing the best information. That's an important tidbit to keep in mind, especially when you consider that I'm out of the loop regarding what you guys do and where you go."

"Wait a damn minute," Kane objected, shaking his head as if Mac had just switched from English to Yiddish. "It's *your* agency. You're a congressional appointee. That borders on treason."

The director did not argue the point. "Oh, it more than borders on it—it straight out violates my airspace. But going after this right now is political suicide. It'll look like a power play, and the spin will be that I'm trying to give Armstrong a leg up in return for a cushy position in the new administration if he wins."

"Maybe, but you still can't just take this. Fuck appearances!" Kane pounded his fist on the table so hard Lilly feared structural failure.

Mac gave Kane a controlled, mirth-free grin indicating he had already considered all this. "Agent, even more than when I told you this at the White House, you need to see the big picture. The Democratic presidential candidate was shot and nearly killed less than two weeks before the election, and we still don't know much about who did it. The investigation into that shooting, perhaps the most critical investigation in the history of the FBI, is being run at least partially behind my back. The two agents who have made the most progress on this case are being waylaid professionally by elected officials and threatened personally by self-appointed super-patriots, and we aren't sure who's directing them." He paused, allowing the agents to digest the information he'd just presented. "If I asked you to paint me a picture with that information, how would you title it?"

Lilly got it just as Kane did, and their jaws dropped in unison. "Coup d'état," Kane breathed.

"Can you see it?" Mac asked with sarcastic reverence. "A work in oil on canvas hanging in the Capitol Rotunda, maybe right next to Trumbull's *Declaration of Independence*. The day the country was born, and the day it died." His voice went back to normal. "So, you'll forgive me if I'm not worried as much about me being professionally wronged as I am about preserving the republic."

"Sorry, sir," Lilly mumbled. "But we still need to figure out what they'll do to stop us."

"I've not been ordered to take you off this case, but I don't think that matters. Truth be told, I'm not sure I'm ever going to get that order, but you'll likely be removed from the case—permanently."

"Are you saying that POTUS or the AG has issued orders to eliminate us?" Lilly asked.

"No, I don't know that. But I've gotten some intel that suggests at least one group has orders to deal with you. These aren't the kind of people who make idle threats, and they don't stop until they've fulfilled their mission. Hence my off-the-chart-high remark."

"That's great," Kane commented, but Lilly ignored him. She couldn't believe her ears. It was one thing to go after criminals, to have the upper hand and be the aggressor, but the idea of an enemy who might attack *them* without warning clouded her mind with worry. When would these maniacs strike? Tomorrow, next month, next year? How many would there be? How would she know when they were finally defeated? Would they show up in her bedroom in the middle of the night, run her off the road, or maybe shoot her from a mile away as she walked into the supermarket? How long would she have to be on guard?

"Okay, okay," she mumbled to herself. *Focus! You have to get a grip!* She looked up at the director, but no cogent questions came to mind. In desperation, she looked over at Kane, but he seemed not to notice her consternation.

"We can handle groups like this," he declared—a bit arrogantly to Lilly's way of thinking. "We already did once."

"No we can't. They're furious at us and they have friends. Lots of them. They'll keep coming and coming and they won't stop until we're both dead," she told them, vaguely aware of the way her voice trembled. "We're screwed."

Both men turned to look at her with befuddled expressions.

"No, we're not, Lilly," Kane told her after a moment. "We just need to think it through."

"A swarm of enraged militants just declared war against us, Kane. Not against the Secret Service or the FBI or even the United States of America. Against the two of us."

"It's not a swarm. Mac said it's probably just one group."

Lilly shook her head. "You know how these guys work. 'Brothers to the end' or some shit like that. They'll back each other up, and you know how many of these guys there are!"

"Not only are you overreacting, you're making assumptions. We just have to come up with a plan to fight back."

"What kind of plan is going to help us now?" she asked, the volume of her voice escalating.

"I don't know yet!" he snapped back. "You need to get a grip on yourself."

"A couple dozen skilled snipers are coming for us," she told Kane, the pitch of her voice rising to a level where glass feared for its integrity. "That's all the grip we need!"

"Lilly, what is wrong with you? I've never seen you so freaked out." She stared at him, her mind a blank, barely able to comprehend his simple query. They stared at each other for a few seconds before Mac interrupted.

"There's more you need to know," he said.

"More?!" Lilly exclaimed. For a second, she feared she might faint, and pressed her hands on the table to keep from falling forward.

"Someone accessed your jackets at Murray Lane."

"How the hell did that happen?" Kane demanded.

"Inside job, and a good one," Mac answered. "We're still trying to figure out who did it, but this guy knows how to cover his tracks. All we know is that both files were reviewed remotely."

Kane cursed under his breath, but Lilly ignored him in favor of her now-runaway thoughts. "So they'll be able to find us no matter where we run to, no matter how long we hide?" Her stomach tightened and a gout of saliva flooded her mouth. "It's like they have step-by-step instructions on how to off us. This is hopeless." She stared at the far wall, her eyes wide and despondent.

The silence from the two more experienced agents did not give Lilly a good feeling. She could feel Kane's eyes on her, but didn't bother to acknowledge him.

"I've got a place we can go, one that nobody knows about," he finally said. "Secret Service doesn't know about it. FBI doesn't know about it. No one knows about it. I haven't even been there in years except to drive by it and make sure it's still standing. I'm not even going to tell you where it is."

Lilly perked up. *This sounds promising.*

Mac nodded, but his face was still a question. "How confident are you that it's safe?"

"It's better than being out in the open," he responded. Lilly saw him twitch his head her way, and she picked up his meaning.

"In other words, you're doing this because of me?"

Kane nodded. "I don't know why you're freaking out right now, but if hiding out somewhere safe helps get you back on track, that's what we need to do."

Lilly had no choice but to agree. She wasn't sure what had just happened to herself, but her reaction to what wasn't that big of a deal was inappropriate and completely out of character for her. And, best of all, his idea was helping. Her mind was clearing. Now that she could better focus on the situation, a reasonable concern presented itself.

"Yeah, you're right," Lilly allowed. "But, even if this place is totally safe and secure, what are we going to do there? Sit around until we get the all-clear six months from now?"

"Maybe," Kane answered reasonably. "We can let other teams handle the threat."

"The FBI can handle that threat, especially given enough time. And I guarantee you won't be bored in your hideout. If you didn't know what you know now, what would your next steps be?" Mac asked.

"We still have the stuff from Barnett's house back at Murray Lane," Kane responded, "and now we have tons more paperwork from the site in Virginia. We were going to go through it at headquarters to see if we could discover who bankrolled this operation."

"Great minds think alike," Mac answered. "What if I asked you to do just that while you're hiding out?"

"How?" Kane asked. "All we have is paper. If we can't get back to Murray Lane, we'll never be able to electronically access anything beyond that."

The director's smile was reassuring and frightening at the same time. "Do either of you know where I got my start in government service?"

"No, sir," he admitted. "You were a section lead in the FBI when I got out of the academy, that's about it."

"I started with CIA, way back toward the end of the Cold War," he explained. "Serious shit—bugging secure buildings, wiretaps, the tech side of paramilitary information gathering, that kind of stuff."

"I'm not sure what that has to do with anything," Kane responded.

"In a nutshell, it means I know how to work around certain obstacles. In the back of my truck, you'll find those bank records from Barnett's place and the other shooting victims. Along with that, there's a desktop printer and two laptops with thumb drives that have the code generators needed to defeat most complex banking security protocols. Kane, you'll know what to do with them based on your cyber-security work. I'm thinking you guys take it all, go hide out, and find the answers we need. You're likely to learn more about our perp and the groups coming after you."

"I know the FBI has lead here," Kane protested, "but even you can't just take all that. The chain of evidence will be violated."

"I didn't break the chain—not really. I had agents collect it all and I took official possession of it. I'm just reviewing and vetting it—more accurately, I'm having two agents do that for me. These things take time, you know. The chain of evidence is being maintained and all is legal." He shrugged his shoulders.

Kane nodded. "And here I am thinking you were just a political appointee. You crafty son of a bitch."

"Thank you," Mac said, showing a little pride and satisfaction at having outmaneuvered Kane. "I'm just a suit following the rules, all of them." His demeanor turned serious once more. "But, having said that, we don't have time to waste. I need answers from that pile of shit in my truck, and I need them now."

Twenty minutes later, Kane and Lilly, slightly winded from lifting a bunch of heavy boxes, were cruising toward a destination to which Lilly was not yet privy.

Chapter 25 – Dangerous Spaces and Friendly Faces

The interior of Kane and Lilly's SUV was uncomfortably silent as they navigated I-95 through Baltimore and northeastern Maryland. Lilly replayed her mental breakdown over and over, but not only could she not figure out why she'd reacted with such histrionics, she could feel Kane judging the shit out of her. By the time they drove over the wide expanse of the Susquehanna River, Lilly couldn't take it anymore. "You might as well say it, Kane."

"Say what?" he asked in a casual, slightly disinterested tone.

"Don't screw around, Kane. I wigged out for no good reason back there, and you're pissed we have to hide out because of some irrational fear I didn't know I had."

"No, I'm not pissed at all. I'm actually pleased—for two reasons."

His demeanor irritated her as much as her own perceived weakness. "What the hell does that mean?" she snarled.

Kane kept his eyes on the road, but his next words were in his business voice. "It means that you ended up helping the situation. Regardless of why, your little hissy fit made me reconsider our goal. As you've noted in the past, I stayed true to form and was ready to attack the problem with guns blazing, but winning that battle might cost us the war. Your reaction made me pause because I had to settle you down, and that made me remember my safehouse. Going there to analyze all this data is the right play, even if we got there somewhat unconventionally."

Lilly was completely unprepared for that, but it made sense. She would have preferred to express herself through logical terms and make a solid case for restraint, but that wasn't the way it went down. Objectively, it was just as Kane said; her reaction led to the best course of action.

So why do I still feel like I failed? "Well, I guess that's good in the end, but what's the other reason?"

"Ah, that. It also made something break my way."

"What? How?"

Kane glanced at her sidelong, and his superciliousness smirk made it nearly impossible for Lilly to refrain from slapping him. "This whole time, you've been the one giving me good advice. Telling me to keep my cool with the higher-ups. Telling me to keep it together when we were about to be shit-canned. Showing me just how much of a jerk I'd been because you're female.

"But then you went and lost it over something that isn't really the disaster you made it out to be. And I had to square you away. Honestly, it feels good to know you're not perfect. When all this is over, we can figure out how to address your issue properly, but right now I get to gloat a little, and I can't say that bothers me one bit." His previously-arrogant grin had changed into a full-blown smile during his diatribe, and it convinced Lilly that, while he was having a little fun at her expense, he would help her with whatever had sent her wildly off-course. For the first time in a couple hours, she felt like herself again.

"Well, enjoy it, because this is the only win you're going to get."

***

"You want to tell me where this super-secret hideout is?" Lilly finally asked when Kane turned on to Route 40 just after going over the Delaware Bay.

"It's in Jersey, about an hour from here. I could tell you exactly where, but I doubt you've heard of it, so there's no point. And we are making a quick pit stop first."

"Well, of course. We need food and basics. I get it."

"Okay, two stops."

"Why two?" Lilly asked.

"I need to pick up a close personal friend of mine. He's going to join us at the safe house." He couldn't help but grin when he said it and, although Lilly eyed him suspiciously, his expression seemed to alleviate the worst of his partner's concern.

"Who? And why? And how do we know we can trust him?" she queried.

"Oh, he's *very* good at keeping secrets. In fact, he's incapable of revealing any sensitive information, even under the most intense interrogation. He lacks the vocabulary."

Lilly got it then. "I should have known you were a dog person."

"Guilty as charged."

"Lemme guess. It's a little foo-foo Pomeranian. Or a French Bulldog, right?" she teased.

"Yeah, something like that."

***

Doggone Right! Day Care was marked by a small sign at the start of a skinny gravel road. "Come on," he invited Lilly when he parked. "Don't you want to meet Jay?"

"Jay? Creative name," Lilly told him. She thought it hysterical that big bad Kane Logan would have such a cute little dog with such a bland name, but far be it for her to judge.

"I got him when he was a few months old, and that was his name. I didn't want to change it, so there you have it. I think it suits him."

"I'll bet. I just can't wait to snuggle him."

"Yeah, I'd love to see that." They entered the lobby.

There were two women behind the counter. "Mr. Logan!" one of them exclaimed.

"Hey, Brittany." He introduced Lilly quickly. "How's our guy?" Maryanna, the brunette, left the room to fetch the canine, setting off a cacophony of barks and yelps.

"Jay-bird misses you lots but he's having all kinds of fun anyway! I know how happy he'll be that you're back!"

"Jay-bird?" Lilly asked.

"That's my nickname for Jay," Brittany answered. "He's my favorite dog here. My Jay-bird," she recited almost musically. "You want this on your card?"

"Please. And can you add two bags of his normal food?"

"Sure thing. I'll have them brought out to your car." She disappeared behind a set of double doors.

"Wow," Lilly commented. "He seems like a popular little guy here."

"Oh, he's popular all right." He seemed like he was trying to reign in a case of the giggles, and that was making her nervous. She just couldn't put her finger on why.

Those thoughts died a quick death when she heard a pounding noise accompanied by the skitter of nails on tile. The doors slammed open to reveal a black grizzly bear with a long tail, a head the size of a beach ball, and huge fangs in a gaping mouth. It turned the corner and charged Kane like a bull.

"Jay!" Kane yelled, and the monster half-jumped, half-crashed into his arms with a force great enough to shove the agent back two steps. Jay yelped and licked his owner before getting down and doing a crazy butt-shimmy dance in a complete circle around Kane, barking and howling like he'd known no greater joy in his life.

Kane smacked him—hard—on his ass, and for a moment Lilly thought about protesting his abuse of this beast/pet, but Jay seemed to love it, backing up into Kane for more maltreatment. His owner obliged, sending him into a whooping growl of what sounded like pure ecstasy. This continued for several seconds, even after Brittany rejoined them to watch the insane reunion.

Then Jay noticed the other person in the room.

Lilly instinctively took a step back as Jay approached her. Even with his head lowered and his body in a submissive pose, he was intimidating. He sniffed her legs, and Lilly prayed it was an attempt to get to know her rather than see how much quality meat was on them. She must have met some basic criteria of his, because he jammed his enormous head into her hand and barked. She jumped.

"He wants you to scratch behind his ears," Kane explained.

"Anything you say—just don't let him eat me!" She pressed her fingertips into his head just behind his half-floppy ears and worked the flesh but was confused when Jay continued to push up into her fingers.

"Not like that," Kane said, disgust in his voice. "Use some force. Like you've got a pair."

Lilly, feeling the dense bones of his skull indicating this dog could likely take more abuse than she could dish out, dug her nails into the short fur and was rewarded with a rumbling moan that sounded like a two-stroke outboard engine stuck in reverse.

"That's better," Kane said, so she continued until Jay had his fill, at which time he resumed his happy dance around his owner. Kane enjoyed the reunion for a moment before the trio headed back to the truck. Jay jumped in the back seat.

"That was a dirty trick," she said without animosity.

"You like to make assumptions," he gloated. "Far be it from me to correct Her Highness."

Lilly leaned away from Jay's massive head as he licked her cheek affectionately from the back seat. "Oh, blow me," she told Kane, laughing.

***

Kane smiled as Jay finally settled down for the ride. He usually ran himself ragged at daycare, so he'd enjoy the rest. They headed west, back in the direction they'd come from, for about thirty minutes, moving out of the suburban Atlantic City area and into the rural farmlands of Cumberland County. After what seemed like forever, Kane made a left turn into a long, single-car-width trail with a mailbox and a sign that read "Pitted Field Farms" at the entrance. They drove for about a mile through the yellowish-brown of recently harvested crops until they came to a small, dilapidated house with a large open carport next to it. They got out and Jay took off to race about the property.

"You live here?" she asked.

"No. I live much closer to Jay's daycare, in Egg Harbor. My uncle left me this place just after I joined the agency, but I don't have any interest in farming, so I created an S-Corp through a trust and hired a farming manager. He hires crews, they manage and farm the land, and we split the profits. Essentially, I'm an absentee landlord, but for vegetables instead of people."

"Cool. What do you grow here?"

"Hell if I know. I think we rotate different crops each year—keeps the nutrients in the soil or some damned thing. Mr. Foley is the farming manager. I let him run this place, and we make money every year, so I don't ask.

Lilly shook her head. "How cynically enterprising of you. But why are you so confident that no one will be able to trace this back to you?"

"I did a lot of work to hide my name. I made the paper trail purposefully serpentine, enough so that only someone like you could trace it. Call it paranoia, but I always suspected I'd need a place like this."

"I knew you were a geek," Lilly said behind a little chuckle before her voice turned serious. "But I guess that's a good thing, now that we've got a safe hideaway."

"It's a fair trade—you do my science homework and I show you the cool places in the woods where we can hang out and drink beer." Jay raced back up to Kane to report that the area was secure with a single bark. "Let's get all this shit inside and get started."

***

As small as the cabin looked from the outside, the internal dimensions made it feel like a World War I submarine, with one tiny kitchen, a claustrophobic living room, one bathroom where you could brush your teeth while sitting on the toilet, and two bedrooms barely big enough for a twin bed each made up the layout.

And it was a mess. Dust that probably dated back to the Hoover presidency coated every substance, and now Lilly understood why Kane had insisted on buying so many cleaning products at the Acme in Vineland. She was far from a neat freak, but figured there were more weaponized strains of bacteria on the kitchen counter alone than the military had stored at Fort Detrick. Before she cracked open a single box of bank records, she grabbed a roll of industrial-strength paper towels, a spray bottle, a bucket of Pine-Sol, and started scrubbing. Using a divide-and-conquer method, they got the house to a livable state in about ninety minutes.

Lilly collapsed on one of the two chairs in the living room which, along with the loveseat, comprised the furnishing for the room. "There's nothing I love more than starting highly complex and critical case research after cleaning a house, getting no sleep, being in a to-the-death fight with my partner, driving six hours, having my boss telling me half the world is coming to kill me, having a mental breakdown, and unloading twenty boxes chock-full of heavy paper."

"Good, 'cause you got five more minutes before we get started."

"Five minutes? Jesus!"

"Democracy cannot wait, agent," Kane taunted. His head lolled back as he spoke.

Lilly rolled her eyes. "Oh my god, Kane, shut up. I'm in no shape or frame of mind for a pep talk from Uncle Sam."

"Well, maybe this will help motivate you." He grabbed one of the laptops and started tapping on the keyboard. "Or at least make you feel a little safer." He held it up.

Lilly saw an array of eight scenes, each showing one-half of each side of the property border. The images were grainy black and white, but they would certainly show anything big enough to be a threat. "Not bad. You've got the perimeter covered pretty well. But who's going to watch it? Jay?" The enormous canine looked up at the mention of his name but, neither smelling nor seeing food, lost interest and let his head sink back down on his paws.

"When anything close to the size of a man passes through the frame, I get an audible alert on my phone and through the system."

Lilly nodded her approval. "What did you say before about being paranoid?"

"You're only paranoid until someone does something to you. Then you're a progressive thinker who anticipates issues." He smiled crookedly. "And right now this progressive mind says we need some coffee. How about I get that started while you set up your organizational structure."

"Deal." Kane left the room and Lilly started her computer, picked up one of the blank pads that Mac had thoughtfully supplied, and lifted the lid off the first box. There was enough information here to occupy a team of forensic auditors for a month, but they didn't have anything near that kind of time. *Well, pressure makes diamonds.*

Fifteen minutes later, when Kane returned with two mugs of coffee, she was beginning to regret her cavalier attitude. Just a cursory glance at one pile of documents suggested far more hours of work than she cared to calculate.

Kane set the mugs on the tiny end table and looked at Lilly's notepad. "What kind of organization is this? It looks like my four-year-old nephew set this up."

"Hey," Lilly answered, a tiny edge on her voice, "this is what I've got so far. Give me some time."

"Sorry, you're right. Tell me what you need—but maybe don't have any coffee, okay? You seem tense."

"I'll give you tense," Lilly responded, taking Kane's joke for the stress reliever it was. She took a sip of the brew. "Yuck. This is like mud."

"The agency isn't paying us to sleep, so I made it strong."

"Strong enough to cut with a knife." She looked into the cup before changing the subject. "I need you to start reverse-searching the deposits I mark. Find where they came from, match the numbers, do your best to get a personal ID, and collate your ass off."

Kane rolled his eyes. "And I thought this was going to be boring."

***

So, this routing number is 383 757 185. Or wait, is that the account number? Kane blinked and shook his head. The numbers and letters were starting to run together like Salvador Dali had painted them, and exhaustion was hurting his focus. Except for one break to feed Jay and let him out, and another to wolf down an "Italian" sub (with fucking *mayonnaise* on it!), he'd been going nonstop for almost seven hours. Combined with the total lack of sleep the previous night and all the stress and travel, he wasn't going to make it much longer.

Lilly appeared to be a different matter entirely. Armed with three different color highlighters and a regular pen, she was churning through bank statements like their mere presence was offensive to her. Every document was either decorated with a colored stripe or notated on a pad before ending up in one of the 100 or so piles she had created on every surface. With so much information, sooner or later he was going to incorrectly enter a critical number or some other pertinent fact and miss the one lead they needed.

"Uncle, Lilly, uncle. Holy crap, how can you keep going? Are you a cyborg?"

She looked up at him, and it was clear her mind was so deep in the data that Kane's intrusion was unwelcome and confusing. It took a second for her to process Kane's words.

"Sorry. I get like this, but you're right. We need a break." She made a final notation on the document she was holding, dropped it in one of the piles, and then came over to plop down next to Kane on the loveseat.

"Did you get anywhere?" Kane asked, not sure he'd be able to understand her answer.

"Kind of. Lots of connections, money moves disguised to avoid the SEC reporting requirements, but I can't find a clear source. Not yet, anyway."

"Well, I wouldn't worry too much," he answered. "We've got at least ten more boxes full of exciting bank statements, checks, and receipts. You'll find it."

"If it's there," Lilly countered. "Remember, we have no idea why all this shit was where we could get our hands on it. What's to say someone didn't stuff these boxes to throw us off the trail, to make us spend time and effort looking for something that isn't there?"

"Do you think that's the case?"

"No. Too much work for an assumed payoff." She shifted gears. "What did you find?"

"I have no idea. All I can tell you is I have fourteen folders on this system with about four gigs of data in each. I need you to make it make sense."

"Any names?"

"Yeah, lots. A few showed up more frequently. I've got them separated."

"I knew you were good for something, Kane. Once we're all done, you can run the names and I'll try to find some pattern in the numbers. That's what—" Her phone rang, startling them both. She pulled it out. "It's a D.C. number," she told him before answering. "Agent Alexander."

Kane couldn't hear the other side of the call, but Lilly instantly looked confused. "That's okay, sir. We're burning the midnight oil trying to find some leads." She looked at him and mouthed *Voight Stafford* to him. He tried to lean in to hear what Armstrong's chief of staff had to say, but Lilly shooed him away and stood up.

"No, sir, he's in the shower...I see. Are you sure we shouldn't both be part of that conversation? I understand, but you have to admit that's highly unusual, sir—especially considering you are not an agent or part of the agency in any way. Yes, sir, that does make a difference. I see. Well, since the order comes from him, I'll be there at 6:30. Thank you."

She hung up the phone but stared at it for a minute, like she doubted that the conversation had ever happened. "That's some weird shit."

"What happened? Was that really Stafford?"

"Yeah." She sat down, still clearly bewildered. "He wants to meet me—and only me—tomorrow morning at DNC headquarters in Washington at 6:30, and it wasn't phrased like a request."

"He can't give you an order," Kane protested.

"He claims it came from Brent Douglas."

"That doesn't make sense. And why just you?"

She shrugged. "No idea. That's why I said you were in the shower. He said he wanted to be sure we could speak privately, and I thought it was best to hear what he had to say."

"Good idea on your part, but still—he has to understand that you would tell me about this."

"Stafford said I should tell you this is an emergency about another case that requires my presence, and that you can call Douglas if you want to confirm."

Kane rolled his eyes. "Stafford probably thinks Douglas can intimidate me." This new issue brought him back up to full speed mentally. "This is damn unusual. Why would Stafford do this? He knows I'd question it."

"Well," Lilly noted, "first we have to understand what Douglas is really thinking—if he's even involved, which we don't know yet. It changes the calculus here."

"I don't think it does," Kane said after a minute. "There are zero reasons for Douglas or Stafford to talk to you separately from me. Now, if Stafford is lying and using his name as leverage to get you to meet him, he clearly doesn't understand basic agency procedure, but he's not that dumb. He'd know we'd consider this so unusual that we'd likely refuse it—or at least confirm it. Director Schultz doesn't know shit and doesn't do shit. Stafford might think we won't go to him, but he'd be an idiot to think we wouldn't seek confirmation from Douglas. Far too risky. For that reason, I say Douglas is at least marginally involved."

"Then why not have Douglas call us?"

"Douglas and I had words, so he thinks I'll tell him to screw off. You're younger, so he might think he can intimidate you."

"I'm not in your court yet on that one, but for the sake of argument let's go with that. Stafford is an arrogant dick, but he has a vested interest in us solving this case. Maybe he has info that will help the investigation but doesn't trust you?" Lilly theorized.

"I'd say maybe to that, except he's still got his head so far up the president's ass they can eat the same cheeseburger at the same time. Why not share his info at the highest level first?"

"Or maybe he wants to be in control. Then he can look like the hero if we do solve this."

"Fuck," Kane cursed. "We're speculating like rookies. We don't know shit."

"Let's reset from what we think we know to what we do know. If I follow the plan, I'll leave here by myself real early tomorrow. We're both way short on sleep, so our judgment might be impaired. I'll drive to Washington, have a meeting about who knows what, and I'll return here probably by noon. You'll stay here and work. What are the definitive takeaways from that?"

Kane was stymied by her question. Opponents, even stupid ones, followed a set of rules that had some kind of logic, but he couldn't find a theme here. He felt like he was playing Hearts and led with a club, only to have the other guy put a live chicken on the table and declare victory. *What would this move accomplish?* Nothing. Except...

"It separates us."

"What? You mean physically?"

"I do. Separately, we're softer targets." The advantages of working as partners in almost any dangerous or emergency endeavor were well-documented—ideas flowed faster, dangers were spotted easier, courses of action were validated, and so on. Most critically, together they could cover each other's backs. Only the rarest of loners worked better by themselves and, despite their occasionally contentious battles, he and Lilly were synched up like they'd been partners for a decade.

"That makes more sense than anything else we've come up with," Lilly agreed. "Question is, what do we do about it?"

Kane got up, wincing at the pain in his leg. "If you go, we are both in greater danger, but we have an opportunity to figure out whatever game they're playing. That danger is mitigated by the unlikelihood that they know where we are, so it's not like they're sitting at the end of the road waiting to take us out."

"Good point," she added. "We can't be in that much danger if they can't find us."

"Yeah, but they'll find you. That's a big risk."

"But, if I don't go, then we still don't know what's going on and we've tipped our hand that we're worried about something," Lilly concluded. "That's giving away any advantage we might have."

"So the smart money says you go."

Lilly looked at the low ceiling with partially fabricated exasperation. "Somehow I knew we were going to reach that conclusion."

"Hey," Kane told her, "you can't argue with the data."

"I know, but every time you review the data I seem to lose sleep. Why is that?"

"Luck of the Irish?" Kane quipped.

"I'm not Irish."

"I wasn't talking about you."

"Clearly. I better get some shut-eye. I've got a long drive coming up in," she glanced at her watch, "about six hours."

***

"Anything?" Doyle asked Reagan. They were getting close to the D. C. metro area, and Ethan was getting impatient.

"Zip," he answered, staring at a laptop. "They ain't in the area."

"Expand the search," he ordered his lieutenant. "I doubt they found the bug, so that means they have to be somewhere close."

"I'm already out to 100 miles," Reagan protested.

"Then go out to 200! We are going to find these fuckers. They're around here somewhere!"

Reagan blew out his breath and widened his search.

Sunday, November 5

Two Days Before the Election

Chapter 26 – One Battle, Two Battlefields

Lilly kept the headlights off as she turned out of the driveway and headed west for several miles. If anyone had been watching for her, they would have been hard-pressed to see the little black Nissan Versa they'd rented in the dark in such a rural setting. Only when she neared the tiny borough of Woodstown and risked dealing with traffic did she flip them on.

Her drive was uneventful. There weren't many cars out this early, so she made good time. But her tension increased as she neared D.C. *What would they ask of her?* Lilly knew only that she had no idea what to expect, except that she'd likely have to think on her feet to turn the situation to her advantage, if that was even possible.

She parked in the South Capitol Street lot and entered DNC Headquarters, the same building where she'd met Kane and started this amazing adventure. That was only seven days ago, but she felt she'd aged a year in that time. The security guard verified the appointment and escorted her to Stafford's outer office. It was empty; not even the receptionist had arrived yet.

Within a minute, the door opened, revealing Stafford and Douglas. She greeted them both noncommittally. "Agent, thank you for coming," Stafford said, clearly trying to moderate his pretentious tone, but it didn't work. He came across as a member of the Royal family trying to talk to a filthy peasant commoner.

"No problem, sir. I'm sure this is absolutely critical." She took a look around the office. It was pretty standard stuff for a high-ranking political appointee, with a nice mahogany desk, a low conference table for informal meetings, and numerous bookshelves. Like nearly every high-level executive in the Washington political scene, Stafford had a wall behind his desk replete with awards, certifications, pictures with VIPs, and various other items meant to impress and intimidate the person facing them.

"Please have a seat." He gestured to the low coffee table, and Douglas brought over a tray with a silver coffee service and three elegant cups.

"Thank you, sir." By choosing the conference table and not his desk, as well as being served by her boss, they were trying to put her off her game. To test how far that went, she looked over at that wall before sitting and focused on one shelf with numerous personal pictures. "*Simpsons* fan, Dr. Stafford?"

"Excuse me?"

"Well, if I'm not mistaken, those pictures on the middle shelf are you with Hank Azaria, Harry Shearer, Yeardley Smith, Nancy Cartwright, and several of Dan Castellaneta. They are most of the Simpsons voice actors, so I have to assume you're a fan of the show."

Stafford appeared thrown by the question but recovered with a smile that seemed unnatural and forced. "Guilty as charged, agent. The show, especially the earlier seasons when it was really good, is a silly little stress reliever. I've watched it for years. I need that belly laugh once in a while, which I'm sure you can understand."

"Oh, absolutely. Who's your favorite character?"

"Krusty the Clown, by far. I love how cynical he is, considering his *raison d'etre* is to entertain children, even though he barely tolerates them otherwise. I think it speaks a bit to our current political system, don't you?"

Lilly nodded, not surprised that his statement equated the candidates and elected officials to a clown and the voters to whom they pandered as children. *How amazingly condescending of you.* She smiled and nodded as if tacitly agreeing. "Fascinating analogy, sir. And that explains all the shots of Castellaneta." He was the voice of Krusty.

"Cartoons and relevant analogies aside," Douglas spoke up, "we are on a bit of a schedule here." *Hello, Mr. Bad Cop.*

"Yes, of course," Stafford said, losing whatever personability the brief discussion had given him. "Agent, Deputy Director Douglas and I want to make one thing very clear."

"And that is?"

"Your work, your efforts, your conclusions, everything you've done regarding this unique case, all have been superlative in every way. Nothing we are going to discuss here should be construed as a denigration of those efforts."

"Thank you, sir. But that suggests there are problems with the investigation."

"I won't mince words," Douglas said. "The problems are with Agent Logan."

"How's that, sir? He's been nothing but an exceptional partner and the consummate professional."

"It might seem that way, but everything I've heard and seen from the two of you points to you developing the leads, recognizing the connections, and setting the strategies. Kane is tagging along and sensationalizing things to make himself appear relevant. I'm sure that, by now, you realize Logan is not exactly someone in good standing with the agency."

They do want to separate us. Kane had been right, but in the wrong way. Douglas, with Stafford's help, wanted to drive a wedge between them, to turn them against each other, to sell one out and wreck their partnership which would destroy the credibility of their investigation *and* end Kane's career once and for all. *But why?*

"Pardon me, but I don't think you're cognizant of the great work Agent Logan has done. It's not just about who connects the dots. Without Kane, his experience, his conjecture, his analysis of my ideas, and the basic discussions we've had, we wouldn't have made the progress we did." She turned to face Douglas more directly. "Sir, as an agent yourself, you have to recognize the value of collaboration."

"I do," Douglas reassured her. "But I also see a veteran agent using that collaboration to take advantage of a young, fairly inexperienced agent for his personal benefit."

"I don't see that." She let the edge in her voice come through; she was playing them for a reaction, and acting emotionally would reinforce their belief that she *was* young and easily influenced. It didn't hurt that Douglas's comment pissed her off.

"Agent Alexander," Stafford interrupted, "but you are the only one who doesn't. I agree with Agent Douglas, and both Director MacMurray and the president concur. You might want to trust our 140 years or so of accumulated experience on this. You have two law enforcement officials and two lawyers in that mix." The president had been a prosecutor long before he entered politics.

Lilly tried a new tack to see what response she'd get. "For the sake of argument, let's assume this is happening the way you say it is. How or why does that impact the results of our investigation?"

"Whose decision was it to release Scott Barnett after he shot up Logan's car, agent?"

"Kane made that call. I agreed with it."

"And who decided to leave the camp in New Hampshire rather than call in a team to arrest potential suspects?"

"Again, that was Kane's, but that was because we feared for our lives."

"Tell me which of you made the connection between Park's assassination and the other five assassinations."

"Sir, that was me, but we all know that's merely because of my gift of memory."

"And Kane also presented the information you developed to the president and the ranking executives of the FBI and Secret Service. How convenient."

"I was a bit nervous. Kane knew that, so he took the lead. He presented our findings accurately."

"And how many times did Agent Logan take action without getting either pre-authorization or reporting in?"

"Look," Lilly said sharply. "This is an incredibly fast-moving case with national security implications. We do not have the time to give everyone and their brother's uncle an update every time we take a crap... sir."

"Agent, it's admirable that you are trying to defend your partner, but when the president asks for frequent progress reports, you give them to him." To Lilly's ear, Douglas sounded aggravated with her insistence. *Good.*

"Would the president like to know what color socks I put on this morning, or would he like to let us get things done so he can announce an arrest has been made?" She turned to Stafford. "And you, sir. Do you want to catch the people that nearly killed your friend and candidate, or know where we are every second of the day?"

"We want both," Stafford responded, "and we're getting neither. That makes President Sharpe look the fool." *Why the hell is he worried about Sharpe looking stupid?* She pushed a little harder.

"With all due respect, sir, neither of us answer to you, nor are we obligated to follow your direction."

Stafford eyes flashed what looked to Lilly like anger, but Douglas was the first to respond. "You do answer to me, Agent, both of you, and I am in alignment with Dr. Stafford's position."

With his concession to Stafford's authority, Douglas had just exposed his belly to him. *He's not in control here.*

Stafford nodded in agreement with Douglas's supplication. "Therefore, when the president asks for the same thing I want, that qualifies as both. And Agent Logan ignored those orders save one time."

Douglas picked up the narrative. "Agent," he said in a voice tinged with weary finality, "all this points to a narcissistic agent who is more focused on advancing his career than solving this case and using you to do it. You are an incredibly intelligent person. I can't believe you don't see the pattern."

Yeah, I see a pattern—of lies.

***

"Got a hit!" Reagan said, the relief in his voice apparent. The way Doyle had been riding him the last hour, he was beginning to worry for his safety.

"About time. Where?"

"Somewhere in Jersey, way down south, near the Delaware Bay."

"Are you sure? What the fuck would they be doing down there?"

Reagan's voice matched Doyle's. "You didn't ask me for an analysis of why they're down there. You asked me to find the bug, and I did that."

"Okay, okay," Doyle conceded. "After what they went through, they might be hiding out." He jerked the truck in the direction he knew Route 95 to be. It would probably take another three hours to get there, which would make for a tired team, but Kane and Lilly would be sleeping when they arrived. With a little luck, two double taps at close range would satisfy the need for revenge that burned in Doyle's belly.

He would, of course, wake them first. They needed to know who they had crossed, and why that had been a mistake.

***

Lilly sat with her elbows on her knees, her head sagging in despair after hearing examples of Kane's transgressions. They were, at the least, stretching the truth. Using what she knew of the man, she felt comfortable calling them outright lies, and she would not fall for them.

But that would remain her little secret.

She looked up, eyes pained. "Are you sure? I hear what you're saying, but every instinct I had told me that he was on the right side."

Stafford reached out and patted Lilly's forearm in a very paternal, very patronizing manner. "Agent, I'm slightly out of my depth here, but I'm sure you know when a suspect or a criminal is lying to you, right?"

"Of course. That's my job." *It's funny you don't see the irony in that.*

"And it's Agent Logan's job too, right?"

"Sure."

"And, with his extensive experience, he knows everything you know and then some?"

"I... guess so."

Douglas took over. "Kane gaslighted you. You aren't the first person he's done it to, but with your help we can make you the last. The question is, will you do what has to be done?"

Lilly forced a stunned appearance. "You know Kane saved my life, right?" That wasn't exactly true, but truth seemed to be what you made it right now. "And you want me to betray him. Do you understand what you're asking of me?"

"I do," the deputy director answered. "Sometimes agents have to make hard choices. You have a doozie in front of you right now. I'm asking you to put our country, our electoral system, and our way of life ahead of the pride of a man who is more concerned with personal gain than his oath to uphold the Constitution."

Laying it on pretty thick, aren't you? "I don't want him hurt or disgraced. Discharge him, but I won't participate unless I have your assurances as gentlemen that he will be treated properly." She almost choked as the word "gentlemen" came from her mouth. "Not negotiable."

The men nodded to each other and Douglas responded. "Agent, your loyalty to Kane, despite what you now know, is why we felt comfortable approaching you this way. You have a bright future with the agency."

"Doesn't change the fact that I feel awful." That wasn't entirely a lie. *What if I had to do this for real? Are these the kind of people I want to work for?* That was a question that she would address another day.

"I know you do. And you have my word that Kane will be just fine." Douglas gave her a smile that was far too bright and merry considering the circumstances. "Now, do we have an agreement?"

Lilly looked at both men, using the harshest stare she could manage. They were full of shit, but she knew it. *Advantage: Lilly.*

"Yes. What do you need me to do?"

***

Kane watched the ethereal shape of the car disappear into the darkness as it headed toward the road, wondering if he'd made the right call. Sure, it all made sense in the living room, but now he was less certain.

He sighed and scratched Jay's head. "C'mon, bud. Let's get some more rest." Jay gave a little whimper indicating he did not wish to turn away from the car. "I know, but she'll be fine." Jay twisted his head and raised his floppy ears, questioning that statement.

"Yes, she will. She's a big girl," Kane protested. "Stop looking at me like that." He caught a glint of red as Lilly tapped the brakes before turning onto the main road.

"She's on her way. Can we go in now?" Jay took one more look behind him before reluctantly following Kane back to the house. Kane was forever amazed by the way Jay seemed to fully understand what he was thinking and feeling, even if he didn't.

Worry and concern notwithstanding, he needed a few more hours of rest if he was going to effectively do his job. He checked that his camera system was still working, kicked off his shoes, and slid back under the covers. Jay, with only one human in the house now, was not interested in the cold, hard floor between the two bedrooms.

"Yeah, c'mon." He patted the bed and Jay jumped up, pushing Kane slightly out of the way as he curled up at the foot of the mattress. Once the dog established his territory, Kane drifted off without another thought.

It seemed only a second had passed before his eyes popped open. It was still dark in the small room, but he could just make out Jay's rear end, tail elevated in full alert, in the hallway. He was about to call out to him to stop worrying about the damn raccoons or chipmunks or whatever was outside when his laptop let out a series of five intermittently spaced chirps.

Uh-oh. He tapped the mouse and saw a notification that one of the cameras had picked up movement and had been trying to alert him every ten seconds. He clicked on the appropriate camera view and rewound to see a blacked-out pickup truck slow as it passed his driveway and then pull to a stop. Shortly afterward, five figures exited the vehicle to form one group of two and another of three. The teams separated, with the team of two going north and the larger one moving south before approaching the house.

Kane checked the time stamp while pulling on his shoes—this all happened about two minutes ago, meaning they could likely traverse the distance to the house in about four more minutes if they were so inclined. Thinking Kane and Lilly to be asleep, they would not be slowed by caution or concern of making a little noise.

The first thing he had to do was put Jay in his bedroom. Whoever his uninvited guests were, Kane doubted they were unarmed, and if any of them saw Jay coming at them with those dinosaur-sized fangs at the ready, they'd shoot first. Jay didn't want to go, but Kane used his (barely) superior strength to pull him into the room and shut the door.

He grabbed one of the ARs from its case and screwed the suppressor onto it. It would reduce the sound of the shots a bit, maybe enough to introduce confusion for a second. With luck, dropping a couple of them might encourage the others to beat a hasty retreat.

Kane army-crawled to the front window, his leg howling as he dragged the wound over the uneven wood. Poking his nose up to the slightly open window he saw the moon hanging in the western sky, illuminating the broad stretch of open ground just enough to allow him to visually track them both. He decided the smaller group to his left was first.

It was harder to make out the shapes of the individuals through the scope, but their quick motion helped. Had they been stealthier, he'd have had to wait much longer before picking his shot. But someone barely 300 yards away moving like he was hurrying to catch a bus was the very definition of a dead man walking the second Kane put his sights on him. Letting out his breath, he squeezed the trigger.

The crack of the shot was loud enough that he wished he'd worn ear protection, but such details had no bearing on the flight of the bullet, which put the target on his back and kept him there. His partner, stunned and disoriented, looked around frantically for a second—long enough for Kane to shift his aim slightly and eliminate that threat.

Purposely ignoring the fact that he'd just ended two lives, he followed his training and pivoted his body, shifting to the larger group to the south. As expected, the second shot had convinced them that a gun had been fired, causing them to drop to the ground and disappear from sight.

Got to get them moving. Not anticipating a hit but hoping for one, he took another shot in the general area where he'd last seen the group. There was no way to be sure, but the dearth of movement and noise meant he'd likely drilled a tiny hole in the ground and nothing more. The stillness, however, was more telling in that it suggested these people had training enough to not panic and run despite being shot at. That made them pros, and he was outnumbered.

A small-caliber bullet cracked against the house. It didn't sound too close, meaning it was as much of a let's-see-what-happens shot as Kane's was, but it told him they knew he was in the house. *Time to move.*

He pulled back, being careful to stay below window level while crawling out the back door. A second shot whined near one side of the house, followed by a third at the other side. *Dammit.* Their strategy was obvious. Fire rounds on both sides of the house, make sure Kane knew he was exposed if he tried to escape in either direction, and use a pincer move to corner and eliminate him.

He needed information. Inching to the corner of the house, he laid his rifle on its side to keep as low a profile as possible and contorted his head to look through the scope. Doing so was a pain in the ass, but as soon as he got a visual, he realized his efforts were worth it.

He saw nothing until a flash from a barrel confirmed the location of at least one of them. Surprisingly, he was aiming a pistol, not a rifle, in his direction.

A pistol at a couple hundred yards? That was idiotic. Such shots were possible, but hardly practical, especially in the dark. Why not bring a rifle?

'Cause they didn't expect to need one.

These people hadn't come here expecting a gun battle. They expected Kane and Lilly to be asleep, to break into their rooms and put a round right between their eyes. They'd either not brought long guns or left them in their truck and now couldn't get to them. This wasn't a game they'd expected or anticipated.

But they should have been coming in a lot harder. They still had a three-to-one advantage with Kane pinned to a fixed location; basic infantry tactics said to push forward, hem your opponent in, and finish him off. Why weren't they?

They don't know Lilly's not here. They were looking for another person they would not find. That would make them cautious and tentative, and he could exploit that.

He rose to one knee, poking just enough of himself around the corner to get a clear line of sight. Several more shots rang out; none were close to him, but he didn't dawdle, as a lucky shot was not out of the question. It was hard picking out the prone figure against the dark ground out at that distance through the scope, but Kane kept his other eye open enough to see a flare of light as his opponent fired once more, marking his location like a lighthouse. He squeezed once, and all movement in the area ceased.

He pulled back as soon as he confirmed the impact. Taking cover by pressing himself against the ancient asphalt shingles of the house, he looked for any motion in every direction. Seeing none, he sprinted as quickly as he could on his injured leg to the corner of the open carport, where he did more reconnaissance on the front of the house.

Nothing.

Not good. There was no telling if he was in someone else's sights right now, and that put him back on the defensive. Kane moved a few more steps until he was leaning on the front passenger-side door of the SUV. Even though he could see at least half of the property, there was no movement.

A gentle *snap* sounded behind him. Turning as slowly as he could, he saw a man's head through the glass of the truck. Kane froze, but the man appeared to be looking behind the house and ignoring the carport. Seeing nothing untoward, he took a few steps around the corner. Kane lowered himself to one knee, drew his pistol, and waited as the figure cleared the back of the vehicle, still staring directly ahead.

On his first day of Marine Boot Camp at Parris Island, his senior drill instructor had asked (screamed) a simple question; what gets most Marines killed? The raw recruits came up with all kinds of answers, but not the correct one. "All right, I'll tell you maggots. It's bein' stupid. And I hate Marines that get dead because they did something stupid."

His DI would have hated this guy.

Kane raised his weapon, lined up his sites, and dispatched intruder number four with a single round to the side of the head. One left.

But where to find him? Kane decided it was time to employ a little psychological warfare. After all, he'd put down eighty percent of the attacking force by himself; the remaining guy had to be shitting his pants or very angry. He returned to the back of the house. "Hey, asshole!" he yelled. "I took out most of your team and I'm not even sweating! Can you at least make me work a little?!"

The response was not as interesting as the voice. "I'm not so easy a kill as they were, Kane!"

"Ethan Doyle! I'm flattered—you seem to have developed quite a crush on me!" *Shit.* He moved into the house to confuse Doyle, at least briefly.

But being here felt wrong. Inside, he was trapped, limited, cornered. He needed to be outside, to move, to run if needed or attack if possible. *Back or front?* He'd last yelled from the back. Was Doyle headed that way, or already there waiting to ambush him? Or was he out front? Whatever else he was, Doyle was no coward, nor was he stupid. He would neither back down nor make a dumb mistake.

His instincts told him to stay mobile, and that the range no longer called for a rifle. He removed the magazine and set it aside in favor of pulling his pistol from its holster. When he opened the front door he found himself looking into the eyes of Ethan Doyle.

They stared at each other for a nanosecond that lasted forever, like a time-compressed old west showdown, where the first man to move gave away the advantage. Kane didn't know who took the initiative, but they both tried to block the other's gun hand, sending both weapons flying to the ground without a shot being fired.

Doyle wasn't as tall as Kane, but he was more solidly built, allowing him to use his leverage and push Kane against the door jam. Both men threw a couple of poorly aimed punches that did little damage, but the forces involved in the wrestling match were wearing Kane and his damaged leg down rapidly. His opponent did not appear nearly as winded as he felt.

Trying to push himself off the house, Kane lost his footing, giving Doyle the advantage he needed. He used Kane's momentum to toss his upper body to the left and over his leg, dropping him on his back. Doyle scanned the area, and when he found and picked up one of the guns, Kane knew he was finished; his opponent was several steps away. All he had to do was aim and pull the trigger.

The crack of splintering wood reached his ears just as Doyle was bringing the weapon to bear. Thudding footfalls and a roar that could have come from any of the three heads of Cerberus identified the approaching maelstrom as Jay. Kane barely had time to ponder why he'd ever thought a mere door would stop his dog before Doyle turned.

Kane caught a glimpse of his obsidian friend in mid-air, maw open, fangs ready, but what struck him was the fury in Jay's eyes. He'd never seen him so animated, so enraged, so ready to do battle.

Doyle got his gun arm around just as Jay's front paws pounded into his chest. He heard the gun discharge, followed by the high-pitched yelp of a dog in pain and the *oomph!* of air being driven out of a man's lungs. Both bodies thumped to the ground.

Kane rolled over to see both Doyle and Jay lying in heaps about five feet apart. Doyle was moving, trying to rise, but Jay was still. A scorching fear that turned to white-hot fury ripped through his body and set it afire.

"MOTHERFUCKER! YOU SHOT MY DOG!" Forgetting his leg and ignoring his exhaustion, he sprung to his feet like a gymnast, grabbing Doyle's collar and yanking him up in one move. *"YOU SHOT JAY!!! YOU BASTARD!"* Doyle appeared to be getting his wind back, but he was in no condition to fight or even defend himself.

That didn't matter to Kane. Holding his adversary with one arm, he cocked the other back and used every muscle in his body to deliver hundreds of pounds of pressure almost entirely through the first two knuckles of his fist to Doyle's face. He felt bone crunch and splinter.

But that wasn't enough, not for Kane, not for his blood-lust revenge. He lost count of how many punches he threw, but only when Doyle's shirt tore loose from Kane's grip and his limp body collapsed against the house did the agent realize his opponent was dead. He spit on Doyle's body as the pain from his leg reintroduced itself, and then he remembered the reason for his attack.

Kane lunged for the porch light, flipping it on before diving to the ground to see how badly hurt his friend was. To his partial relief, Jay's eyes were moving and he was breathing heavily, but those eyes appeared unfocused and he was still lying on his side, signs that something wasn't right. He laid a hand on Jay's shoulder.

"It's okay, boy, I gotcha. Where ya hurt?" He started running his fingers gingerly over Jay's body, hoping to find the entry wound, but nothing materialized. He didn't want to roll Jay over, fearing hurting him worse, but he knew he had to. Before he could, he noticed something shiny on Jay's head just in front of his left ear. He touched it. It was blood from an opening about an inch long.

No. Not a headshot. Kane could barely stand to probe the wound and discover how bad it was, but he needed to know if his pal had any chance, so he did the unthinkable. Using his pinky, he pushed through the cut as gently as he could but stopped in confusion when his finger failed to enter more than a millimeter. Jay yelped and looked up at him.

Confused, Kane pulled his hand away. Unsure of his next option, he looked around a bit helplessly and saw his gun, the one Doyle had picked up, lying on the ground with blood on the butt of the magazine, bringing it all together. Upon hearing Jay's battle roar, Doyle had swung around in terror, leading with his gun to shoot the beast, but instead struck Jay with the butt of the weapon hard enough to break the skin. The impact caused him to discharge a round, making Kane assume Jay had been shot.

"Is that all, Jay? Just a cut on the head?" he asked, his voice shaky and tinged with relief that he wasn't sure was appropriate yet. Jay's eyes seemed to clear, and he got to his feet a little slowly. Turning in a complete but wobbly circle, he shook his head, sneezed and, after a pause, wagged his tail and pressed his enormous cranium into Kane's chest—his go-to move when he wanted to be petted.

Kane complied instantly, simultaneously rubbing Jay's muscular torso but finding no other injury. Still, a head injury was a head injury, so he remained worried about the dog's health. "Good boy, but we're still going to the vet. Right now." He earned himself a look as he used the dreaded v-word, but Kane didn't care. "Yup. Let's go." He made to stand but was overcome with emotion, grabbing his big goon buddy around the neck, unable to stop the tears that overwhelmed him. The canine allowed the embrace for a few seconds before twisting his head slightly, delivering a sidelong lick of affection to comfort Kane. "Thanks for that, boy," he said as the emotion passed, "but we're still going." Jay grumbled but followed his owner a bit unsteadily toward the carport after Kane retrieved his weapon.

Kane had to help Jay get in the front seat, something he normally didn't need to do, making him sure of the need for the trip. Despite that, he hesitated. There were five dead bodies —that he created—and numerous weapons scattered about his property, and it was irresponsible for him to just leave such things unsupervised. With a curse, he placed a call.

"New Jersey State Police, Bridgeton Barracks, Sergeant Gutierrez speaking."

"Sergeant, this is Kane Logan." Years before, he'd introduced himself as a matter of professional courtesy to the local and state police.

"Yes, what can I do for you?" He sounded impatient.

We've got ourselves a new guy. "I'm a Secret Service agent, and I can tell you about those shots that everyone's calling in about."

That did the trick. "What do you have for me, Agent?"

Kane gave him a brief rundown of what had happened and what they would find upon arrival, including a request to not touch the papers in the dwelling. He heard the trooper sending instructions to his cars. "Thank you, agent. We should have a unit to you shortly. Please wait there for a debrief."

Kane expected that. "Sergeant, I'll wait for his arrival to maintain the continuity of the crime scene, but I have an injured member of my team and will be taking him for medical care as soon as your man gets here." He crafted the phrase carefully to ensure the species of the "injured member" remained vague. Who knew if this guy was a dog person?

"Agent," Gutierrez said without a ton of conviction, "I can have an ambulance there in a minute or two. Can we take that route instead?"

Kane played the card the trooper would have to respect. "If it was a member of your team, would you wait?"

That worked. "Please get back to the scene ASAP, sir."

"Will do, Sergeant." He terminated the call just as a unit screamed into his driveway. Kane pulled forward slowly to meet the trooper, his own emergency lights flashing, and pointed out where he should look. Without a second thought, he floored the truck and turned east to the nearest veterinary hospital, wondering if any of the other troopers would be dumb enough to try and stop him.

Chapter 27 – Enough to Drive You Crazy

Lilly sent a text to Kane indicating she was on her way back, leaving out details about the meeting. Unless one of them believed there to be an overt physical threat to the other, whatever happened could wait until they were together.

She tried to think through what had just happened, but the surreal nature of the meeting made conclusions elusive. Outlandish scenarios occupied her thoughts when, near the ranch, she encountered a sheriff's deputy blocking the road, signaling for her to stop.

"I'm sorry, Ma'am, but the road is closed right now. Can I suggest you follow the detour signs to Route 40?"

"I'm Agent Lilly Alexander with the Secret Service," she told him, holding up her ID. "My destination is about a mile down this road, and I need to get there."

He scrutinized her badge. "Are you here for the investigation?"

Lilly hid her confusion. "Yes, that's me."

"We were told an agent might be coming by. I'll call the next checkpoint for you so they will let you right through."

She thanked him and floored the underpowered car. Lilly did not like the way he'd phrased his question. What needed to be investigated? What was so serious that they were blocking the road a mile away? Had Kane been hurt? By the time the next officer waved her onto the farm road entrance, she was almost a basket case. Seeing knots of officers standing around what looked to be covered bodies by the driveway did not help her disposition.

She parked near the house, looking for whoever could give her information the fastest, but that effort was waylaid by a loud bark and the sight of Jay, his head covered in some kind of white bandaging, charging her at full speed from the door of the house.

Lilly cringed, worried he might crash into her. Due to some preternatural understanding that he outweighed her by a fair margin, however, he skidded to a stop right in front of her and pushed his bulbous head into her hip.

With the bandage, she wasn't sure if scratching would hurt him, so she settled for patting his back. "Where's Kane, Jay?" In short order and to her unfathomable relief, she saw her partner come limping out the front door of the house with a New Jersey State Trooper in tow. Seeing how he struggled, she met him halfway. Jay barked several times at Kane, clearly pleased with himself for delivering Lilly.

"What the hell is going on here?" she asked, not bothering to mask her concern.

"It's been, shall we say, quite a morning." He gave her a quick run-down of events. Lilly could feel her jaw dropping and her eyes widening with each detail he offered. *Five on one? Damn.*

"Do you think that's why I was called away?

"No. I think it was a coincidence." He dropped a small black item, about the size of a flash drive, into her hand. "This is a tracking device. The cops went over the truck and found it tucked up under the back bumper. My guess is one of Doyle's people put it on when we were at the house in Virginia wandering through the forest, kind of as a backup plan."

"Great. Now this location is compromised too. We're running out of hiding places, Kane."

"Maybe, maybe not."

"Are you nuts? You remember what Mac told us? How can you be sure Doyle didn't sell our location to the highest bidder?"

Kane appeared unconcerned. "This wasn't about selling us out or having us eliminated by someone else. This was about revenge."

"Sounds like an awfully petty reason to commit murder."

"Not to Doyle. We cost him his camp, probably a lot of his clients and weapons, everything he needed to be the patriot and savior of democracy he fancied himself to be. He chased us all the way to Virginia but didn't get us there. I think he took matters into his own hands by bringing his team here for some payback." Kane's voice and face became as dark as an approaching storm. "But they lost."

"Nice theory, but are you willing to gamble our lives—including Jay's—on it?"

"Yeah, I am." He leaned back against the wall, assurance radiating from him. "Why would Doyle tell anyone else where he's going to commit murder to make a few bucks, and then come here and do it himself? Why would he and his men walk all the way here from the road with silenced .22 pistols and not bother with the bigger guns in their truck? They expected to find us asleep, without a dog, and finish us quiet and quick. They weren't planning for a fight. Hell, Doyle left his keys in his truck."

He makes a compelling case. Still... "I need to be sure, Kane. I'm not sure yet."

"The sheriff's office has a cover story going out that the shots were a farmer shooting at coyotes that were attacking his livestock. The state troopers have agreed to station a unit here at all times. My alert system is still in place, and it worked like a charm last night. And my man," he scratched Jay's neck, "will back that system up. We're perfectly safe here."

Lilly shook her head, impressed with Kane's methods. "How do you do that? It's like you live a second life as some evil criminal mastermind conjuring up all kinds of horrific scenarios and pointing out how bad things are gonna get, but then you just tell me it's all gonna work out in a calm voice and flash that charming smile, and you make me believe you both times."

Kane tilted his head to the side. "Maybe it's because I have an honest face."

His confidence was infectious. "Now I know you're full of shit," she told him with a laugh. "Okay, we stay."

***

It seemed to take forever, but eventually the troopers and detectives finished with their questions and work. Only then did Lilly sit down with Kane and explain in detail how Douglas and Stafford had asked her to send the case off on a tangent by sharing fake information with her partner.

"Those motherfuckers," the agent growled. "I shoulda strangled Douglas in his office the other day."

"Your penchant for violence notwithstanding," Lilly responded, "how do we handle this?"

"I don't understand their end game, but we really don't have to care about what those two said. Let them think they did something. We need to focus on the big questions—why someone undertook this whole assassination."

"Isn't it obvious? Someone fears an Armstrong administration enough to kill him. Doyle fits that profile perfectly."

Kane shook his head. "I don't mean why someone drugged the shooter to take the shot. I mean the why behind the entire plan. This shooting wasn't about an implemented policy. A candidate doesn't do that, so the shooting was political in nature. Whoever committed this crime—Republican, Democrat, Libertarian, Chinese, Martian—was smart enough to do so when there wasn't much time to solve it. There is a bigger end game going on here, and we can't see it yet."

"But what?" Lilly asked. "The odds were against him winning, so why risk the shot? It actually might have backfired—being shot might be the best thing to ever happen to him because that bullet gave him a ton of sympathy votes. Why take that chance when your side is winning?"

"And yet there *was* a reason," Kane said slowly. "You've got a drugged operative who will follow any command, yet you go to all this trouble to set up an outrageously difficult shot, one that ultimately failed. Why not just insert your dude in the crowd and take your chances with a .357 from three feet so it's a sure kill, and then instruct him to blow his brains out so he can't answer questions? Like you said, with the miss, you ended up helping the guy you tried to kill. Seems kind of... counterintuitive." He snapped out of his trance and looked more pointedly at Lilly. "Will you remember this conversation?"

Lilly snorted derisively. "What do you think?"

"Good. We might need to revisit these details sometime later. But, to my point, if the polls open and we don't have anything further, the 'wrong' man might be elected president. We need something *very* concrete as soon as possible, or all the work we've done might be for nothing. You and I may be the only two people with the ability and information to do that."

"Well, at least there's no pressure," Lilly scoffed.

"I know. But every second we chat about it is another second we don't have any proof." He pushed himself to his feet, the weariness flooding through him once more. "Goddamn, we're both going to need some rest soon. Maybe a power nap."

"Last time you talked about us getting some sleep," Lilly responded with a frown, "I drove three hours to get lied to and you had a gun battle against five men. Maybe let's not make plans for rest right now."

"That's good thinking."

***

Lilly took a few deep breaths to rejuvenate herself as she walked through the room, checking each of the piles she'd created, with Jay trailing behind her like an auditor, sniffing each accumulation of paper to confirm that she'd done her job properly. It was a technique she used when she had to return to a process, and in under ten minutes her brain was back to classifying and organizing names and numbers at peak efficiency.

It was demanding, repetitive, and a mind-numbing jumble of data. Lilly, though, found order in the chaos. Humans, no matter how smart they were, were slaves to habit. Computers with artificial intelligence found many of the patterns, but not all of them. The masters, the Rembrandts, who could develop and use a system that computer algorithms couldn't see, they were her prey.

As good as she was, she needed Kane and his computer to move back in time through the chain. Lilly could only go through so many steps with just paper, so when she hit the inevitable wall, she delivered yet another sheet to her partner, who used his experience with cybersecurity and the (probably illegal) code on the thumb drive to break through bank firewalls to see what led to the transactions Lilly had identified. The printer pumped out reams of paper covered in columns of money and account numbers.

After she delivered the twentieth or so sheet of the day, Kane rolled his eyes. "C'mon! Every page you give me generates a couple hundred records I've got to track, download, and organize. I can't keep up. What the hell are you trying to do to me?"

"Just doing my job," she replied. "You've got the computer—I should be the one having trouble keeping up with you!"

"You *are* a computer," Kane told her, a combination of awe and anger in his tone. "I can't type as fast as you think."

"Buck up," she teased. "I've only got two more boxes of documents after this one, and then I can start working with you. How much do you have so far?"

Kane held up a sheaf of paper. "Enough to last us until Christmas—next Christmas."

"Funny. Don't forget, that's only round one."

Kane's face spoke of fear and agony. "How many rounds are there?"

"As many as there need to be. I know this isn't quite as glamorous or exciting as running around the countryside and exchanging gunfire with everyone who looks at you sideways, but it solves crimes just the same."

"It may solve a lot of crimes," he grumped, "but it's boring as shit."

"You never chased a money trail, Kane? You know that was the original purpose of the Secret Service, right? To fight counterfeiting."

"Thanks for the history lesson. Yes, I knew that, but I never actually did it myself; I was always better at planning and being on protection details."

"Yeah, you strike me as the 'screw this desk work, let's shoot someone' kind of agent."

"Considering how hard you are geeking out on pages of numbers, I wouldn't make that sound like such a bad thing. I knew you were good at this, but it's like you thrive on it."

"'Thrive' might not be the right word, but yeah, I'm in my element. And, since we spent most of the investigation working in your wheelhouse, I can't say our current situation upsets me too much."

"Sadist."

"Pussy."

They stared at each other for a second, feigned irritation on both faces, before cracking up with far greater intensity than the friendly insults warranted. Lilly collapsed on the love seat next to Kane, not caring just how close it put her body next to his but noting that he slumped against her. Jay got up and came over to sniff the situation to ensure everything was on the up and up. Finding the arrangement acceptable, he laid back down with a groan of fatigue.

They sat silently for a few minutes. Lilly let her head loll back, luxuriating in resting her brain. Like Kane, she had finite reserves, and they were being used up far more quickly than normal due to her lack of sleep. Worse, Kane's solid, warm body that smelled vaguely of spice and leather brought a feeling of comfort she'd not known for some time.

There was work to do, but it would have to wait just a bit longer.

Chapter 28 – Doggy Style

Lilly tried not to rush Kane, but he seemed to be moving as fast as cold lava. *How fucking hard could it possibly be to get through these last twenty-seven transactions?!* She took a deep breath. Kane was doing his best; impatience wasn't going to help that.

She checked her watch. It was almost two a.m., which meant they'd been working for better than nine straight hours with nothing more than bathroom breaks. Lilly had performed what she modestly considered a Herculean effort, even for her; finding what should be the last step in the trail, where the money had first been deposited into a bank of any sort. At least, if they got a name and some related information, they could get a search warrant and start asking pertinent questions.

Finally, Kane tapped the keyboard with great relish, and the printer started whirring once more. "Confirmed. Every one of those last transactions goes back to the same account at CreditPlus Bank."

"I've never even heard of that bank," Lilly commented.

"They're pretty small. Mostly online, with eight brick-and-mortar locations in the D.C. area. And this account was opened at the branch in Bladensburg, Maryland." He pulled the pages off the printer and scanned them. "Looks like a ton of deposits spread out over the last thirteen months."

Lilly leaned in to see, not thinking much about how her hands gripped his shoulders until his slight movement made them ripple under her touch. Belatedly, she realized she was also pressing her breasts into his upper back—and how he didn't even try to move away. Of course, she didn't either.

Keep it together. She forced her mind back to business. "Over three million bucks worth of deposits. That's a lot of transactions, especially at," she did some rough math in her head, "an average of $8,000 per deposit. Like 400 or so. Two every business day for over a year."

"But why do so many deposits?"

"Probably to fool SEC investigators. A lot of the deposits were only a few hundred dollars. That's a fairly standard way to avoid SEC regulations about reporting deposits over $10,000 or structuring them in a way to avoid that regulation. Put enough noise in the deposit stream and that dog won't bark. Whoever did this knew his or her shit." She reached the last page in the list of account activity. "And... yup."

"What?"

"Starting in the spring, you start seeing the payouts, right when the recipient accounts started showing the money coming in." Lilly grabbed another form and handed it to Kane. "Can you look up this account from Mountain West Bank?"

Kane entered the information. "That account belongs to a Mr. Argen L. Collins at 6744 Oasis Road in Sand Hollow, Idaho. It was opened in January at the branch in Nampa, about ten miles away from his house."

"Is that a good name?"

More typing. "Looks like it. The address is a real place—it's a run-down house with a bunch of other buildings, and it's in the middle of nowhere. And we have a social security number, driver's license, hunting license, even tax returns, all valid. Best of all, he's not dead."

They shared a look. No further communication was needed; they might have just IDed the shooter. He would soon be visited by a couple of agents for a friendly chat. "Another nice pickup, Lilly."

"Thanks."

"Anything else?"

"Nothing surprising," she told him. "The account is almost empty. There's only nine grand left, and the last activity was three weeks ago."

"That fits. The original money man is done using it."

"Who's our lucky contestant?"

Kane printed one more page as he read off the screen. "This account was opened by one Rory B. Bellows, 1132 Geaton Drive, Upper Marlboro, Maryland. Social Security number 761-05-1450."

"Tell me we're two-for-two."

"Nope. Not only is that not a valid address—there is no 1132 on Geaton Drive in Upper Marlboro—but I don't get a single hit on that social."

"Whoever it is, he's our guy. Well, his alias anyway. Maybe Mr. Collins can ID him. We'll go to the bank branch tomorrow to get a description and do interviews."

"Definitely. Meanwhile, how else can we figure out who Mr. Bellows really is?"

Lilly pulled the page off the printer. In addition to the information Kane had read off, it had a poor-quality image of Bellows' signature. She wasn't a graphologist, but the bold strokes, large letters, and the right-slanted "L's" suggested a confident person—likely a male—who felt in control of the situation.

One other item caught her eye; a few tiny smudges around the signature. They looked to her like asterisks. She handed the page over to her partner. "What do you make of these little marks around the name?"

Kane frowned. "Looks to me like a couple of bugs got squished on the signature card," he half-joked, frowning as he enlarged the image on the screen. "I think they're stars."

"Like a Star of David?"

"No, like a five-point star, the kind you draw real quick and easy without lifting your pen." He turned the laptop around so she could see what he meant. They looked like childish doodles.

"Oh. Weird."

"Yeah, real weird. Now our suspect is a third-grade girl?" Kane sneered.

"No, it's just a personality quirk. Keep it in mind—you'd be surprised how many connections I've made based on stupid stuff like this."

"OK." Kane did not sound convinced. "In any case, it's time for some shut-eye. We'll report to Mac in the morning and determine what to do with all this shit then."

"Sounds good."

Kane shifted his weight like he was about to get up, but stopped. "I don't want to sound condescending, but you've done incredible work here. If you were on my detail, I'd put you in for an ESA."

"Really? You think this was exceptional service worthy of an award?"

"Absolutely."

Lilly smiled at him, pleased at the compliment. But her gaze lingered. Perhaps it was the exhaustion or stress overwhelming her, but her mind shifted out a of personal paradigm into something more... personal.

And Kane didn't look away. Instead, a curious little smile creased his mouth, one that made her think about how full and voluptuous his lips appeared. "We've earned some time off the clock. Both of us."

There was no missing his message. Lilly was more than interested but wasn't sure how to respond. As she tried to decide, Kane twitched an eyebrow ever so slightly and stepped away.

"C'mon Jay, let's go out before bed." He brushed by her, ensuring their bare forearms would touch. Sparks flew, but they did not help her make a decision. Kane studiously ignored her while waiting at the door for Jay to take care of his business. When the dog trotted back in, Kane threw one more come hither glance her way and retreated to his room.

What the hell should I do? He was interested, and so was she, but moving forward was still a blatant violation of protocol and the rules of common sense. She heard him banging around for a minute before the creak of mattress springs signaled he'd gotten into bed, and the light clicked off. *Did he think that was an invitation? Was it? Should I accept it?* Desire warred with pride for a couple of seconds, but eventually pride won. She walked right past his room and to her own, flicking on the light. Almost as an afterthought, she left her door open a crack.

Lilly took her time undressing, growing irritated as the moments passed. She fully grasped the contradiction of being annoyed with him for acting in exactly the same fashion as she was, but this was no time for logic. He had started all this, so that stubborn bastard was going to come to her one way or another.

As she pulled off her top, Lilly heard movement coming her way. However, the multitude of footfalls announced who was moving about. Jay pushed the door open and came over to her. She sat down on the bed to pet him, oddly self-conscious about being topless.

Jay didn't seem to care, laying his enormous cranium on her thigh and looking up at her. "Did Kane send you in here to get me to come to his room?" she whispered, half-serious. She wondered if the technicality justified her going to him. *I'm not doing what Kane wants. I'm doing what Jay wants.* Lilly smiled to herself at the absurd but not quite rejectable idea.

As she looked into his eyes, she had an inspiration. Reaching over to the tiny nightstand and opening the drawer, she found what she hoped would be there—a notepad and a pencil. Ripping off a sheet, she scribbled out a short message and tucked the paper in Jay's collar. He tried to look to see what she'd done but didn't seem overly concerned.

"Go see Kane, Jay!" She infused enthusiasm into her voice, making him pick his head up and tilt it at her. "That's right! Go ahead!" She would have sworn he gave her a knowing smile before turning and heading out of the room.

***

Why do I do stupid shit? Kane sat on his bed in his boxer shorts with the lights out, leaning against the headboard, wondering what had possessed him to hit on his partner.

Yes, Lilly had dropped some very clear hints. Yes, she'd grabbed his package the other day and then made a comment that could only be interpreted one way. Yes, she'd pushed her tits into his back a few minutes ago and kept them there.

She wanted him; maybe not quite as much as he wanted her, but any dummy with a pulse could see it. And she was across the hall. Why was he still sitting *here*?

Duty. Rules. Protocol. Federal law. Obedience to an agency and a system that had fucked him over. Hadn't he given enough of himself?

Everything about her attracted him. She was smart, she was tough, and she was self-confident. Those qualities made her more appealing than any woman he'd ever remembered. Even the way she aggravated him to no end was exciting. The fact that she was gorgeous was just a bonus.

So be a man! He longed to go to her, but self-discipline was a hard habit to break. It would be so much easier if she'd just come to him, but that seemed out of character for her. *Am I going to blow this by being stubborn and worrying about shit that doesn't matter anymore?*

Jay treaded back into the room, but Kane barely noticed. He was a little antsier in a less-familiar space, so his moving about was hardly unexpected. He placed his hand on the back of Jay's neck, looking down when he felt the sheet of paper under his collar.

"What d'ya got there, Jay?" Pulling it out, he grabbed his cell phone and selected the flashlight to illuminate the scrawl on it.

I don't know what's holding you up, but Jay thinks you should join me.

Jay was watching him as he read the sentence, and when Kane looked back down at his pet, he knew it was all over. If Jay had been blessed with vocal cords, he would have been asking his owner what the hell he was waiting for. Kane smiled despite knowing how badly

Lilly had outmaneuvered him. He could resist her (well, maybe) but he could never resist an entreaty from Jay, and Lilly had picked up on that.

"Thanks, boy," he said quietly, patting the mattress. "C'mon up." Jay needed no further encouragement, spreading out across the comforter like he knew he would have the bed to himself for the rest of the night.

This ought to be an interesting encounter. Not eager to supplicate himself but motivated to enjoy the benefits of such humiliation, he rose and walked the few steps to Lilly's door. Unsurprisingly, it was cracked open, so he rapped twice on the door frame and stepped in.

His partner stood by the head of her bed wearing nothing but a pair of panties, accentuated by a sultry smile and the raised eyebrows of a gloating victor. Kane took in her body, bathed in the warm, libidinous light, and it was all he could do to stop in the doorway.

He kept his eyes locked on Lilly, deliberately avoiding looking at her exposed (and damn-near perfect) breasts, instead holding up the piece of paper. "Do not," he said directly but with a soft edge, "use my dog to send me sex notes. He is not my pimp."

Lilly bit her lower lip and tilted her head, appearing far sexier than he'd thought possible. "A girl's gotta do what a girl's gotta do. Now, are you going to stand all the way over there, or are you going to come here and take care of business?"

Her perfect question eliminated any hesitation. Dropping the note on the floor, he stalked over to her. She took one step herself, which he took as a tiny concession, and it made him smile as they pressed their bare chests together. Kane gripped the back of her head, tilting it slightly so he could push his tongue into her willing mouth more easily.

Their kiss was urgent and intense. Lilly seemed determined to make him pay for his stubbornness, but the way she moved her body to straddle his thigh made that okay. Her fingers dug into his back.

She pushed his head to the side, and for a second he feared she might accidentally try to kiss the still-healing injury on his neck, but she avoided the area entirely in favor of his ear, which she caught between her lips, nibbling the flesh and running her tongue over the contours of the lobe. His eyes crossed as her mouth worked its magic.

Lilly's hand left his back, sliding over his hips to rest on Kane's erection through his boxers. She moaned into his mouth upon feeling his hardness, giving him a boost of confidence he didn't need. He pushed himself into her hand, making sure she got the full benefit of his hard-on. "Yeah," she breathed, "that's what I expected." With far less blood than normal entering his brain, it took him a second to remember how she'd grabbed his package the other day.

Lilly took a step back. Much to Kane's consternation, his hips followed her hand without conscious direction, making him feel like he was being pulled by an invisible leash.

"Getting a little eager?" she taunted, making sure she maintained a whisper-soft grip on his member.

"Being a bit of a tease?" he countered.

She laughed, the sound rich and wanton in his ear. "You gotta earn it."

Kane stepped into her, using his hips to turn her back toward the bed. "Maybe I'll just take it." He'd barely finished the last syllable when he used his superior size and strength to push her to the mattress. "What do you think about that?"

Lilly went down, but she retained enough control to land gently and prop her upper body up on her elbows. Her eyes were aflame with perfervid lust when she shot Kane a vicious smile. "You'll play hell trying."

So that's how this is going to go? Kane wasn't fazed. She'd demonstrated her rebellious streak often, and she was pushing his buttons like she wanted to be overpowered. He was more than willing to oblige.

He swooped down on her, but she was ready for the move, forcing her thighs together just before he could push his lower body between them. Kane grunted in mild pain as his erection, having nowhere to go, jammed awkwardly into her upper thigh. He slid off to the side, his passionate and aggressive move ruined, but even before he looked back up he could feel her unspoken taunt. *That's the best you've got?*

She may have been tough and ready for his advances, but he was stronger—by a wide margin. With a deft move that Lilly either wasn't expecting or was hoping for, Kane grabbed her right arm and, using it as leverage, pulled on her ankle with the other hand to roll her onto her stomach.

"Oof!" In an instinctive move to regain her leverage, she opened her legs, and Kane used that opportunity to put a knee between them, ensuring they would remain apart. Lilly kicked her heels up and swatted backward with her hands, but she was swinging blindly and none of her attempts came close to connecting.

Kane leaned in, pinning her upper body to the bed and putting his mouth to her ear. "I think you need to learn your place." His words sounded animalistic to his ear, but the way her body flushed with heat told him he was in safe territory in this improvised role play.

"Drop dead," she moaned. He rose and, still holding her in place, grasped the waistband of her wispy panties. He intended to yank them down to her thighs, but in the heat of the moment his raw power tore the delicate fabric and they came off her body in a shredded heap.

Such violence was not Kane's intent, but doing so caused a primal surge of power to flow through his body. Caught up in the heat of the moment, he held them a few inches from her face. "You see what you get when you fight me?"

***

The ripping sound of her panties as they were removed so savagely was indescribable. She loved it. And when he held them up and taunted her with his misogynistic question, her vision tunneled and the breath drained from her lungs. She had not planned for their sexual encounter to devolve into such a struggle for power and dominance, but that's how it had gone, and Kane seemed more than willing to indulge. She might have protested, but any sounds that came out were little more than useless blather.

A *whooshing* sound confused her for an instant, but that confusion was interrupted by a sharp sting on her right ass cheek. *What the hell?* When it was repeated on the left, she knew exactly what was happening; Kane was spanking her. A flood of wetness exploded between her legs. Normally, Lilly would never have allowed such a thing, but for some unfathomable reason having Kane inflict such humiliating pain/pleasure drove her to a level of ecstasy she could barely comprehend.

She wriggled violently but had no real desire to escape the electric handprints that were setting her ass ablaze. It didn't matter; Kane controlled her effectively with what seemed like minimal effort as he rhythmically applied the punishment.

Lilly panted as the red-hot pain flowed into her body, sending an electric charge right to her most sensitive zones. It was delicious and erotic and so very powerful, pushing everything except the crisp sting on her backside and the flowing arousal between her legs into the distant recesses of her mind.

Her nipples grew rock hard as her excitement expanded throughout her body, and they rubbed against the not-quite-soft fabric of the bedspread, just adding to the multitude of stimuli attacking her from all sides.

The strikes stopped, and Kane used both hands to pull her hips up so she was on her knees with her face still pressed into the mattress. Twisting her body, Lilly could see his patented look of arrogant victory, as if he never doubted just how easily he could control her—and inflame her desires while doing so. *Oh, hell no.*

A few minutes ago, she'd told him he needed to earn it—even though she'd been uncertain what "it" was. Compliance? Submission? Capitulation? No matter how she defined it then or now, the requirement still applied.

With blinding speed, Lilly pushed her upper body off the bed and swung her leg up and over Kane's head. His face registered surprise at her flexibility. Before he could get his mind around her actions, she'd raised the other leg to lock them together around his neck.

Already leaning forward and hardly prepared to defend himself, Kane lacked the balance and the strength to resist as Lilly flexed her thighs and started pulling him—or, more importantly, his mouth—down and in toward the center of her arousal. "You see what *you* get when *I* fight?" she growled.

Her lover appeared vexed at having his last taunt used against him, but caught her meaning, and her intent, quickly. With a look that was one percent challenge, one percent concern, and ninety-eight percent lust, he grabbed her legs and worked to pull them apart. It did little good; her limbs were well-positioned and strong enough to keep him, though bigger, in check. Had Kane really wanted to break free from the hold, he would have had to hurt her, and Lilly knew that wasn't on the agenda, so she proceeded. As that strong, sexy jawline was pulled inexorably down between her legs, she saw his eyes glaze over with lecherous thirst just before their two very different sets of lips touched.

Lilly wondered just how defiant Kane would remain, but his tongue snaked out without hesitation and caressed her with a delicious mix of pressure and tenderness. Arching her back, she let out a guttural cry of passion and a desperate need for further gratification. Lilly directed his efforts by flexing the insides of her thighs. Kane's grunts of discomfort as he obeyed her unspoken orders gave her a rush of power and authority that only amplified the sublime ecstasy tearing holes through her soul. Being in control suited her.

Distracted by the killing pleasure, she allowed her legs to relax and open, giving Kane an opportunity. Rising, he grabbed her thighs and pulled her backward so her ass dangled off the edge of the mattress, at a perfect height for his erection. He pushed his boxers down and kicked them to the corner, allowing his rock-hard shaft to point at her like a ceremonial sword.

"Got anything to say now?" he sneered. Lilly could see Kane was back in his element, and it gave him an aura of invincibility that drove her wild. The ragged bandages around his leg and neck just amplified his warrior affectation, and it forced the words from her mouth.

"Yeah," she told him. "Fuck me. Fuck me now, Kane."

"That's better," Kane said—rather brazenly in her opinion, considering all the effort he'd put in to get to this point.

"You better be worth all this work," she snapped back.

"Oh, I will be," he assured her. "Now shut it." To forestall any further discourse, he repositioned his body and, with one strong, steady thrust entered her to the hilt. Had Lilly not been totally soaked or even slightly unprepared, it might have been painful, but in her current state she took everything he offered and reveled in the sublime pleasure that only two people in perfect sync could generate.

Kane gave her a second to grow accustomed to his presence, but when he started fucking her, he held nothing back. Lilly felt how easily he moved her body, making her feel like little more than a toy to be used for his satisfaction—and at the moment such objectification didn't bother her. Each stroke was an onslaught of transcendent bliss that pushed her ever closer to an epic orgasm.

His breathing became strained and ragged. She did her best to twist her hips into him; it was hardly fair for her to just take everything he was giving without offering something in return.

"Oh, goddammit!" he yelled. Lilly took satisfaction at how her body, her gyrations, and her soft flesh excited him as much as his ministrations did her and made him cry out. She wished to give him a signal that she was nearly there as well, but the wave built rapidly and her vision tunneled. She matched his rhythm, desperate to make the most of the indescribable moment, and when her climax crested it sent shock waves throughout every part of her body.

Kane sped up just before he exploded, crying out with the heat of the moment, and his body resonated as it was overtaken by the same forces that flowed through Lilly. She gripped the comforter as tightly as she could, her eyes clenched shut to avoid anything that might interfere with the sweet, sensual flavors accosting her mind, body, and soul.

Finally, Kane slid off to the side, and Lilly collapsed back on the mattress. With her last vestige of strength, she rolled over to face Kane, and they re-oriented themselves so they were entirely on the bed. They exchanged no words; they simply weren't necessary. She glanced at him as she panted, desperate for oxygen, and saw the same level of fatigued bliss on his face. Lilly was far too hot and sweaty to require any blankets, and in a few seconds their powerful huffs became the deep, slow breaths of slumber that only came after glorious and ardent sex.

Monday, November 6

One Day Before the Election

Chapter 29 – Who Is Rory?

Lilly felt the rhythmic rise and fall of the warm chest under her head. The gentle, soothing motion tried to pull her back into blissful slumber, but the vague soreness of her upper thighs and hips reminded her of recent, blinding pleasure. *Wow. Just wow.*

She was far from a virgin, but last night she'd finally learned the difference between making love and *getting fucked*. Their passionate encounter had been rough, even brutal, but it had been far from a callous encounter. Kane seemed to know on an elemental level that the intense, primal event had been necessary to dissipate the blistering sexual tension between them. It had been glorious and violent and erotic and exactly what she'd wanted—even if she'd not known it beforehand.

She opened her eyes, glancing over at the man who had set her body afire. He needed a shave and his short hair was tousled and messy, but the unkempt visage just added to the powerful mystique. Sliding her hand down his muscular stomach, she ran the tips of her fingers through his pubic hair gently until he stirred. “That’s nice,” he mumbled before opening his eyes fully and adjusting his body. “How are you?”

“About as good as you might imagine. Maybe a little sore.”

Kane grimaced. “I’m sorry if I got a little rough. I felt like you were kind of jousting with me, sending me signals to keep pushing.”

“Don’t you dare apologize,” she told him. “You read me perfectly. That was just what I needed. Walking a little funny for the rest of the day is a small price to pay for it.”

He arched his eyebrows. “Just don’t let anyone notice your gait. We broke more agency rules last night than I care to count.”

“I know. You better hope I’ve got a clean pair of panties because you wrecked the pair I had on.”

“Oh well,” he said with a languid grin. “Maybe you shouldn’t wear any today.”

“Hey buster, if I’m going commando, so are you. This is an equal-opportunity partnership.”

Kane shook his head as he pushed himself to a sitting position. “There’s always gonna be a catch with you, isn’t there?”

“Count on it.”

***

Kane and Lilly sat down at the table a few minutes later, having made themselves as presentable as possible. After a brief discussion, they each took one of the pending tasks and jumped into action.

Lilly got up and started collecting the piles of documents they had created over the past two days. If by some miracle they made an arrest, these papers would be crucial in ensuring the chain of evidence needed to get a conviction, meaning that she couldn't just drop them back in their boxes haphazardly.

Kane placed a call to Director MacMurray, bringing him up to speed on what they had and their next steps. "That's decent work in short order, Logan," Mac said when he finished his summary.

"Thank you, sir, but the real credit goes to Agent Alexander. She's a damned machine with this stuff." He saw Lilly turn and flash him a grin at the compliment. *I never got such a fetching smile when calling a woman a machine.*

"Apparently. I guess she's been more of an asset than we realized."

"And then some." He shifted gears quickly. "How do you want us to handle the search warrant?"

"What county?"

"Uh, Prince George's."

"Good. I know a few judges there. I'll make a call. Use the template to write it up and I'll text the address of a judge who can sign it."

"Great."

"And I know you know this, but we are under serious time pressure."

"Understood. We are going to do our best."

"I know you will." He paused. "Kane, we need one of your miracles here."

Nothing like being asked to resolve an impossible situation one more time. Despite everything, he was still being implored to heroically save the day. With a quick look of exasperation skyward, he moved on to his next topic, giving a quick account of his adventures from two nights ago.

"Doyle?" Mac asked. "The guy from the camp?"

"Yes, sir. He had quite the hard-on for me."

"Where was Agent Alexander during all this?

"Well, that takes us to a new and really interesting story." He relayed Lilly's impromptu meeting with Douglas and Stafford.

Mac was silent for a second. "There's an angle here we're not considering. Stafford, he might not have figured this all out, but Douglas couldn't be so dumb to think that Alexander wouldn't go to you about this, or her SAC, or even to me." He paused, and his next words were more measured. "And you're absolutely sure that she heard him correctly?"

"Sir, I haven't the slightest doubt about Lilly's recollection. She could probably tell you the number of pinstripes on Stafford's overpriced suit."

"What was Lilly's take on it? And yours?"

"Lilly is certain they're playing some sort of game, and I agree with her, but we don't have a clue as to their goal. If there's one man in the world who wants this solved, it's Voight Stafford, so why try to discredit me? If I'm poisoning the investigation that badly, ignore me.

"And Douglas," he continued. "Yeah, I'm not on his Christmas card list, but he's in line to be the next director, so it's in his best interest to have two Secret Service agents run this down. And, again, if we don't get it done, no loss. But, even if we're wrong, we have developed real leads, making it nonsensical to do what they did." He stopped as a very confusing—and troubling—thought exposed itself. "Unless..."

"Unless what?"

"Sir, I'm just throwing this out, but their action smacks of desperation. And the only reason you'd be getting desperate is if you didn't want someone to figure this out."

"That follows," Mac agreed. "So?"

"We are trying to figure out who committed the crime. The only person who would want to prevent that is, well, the criminal."

"Whoa. Douglas is a conniving little prick, but you need a lot more to accuse him of being behind this. A *lot* more."

Kane nodded to no one. "You're completely right. All I have is an idea backed up by theory and a few equivocal thoughts. I bring it up only as something to keep in mind."

"Duly noted. I'll keep that thought tucked away unless something changes. And, while this is great conjecture, it doesn't get you moving any faster. If you get something out of the bank visit, unless it's a quick win, kick it back to me."

"Sounds good."

"And, no matter what, text me your next steps as soon as you know them. I have a meeting with the president at 11:00 today. I don't know what's going to come of it, but I don't expect good news about you. So keep a low profile—if I can't find you, I can't give you bad news."

"Don't I know it. Anything else?"

"No, sir."

"OK, get going. Good luck." The line went dead. Kane pulled up the standard template that federal agents used to craft search warrants on his computer and filled it in.

He next checked on Lilly, who was a little more than halfway done with her work. "Learn anything new?" she asked.

Kane ran her through the conversation, including his outlandish speculation about Douglas, noting that her reaction was similar to the director's. "Mac's got a meeting with the president at 11:00. Figure we'll be pulled at that point and I'll be shit-canned."

Lilly frowned. "If Sharpe pulls us, can we legally continue to investigate the crime?"

"I don't know. I know if we don't hear the order, we can't obey it. Until that happens, we keep working. Everything else will sort itself out one way or the other."

She paused. "Yeah, but will it work out with a bang or with a whimper?"

"I think that's up to us."

***

With the truck packed, Kane, Lilly, and Jay sped eastward back to Egg Harbor. Leaving their snug little hideout meant Kane couldn't care for or protect Jay properly, something he explained to Lilly when they made a right instead of a left upon leaving the driveway. When they arrived, Jay raced through the door to the boarding area and started making his usual racket. Kane felt the normal pang of guilt over leaving his buddy, even though he enjoyed being there. But he couldn't waste time feeling blue—there was work to be done.

Kane blatantly violated every speed limit sign he saw, and far earlier than the GPS had originally indicated, they pulled up in front of the home of the Honorable Carolyn T. Gainey, Circuit Court Judge for the Seventh Judicial Circuit of Maryland. As they hopped out of the car, Lilly was a bit startled to see a woman, probably in her forties, exit the front door in her bathrobe. She looked flustered as she approached them. "Are you Agents Alexander and Logan?"

"Yes," Lilly responded. "Judge Gainey?"

"That's right. Do you have the warrant?"

"Yes, Your Honor." She handed over the document. "Is everything all right? You seem a bit out of sorts."

The judge started flipping through the page rapidly, delaying her response. "What? Oh, yes. I've got a sick kid upstairs, and getting a call from the FBI director for a warrant before I woke up threw me." Lilly watched her eyes dart back and forth over each page, so quickly that it took the woman barely a minute to go through all twenty-two pages of the warrant. She scrawled an illegible signature on the last page, wrote the time next to it, handed it back to Lilly, and went back into her house without another word. With a shared glance of surprise and a shrug, they jumped back in the truck and roared over to the Bladensburg CreditPlus branch.

Grabbing their laptops, they entered the building and flashed their badges. "We need to speak to the branch manager right now please," Lilly told the desk representative. On the drive over, they had decided that Lilly, with her better understanding of this part of the investigation, should drive the conversation. Within fifteen seconds a woman walked out of an office and extended her hand to greet them.

"Hello. I'm the branch manager, Teresa Pierce. How can I help you?"

"Is there somewhere we could speak in private? This is an extremely sensitive matter, and time is of the essence."

"Certainly." She led them into her office and shut the door.

Lilly handed over pages summarizing the account information as well as the search warrant. "We need to know everything you can tell us about this account—most of all, we need to identify the person who opened the account. That name is almost certainly an alias."

Pierce looked at the sheet. "How do you know that?"

"The social security number is not valid, and that address doesn't exist," Lilly told her.

Pierce took time to study the warrant, spending more time than the judge. "Let's see what we have." She tapped on her keyboard. "Everything on your sheet matches my information."

"Can we speak to the bank employee who opened the account?" Lilly asked.

"Sure. That would be... oh, I'm sorry. That's not possible. The employee, Andy Hartsdale, died in a car crash a couple of weeks later."

Lilly glanced over at Kane, who raised his eyebrows. *Not a coincidence.* "Do you know what happened?"

"Not exactly. No one saw the accident. It was during a downpour, and he must have lost control. He rolled several times and the car caught fire."

Lilly bit her lip in frustration, contemplating her next move when Kane spoke up. "Is there anything you can give us, anything at all about the account that might lead us to a real person?" He came across as desperate, but Pierce tilted her head back and seemed to be thinking.

"Maybe." She entered more details into the computer, nodding after a second. "This might help. They did a lot of ATM deposits, and we always capture a picture of the person when they use the machine." She spun her monitor around to show the agents a list of transactions with thumbnail images next to them.

"Can you collect those images and give us copies?" Lilly asked.

"I'm sure I can." Pierce clicked around in the program. "Yup, here we are. Give me a minute and I'll have a .ZIP file for you."

Lilly handed over a thumb drive. "If you could put it on here, that would be great."

Pierce took the proffered item, inserted it in her computer, and loaded the files before returning it to Lilly.

"Thank you. One last request. Is it possible for us to get a few minutes in a private room? This is good information and we need to act on it right now."

"I think so. Let me make sure the conference room is clear." Pierce left the room.

Kane turned to Lilly. "NGI?"

"Yup." She jammed the drive into her laptop. "It's as good a place as any to start." The Next Generation Identification system used facial recognition software to identify anyone with felonies at the state or federal level.

Pierce returned. "The conference room isn't scheduled for several hours, so you are free to use it. I'll make sure you aren't disturbed."

"Thank you. We won't be long," Lilly told her. They set up on a large wooden table and started reviewing the digital images as quickly as they dared.

It became apparent that two men were making the drops. One was a muscular, light-skinned Black man with short hair, a nose ring, and gauges in his earlobes. The second man was much skinnier, white, and had his arms, neck, and even his forehead decorated with garish tattoos. Both were usually dressed in plain hoodies over crisp white T-shirts. In a few shots, the agents could see that their pants were exceedingly baggy.

"Do either of these guys look like they have the means to set up an account with the idea of pumping millions of dollars into it?" Kane asked rhetorically.

"No way."

"These guys are cover so they don't expose the real bankroller."

Lilly sighed, once again frustrated. "Well, it's better than nothing. Pick the best few photos. We'll run 'em and see if we get a hit."

Kane nodded. In a few minutes, they had enough reasonably clear face pictures of their suspects. Kane loaded the photos and initiated a search. It took about four minutes before they got results.

"Two hits. The Black guy is Jerome Carter, twenty-five, numerous arrests for possession, intent to distribute, a couple of B&Es and assaults, possession of an unregistered firearm. His friend is Patrick Owens, twenty-seven, pretty much the same rap sheet."

Lilly shook her head as she looked over Kane's shoulders. "Both committed violent crimes with guns. Why the hell are they on the street?"

Kane dug into the file a little deeper. "Looks like they were both doing a stretch in D.C. Central Detention before they were suddenly paroled for good behavior due to 'overcrowded prison conditions' in September last year. If I remember correctly, that's when all the deposits started, right?"

"The first one was October 2nd," Lilly confirmed. "And it wouldn't shock me in the least if Mr. Rory Bellows had a lot to do with that, which makes me wonder just how he pulled it off. Any other charges outstanding on these guys since their release?"

"Nothing, not even a noise violation. Model citizens, both of them. They make every meeting with their parole officer."

"Do we have addresses?"

"Yup. They live together in an apartment in the Brentwood area of D.C."

"And that's about five miles from this branch," Lilly noted. "How convenient."

"Yeah, for us too." He started packing up his computer. "Let's pay them a visit."

Chapter 30 – Dangerous House Calls

The Brentwood area of northeast Washington, nestled between Route 1 and Route 50, was one of the higher-crime areas in the city. With the enormous Amtrak maintenance facility and the Brentwood Rail Yard dominating nearly a third of the neighborhood and trains coming and going at all hours of the day and night, the noise and diesel fumes were sufficient to keep property values down and allow for urban blight to dominate most of the homes.

Kane maneuvered through the twisting streets until they parked in front of 2514 16th Street, which turned out to be a gray two-story brick row home. Their black SUV with government tags drew stares from many of the pedestrians out and about on the cool autumn day, but Kane knew they would keep their distance.

Apartment 3 was on the second floor, so Kane and Lilly ascended the creaky staircase to the landing. The faint thump of bass could be heard coming through the walls, masking their approach. As they got closer, Kane crinkled his nose at the overwhelming smell of marijuana. He tapped his nose at Lilly, who nodded. As if on cue, raucous laughter erupted from the apartment.

They drew their weapons and pointed them at the ground. "United States Secret Service! Open the door!" Kane used a practiced voice, one that was not quite hostile but still projected unquestionable authority. To neither Kane's nor Lilly's surprise, everything went silent for about three seconds, followed by sounds of frantic scuffling. "Right now!"

Still nothing. Kane nodded to alert Lilly as to his next move before taking one step back and kicking the door with the bottom of his foot. The hollow door failed, allowing them to charge in with Kane in the lead and Lilly hot on his heels. Their suspects were standing by the couch with wide, glassy eyes and a sheen of sweat on their foreheads. The skinny white man had his hand jammed between the cushions.

"FREEZE!" Kane and Lilly shouted the command in perfect unison. Momentarily, both were handcuffed, sitting cross-legged on the floor. Lilly pulled the cushions off to reveal a cheap Taurus .22 caliber pistol exactly where Scumbag Number One had been digging. "Look what our friend was reaching for," she said before clearing the weapon.

"Look, man," the skinny guy remarked. "It's just some pot. I got scared."

"It's not just pot, asshole," Kane told him. "You now have a weapons charge." He let that statement hang in the air for a second before proceeding. "All we want is some information. If you cooperate with us, maybe we forget that the gun ever existed. Maybe." That was a bald-faced lie, but this skinny little degenerate didn't need to know that.

He looked back and forth at Kane and Lilly several times. "What do you want to know?"

"You're Patrick Owens, right?" Lilly asked him. "And you're Jerome Carter?"

"Yeah," Owens answered, but Carter remained silent.

"You made cash drops at the CreditPlus bank ATM in Bladensburg for over a year," Lilly said.

"Yeah."

Carter glared at him. "Man, shut the fuck up!"

Kane turned in his direction. "Bad advice, Mr. Carter. Do you have any idea how long of a sentence you'll get for pointing a gun at a federal agent?"

"I didn't point no gun at you!"

"That's... not how I remember it. How about you, Agent Alexander?"

She smiled sweetly at Carter. "Me either."

"Nah, man! That's bullshit and you know it!"

"The only thing I know is that people are going to believe me over you, Mr. Carter." Kane trained his focus back on the other man. "Now, Mr. Owens, tell us who you were doing that for."

Owens looked unsure for a brief moment before making his decision. "Like I don't know his name, but he met us when we got paroled, right outside the courthouse. He told us he was the one that got us out, so we owed him."

"And he told you about the deposit plan?"

"Yeah. And he said if we stayed out of trouble and did our job, things would be great, but if we fucked up, we'd be in super deep shit."

"And you didn't ask any other questions about it?" Lilly inquired.

Owens looked at her like she was a moron. "Why would I? He gave us a wad of cash right then, and every time we did a deposit he put extra bills in the envelope for us—like a couple hundred a day. And we never paid any rent. All we had to do was go to the bank, drop the money in the ATM, and pocket the rest. Like thirty minutes a day, tops. It was a lot better than getting sent back to prison."

"What's he look like?"

Owens shrugged. "Can't say for sure. He's older, maybe fifties or so, thin. The only time I looked at him in the daylight was the day we got sprung, and he was wearing a hat and sunglasses."

Kane pounced. "You saw him dozens of times but you don't know what he looks like? Bullshit."

"No, man! He'd call us real early, like before the sun came up, and one of us would walk down the street. He'd pull up in this old car, we'd hop in the back, and there'd be two envelopes lying on the seat—one for us and one to deposit. Then he'd drive about a half mile down the road so we could get out, and later we'd do the deposit. He didn't talk or even look back at us."

Shit. That's smart. It also dead-ended them once more. The generic description that Owens gave him was of almost no use. Kane turned away.

Lilly, however, persisted. "When you talked with him that first day, what do you remember from that meeting?"

Owens rolled his eyes. "I just told you what he looked like. Da fuck else you want?"

"Anything you might remember. How tall? A birthmark or a tattoo. His shoes. Anything." The punk looked down, trying to recall something that would help him curry favor with his interrogators.

"He had some weird-ass accent," Carter blurted.

"Weird how?" Lilly asked him.

"Like a snooty rich dude. All 'tut-tut' and stuff. Like Richie Rich."

Kane and Lilly shared a look. To these guys, anyone who spoke grammatically accurate English probably sounded like a noble lord.

"Fine." Kane walked to the other side of the room and made a phone call while Lilly tried to extract any more information. Shortly after Kane completed his call, two Washington police officers came into the apartment. "Hey!" Owens protested. "You said you wasn't gonna call the cops!"

"I said no such thing."

"Told ya," Carter spat. "You can't trust the fucking feds either."

Once the police were inside, the two agents handed over Carter's gun and retreated to their truck.

"What now?" Lilly's voice was low and hopeless.

Kane wanted to raise her spirits like she'd done for him several times, but he had no good answer to her simple question. "Not sure. What do we have?"

Lilly blew out her breath. "We've got two jerkoffs who are a dead end in the chain of evidence. We have a vague description of a middle-aged guy with some kind of rich accent, who seems to have enough juice to get two guys out of jail and afford an apartment for a year or more. He drives some kind of old sedan so he doesn't stand out. Basically, nothing."

He had to agree with her assessment. For the first time in this investigation, he had no leads or ideas. "Yup. Goddamn it. Those clowns were useless. I don't know where we go from here." He stared over the hood for several seconds, turning only when Lilly's head came up like a shot.

"I do," she said.

***

Lilly figured they were about done. Whoever had masterminded this shooting had covered his tracks too well. Maybe someone else could find a lead, but she and Kane were either too close, too tired, or too confused to proceed.

She barely heard Kane's last words, but her unconscious mind grabbed onto something. *Clowns? How could that possibly be important?* It had to be exhaustion. Still, she allowed her mind to work. Clown faces appeared: Bozo, Clarabell, Ronald McDonald, Krusty, Pennywi–. *Wait. That's it.* She felt a burst of energy and turned to her partner, her face alight with inspiration. "I do."

Kane side-eyed her. "You do what?"

"I know who Rory B. Bellows is," she said confidently.

"How? Those guys gave us absolutely nothing to work with."

"When I was in Stafford's office the other morning, I wanted to get a feel for where their heads were, so I made a little chit-chat. On the wall behind his desk, Stafford has the standard bunch of 'famous people who like me' pictures, and several of them were with the voice actors from *The Simpsons*."

"The cartoon?" Kane sounded incredulous. "What the hell are you talking about?"

Lilly forged ahead. "Yes, the cartoon. Do you know who Dan Castellaneta is?"

"No."

"He does a lot of voices on the show. He does Homer, Grandpa Simpson, Barney Gumble, and others. He also does Krusty the Clown, and Stafford said that was his favorite character."

"So? So what?!"

"Season seven, Episode fifteen. Bart the Fink. Krusty writes Bart a check, but when Bart cashes it, he accidentally exposes Krusty as a tax cheat. Krusty fakes his death to get out of the IRS debt. Bart feels guilty about being responsible for Krusty's death and starts thinking he sees him everywhere. He and Lisa search for him, but they have no luck. When they are leaving one place, Bart sees a check taped to the cash register under a 'Do Not Accept' sign. It's signed by Rory B. Bellows, but Bart recognizes the signature as Krusty's *by the little stars around the name*—just like the first check."

Kane squinted. "Wait. Like the signature on our account?"

"Yes." Lilly took a deep breath. "Stafford likes Krusty the Clown. Krusty uses the name Rory B. Bellows to hide out from the IRS. In the show, Rory's signature on that check has little stars around it. The real account signature had little stars around it. Only the hard-est-core *Simpsons* fans would know the name Rory B. Bellows and the stars—hell, the episode aired like twenty-six years ago—and Stafford said he's watched the show since it started. Add to that, our two depositors said their guy had a rich, snooty accent. Who do we know that has such an accent?" Kane looked like he might be catching on, so she brought it home. "Rory B. Bellows is none other than Voight Stafford."

Kane stared at her as he processed her statement. Three times, he started to speak, but each time he stopped before a word came out. After nearly a minute, he shrugged. "Everything you said fits. But that begs another question. What possible reason could Stafford have for bankrolling an effort to have his candidate and friend killed?"

The sobering question put a wet blanket over Lilly's enthusiasm. "I can't explain that part. But, motive aside, the facts we have point to Stafford being behind all of this. We might not know the why, but we know the who."

Kane started nodding, gently at first but then more firmly. "Every time you're sure, you end up being right. And that makes me nervous." He started the truck and pulled away from the curb.

"Where are we going?"

"I don't know and I don't care. If this is Stafford's doing, I'm not cool being a stationary target, so we're going to stay on the move until we figure out what to do next."

"Maybe we should call Mac?"

"Good idea. Go for it." Lilly dialed his clandestine number, only to have the call go directly to voicemail. "Shit. What time is it?"

"Quarter after eleven."

"Mac's in with the president right now. We're probably getting fired as we speak."

Lilly's nostrils flared. "You know what, Kane? I don't care who fires us—at this point, nothing short of a gun pointed at my head is going to stop me from running this down."

Kane appeared surprised at the vitriol in her voice, but the intensity of his response matched hers. "Couldn't have said it better myself."

Lilly smiled; in that moment, their partnership solidified into an unbreakable bond. Despite the dangers they faced, confidence flowed through her. There was nothing they couldn't handle.

Her phone rang, and the screen showed it was Brent Douglas. They shared a knowing look. With her recent revelation, Lilly's clandestine meeting with Douglas and Stafford now took on greater gravitas. Lilly accepted the call. "Alexander and Logan."

"You did it this time," their boss said without preamble. "Both of you. Did you think I wouldn't find out that you forged a search warrant using the name of a circuit court judge?"

Lilly glanced at Kane, her face a question, and had the look returned. "What the hell are you talking about, Brent?" he asked.

"Don't play stupid with me. The manager at CreditPlus Bank in Bladensburg called us to confirm that the warrant was valid, which was a smart move. Judge Carolyn Gainey just told me she never got a request to sign a warrant, never met you or Agent Alexander at her house, and never signed anything. In fact, a dozen people can confirm she was in her chambers by 8:10 this morning, planning the day with her deputy, so the 8:38 a.m. time on the warrant is invalid."

"Sir," Lilly chimed in. "That can't be accurate. I literally handed her the warrant myself and watched her review and sign it."

"I just explained why you couldn't have done that, Agent Alexander. I thought you had a bright future, but it looks like I was mistaken."

"That is insane. Someone is bullshitting you."

"I know. I'm talking to them."

She hit her boiling point in a heartbeat. "I don't care what you think you know! Don't you *dare* call me a liar!" From the corner of her eye, she saw Kane blanch, then chuckle.

Following a pause, Douglas' responded, his voice oddly robotic. "Kane Logan and Lillian Alexander, you are under arrest. You are to report to the nearest police authority and turn yourself in, where you will be read your rights. I advise you not to say anything further at this time."

Lilly was not done. "And I advise you to go screw yourself. You want to arrest me, come and do it yourself." Without even looking at Kane, she pressed the End Call button on the display. "Drive, Kane. Head for the hills." Her partner needed no further prompting, pushing the accelerator down and making a skidding turn north to head for the Maryland suburbs. Lilly turned off the GPS on her phone.

"I guess we're really all in now, huh?" Kane asked.

"I'm sorry," Lilly said sincerely. "I could have handled that better."

Kane shook his head. "Forget it. I would have blown my stack if you hadn't. But I still don't have the foggiest idea what he was talking about."

"Right? I'm not crazy, am I? I was there when that judge signed our warrant this morning, right?"

"I saw what you saw," Kane confirmed before his face changed. "Find an image of Judge what's-her-name."

"Carolyn Gainey."

"Yeah. Her." Lilly started tapping on her phone.

"What are you thinking, Kane?" She had no idea how a picture of the woman they'd met a couple of hours ago would help them in any way—at least not until she saw the image. "What the...?"

The woman on the screen was Black. The woman this morning had been white.

Without a word, she showed it to her partner. He took a glance. "Who the hell is that?"

"Circuit Court Judge Carolyn Gainey."

"Oh shit," he breathed. "Are you sure?"

"Google seems to be fairly confident. There's like six more pictures of her, all the same." She stared at the screen like her eyes were lying to her. "I don't understand. How is this possible?"

***

Kane drove as fast as he dared while running through the possibilities that would explain the conundrum they now faced. *Be logical. Work the facts.* It took critical moments to eliminate impossibilities and boil things down to the basics.

"The way I see it, this can only go one of two ways. One, Mac sent us to the wrong address on purpose because he wanted to screw us and knew the woman that lived there was willing to impersonate a judge.

"Two, because Mac is working with us on the sly, he's using an unencrypted phone that someone has hacked into. His call to real judge is intercepted by fake judge. Real judge goes to work. Fake judge sneaks in the house, meets us, and signs. Thoughts?"

Lilly frowned. "Honestly, the first one seems more realistic, but my gut instinct is that Mac is being straight with us. When he called me the other morning down at the crime scene, he sounded sincerely sorry for being such a dick the night before."

"Concur."

"But your second idea seems kind of farfetched."

"After all the shit we've seen go down in the past week or so, you think *this* is too much to be believed?"

"Maybe not," she conceded, "but that seems like a lot of lucky decisions."

"More like very informed ones. Let's stay with your theory that Stafford is the head cheese in all this. He is clearly concerned that we're close to a major breakthrough; that's why he had you come to his office by yourself. He's close to the president and is working with Brent Douglas in some way, so he knows we aren't going through them."

Lilly nodded. "Maybe it's not as off-the-wall as I thought."

"Let's test your theory. See if Mac is out of his meeting and put it on speaker."

Lilly did as requested, and this time Mac picked up. "Hello?"

Before anything, Kane wanted to establish the paradigm of the call. "It's me. Any questions I shouldn't ask?" *Are we fired?*

"Yeah, lots of those." *And how.*

"Gotcha. And there is another topic that simply will not wait for our regular meeting." *Others are listening in, so I can't speak freely.*

"Make it quick. I'm up to my eyeballs over here." *I'm listening.*

"Sir, this is hot. Next-level hot. We need to meet ASAP." *Do not do what I'm about to tell you to do.*

"OK. Where?" *I'll stay put.*

"Fort Slocum Park, at the pavilion on the southeast side." *Right out in the middle of everything.*

"I'll need about twenty minutes to get there." *Do you need time to set something up?*

"That works, sir. A couple extra minutes won't matter." *Time isn't the issue.*

"Understood. The pavilion at Fort Slocum?" *The location is the key?*

"Yup. Keep your eyes peeled." *When you learn what happens there, you'll understand.*

"Done. See you then." The line went dead.

Lilly looked confused. "You think it's a good idea to go meet Mac at a location we just announced over a phone that you think is hacked?"

"No, it's a terrible idea. That's why we're not going. Neither is Mac."

"But—" Lilly caught on then. "Gotcha."

"If I'm right, the area will be filled with undercover police and uniforms just waiting to pounce on us. Mac will hear about that and figure out his phone is compromised." He turned west. Fort Slocum Park was north of their current location.

"Fast and loose, Kane," Lilly said with an admiring smile. "Just how I would have played it."

"We're rubbing off on each other," he responded with his own grin before getting back to business. "We have two main tasks right now: make sure we don't get spotted, and figure out what Stafford's motive is. Let's focus on that."

"Deal." Both fell into silence and Kane worked to blend in with traffic.

Once Missouri Avenue turned into Military Road, the traffic thinned, allowing Kane to speed up. By the time they entered Rock Creek part, he began to relax a little bit. Being on a less-used road minimized their chances of being spotted. It wasn't perfect, but it would have to do until they came up with a plan. "Any ideas about our next moves?" he asked.

"The only idea I have," Lilly said, caution radiating from her voice, "is that if Stafford had Armstrong killed, Zach Holland becomes the presidential candidate. He is Armstrong's vice-presidential candidate."

"OK, but it's smarter to wait until after the election. Holland might lose because he's less known."

"Maybe it's a coordinated effort to get the sympathy vote for Holland."

Kane looked at her. *Sympathy... sympathy.* The idea fit—somehow. He had a vague recollection of bringing up the same concept recently but couldn't pin it down. "Did you or I say anything about sympathy recently?" he asked.

"What are you getting at?"

"I'm not sure. But something about playing an angle to garner support or sympathy, helping Armstrong. I just don't know how."

"Gotcha. Give me a minute." Lilly closed her eyes, and Kane waited patiently.

"I think I have something for you," Lilly told him after about ninety seconds. "At your farm, when I got back from the meeting with Stafford and Douglas, we were talking about what they had been trying to accomplish and I said, '... being shot might be the best thing to ever happen to him because that bullet gave him a ton of sympathy votes.' Then you talked about making it a sure kill because the tough shot was risky. 'With the miss, you've actually helped the guy you tried to kill.' That's all I've got."

Kane nodded but remained confused. Perhaps Stafford had jumped on the opportunity to exploit the shooting, as anyone might. Such an event was a gift from the heavens, but even the best campaign manager couldn't make a dead man president. And the evidence still pointed to Stafford having engineered the shooting. It was like he knew how good the payoff would be....

Holy Machiavellian shit. "I've got it," he said.

"What?"

"I know what Stafford was up to. *Is* up to. His plan is perfect, and it's been executed perfectly every step of the way. Damn," he said, his voice filled with awe.

"Wanna fill me in?"

"Do you know what Munchausen Syndrome by Proxy is?" Kane asked. Before she could answer, her phone rang. The dashboard display showed a number that she did not recognize. *Should they answer?* Throwing caution to the wind, Lilly tapped the screen. "Yes?"

"Alexander?" It was Mac's voice, causing Lilly to exhale heavily.

"Yes sir. I was hoping it was you using another phone."

"Since they've hacked into my personal phone, I just destroyed it and activated one of my backups. What's your status?" Kane jumped in and brought him up to speed, briefly sharing Lilly's theory.

"Wait," Mac said when he finished. "Why the hell would Stafford try to kill his candidate?"

"That's the question of the day. I just developed a few solid thoughts about that, but we don't have the time to explore them right now."

"Yeah, gotcha." He shifted gears quickly. "So they probably know I'm working with you against orders."

"Seems that way."

"Dammit. These guys have all the bases covered. Worse, D.C. police put a BOLO out on you. You won't last an hour out in the open."

"That's probably optimistic," Kane told him. "Honestly, I don't know that we have any good options, so we're just staying mobile."

"Standby," Mac said. Lilly could see the worry lines on Kane's forehead as he scanned the traffic for black-and-whites or unmarked cars. She felt as concerned as he looked.

Finally, the director addressed them again. "I'm texting you a location. How quick can you be there?" Lilly entered the information into the map application on her phone. It pointed her to a spot in the woods near the Chesapeake and Ohio Canal.

"Ten minutes, sir," she told him. "If we don't run into any bogies."

"Understood. Fast as you can." The call terminated.

Lilly told Kane where he was going, and he adjusted his route accordingly. "What do you think he has in mind?" he asked.

"I don't know, but I'm glad he has something because we are well and truly screwed without an idea. I hate needing help, but right now we do."

"Agreed. It better be a winner." They lapsed back into silent vigilance, eyeing every car they passed until they got to their destination, a dirt parking lot near the canal. Normally frequented by hikers, it was currently deserted on this mid-afternoon workday. Ignoring the sign forbidding vehicles on the path, they drove over the footbridge, wincing as it groaned under the truck's weight, and proceeded down the canal towpath for about a mile. As they closed in on their destination, both Kane and Lilly peered into the forest until they spotted a vehicle similar to theirs through the leaves.

Mac and his driver stepped out as they pulled up. Lilly noted that this was not the same driver she'd met at the Alternate Seneca location.

Without a word, the anonymous agent headed to the back of their truck and started transferring the boxes of paper evidence into Mac's SUV.

"What's he doing?" Kane asked the director.

"That truck is your kryptonite right now. You need a different ride, so Agent Martin is going to take your vehicle for a little spin. Of course, we're going to keep the evidence in my truck with us, while he does everything he can to draw attention. That should give us a few extra minutes, and we might need that time to enact my idea."

"I'm glad you have something, sir," Lilly told Mac. "What's the plan?"

"First, tell me why I should be arresting Voight Stafford, and then please explain how your scenario makes the slightest bit of sense."

Lilly took the first part, walking MacMurray through the string of connections, ignoring his expressions of disbelief, skepticism, and amusement until she summed it all up. Just like with Kane, she waited patiently, a slightly bored look on her face, as Mac tried—and failed—to come up with anything that could poke a hole in her theory.

But then she offered a concession to reality. "While I'm certain of the evidence, I can't explain the 'why' part." She gestured at her partner. "Kane started babbling about that during our drive, but we didn't have time to discuss it."

Mac shifted his focus. "Perhaps you could enlighten us, Agent."

Kane nodded. "Sir, when we talked outside the White House the other day, you told me that perception was reality. Keep that in mind as I explain this. It's total bullshit that, oddly enough, makes perfect sense." He provided his idea as Mac listened in amazement.

"That might be the god-damndest thing I've ever heard. And, like you said, it makes so much sense it's almost frightening. But we're going to need something else to take this from theory to fact."

"Did you pick up that guy in Idaho, the one who got payments but isn't dead?"

"Yeah. And we've got two field agents talking to him right now, with another team ripping his life apart over the last year."

"Wanna bet he tests positive for the drug?"

"That's a safe bet." Mac paused, and when he spoke again, his voice was thick with admiration. "You two, you nailed this. I'm damn impressed. Sharpe and Douglas may have fired you, but you guys have a standing job offer with the FBI until the day I retire." The two (recently) ex-Secret Service agents shared a look of mutual satisfaction.

"Thank you, sir," Lilly said.

"One thing I don't know," Kane said. "What about Douglas? I honestly can't say if he's really involved in this or if Stafford is tugging him along like a puppy."

"He's an annoying little bastard," Mac said, "but I don't see him as having the brains or the balls to be a part of this. He isn't motivated by anything beyond being named Secret Service director and settling a petty score by getting rid of you, Kane. I think we can figure everything out by his reaction when we show our cards."

"And how do we do that? We have to make this information available to the public *before* election day," Kane pointed out. "And that's tomorrow."

Mac's grin hinted at the evil it contained. "I've got a great way to get Stafford to hang himself."

Chapter 31 – Shock Wave

Voight Stafford sat in his expansive office alone, reviewing Armstrong's itinerary for the following day. The events were just as he'd specified—short duration to account for Armstrong's still-limited stamina, with friendly crowds to make it obvious that *everyone* loved him, and a promise by media-friendly assets to keep the questions easy. Victory was likely but not assured. Last-minute votes could matter.

His phone *dinged*, indicating a text. Every politically relevant person, knowing what Stafford knew, was trying to get their foot in the door just before the elevator headed up to the very top floors of power. Some the chief of staff would embrace, some he would put off for now, and some he would ignore entirely.

But this text was a different beast altogether.

I know everything you did, and I can prove it. I can destroy you and Armstrong. You'll be in jail and he won't be able to get elected as an alderman in Nowhere, Kansas. I'll be at your office at 4 p.m. today to talk.

Stafford did not react physically. It was a good habit to cultivate, especially in politics, even if the wheels were falling off. Without knowing who sent the text, he wasn't sure how bad things were—but at the least several lug nuts were loose and the tires were wobbling.

Who is this, and what do you think I did?

Don't play games with me. You know exactly what I'm talking about. The more you jerk me around, the more it will cost you. 4 p.m.

Stafford drummed his fingers on his teak desk. Who could possibly make such an accusation and have anything to back it up? He was the only person who knew the whole story and was quite sure he'd left nothing to chance.

He stopped that train of thought. "Quite sure" was a dangerous way of thinking. With slightly more than eighteen hours to go until the polls opened, and with literally everything on the line, making assumptions was irresponsible.

Changing his focus, Stafford considered the timing. Why now? Why not after the election? The inference was that the threat could be used to swing the election to Sharpe, which narrowed down the list, but not nearly enough. Whoever it was, Stafford likely already knew him in some capacity, and that person had the confidence to come directly at him, marking him as someone with power and authority.

He checked his watch: 2:50. He didn't have time for academic consideration of the situation. He placed a call, and Brent Douglas picked up on the first ring. "Hi, Voight. What's up? I'm kind of busy."

"I might have a problem."

"What kind of problem?" Stafford explained the text. "What could they accuse you of?"

"I can't imagine. I've got nothing at all to hide."

"If you have nothing to hide, then you shouldn't be worried about the threat," Douglas pointed out.

Stafford *harrumphed* gently into the phone. "This is D.C.," he reminded Douglas. "You don't have to commit crimes to be accused of being a criminal, and voters don't require facts to change their vote. Hearsay and rumor will do that just fine. More importantly, you know what any suggestion of impropriety would do to the senator and, by extension, your appointment as director."

The veiled threat was met with silence for several seconds. "What do you want to do?"

"Well, we need to hear what kind of nonsense this person has so we can get out ahead of it, and we need to contain any leaks. I would like you to handle the takedown personally."

"OK," Douglas agreed. "We'll get them on tape making their accusations, and then I can arrest them right in your office. That way we can control any narrative they're trying to spin so the press doesn't get wind of it."

"Very good. I'll see you at quarter of four."

***

"Any last questions?" Mac asked the agents as Kane parked in the Democratic National Committee parking lot.

"Nope."

"No, none," Kane lied. The director's plan was clever—too clever—but dangerous times called for risky moves.

"Let's go." They got out of the truck as one, with Kane to the director's front right and Lilly behind him and to the left in a standard cover formation. As much as they wanted to appear to be protecting

Mac, they were really protecting themselves. If anyone recognized either agent, things could get dicey quickly. Kane scanned the building, looking for the black line of a rifle trained on them, but all the facing windows appeared to be closed.

Mac texted as he walked. His phone beeped back at him a few seconds later, and he slowed to read the response. "Armstrong's headed to Stafford's office in a minute," he said, his voice just loud enough to be audible. Both agents acknowledged the information but did not lose focus. There were too many ways things could go south.

***

Stafford's desk phone sounded, and he pressed the intercom button. "Yes?"

"Sir, Director MacMurray is downstairs at reception and says he needs to see you right away."

Stafford's eyes narrowed slightly. MacMurray checked all the boxes—he could know at least part of the real story, he had Stafford's contact info, and he had the horsepower to walk into his office and make threats. "Did he say why?" he asked, looking at Brent Douglas, who shrugged.

"No, sir. He just said it's vital and he must deliver the information personally."

"Very well. Send him up." He killed the connection.

Douglas stood. "It's not going to be easy for me to arrest the director of the FBI," he pointed out.

Stafford gaped at him. "Why? He's committing a crime!"

"Think it through. If I put MacMurray in cuffs and try to walk him out of here, his protective detail won't just accept that, not without knowing exactly what's going on, and I can't guarantee they'll take my word for it. They sure as shit won't take your word. Their orders are to protect him from all threats, period."

"So wave them off. Jesus, do I have to do *all* the thinking here?

"It's not that simple, Voight! Agents take an oath, and it isn't just some nonsense. They take it seriously, and if they don't know why he's being arrested or don't feel it's valid, they will defend him."

"Don't they work for you?" Stafford asked in a voice suggesting he was impugning the deputy director's manhood.

"Yes, but they aren't fucking robots. We teach them to question everything."

Stafford's sigh was a combination of disgust and disdain. "I'm not sure Senator Armstrong will be comfortable with a director of the agency committed to his safety if he can't control his agents."

"And I'm not sure that he'll be comfortable being protected by mindless drones who shit their pants if someone tries to push them around!" He appeared to want to say more, but stopped himself. "Don't worry," he said in a far-calmer voice. "I'll handle it."

"I hope so."

***

Kane, Lilly, and Mac stepped out of the elevator just in time to see the senator enter the hallway, flanked by his own protective detail. The four agents shared a subtle look of greeting, but Kane didn't recognize them, and they did not appear to know him. Exactly as hoped.

"Pat," Armstrong asked the director, "what the hell is going on?"

"Let's wait for the meeting, sir." Armstrong, although he had to be expecting just that response, still pursed his lips in frustration.

Kane took the lead, stepping into Stafford's outer office and clearing the room. In an effort to keep the executive assistant calm, he had not drawn his weapon, but his hand was in position. Stafford's secretary was expecting MacMurray, but the senator and his detail seemed to throw her a bit. She stared at the entourage until the director prompted her with a look. She pressed the intercom. "Sir, Director MacMurray and Senator Armstrong are here to see you."

A brief pause ensued. "Do I have a meeting scheduled with the senator?" Kane could almost hear the gears turning in the chief of staff's head through the phone as he processed this new information.

"Not on my schedule, sir."

"Send in the senator. The director will have to wait."

"Dr. Stafford," Mac said loud enough to be heard over the device while looking at Armstrong, "I strongly suggest you meet with us both at the same time."

"Very well." A faint scuffling sound came over the device. Armstrong seemed not to notice, but Mac leaned in as if to hear it a bit better, and he shot a quick look at Kane and Lilly. "Send them in."

"Yes, sir." With a nod, she pressed the button under the overhang of her desk. Kane, without trying to look obvious about it, backed up a step to ensure he wouldn't be seen when the door opened. Lilly followed suit, earning them an odd stare from the other two protective agents, who followed Mac through the door ahead of Senator Armstrong.

As soon as the door shut behind them, Kane looked over at the secretary. "You should take a break," he suggested. "Right now." The woman gave him a curious look, and Lilly nodded earnestly, even angling her head to the door and patting her gun. That was enough for Stafford's assistant to leave the office.

"You ready for this?" Kane asked his partner. "Remember, it could go sideways fast."

"Are you?" she asked rhetorically. "And does it matter? It's not like we've got a choice."

"No, we sure don't."

***

Stafford was standing behind his desk when the four men entered. Armstrong's detail found unobtrusive spots on opposite walls, but their body language suggested they felt the tension in the room.

Stafford kicked off the conversation. "You gentlemen have me at a disadvantage. Director, I'm not aware of anything happening that requires us to meet in person. And Sam, while you are always welcome in here, I'm sure you're far too busy to make a surprise social call."

"This isn't a social call, but I don't know what I'm doing here either. The director texted and asked me to meet him here."

"Well, Director," Stafford said, "it would appear you have the floor."

Mac took a deep breath, one dramatic enough that the agents against the wall took notice and looked at Armstrong. "Senator, what I'm going to tell you is the most amazing tale you are ever going to hear, but I am 100 percent certain it's true." With that, he took the three steps over to the door and opened it.

***

Game time. Lilly followed Kane into the office and pulled the door shut behind her. When she faced the desk behind which Stafford stood, she took no small satisfaction at seeing the look of shock on his smug face. "What the hell are *you two* doing here?" he asked like he'd attended their open-casket funeral that morning. Before they could respond, however, the door to Stafford's private bathroom blew open and Brent Douglas surged through the opening, his weapon drawn. He pointed it directly at Kane, but his angle was such that he would barely have to adjust his aim to get Lilly with a second shot. "You two are under arrest! Drop your weapons!"

Kane, Lilly, Mac, and both of Armstrong's protective agents reacted instantly, pulling their service weapons. After a few seconds of bodies twisting and heads swiveling, everyone with a gun had a dance partner. Kane and Douglas faced off, while Mac took one of Armstrong's agents and Lilly took the other. Stafford's eyes went wide while Armstrong, more in the line of fire from Lilly, instinctively twitched and ducked.

"I said you're under arrest!" Douglas bellowed. "Both of you! Put your weapons on the floor and take two steps back!"

"Not gonna happen, Brent," Kane told him.

"Douglas," Mac said without taking his eyes off his target, "Agents Logan and Alexander are operating under my authority right now. You will not be arresting them."

"I've got an order from President Sharpe to bring them in! If you try to stop me, you will also be arrested."

"The president has no authority to order the arrest of these two agents, and I outrank you. Now stand down! That's an order."

Lilly was barely keeping her cool. Not in her most pessimistic imagination had she envisioned the epic Mexican standoff she found herself in. She met the eyes of her counterpart and saw that he was just as scared as she was, but also that he would not hesitate to defend his principal. *Shit.*

"Lilly," Mac said, "I suggest you start talking."

Right. She took a deep breath to settle down. "Dr. Stafford, it gives me great pleasure to tell you that we're here because of your arrogance and hubris."

"Mine?" Lilly chanced a quick look at him and noted that he appeared well and truly surprised. *Good.*

"Yes, sir, yours. You were in the room when Secretary Carlisle put me on this case, and she spoke about my eidetic memory. You underestimated that, sir—or should I say Mr. Rory B. Bellows?" This time, she looked directly into his eyes as she delivered the last part of her sentence and was rewarded with seeing the color run out of his face.

"Who is Rory Bellows?" Armstrong asked.

"Why don't you ask your chief of staff, Senator?" When Stafford did not speak, she plunged forward. "No answer? That's fine. I'll fill him in for you." She gave her short but effective speech for the third time, being sure to use graphically clear terms that would convince a kindergarten class.

When she brought it home, Lilly swept the room to see the reactions. Kane and Mac were angry but composed. Armstrong's agents were still all business, but their eyes were as big as dinner plates. Douglas and Armstrong, predictably, looked like they'd just been sucker-punched in the gut, moving their stunned gazes from Kane to Lilly to Stafford.

Stafford's face was at once the most guarded and the most descriptive. At first glance, nothing seemed to have changed, but upon closer inspection, there were differences—subtle ones that stood out to Lilly like lighthouses in a fog bank. His upper lip trembled just a bit, and the muscles in his jaw flexed.

His eyes, though, told her how perfectly she'd nailed the situation. His gray pupils burned at her like those of a vengeful god. Had there not been guns everywhere, Lilly expected he would have sprung across his enormous desk and tried to strangle her. She allowed one corner of her ruby-red lips to curl up in a tiny smile and winked at him.

Stafford's eyes grew wider for just a second, but he almost instantly took back control of his outward emotions. With his next words, Lilly would have believed that her speech had never happened. "That's a fascinating theory, Agent Alexander," he said in the calm and measured voice of a man in charge, "but what would I possibly have to gain by hiring someone to shoot my candidate?"

With the question being an absolute requirement of the conversation, Lilly had already crafted her reaction. Stafford felt he once again had control of the narrative, and she reinforced that idea by allowing a hint of doubt to come over her face. She almost laughed out loud as Stafford took note of it and gained further confidence, but that wouldn't do. Instead, she looked away.

"Kane?"

***

Kane did a quick assessment of his target. Brent still had his weapon pointed at him, but his aim had drifted a bit, and his expression indicated that his ardor had cooled, so he took a calculated risk. He holstered his weapon and leaned on the back of one of the guest chairs.

"You know, sir, I asked that very question when Lilly shared her theory with me, because I couldn't understand what would motivate you to do such a despicable thing. But she convinced me, and it led to a thought. Have you ever heard of Munchausen Syndrome by Proxy, sir?"

Stafford furrowed his brow at Logan. "There was that stupid movie like thirty years ago—Baron Munchausen or something."

"There was, sir, but that's not what I'm talking about. Munchausen Syndrome is when someone harms themselves, pretends to be ill, or makes themselves ill to get attention from others.

"Munchausen Syndrome by Proxy is similar, but it's far more evil. It's when someone—usually a parent—either hurts or makes their child ill so they can garner sympathy at having to deal with the situation."

"Agent, get to the point," Stafford ordered, but he appeared as interested in Kane's ideas as much as anyone.

"People with this condition are mentally ill, so they deserve our sympathy and treatment. But you, sir, you applied this concept to satisfy your out-of-control desire to get your man into the Oval Office, whatever it took.

"For most of this investigation, we all assumed that the shot was *this close* to perfect, that the shooter had come within about a foot of decapitating Senator Armstrong from an impossible distance. We were all wrong." He leaned forward.

"All the practice locations, all the shooters you hired and paid, all the expert snipers you got to train them, all the drug cocktails they were given, were for one purpose—to have your shooter do precisely what you needed. And he did.

"The shot was *exactly*—down to the millimeter—what you planned. Of course you didn't want Armstrong dead, but you needed him to be shot and seriously injured. You knew how the American people would react, and you were completely right. He had to get hurt, but he had to survive, because the resulting sympathy would send his numbers through the roof. Now you've got even his staunchest enemy feeling sorry for him, so much so that President Sharpe himself might vote Democrat. Armstrong is the innocent proxy, but you are the mastermind manipulating the public to make him president."

Kane turned to the others. "It was, literally and figuratively, a perfect shot."

The room was deathly silent. Lilly's news had stunned everyone, but Kane had just dropped a hydrogen bomb, and the fallout hadn't even started to spread.

Armstrong recovered enough to speak. "Voight, is this true?" His chief of staff turned his head slowly in the direction of the question but said nothing. His silence spoke volumes.

"How could you? You've been my friend since college. You were the best man at my wedding. What the hell were you thinking?!"

Stafford regained himself. "Six years ago, just after you gave your acceptance speech in Boston as senator-elect, do you remember the conversation we had in your hotel room?"

Armstrong took a second to think. "About going for the presidency?"

"Yes. Do you remember what I asked you, and how you answered?"

"You asked me if I wanted to be president, and I said 'Hell, yes.'"

Stafford nodded. "And what did you say when I asked how far you were willing to go to get there?"

Armstrong closed his eyes. "As far as I have to."

His friend nodded. "I went as far as you had to. We were down in the polls, so I made it happen. And because I did, you're about to be president-elect." He looked triumphant, convinced he'd done the right thing for the right reasons, but the self-satisfaction faded as he saw unimaginable pain around the eyes of the senator.

"Voight, I can't believe I have to say this, but I want to be president because I think I can help this country. You can't do that by hurting people or using them as pawns to get some votes." He turned his attention to Kane. "Agent, I want the truth—did his actions, directly or not, result in dead people, dead Americans?"

"Yes, senator. At least a dozen—perhaps more."

Armstrong went pale, and he appeared unsteady on his feet for a second. He braced against Stafford's desk. "You absolute motherfucker. Politics is dirty pool, but not like this."

"Sam," Stafford said earnestly "I had to do it! We were trailing everywhere in the polls. If I hadn't done this, you might never be president! We would never have been able to accomplish anything if I hadn't done this!"

"It's not worth it, Voight. I'm not even so mad about you having had me shot as the fact that you *killed* people. How am I even morally qualified to hold the office of president now? I'm not sure I can face my wife!"

"Nancy will understand. The country will understand. I thought this through. You didn't know what was happening. You can say that, and you won't be lying. You're going to be elected because you're the best man for the job. When you take office, you can pardon me." He stepped up to the senator. "I did all this for you, Sam. For us. For the good of the country."

Armstrong looked down at the shorter man with contempt. "No. You're done. If I'm elected, if I don't resign on day one, I'm not going to pardon you. I'm going to make sure you get everything that's coming to you." He turned away.

"Sam?!"

"No, Voight. You're fired. You crossed a line so... so set in stone that I can't even get my head around it." He looked at MacMurray. "Get this piece of shit out of the building," he said before leaving the office. Voight Stafford stared at his retreating boss like a loyal dog watching his owner leave him at the pound.

Mac produced a pair of handcuffs and handed them to Kane. "You guys hook him up and walk him out."

Lilly holstered her gun and joined Kane, who took great pleasure in wrenching Stafford's arms behind him so she could slap the cuffs on his wrists and double-lock them. Once they were secure, each agent took an arm and moved him toward the door.

"With pleasure, sir."

***

The "Special Report" screen popped up on every major network as well as the news channels. In each instance the newscasters reported that they were cutting live to the J. Edgar Hoover Building for a press conference of critical importance.

"Yes, Chris," the CNN on-scene reporter said into the camera, an unoccupied podium in the background. "We're in the press briefing room of the Hoover building, and we've been told that FBI Director Patrick MacMurray will be making a statement within moments. Although we were given no indication as to the topic, the assumption is that there has been a breakthrough in the investigation of the assassination attempt on Senator Armstrong. In the days since the shooting, there has been little information forthcoming on the topic, so we cannot—here comes the director." The camera shifted to show MacMurray striding to the raised platform.

Mac placed a single sheet of paper on the lectern and cleared his throat. "I'm going to make a statement in several parts. Please hold all questions until the end.

"First, Secret Service Director Adrian Schultz has advised me that he has accepted the resignation of Deputy Director Brent Douglas, effective immediately. This was at the request of the deputy director solely for personal reasons. I wish to stress that this is, in no way, associated with the other items I am about to relate. A senior agent will assume his position on an interim basis."

"Next, we have arrested a Mr. Argen Collins of Sand Hollow, Idaho in connection with the shooting of Senator Samuel Armstrong. Since Senator Armstrong is, of course, both an elected official and a major presidential candidate, Mr. Collins has been charged with attempted murder, a federal crime under Title 18, Section 351, Subsection A of the United States Code."

He took a deep breath. "We have also arrested Dr. Voight Stafford, Chief of Staff for Senator Armstrong, and charged him with conspiracy to commit murder in the shooting of Senator Armstrong. This is also a federal crime under Subsection D of the previously referenced code."

Most of the reporters in the room, even the seasoned veterans, shared looks of unfettered amazement with their colleagues at this last disclosure. The press was a cynical bunch, and in Washington that was multiplied a hundredfold. But, if a group of people could be described as uniformly dumbfounded, the open jaws and wide eyes of these journalists made that definition applicable. "Any questions?" Mac asked the room.

He blinked and leaned back in an instinctual response to the cacophony of three dozen shouted questions that hit him like a sonic boom.

Epilogue – All About the Timing

After delivering Stafford to FBI headquarters, Kane and Lilly jumped right into the required paperwork. When Mac walked into the office a few minutes later, he did a double-take.

"Hey!" he barked.

His tone got their attention. "What?" Kane asked.

"You two were exhausted when I saw you at the safehouse the other day, and I doubt you got much sleep in the interim."

"You know the drill, Mac. This shit isn't going to fill itself out."

"You'd be amazed at what might happen to it. So, as of right now, you two are off duty until Monday."

"You know we can't do that," Lilly told him.

Mac sighed dramatically. "Agent Alexander, I'm quite sure you remember what I told you about questioning my orders. Do I need to reinforce that?"

"Um... I guess not."

"So you two are out of the office until Monday morning. In the meantime, get some rest—and by that I mean at least some of it in separate beds."

Two mouths dropped open. "You know?"

"I'm old, but I'm not dead yet," Mac responded. "Plus, you've more than earned it. Dismissed." Without giving them a chance to respond, he headed to his office. The two agents shared a look before leaving the Hoover Building like it was burning.

On the way to the car, they talked about what they should do with their unexpected free time—mostly where they should crash. Lilly naturally assumed it would be at her place, as Falls Church was a short drive, but Kane had other ideas.

A little over three hours later, she watched (with much less trepidation this time) as Jay blasted through the door of *Doggone Right!* daycare and violently showed his affection to his owner before greeting Lilly in a slightly more reserved manner. Jay eagerly raced up to their truck and danced around waiting for someone to open the door.

***

Kane lay against the pillows piled against the headboard, bare-chested with the sheets down around his waist. To his right, Lilly snuggled up against him, her naked body similarly exposed. It was late. Actually, it was very early; the deep indigo blue signaling the approaching dawn was just beginning to show through the east-facing windows of the bedroom.

Despite the hour, they weren't sleepy. Only minutes ago they'd finished their third frenetic and highly satisfying bout of lovemaking since dinner. Kane found it quite kinky that Lilly got turned on watching the dry political reports of which states were for Sharpe and which were for Armstrong, but it didn't bother him enough to turn her down when she used those enormous blue eyes to invite him to entwine himself with her body once again.

Jay had settled in his bed in the corner, snoring softly. To both Kane and Lilly's surprised amusement, each time they began another round of amorous activity, Jay had risen, huffed, and headed out of the room as if not wanting to be exposed to such perversion. Now that his humans had settled down, he was taking advantage of the silence.

While three times in one night was a record for both of them, any thoughts of hitting for the cycle were on hold. A round of predictions was coming soon.

***

The extreme sympathy vote that Stafford had worked so hard to cultivate evaporated in the hours following the arrests. Phone polling indicated that many people who had felt bad for Armstrong were put off by the revelation of such extreme corruption and immorality. Suddenly he wasn't trustworthy.

Stunned by Stafford's betrayal, Armstrong made the tactical error of not getting in front of the television cameras that night. Word from inside the campaign described Armstrong as too shaken, making him unable to speak on the topic. The press release that his campaign put out sounded for all the world like the dry political double-speak used when someone got caught with his pants down (literally or figuratively), and the voting public didn't like it.

After a sleepless night of discussions, contemplation, strategizing, and encouragement from the rest of his team, Armstrong regrouped.

Staffers made early calls and got other guests and topics bumped from the top early-morning shows like *Good Morning America, Today, CBS This Morning,* and even *Live! With Kelly and Mark* in favor of the man at the center of this amazing story. Both the shows and the campaign flooded the internet and airwaves with word of these interviews, ensuring a massive audience.

In each show, the senator made a brief statement about how betrayed he felt and that he understood the American people felt the same way. He then invited questions, telling viewers that the hosts were free to ask absolutely anything, and they did not hold back. Even though he fumbled a few answers, the approach displayed a candor that resonated with most of the audience.

With all that, he saved his best punch for the end of each interview. "If you, the American people, feel that I am not worthy of the office of president because of these recent events, then you should follow your instincts and give your vote to another candidate."

It was an eloquent line and a masterful piece of damage control. By the time the East Coast headed to the polls, many of those who had jumped off his bandwagon after the arrests reversed themselves and indicated a willingness to have Armstrong as their president.

***

Lilly shuddered as Kane ran his hand along her side gently. "What do you think he's going to say?" he asked.

"I don't know," she answered, conflicted as to how she felt about how things were playing out. She'd tried not to worry about it most of the evening (Kane's efforts over the past few hours had been *very* distracting—and satisfying) but now it had taken up residence in her head and couldn't be ignored any longer. She felt the muscles in her face tighten with unease.

Kane muted the television. "What's bugging you?"

Lilly sighed. She should have known he'd pick up on the change in her disposition. "It's just... did we really accomplish anything?"

"Of course we did. We solved a crime and brought the perpetrators to justice. That's our job."

"Yeah, I know," she admitted. "But we didn't bring things back to the status quo. The assassination attempt still influenced voters tremendously, and the arrest we made may have handed the election to Armstrong."

Kane squinted at her. "Are you saying you're pro-Sharpe?"

"I'm not pro one or the other. I'm saying that all of our hard work, the danger, the risk, all of it, didn't matter in the end." She shook her head in frustration.

"Lilly, we can't fix everything. Once that bullet hit Armstrong, everything about the election changed permanently. Sometimes we can prevent these things, but sometimes we can't, and this was a time we couldn't. But we did the next best thing. By exposing Stafford for the piece of shit he is, we gave the public all the information there is and, even more importantly, we removed a criminal from a position of extreme power.

"Yes, a lot of people changed their minds based on the shooting, but this is a free country. People base their vote on a lot of things. Some of them are valid, some of them are idiotic, and some are irrelevant. You can't control that."

Lilly gave him a wry look. "Sage advice. You're getting smarter."

"Someone I know recently told me not to worry about every little thing. I'm just returning the favor."

"That someone sounds pretty smart," she said, feeling the apprehension leave her body in favor of a more amorous sensation. "I think you should listen to him... or her."

"We'll see." They leaned in, mouths open, but were interrupted when the television screen, which had been alternating between talking heads and a map of the country, changed drastically to display a large banner at the bottom.

CBS NEWS PROJECTS SAMUEL B. ARMSTRONG ELECTED PRESIDENT.

www.ingramcontent.com/pod-product-compliance
Lightning Source LLC
La Vergne TN
LVHW050918080826
845145LV00001B/129

* 9 7 8 1 9 6 8 7 5 9 3 3 9 *